W9-CDD-379

Return to the Whorl

BY GENE WOLFE FROM TOM DOHERTY ASSOCIATES

Novels
The Fifth Head of Cerberus
The Devil in a Forest
Peace
Free Live Free
The Urth of the New Sun
Soldier of the Mist
Soldier of Arete
There Are Doors
Castleview
Pandora by Holly Hollander

Novellas
The Death of Doctor Island
Seven American Nights

Collections
Endangered Species
Storeys from the Old Hotel
Castle of Days
The Island of Doctor Death and Other Stories and Other Stories
Strange Travelers

The Book of the New Sun
Shadow and Claw
(comprising *The Shadow of the Torturer* and
The Claw of the Conciliator)
Sword and Citadel
(comprising *The Sword of the Lictor* and
The Citadel of the Autarch)

The Book of the Long Sun
Litany of the Long Sun
(comprising *Nightside the Long Sun* and
Lake of the Long Sun)
Epiphany of the Long Sun
(comprising *Caldé of the Long Sun* and
Exodus from the Long Sun)

The Book of the Short Sun
On Blue's Waters
In Green's Jungles
Return to the Whorl

Return to the Whorl

VOLUME THREE OF THE
BOOK OF THE *S*HORT *S*UN

Gene Wolfe

A Tom Doherty Associates Book
NEW YORK

This is a work of fiction. All the characters and events portrayed in this novel are either fictitious or are used fictitiously.

RETURN TO THE WHORL

This book is printed on acid-free paper.

Edited by David G. Hartwell

A Tor Book
Published by Tom Doherty Associates, LLC
175 Fifth Avenue
New York, NY 10010

www.tor.com

Tor® is a registered trademark of Tom Doherty Associates, LLC.

Library of Congress Cataloging-in-Publication Data

Wolfe, Gene.
Return to the whorl / Gene Wolfe.—1st ed.
p. cm.—(The book of the short sun; v. 3)
"A Tom Doherty Associates book."
ISBN 0-312-87314-X (alk. paper)
1. Interplanetary voyages—Fiction. I. Title

PS3573.O52 R4 2001
813'.54—dc21

00-048811

First Edition: February 2001

Printed in the United States of America

0 9 8 7 6 5 4 3 2 1

Respectfully dedicated to

Teri and Al

Proper Names in the Text

Many of the persons and places mentioned in this book first appeared in *The Book of the Long Sun,* to which the reader is referred. In the following list, the most significant names are given in CAPITALS, less significant names in *italics.*

AANVAGEN, the protagonist's hospitable jailer in DORP.
Colonel *Abanja,* a Trivigaunti officer.
Antler, a son of SMOOTHBONE by his second wife.
Auk, the thief who once coached SILK in burglary.
Sergeant *Azijin,* a legerman of DORP.
BABBIE, a tame hus belonging to *Mucor.*
Bala, Sinew's wife, on GREEN.
BEROEP, a householder of DORP, AANVAGEN'S husband.
Caldé BISON, Maytera MINT'S husband, presently caldé of VIRON.
Blanko, an inland town.
Blood, a crime lord killed by SILK, *Mucor's* adoptive father.
BLUE, one of two habitable planets circling the SHORT SUN.
Blazingstar, a magnate of NEW VIRON.
Calf, one of HORN'S brothers, a shopkeeper of NEW VIRON.
CAPSICUM, *Marrow's* mistress and executor.
Chenille, the woman who accompanied *Auk* to GREEN.
Cijfer, Captain WIJZER'S wife.
Cilinia, Typhon's eldest daughter.
Cowslip, one of HORN'S sisters.
Cricket, a boy, *Cowslip's* son.
DAISY, a fisherman's daughter taught by NETTLE.
DORP, a coastal town north of NEW VIRON.
Echidna, a goddess in the *WHORL* and the patroness of GAON.
Eco, a former mercenary, *Mora's* husband.
Endroad, a village subject to VIRON.
Eschar, a magnate of NEW VIRON.
Flannan, one of PIG'S friends, a Flier.
GAON, a town of BLUE governed for a time by the narrator.

Gib, one of the colonists who accompanied *Auk* and *Chenille.*
GREEN, one of the habitable planets of the SHORT SUN.
Patera *Gulo,* the Coadjutor of VIRON.
GYRFALCON, a magnate of NEW VIRON.
Judge HAMER, one of the five judges who rule DORP.
Hammerstone, a soldier of VIRON, OLIVINE'S father.
Hare, a criminal, originally of VIRON.
Hari Mau, the new Rajan of GAON.
He-Pen-Sheep, a hunter.
HIDE, one of HORN and NETTLE'S twin sons.
Hierax, in the *WHORL,* the god of death.
Honeysuckle, a servant in the palace of VIRON'S caldé.
HOOF, one of HORN and NETTLE'S three sons, HIDE'S twin.
HORN, the chief author of *The Book of the Long Sun.*
HOUND, a shopkeeper of *Endroad.*
Incanto, the name by which the narrator was known in *Blanko.*
Inclito, the Duko of *Blanko.*
Patera *Incus,* the Prolocutor of VIRON.
JAHLEE, an inhuma freed by the narrator.
JUGANU, an inhumu freed by the narrator.
Krait, an inhumu adopted by HORN.
Kypris, the minor goddess who invited SILK to unite himself to PAS.
Private *Leeuw,* a legerman of DORP.
LIZARD, an island north of NEW VIRON.
LONG SUN WHORL, the interior of the *WHORL.*
Maytera MARBLE, an elderly chem.
Marrow, a magnate of NEW VIRON.
Merryn, a witch.
Maytera MINT, a leader of the rebellion that overthrew VIRON'S governing council.
Molpe, in the *WHORL,* the goddess of the winds.
Mora, the daughter of the Duke of *Blanko.*
Mota, one of *Hari Mau's* followers.
The *Mother,* a Vanished Goddess.
Mucor, a woman possessing paranormal powers, Maytera MARBLE'S granddaughter.
Musk, a Vironese criminal, now dead.
Nabeanntan, a mountain town of the LONG SUN WHORL.

NAT, a magnate of DORP.

The NEIGHBORS, the earlier inhabitants of BLUE, also called the *Vanished People.*

NETTLE, HORN'S wife, the mother of HOOF, HIDE, and *Sinew,* co-author of *The Book of the Long Sun.*

NEW VIRON, a town on BLUE founded by colonists from VIRON.

OLIVINE, a chem, Maytera MARBLE'S daughter.

Onorifica, a servant girl in the household of the Duko of *Blanko.*

OREB, a talking night chough.

The OUTSIDER, the god of things outside the LONG SUN WHORL.

Oxlip, one of HORN'S sisters.

Pajarocu, a phantom town on BLUE'S western continent.

Parel, a servant girl of DORP.

PAS, the father of the gods of the LONG SUN WHORL.

PIG, the name assumed by a blind wanderer.

QUADRIFONS, the god of doors and crossroads, and much else.

Patera *Quetzal,* an inhumu, once the Prolocutor of VIRON.

Patera REMORA, the Prolocutor of NEW VIRON.

RAJAN, the title of the ruler of GAON.

Rajya Mantri, an advisor to the RAJAN of GAON.

Maytera ROSE, an elderly sibyl, now dead.

Roti, one of *Hari Mau's* followers.

General *Saba,* a Trivigaunti officer.

The *Seanettle,* a yawl, a kind of two-masted boat having a mainmast and a small mizzen.

SEAWRACK, the young woman given to HORN by the *Mother.*

Shadelow, BLUE'S western continent, so named by HORN.

Patera SILK, a former caldé of VIRON.

Sinew, the oldest of HORN and NETTLE'S three sons.

SHORT SUN, the sun orbited by the *WHORL.*

SMOOTHBONE, a shopkeeper of VIRON, HORN'S father.

Spider, a spy-catcher of VIRON.

Stag, a son of SMOOTHBONE by his second wife.

Captain *Strik,* a trader of DORP who once befriended HORN.

Mysire Advocaat TAAL, the advocate engaged by BEROEP and others to defend the narrator.

Tallow, one of HORN'S brothers.

Tansy, HOUND'S wife.
Tartaros, PAS'S loyal son, the god of thieves and commerce.
Thyone, a minor goddess of the LONG SUN WHORL.
Tigridia, a client of the Honorable Order of the Seekers for Truth and Penitence.
Tongue, one of HORN'S brothers.
Trivigaunte, a foreign city south of VIRON ruled by women.
Caldé *Tussah,* SILK'S adoptive father.
Typhon, the ancient tyrant whose personality became PAS.
VADSIG, a servant girl in AANVAGEN'S house.
Vanished Gods, the presumed gods of the NEIGHBORS.
Vanished People, another name for the NEIGHBORS.
Mysire Advocaat *Vent,* the advocate assigned the narrator by the court.
Versregal, Captain *Strik's* wife.
VIRON, the city in which most of the action in *The Book of the Long Sun* took place.
Private *Vlug,* a legerman of DORP.
Wapen, a discontented young man of DORP.
Weasel, CAPSICUM'S grandson.
The *WHORL,* a spaceship whose vast interior cavity constitutes a small world—originally, an asteroid.
Captain WIJZER, the trader from DORP who directed HORN to *Pajarocu.*
Willet, the name assumed by a Trivigaunti spy.
Master *Xiphias,* an old fencing master.
Ziek, a merchant of DORP.

To My Hosts,

I am the silent presence in your house, the young woman who lies abed by day as by night. The woman who is to be brought before your judges, sleeping.

Tried, sleeping.

And condemned, still sleeping, to slide down into death.

Have you wondered whether I breathe at all? Do you sometimes lay a feather on my lips? I think you must. I feel you at my bedside.

None but my father can wake me.

Ask Aanvagen.

Let him sleep in a chair beside me, and I will wake.

Ask Aanvagen.

Let him hold my hand in his. Call him Horn, for the sound of that horn will awaken me. Let him come to me, and you will see me wake.

Ask Aanvagen.

Jahlee
your
sleeping
guest

1

The Bloodstained Men

We have been journeying by guess, and it is high time we admitted it. Thus I admit it here. All things considered, we have been fortunate; but unless we are favored by the Vanished Gods of Blue far above most, it cannot continue.

In this third book, which will surely be the last, I will begin by saying that, and telling you who we are; but first I should mention that the bandits are all dead, and that I, rummaging through their loot, have discovered this paper—an entire bale—and am making haste to use it.

His thoughts seemed to have nothing to do with the dead woman, her coffin, or the hot sunshine streaming through the open door into the poor little room. There was a pattering, as of rain; moisture splashed his ankles, and he looked down and saw blood trickling from his fingers to splash into a small pool at his feet.

His son had deserted him.

He was wounded. (No doubt the blood was from that wound?)

He lay in the medical compartment of a lander, though he was standing now, his blood dripping on worn floorboards. The bier was for another, it seemed, and the other was a middle-aged woman, and was already dead.

A knife with a worn blade and a cracked wooden handle lay at his feet. Reflexively, he bent to pick it up, and recoiled from it as if from a coiled snake. Something screamed in the emptiness, something deeper than resentment and thoughts of water, food, and healing.

He backed away from the knife and stumbled through the open door into the darkest night ever known.

We are four, a number that includes Oreb but excludes our four horses and Jahlee's white mule. Oreb is my bird and often a nuisance, as he is at this moment, trying to wrest one of his old quills from my fingers. "It's no use, Oreb," I say. "I want to write—have just started a new book—and I won't play with you at all unless you behave yourself."

"Good bird!" He means himself.

Have I mentioned Hide? Looking over this sheet, I see I have not. Hide is the fourth member of our party and my son, one of three. He is of medium height, not bad-looking, solid, muscular, and rising sixteen. He wears a sheepskin coat shorter than mine, a sheepskin hat, and sheepskin boots that are very well greased now, he having found a pot of mutton fat. No doubt the bandits used it for the same purpose.

The bandits, I should say, are all dead. Even the last. I would like to inter them with some decency, but the ground is frozen. Jahlee suggested burning their bodies, but it would take a great deal of wood, I am sure, to consume the bodies of nine men.

I must have been present when Patera Silk, Patera Quetzal, and Maytera Marble burned Maytera Rose. If someone had asked me about it yesterday, I would have said that I was not, that Nettle and I went away to fight for Maytera Mint after Echidna ordered her to destroy the Alambrera; yet I find that I can very clearly visualize the skull peering from the flames. It seems likely that I am confusing that occasion with some other on which a body was burned.

In any event I am certain they used a great deal of good, dry cedar. Our wood here will be green, and that which is not green will be wet with snow. Hide and I, working hard, might cut that much wood in a week, perhaps. (I in half an hour if I used Hyacinth's azoth—but what folly it would be to let them know I have it now!)

Anything else about Hide? A lot, although I will not try to set it all down. Hide has a twin, his brother Hoof, who looks exactly like him. Hoof is in the south, or at least Hide believes he is. We were tempted to turn south around the marsh in the hope of finding him. It would have been farther, but I wish we had.

I am telling you all this in case the first two books in my saddlebag are lost or destroyed, which is surely likely enough. If you have them, they will tell you much more about me and my sons than I possibly can.

What else should I say? As a traveling companion he is inclined to gloom and pessimism. (He may well think the same of me.) He is not talkative, and is seldom entertaining when he does talk. But he is courageous and resourceful, and has a smile I can warm my hands at.

I see I have already begun on Oreb, so let us take him next. He is smaller than a hen, though his wings are much longer. His feathers shine. His head, bill, and feet are red. He has a most disconcerting habit of leaving me suddenly, when he may be gone for a day, an hour, or (once) the better part of a year. I got him in the Long Sun Whorl before Hari Mau got *me* and put me on his lander.

To be more accurate, Oreb got me as they did, adopting me as his master and sometime confidant. If I did not feed him more than he feeds me, it might be difficult to say who owns whom.

He thought he had gone blind, then that it was death. He had failed to reach the Aureate Path—he would wander in this darkness forever, beset by devils.

Devils worse than the inhumi? Worse than men? He laughed aloud—madness. Madness; and to be mad was to be dead, as to be dead was to be mad, and to be dead and mad was to be blind.

His fingers met the rough bark of a tree, and he discovered for the second time that they were slippery with blood. There were oozing cuts in both his arms and both his wrists. Rummaging unfamiliar pockets he found prayer beads, spectacles, two cards, and at last a handkerchief still folded in a way that seemed to promise it was clean. He started a tear with his teeth, ripped the handkerchief in two, and bandaged his deepest cuts, making himself work slowly and carefully, tightening the clumsy knots with his free hand and his teeth.

Far off, a faint light shone. He stood up, blinked at it, and stared again. A light, a faint point of golden light. When Aster's house had been haunted by her dead child, Remora had laid the ghost with candles and sacred waters, and many long readings from the Writings, urging it between times to go the Short Sun.

So it was said in town, at least; and when he had asked about it, Remora had explained that ghosts, for the most part, did not realize they had died: "An, um, understandable? An innocent confusion, eh? They have never been dead before, hey? The, ah, we religious know. Generally. Informed, eh? Expected. No ghosts of, um, holy augurs, hey? Or, er, sibyls. Not—ah—unheard of. But few. Very few."

Remora walked beside him, speaking into his ear.

"We—ah—anticipate it. Some even pray that it may be hastened, so, er, desirous of the blessed companionship of the Nine. But the, um, ah . . ."

Unbelievers.

"Skeptics have assumed—no evidence, eh? Do you follow me here, Horn? Um, theorize that, er, dissolution? The kind embrace of High Hierax is an—ah—mere sleep. But without dreams. There is in, er, simple fact. No such thing."

Yes, Patera.

"They will not, um, credit it. Because they do not, eh? In every case—ah—recollect their dreams. The, um, goddess of sleep, eh? Morphia. Aspect of Thelxiepeia. She has, um, sagaciously arranged that we—ah—dream? That we shall be subject, eh? Yes, subject. Subject to phantoms—"

He had stepped on something hard and round. He picked it up, and felt dry, dead bark drop off under the pressure of his questing fingers. A fallen branch.

"You see?"

No, Patera, he thought. No. I do not.

"No, um, slumber without dreams, so we may know that sleep is not the end. We who've given over countless, um, delightful hours to prayer are prepared. Know Hierax when he comes, eh? You are a, um, boatman? Sailor?"

Its twigs were weak and brittle, but the branch itself seemed stout enough.

"Steer by the stars, hey? Do you take my meaning, Horn? By the stars by, er, at the midnight hour, and by the sun, um, daylight. Just so. Not, um, myself. Not seaworthy, eh? But so I've been told. Sun, and stars."

He waved the stick before him, discovering a tree that might perhaps have been the same tree to his left and something spongy that was probably a bush to his right. The pinpoint of yellow light called out to him like the driftwood fires the fishermen's wives lit on the beach by night.

"Landmarks. This is, um, crucial, eh? Landmarks. We, um, I spoke of faith. Of hours spent at prayer. Not—ah—natural to a child, eh? You agree? Run about shouting. Play. Perfectly normal. Fidget in manteion, seen them scores of times. You likewise, doubtless."

Yes, Patera. Certainly.

The stick made it easier to walk, and he told himself that he was walking toward the Aureate Path, toward the spiritual reality of which the mere material Long Sun was a sort of bright shadow. He would go to Mainframe (although he had already been there) and meet gods.

"A child, therefore, clings? A child adheres to landmarks, places familial and familiar."

Hello, Molpe. My name is Horn, Marvelous Molpe, and to tell you the truth I ever paid much attention to you. I'm sorry for that now, Molpe, but I suppose it is too late. You were Musk's goddess. Musk liked birds, loved hawks and eagles and all such, and I didn't like Musk, or at least didn't like what others told me about him.

"Hug the shore, eh? These, um, departed? These children who have, um, attained to life's culmination early. The—ah—familiar house, um, rooms. Toy, eh? Even toys. We, er, prattle that they have lost their lives, hey? Said it myself. We all have, eh? Possibly they hope to find them again, like a lost doll. Sad, though. Tragic. Not like, um, exorcising devil, eh? Caldé Silk, eh? Performed the—ah—exorcised. Wrote an, um, report. Some old place on Music Street. I—ah—saw it. His, um, report, that is."

You were the goddess of music too, Molpe. I ought to have remembered that. I could use a cheering song. And I have sung, Molpe. I really have, although I was not thinking specifically of you. Oh, Molpe! Please, Molpe, dear old Molpe, goddess of kites and childhood, doesn't that count for something?

The point of light had become a rectangle. Still very far, and still very small; but distinctly a rectangle. Which god had light? Molpe? Molpe had autumn leaves, vagrant scraps of paper, wild birds, clouds, and all the other light things. So why not light itself?

"Pas, eh? Solar god, er, sun god. Go toward the light, child, hey? Steer by the sun."

What about the stars, Patera? Was Pas the god of stars, too? No, he could not be, because the stars burned outside Pas's whorl.

Not just in manteion, Molpe—but I sang there every Scylsday as a boy.

Miraculous Molpe, wind-borne on high,
Reaches her realm to the lands of the sky.
Dance for us, Molpe! Sing in our trees,
Send us thy breath, the sweet, cooling . . .

The old hymn faded and was gone with his cracked and lonely voice. Tartaros was the god of night and dark places, Tartaros who had been Auk's friend, walking with Auk, his hand in Auk's. There was no god's hand in his own, nothing but the stick that he had picked up a moment before. Was there a stick god? A god of wood and tree? A god or goddess for carpenters and cabinetmakers? If there was any, he could not think of it.

Smoke. He stopped to sniff. Yes, wood smoke. Very faint, but wood smoke.

How hot it was!

He had tried to smoke and salt fish when they had first come to Lizard, and watched his fish spoil afterward, had gone at last, after humiliating himself more than once, to the fishermen and learned their secrets. The smell of wood smoke always reminded him of his failures, of eating the fish that even loyal Nettle would not eat and being violently ill for half a day afterward. It was the dryness, not the smoke (as he had thought), that preserved the fish from decay.

"Tartaros! Can you hear me, Tenebrious Tartaros? Are you listening?" When he had written about Auk, he had shown Tartaros replying instantly to such pleas as those; but here was no book, no story, and there was no answer at all.

This grass-like stuff was wheat, presumably. Some sort of grain. They grew wheat, in that case, in the dark beyond the Aureate Path, the darkness of which the shade was a mere material shadow cooling the whorl, cooling even the breath of Molpe.

Hare had joined General Mint after Blood died, and had told them about the eagle and the old kite maker's praying to Molpe for a wind. The wind had come, he said. The wind, and winter, too. Winter at last, with snow to refresh fields as hot and dry as dead fish hanging over a fire.

How hard the wind had blown, and how bitterly, bitingly cold it had been when they had gone down into the tunnels!

Not like Green. No, not like Green at all.

The bomb had burst, and Hyacinth had feared that their horse had been killed. Hyacinth, freezing cold and a little dirty, so beautiful in the dim light and wind-driven snow that it had been hard to look at her. Nettle had been cheerful and brave; but Hyacinth had been lovely, always lovely and always finding new ways to be lovely even when she was exhausted or shrieking curses. Hyacinth had hated all men, had hated men in the aggregate, because of things that had been said to her and things she had been forced to do for money, humiliations worse than spoiled fish.

He had loved Nettle—Nettle, whose mother had hated her from the moment of conception, as the name she had given her had made only too plain—and had envied Patera Silk Hyacinth (lovely, savage Hyacinth) with all his heart.

He stumbled and fell, got up again, too weary to swear, and looked for the golden rectangle; but it had vanished. He was tired, he discovered. Weak and tired and light-headed, and what was the use? Sighing, he dropped to his knees, then stretched out upon the soft, half-grown grain.

If Hyacinth had indeed been his, he would never have gone to Blue, never have gone to Green, never have died on Green. . . .

For the first time he admitted himself that he was truly dead, that he had died in the medical compartment of the pillaged lander he had struggled so desperately to repair. This was the whorl again, the *Whorl* in which he had been born, and this was the only afterlife he had been granted.

If he had somehow possessed Hyacinth, he would still be in the Long Sun Whorl. He had not possessed her, yet here he was, without the Long Sun.

His eyes shut of themselves, seeing no less shut than open; and the soft cold swirling snow of another day filled his mind, mocking the dry heat of black night.

Wings beat overhead, and a harsh voice called, *"Silk? Silk? Silk?"* But he did not reply.

The third member of our party is my daughter Jahlee. She is of medium height, red-haired and attractive, with a smooth almond-shaped face and a sly smile many find captivating. The white mule is hers; she wears a thick wool gown under a wide, warm, snow-cat coat that reaches to the ankles of her kid-skin boots. The cold makes her slow and sleepy just the same, and she fears—as I do myself—that she may freeze to death like my poor friend Fava.

Jahlee is talented, although it might be unwise for me to say exactly how. She slipped her hands from the bonds as soon as the bandits left us. She can free herself easily from all such restraints, and her big white mule tolerates her, although it is naturally somewhat fearful. Our horses panic if Jahlee rides too near—but perhaps I have said too much already.

About myself, there is less to tell. I am Horn, Hide's father and Jahlee's. I am taller than most, and thin, with a homely, bony sort of face and white hair as long and thick as a woman's. I wear sheepskin boots like Hide's, and a long sheepskin coat over the old dark robe in which I left Gaon.

Now you know all four of us, and I must get some rest.

We hoped to reach the coast today, but there is no sign of it. I asked Hide whether we would not be several days' ride north of New Viron when we reach the sea. He said a week's ride at least. No doubt he is correct, but I would have appreciated more optimism. Since it seems likely that we are north of New Viron, we will pass Lizard before we come to the town. We will pass it, but we cannot reach it without a boat. Much as I would like to see Nettle (and Hoof?), my mill, and the house, I have resigned myself to going to New Viron first, selling our horses and some of the loot, and buying a boat.

Hide and Jahlee are asleep. It worries me, because she sleeps so little, normally; but she is near the fire and as warm as I can make her, with two blankets under and three over her, and her big coat as well. Her face—

I have sent Oreb to look for the sea. He is not as skillful as I would like at estimating distance or gauging the difficulty of rivers, sloughs, and the like; still, he will be able to tell me something of value. Or so I hope. Jahlee might scout for us in warmer weather, and that would be better.

Tomorrow we must find someplace where we can buy more food. If I thought that Jahlee was as hungry as I am now, I would be afraid to sleep.

Hide woke me up to tell me about his dream. He thought it might be important, and perhaps it is. Now he is sleeping again, but I shall sit up until dawn. It would be dawn already if only the sky were clear.

"It was so strange, Father. I didn't know I was dreaming at all until it was over, and it was such a long dream."

I nodded. "People say that when you know you're dreaming you're practically awake."

"Then I wasn't, but I was wide awake the minute it was over, and that was just a minute ago. Maybe I shouldn't have tapped your shoulder like I did."

"It's rather too late to think of it now." I yawned and stretched, believing—then—that I would be able to go back to sleep quite quickly.

"Can I get you something? A drink or something? There's a lot of wine left."

I shook my head, and suggested that he tell his dream, since he had awakened me for that purpose.

"I was in this big, big house. Like a palace. I've never seen a real one, but like the Caldé's Palace you and Mother talk about. Only it wasn't grand like that, it was more like a great big kitchen with lots of rooms. I know this sounds petty silly."

"Dream-like at least."

"And halls and pantries and things, and tables and chairs and a lot of big cabinets of some kind of light-colored wood, smooth and waxed but not, you know, carved or painted very much. Some of the chairs were upside down. I don't smell things in dreams much, but I could smell food all the time, like meat with lots of pepper in it boiling in a pot, and bread baking."

"That was because you were hungry," I said. "People who go to sleep hungry are apt to dream about food."

"I never saw any, but the smell was in the air all the time. I walked around . . . I don't know how to explain this."

"You need not try, in that case."

"I was younger. I couldn't be sure how old I used to be, but I knew I was younger in my dream."

"I'd like very much to have a dream like that."

"I was afraid I'd meet Hoof. I felt like he'd be mad at me for being younger, and he'd be bigger and stronger than I was. I walked a long way, and sometimes I'd see tall men with too many legs going into rooms, but I couldn't get the doors open, and mostly I didn't try. Sometimes they'd be waiting up against the wall where I couldn't see them good because there was a cupboard or something there, and I'd be afraid to look. You're making the little circles again, Father. What is it?"

"Nothing, perhaps. Did you ever get a good look at them?"

He shook his head.

"Did they have long noses?"

"I think so."

"Large ears?"

"I don't know. I didn't ever see their faces very well, but it wasn't anybody I knew. Or I don't think so."

"I understand. Did you look at your hands, Hide?"

"At my own hands? I don't think so."

"We seldom do. Or at least I don't look at mine often. Jahlee must watch hers a great deal more. When we killed the bandits I beat a man to death with my staff."

He nodded. "I remember."

"I didn't think you'd noticed. You were shooting."

"You had to do it, Father."

"No. No, I didn't, and I didn't intend to. It was only that I struck him, several times, I think, and he fell but he kept his grip on his knife. Then he started to rise, and I was afraid—desperately afraid, Horn—"

"I'm Hide, Father."

Although I blush to record it now, I only blinked and stared at him, wondering how I could possibly have made such a foolish error. Oreb saved me, landing on the ground at a point that put the fire between Jahlee and himself. "Big wet," he croaked self-importantly. "Bird find."

"Is it much farther?" Hide asked him.

"Bird find!" he repeated.

I told Hide, "He means that it is far for us but not for him. Is there a town, Oreb, where the land meets the sea?"

"Big town!"

"I see. Are there any before that? One we might reach tomorrow, for example?"

"No town."

I nodded. "Thank you very much indeed, Oreb. You've been very helpful."

He took wing.

"He's still afraid of Jahlee," I told Hide. "I don't believe he has reason to be, but he is."

"So am I, a little. I mean, not on Green or that other place, but here."

I nodded again. "Was she in your dream?"

He shook his head.

"Was anyone, besides the tall men?"

"A little girl named Mora and another one. Do you remember Mora from back when we were staying at that farm Jahlee pretended was hers? You said you knew her before, and she talked like she knew you."

"Of course."

"This little girl looked a lot like her, dark and pretty, you know? And she had a thing here on her cheek." Hide touched the middle of his own.

"I understand."

"They'd been playing with dolls. You know how girls do."

"Yes, certainly."

"They had a lot of dolls and toy dishes and a little table and chairs. The dark one wanted me to play with them, and I said all right, only not that. Then the other one said how about hide-and-seek? So I said all right. Then they said their dolls could play too, whoever was it could look for the dolls, too."

"I see."

"I hid my eyes, you know how you do, and counted to a hundred. You wanted to know if I'd looked at my hands."

"Yes. Did you?"

"Uh-huh. I just thought of it, but I did then. I remember taking my hands down after I counted. They looked younger, too, just like the rest of me."

"Were you wearing a ring? Any jewelry at all?"

He shook his head.

"Do you remember the ring I found in the lander?"

"Sure. Only you gave it to Sinew, not me. I don't think I could have taken it back with me."

"Neither do I. I simply wanted to know whether you remembered what it looked like."

"A white gold ring with a white stone."

I nodded, looked at my own hands, and picked up my staff, which had lain beside me while I slept. "I spoke of killing a man with this. I hadn't intended to kill him, but I was afraid he was going to kill us. I thought he might kill you or Jahlee, and kept hitting him as hard as I could; when the fighting had ended, I looked at him, and he was dead."

"It wasn't your fault, Father."

"Of course it was, and his as well. It was—it is—my fault that I killed him. It is his fault that I bear the guilt of killing him, because he gave me good reason to fear him. But if it could be proved that his death was neither his fault nor mine, it would not restore him to life."

"No."

"After the fighting was over, I noticed I had blood on my hands and realized that it was his. I washed them, and for a moment thought that I had lost the ring Seawrack gave me."

From a branch some distance from our fire, Oreb called, "Bird say. Say girl."

I looked up at him. "What are you talking about?"

"Say girl. Silk go. Go wet!" He flew, quickly vanishing in the dark sky; and Hide ventured, "Maybe he wants to tell Mother we're coming home."

"Perhaps he does. May I ask how your dream ended?"

"Well, I hid my eyes like I said, and after that I looked for a long, long time. Sometimes I saw those tall men. They would be standing still next to something else tall, like one of the cupboards or a big clock or something. But I knew they weren't playing and I wasn't supposed to see them at all, so I pretended I didn't, and went on looking."

"Did you find anyone?"

"Yeah. It took a long time, but I finally did. I opened this one big cabinet, and there was one of the dolls." He fell silent, his face troubled.

"I would think you would have been happy."

"I was. It was just a doll, though. Like a baby, only somebody had carved a face sort of like that one on your stick. Only this was a baby's face, and painted pink. Younger than Bala's baby. You couldn't even tell if it was a boy or a girl."

I said I doubted that it made any difference.

"I guess not. I took it and carried it like a real baby, and tried to go back to base. The place where I'd counted?"

"I understand. Could you find it?"

"Huh-uh. I looked and looked, only I couldn't find them. You know, the little table, and the chairs the dolls had been in. So finally I sat the doll down in a corner and said you're it. I explained about hiding eyes and counting, and looking for people, and then I ran away and hid. There was this great big long sofa with lots of legs, I don't know how many but eight or ten, maybe, and I got down on my stomach and crawled under it."

"Go on."

"There was a little girl hiding under there already. At first I thought it was the one with yellow hair, but it wasn't."

I nodded and said that I was delighted to hear it.

"Then I thought it was the other one, Mora. Only it wasn't her either."

"Who was it?"

Hide looked troubled, and seemed unable to meet my eyes. "I don't know."

"Was that the end of your dream?"

"Almost. We didn't talk, just pushed up close and held on to each other. We were both scared."

"In a game of hide-and-seek? What were you afraid of?"

"Being found, I guess. I was in front and she was in back against the wall, and I wanted to say if she sees me I'll go out and be it, and they won't know about you. Only I didn't. And pretty soon I could hear the doll, walking slow and looking in all the cabinets. And then I woke up and woke you up."

"To ask what your dream meant."

He nodded. "Yeah."

"But there is something about your dream you aren't telling me. Who was the girl under the sofa?"

"I don't know."

"Have you told me everything you remember about her?"

"What did it mean, Father? Do you know?"

"I might guess, I suppose—but I have no intention of guessing until you're willing to tell me everything you remember about it. Are you?"

"I'll think about it," he said, and lay down.

The sea was to his left, cliffs of wet black rock topped with dark and lofty trees to his right. At times he climbed over tumbled stones and fallen trunks. At others, he walked stony beaches with water lapping at his boots. He had gone a long way already and felt he had a long way to go still, although he could not have said how far, or where he was going. A single bird swooped and wheeled over the sea; once it cried hoarsely and he stopped to look up at it, touched by some memory to which he could not put a name.

At last he saw a house, small and primitive, with walls of big timbers and a steep roof of wooden shingles that were curling now, warping from the sea's salt spray and the Short Sun's heat. He made for it, aware that in some fashion he had left the beach, that he was wading, or perhaps walking inland. There was sand under his feet as he approached the house, sand mixed with chips of bark. He tried to rid his boots of it before he went inside, kicking the step gently with his left foot, then his right. He stepped inside . . .

And was home. The table at which they had eaten was there, armless chairs for Nettle and himself, stools for the boys. When Marrow and the rest arrived to ask him to go back to the *Whorl,* there would not be chairs enough for all of them, and someone would carry out the heavy wooden storage box that he had built for winter clothes, and someone else would sit on that.

But Marrow and the rest had not yet come to ask him to go. There was a child asleep in a basket now, the old wicker basket Nettle had woven for herself before they left the farm that had been their share of Blue, the land given them for coming because everyone had wanted land and livestock, even those like themselves who had less than no idea what to do with it. The sleeping child was Sinew. He knew it before he saw its face, before he saw the small silver ring the child wore, or the white stone in the ring.

The inhuma came, a bent and haggard figure that was not a woman, in a gown contrived of yellowing rags. She recalled Jahlee. Had Jahlee come to Blue for the human blood she needed and returned to Green, then come to Blue again? How long had she starved under the stone in Gaon?

The inhuma bent to drink, and he turned his head away and found himself crouching on the sand beside an earlier Horn who was seated on a blanket beside Nettle. Her right hand was in his; with her left, she pointed to a fish jumping far away, invisible against the setting sun but leaving silver circles on the calm swell of the sea. The fear of another pregnancy hung over them both, invisible as the fish but more real.

Nettle said, "Did you ever see anything so beautiful?"

He whispered in Horn's ear. *You.*

"When we were on the airship . . . Do you remember? I went up there alone. Up on the roof of the gondola. I never told you."

"I would have come with you."

"I know. But you were still asleep, and anyway I wanted to do it by myself, just once. It was the day before we got back to Viron, I'm pretty sure."

"It must have been cold," the Horn beside her said.

And he, the walker beside the sea, knew that Horn was thinking of the winter not long past that would soon come again, and the donkey frozen in the little hut he had built for it, and himself standing over it with his knife thinking that there had been some mistake that it could not be real, the donkey had been so young, not yet a year old, and it could not be happening; but back in the log house on the beach Jahlee had drunk her fill. Her fangs had vanished. She had licked the child's face and neck, and had wiped her mouth on the back of her hand, a ragged, painfully thin figure with famished eyes who melted through the doorway and was gone.

"It was, but not as cold as it was in Viron down on the ground once we got there. You couldn't see much sun, because the airship was sailing down the sun."

"I remember," the Horn beside her said.

"Just the same, I knew when the shade started to go up. I could see it in my mind, and the first light came down like gold dust."

The Horn beside her may have spoken then. Or not. If he did, the walker beside the sea crouching next to him did not hear him. *In a moment the sun will be down. The stars will come out, and the wind grow cold. You will go inside and find Sinew, and it will never be the same again. Clasp her to you now. Tell her you love her now, before it is too late.*

It was desperately urgent that he speak—desperately urgent that he be heard and understood. He rolled his head from side to side on the soft, crushed stems of the wheat, conscious that no sound issued from his lips.

His eyes opened. He sat up. It had been so real, all of it; but a dream, only a dream, and it was black night still.

He should lie down again, sleep again; in the morning, the men would expect him to lead them against his son's village.

We have been riding downhill all day. Winter is milder here, although it is still wretchedly cold. All of us would like very much to get inside, even the horses and Jahlee's mule—to escape the cold and the wind, if only for an hour.

We met other travelers today, four merchants with their servants and pack animals. We were glad to see them; but they, I believe, were even more glad to see us, because they had quarreled and were eager to air their grievances. I listened as long as I cold bear it and longer, reminding myself of all the foolish quarrels in which I myself have been involved, often as the instigator. It is educational as well as humiliating, to listen to others voicing complaints like our own. They were all thoroughly bad people of the type to which I myself belong—that is to say, bad people who are pleased to think themselves good.

At last Jahlee threw back her hood, leveled a trembling finger at the one who had been speaking and demanded to know what they wanted us to do.

"To judge between us," said one man, who had spoken less than the others. I believe his name is Ziek.

I explained that it would be quite useless for me to judge unless they would obey me as a judge, and one by one they pledged themselves to do so. Scylla is their principal goddess, I found, just as she was ours in Viron. That being the case I made them swear by Scylla, and by the Outsider, and by whatever gods might still linger here on Blue, and because I saw that had impressed them, by the Vanished People themselves.

When they had done so, I said, "Hear my judgment. You have so embittered yourselves, and forsworn yourselves, and tangled yourselves among competing claims and allegations that no peace is possible among you. There is no need, however, for you to torment yourselves as you have been doing. Am I to assume that you are all going to the same place?"

They were, to a town on the coast called Dorp.

"Then my judgment is that you must go there separately. You," I pointed to the largest of them, a man called Nat who seemed to be the richest too, "are to leave at once. How many of these horses and mules are yours?"

He had sixteen.

"Take them and go. Travel as fast as you can. We will rest here for a time before we follow you. When we ride again, it will be with the blond man in front, the one with the red cap between my son and me, and this one [by which I meant Ziek] behind my daughter. In an hour or so, I will send him ahead just as I'm sending you. In another hour another, and so on."

Nat protested. "What if I'm robbed? One man alone can't resist."

"Of course he can. He may be killed, but that is the risk he runs when he quarrels with his friends. Have your drivers collect your animals and go."

"Man go," Oreb seconded me.

He looked at me for a few seconds that seemed much longer, his eyes blazing with hatred. "I won't!"

"Then arrest him," I told the other three. "You've sworn to do as I tell you. Drag him off his horse and throw him down."

He drew a needler, but I struck his wrist with my staff. We have him still, I regret to say, with a valet, two drivers, eight horses, and ten mules. I had intended to have Hide untie him and remove his gag tonight so that he could eat, but I was tired and Hide was busy unloading and unsaddling our own horses, and hobbling them, and I forgot. From his size and the redness of his face, a missed meal is more apt to help then harm him, I believe. It will be enough to feed him in the morning before we let him go.

I am sleepy enough for two, but before I sleep I ought to say here that here we have four horses, not counting Jahlee's mule. That makes twenty-three animals, not counting Oreb, who seems to have gone exploring: Nat's mount, his valet's and his pack animals, my own mount and Hide's, the white mule, and two pack horses we took from the bandits, loaded with our scant baggage and some loot.

2

Great Pas's Godling

Her husband held the lamp while the woman poured warm water on his wounds. "What happened to you?"

He shook his head, and her husband snorted.

She said, "He doesn't know. Can't you see his face?" Then to him: "You can put that one down now. Hold out the other one. Over the bucket."

He obeyed as meekly as a child.

"Your cousin Firefly—"

"Firebrat," her husband said.

"He didn't know his name after he fell that time."

"You fall?" the husband asked. "Hit your head?"

"No."

"What's your name?"

He hesitated. "Horn."

"Don't want us to know," the husband remarked.

"They're clean now," the woman said. "Lots of people say wash them in wine, but water that's boiled is about as good, and wine costs."

He nodded gratefully.

She picked up the bucket, which was of wood bound with iron, carried it to the sink, and poured out pink water. "Where you from?"

"Lizard." (It had slipped out.)

"Lizard sent you? Who is he?"

"Are we in the *Whorl*?"

Her husband said, "Still here. They're tryin' to run us out, but we'll run them out 'fore we're through."

The woman sniffed. "Big talk."

"Then I'm from Viron. I was born there, and I grew up there." He felt a twinge of fear. "You're not at war with Viron here?"

The husband said, "They don't care about us out here."

"Where are we?" He looked around the kitchen as if the hulking black stove or the strings of onions suspended from the ceiling might provide a clue.

"Endroad." The wife tore a clean rag with a sound that made him think of blood and smoke and the rattle of buzz guns.

The husband nodded confirmation. "Endroad. 'Bout as far from Viron as you can get, without you go into the wild."

"We're not really there," the woman said briskly. "Hold out your arm. That one's starting to bleed again." She wound clean, worn cloth about it. "Take you about an hour to get to Endroad when the sun comes back."

"Nearest place, though," her husband explained.

"Only place," she corrected him.

"I don't want to become a burden to you."

Neither answered.

"I suppose I am already, but when you've finished bandaging those, I'll go."

"Knife cuts?" The husband sounded a trifle more friendly.

"I don't—" He recalled the knife on the floor. How threatening it had looked! "Yes," he said. "I believe so."

"Ah! Tried to fight him off." Slyly, "Was it a godlin'?"

That was a new word to him.

The woman said, "A godling would've killed him."

"Big one would've," her husband agreed.

He wanted to ask her what godlings were, but sensed that he should not. "I saw your light." That seemed safe. "I had gone to sleep in a field. In one of your fields, I suppose. When I woke, it was the only light that I could see anywhere, and so I walked toward it. I—I hope—"

"If you drink you get into these fights," the woman told him severely. "Leave that to the young ones."

"Only house hereabouts," her husband said, " 'cept manse."

Surprised, he looked up. "Is there an augur here?"

"Not no more."

The woman tied the last knot and straightened up. "There used to be. Still belongs to the Chapter, they say." She eyed him narrowly. "Some woman's there now. Came out from the city, I guess. You know her?"

"I don't know." He stood. "What's her name?"

"Don't talk much," the woman said.

Her husband lowered the lamp and set it on the battered table. "She went over there to be friends, but she just shut the door on her. Said she was sick."

"She looked sick, too." The woman hesitated. "Want something to eat? I guess we could spare something."

He shook his head. "I don't wish to impose on you any more. I'll leave now." He glanced at the open window, wincing inwardly at the utter darkness beyond it. "Have you any idea how long it will be until shadeup?"

"Shadeup?" The husband spat through the window.

The woman said, "Forgotten, haven't you."

"Forgotten what?" There was a stick in the corner, a rough stick far from straight that he decided must be his.

"Darkday. Sun goes out. Gone out now."

Vaguely he recalled an incident on Sun Street, the altar in the middle of the street, with the sacred window in which Echidna had appeared, the heat that had followed the darkness, and the blazing fig tree. "I know," he said.

"You'll get hurt." The woman spoke as if the words had been forced from her. "You'll get hurt again. You stay here until the sun comes back."

He looked from one to the other. "Don't you know . . . ?"

"No tellin'." There was anger as well as resignation in the husband's voice. "Gods been blowin' it out to make us go."

The woman sighed. "Something's wrong in your head, or you'd know."

"I'm going to tell you the truth. I mean all the truth. Everything, as I should have from the beginning."

There was a silence. At last the woman said, "Go on."

"I haven't lied to you. I was born and brought up in Viron, exactly as I said. But I've spent over twenty years on Blue."

The lack of any expression on their plain, work-worn faces

seemed to show they had not understood. He said, "Blue is what we call one of the whorls outside the *Whorl.*"

Neither spoke.

"Because it looks blue, you see, when you're high above it in a lander. Blue with streaks of white cloud, really, but you have to be close to see them. From Green it's just a blue dot, when the sky is clear enough for you to see it. I lived on Blue for years, as I said. After that I was on Green for a long time. Or at least, it seemed like a long time to me. I suppose it was actually only half a year or so; but I've been away from this whorl a long time. That's all I'm trying to say."

The woman muttered, "You been where they keep trying to get us to go."

"The gods? Yes. Yes, I have."

The husband asked, "Why'd you come back?"

"To find Silk. Do either of you know Patera Silk? Caldé Silk of Viron?"

Neither spoke. They edged closer together, regarding him through slitted eyes.

The rest seemed remote and unimportant, but he included it anyway. "Also to bring back new strains of corn and seeds of other kinds, and to study certain manufacturing processes. But mostly to bring Silk to New Viron, on Blue."

"Seed corn? Can't give you much, need it for us."

He nodded humbly. "A few would be enough. Six, perhaps."

The husband shook his head like a mule that does not want to take the bit. "Can't spare six ears."

"Six seeds, I meant. Six grains of corn."

"That'd be enough?"

"Yes, I'd be very grateful."

The woman asked, "How'd you get back?"

"I don't know." He found that he was staring at the wide, warped boards of the floor, his head between his hands; he forced himself to straighten up and look at her. "The Neighbors did it. The Neighbors are the Vanished People, the people who used to live on Blue a thousand years ago. They brought me here in some fashion, but I don't know how."

"When did you get here?"

"Yesterday. At least, I've slept once since I got here." He strove to remember. "There was sunlight when I arrived. I'm quite certain of that."

The husband nodded. "Days don't matter much. It's sun, or no sun. If you find Silk, how're you going to take him back?"

"In a lander, I suppose. You said the gods were trying to make you go."

Both nodded, their faces grim.

"So there must be landers left, perhaps landers that have come back for more people. The gods wouldn't try to force you out if there were no way for you to leave."

The husband spat out the window again. "They don't work. That's what I hear."

"I've had some experience of that on Green." He crossed the kitchen, finding his legs stronger than he had anticipated, and picked up his stick.

The woman said, "I'm going to fry some bacon. Haven't done it much on account of the heat. But I'm going to fry some soon as I get the stove going."

"That's very kind of you." As he spoke, he realized that he was more sincere than he had imagined. "I'm grateful—really I am. But I don't need food, and certainly don't need luxuries."

She had pushed back a curtain that had once been a sheet to search nearly empty shelves, and seemed not to have heard him. "I'll make coffee, too. Coffee's dear, but there's enough left for another pot."

He recalled the beverage of his childhood. "Maté, please. I'd like some. I haven't drunk maté in a long while."

Her husband said, "You want that seed corn? We got to fetch it out of the barn." He held a stick of his own, a thick staff more like a club than a cane.

"Yes, I do. Very much."

"All right." The husband leaned his staff against a chair, and rummaged under the table.

The woman asked him to pump, and he did so, heaving the big iron handle up and down until the rusty water was past and she had enough clean water to fill her coffeepot.

The husband pulled out a clumsy tin lantern and lit it from the lamp. "We'll go now. That'll take her a bit." An inclination of his head indicated the stove.

The woman murmured, "Coffee, bacon, and bread." She turned to face them. "That be enough?"

"More than enough. And I'd prefer maté, I really would."

The husband opened the door (letting in the ink-black dark), retrieved his staff, and raised his lantern. "Come on," he said, and they went out together.

"Is it dangerous out here? When the sun has gone out, I mean." He was thinking of the husband's staff.

"Sometimes. Horn, that's your name?"

"Yes," he said. "I'm afraid I didn't catch yours."

"Didn't throw it." The husband paused, chuckling at his joke. "You want that seed?"

"Very much." Something or someone was watching them, he felt—some cool intelligence greater than his own who could see in darkness as in daylight. He pushed the thought aside, and followed the husband, walking rapidly across dry, uneven soil as hard as iron.

"Know how to grow corn?"

"No." He hesitated, fearful that the admission would cost him the seed. "I tried once, and learned that I didn't—I had thought I did. But the seeds you give me will be planted by men who know a great deal. My task is to bring it to them."

"Won't grow in the dark."

He recalled speculating that those denied the Aureate Path might grow crops, and smiled. "Nothing does, I suppose."

"Oh, there's things. But not corn." The husband opened a wide wooden door, evoking scandalized protests from chickens. "Sun don't come back, that's the end for us. You comin'?"

He was staring upward into the pitch-black sky. "There's a point of light up there. One very small point of red light. Is it in the skylands? You have skylands here."

"That's right."

"On Blue the night sky is full of stars, thousands upon thousands of them. I'm surprised to see even one here."

"That's a city burnin'."

He looked down, horrified.

"Some city burns up there just about every time they blow the sun out. You want that corn? You come along."

He hurried into the barn.

"I grow my own seed. Two kinds. You can't let 'em cross. Or cross with any other kind, either. You know about that?"

He nodded humbly. "I think so."

"Cross 'em, and you'll get good seed. Plant it to grind and feed the stock. Don't plant the next, though. You got to go back to these old kinds and cross again. Six, you said."

"Yes. I believe that should be sufficient."

"I'm going to give you twelve. Six ain't enough." Butter-yellow lantern light revealed dry ears hanging in bunches.

"This is very, very kind of you."

"See here? This black kind?" The husband had detached an ear.

"Yes. I thought at first that it only looked black because it's so dark; but it really is black, isn't it?"

"You take it and pull off six. Not no more. I need it."

The ear was small and rough, the seeds small too, but smooth and hard. He rubbed and tugged six free.

The husband retrieved the black ear. "See this?" It was a second ear, slightly bigger and much lighter in color. "This's the other kind I got. Red and white. You see that?"

He nodded.

"The red ones and the white ones are both the same. Don't matter what color you take."

"I understand."

"You can have three red and three white, if you want 'em. Make you feel better. Color don't make no difference though."

"I will, just to be on the safe side."

"Figured. You plant 'em in the same hill so they'll cross. You don't feed that or grind it either. Plant it. Corn'll be yellow or white. Not never red nor black."

He nodded, struggling to detach the first grain.

"Plant it, and next year you'll have a real good crop."

"Thank you. I pray that I can get this seed you're giving me back to Blue safely."

"Your lookout. Thing is, every year you got to grow some black and some red-and-white off by themselves. Got to keep 'em apart and don't let no other corn near 'em. Do like that, and you can grow more seed next year for the year after."

"I understand." He held his hand closer to the lantern, seeing in the mingled grains waving green fields, sleek horses both black and white, and fat red cattle.

The husband retrieved the seed ear. "We're goin' out now."

"All right." Carefully depositing the twelve grains of corn in a pocket, he helped the husband close the big door.

"Wolves come in closer, darkdays," the husband said almost conversationally. "Kill my sheep. Not many left."

He said, "I'm sorry to hear that," and meant it.

"Got two dogs watchin' them. Good dogs. Kick up a fuss if there's wolves around, but I don't hear 'em. Now this Silk."

It had come too suddenly. "Yes. Yes—Silk."

"He was their head man down in the city."

"Caldé. Yes, he was."

"He was good out here. Got my slug gun off him. Years ago it was. Still got it, and three shells I'm savin'. He's not there no more. City people run him out."

"I see. Do you know where he went? Please—this is very important to me."

"Nope." The husband set the lantern on the ground between them. "He was head man a long time. Had a wife. Pretty woman's what I heard."

"Yes, she was. Beautiful."

"Whore, too. That's what they said. That why you want to find him?"

"No, I want him. I want to take him to New Viron, as I said—and Hyacinth too, if she'll come. Don't you have any idea where they are?"

The husband shook his head.

"I'm sure you'd tell me if you knew. You and your wife have been extremely kind to me. Is there anything that I can for you in return? Some sort of work I could do?"

The husband said nothing, standing in silence with legs slightly separated. His heavy, knobbed staff, grasped in his right hand at the balance, tapped the thickly callused palm of his left. The odors of coffee and frying bacon diffused from the open window of the kitchen, tantalizing them both.

"You want me to leave."

The husband nodded. "Go. Go or fight, old man. You got your stick. I got mine, and I'm tellin' you. You goin'?"

"Yes, I am." He held up the dead branch he had picked up the night before and flexed it between his hands. "I certainly won't fight you—it would be the height of ingratitude, and I've offered to leave several times already. I would greatly prefer to leave in friendship."

"Get!"

"I see. Then I must tell you something. I could defeat you with this, and beat you with it afterward if I chose. I won't—but I could."

The husband took a measured step toward him. "It'd break, and you're older than me."

"Yes, I suppose I am. But this stick wouldn't break, not the way I'd use it. And if you really believe the difference in our ages would give me an insurmountable handicap, it is base—very base—of you to threaten me."

When the better part of a minute had passed, he took a step backward. "Thank your wife for me, please; she was kind to a stranger in need. So were you. Tell her, if you will, that I left of my own accord, having no wish to deplete your meager store of food."

He turned to go.

He could not have said afterward whether he had heard the blow or merely known that it would come. He swayed to his right. Whistling down, the knobbed head scraped his arm and bruised the side of his knee. He pivoted as it struck the ground beside his left foot, pinned it with his foot, thrust his bloodstained stick into the husband's face and threw it aside. Half a second and the knobbed staff was in his hands. A quick, measured blow knocked the husband flat. Another put out the lantern.

Once he turned back to look at the lighted windows of the farmhouse he was leaving; but only once.

"Need practice!" exclaimed a man older than himself who popped unbidden into his mind. "Ruins you, fighting! Spoils your technique!"

He had white whiskers and jumped about in an alarming way, but his thrusts and cuts were as precise as a surgeon's with lancet and scalpel, and incomparably faster.

I can't practice now, Master Xiphias. I need this to feel my way along.

That had been the old man's name. He repeated it under his breath, then said more loudly, "Xiphias. Master Xiphias."

Some distance away, a bird called, *"Silk? Silk?"*—its hoarse cry shaped by chance or, as was more probable, his own mind, into the familiar name.

"Yes," he said aloud. "Silk. Patera Silk. And old Patera Pike, who must have been eighty. Also the sibyls, Maytera Rose, Maytera Marble, and General Mint."

The whorl had turned upside down, and suddenly—ever so suddenly—there had been Patera Quetzal, Patera Gulo, and Patera Incus; and Auk and Chenille, Hammerstone, Mucor, Willet, the lovely Hyacinth, and dozens of others. Running and shooting for Maytera Mint, who had continued to wear her sibyl's black bombazine gown, with a needler and an azoth in the big side pockets in which she had carried chalk.

Ginger's hand blown off, and Maytera Marble's cut off. "My mind's slipping," he confided aloud; it was comforting to hear a human voice, even if it was only his own. This rutted, grassless ground on which he walked was probably a road, a road going who-knew-where.

"It's like that first book Nettle tried to sew, the thread has broken and the pages have fallen out. They are gone now—all gone, except for Nettle and me. And Maytera, out there on her rock with Mucor, Marrow, and a few others. Old classmates. Sisters and brothers."

Calf, Tongue, and Tallow had wanted help from him, a great deal of help that his mother had urged him to provide, when he and Nettle had nothing to eat. It was a bitter memory, one that he counseled himself to forget.

"Got to practice!" That was Xiphias in the Blue Room.

How can I get to be a good swordsman, sir? I don't have anybody to practice with.

The sword out at once and pushed into his hand. Xiphias's old, veined hands (still astonishingly strong) positioning him before a pier glass. "See him? Fight him! Good as you are, every bit! Up point, and guard! Parry! Hilt, boy! Use the hilt! Think you've got it?"

He had said yes and thought no. Now he halted, making quartering cuts with the lighter end of the knobbed staff and parrying each the moment that he made it.

"Not so bad," he muttered. "Better than I did down on Green, though that sword was a better weapon."

"No cut," a harsh voice overhead advised. Startled, he terminated his practice; and something large, light, and swift lit upon his shoulder. "Bird back!"

"Oreb, is that you?"

"Good Silk."

"It can't be! By Bright Pas's four eyes, I wish I could see you."

"Bird see."

"I know you do, but that's not much help to me. Not unless something's lying in wait for us like the convicts did for Auk. Is there anything of that kind?"

"No, no."

"Armed men? Or wolves?"

"No man. No wolf."

He recalled the new word that the husband had used. "What about godlings, Oreb? Can you see any of those?"

The bird fluttered, his beak clacking nervously.

"You see those. You must. Are they close by?"

"No close."

"I'd ask you what they are, if I thought there was any hope of getting a sensible answer out of you."

"No talk."

"It's unlucky to speak of them? Is that what you mean?"

A hoarse croak.

"I'll take that for a yes, and take your advice, too—for the time being at least. Are you really Oreb? The Oreb who used to belong to Patera Silk?"

"Good bird!"

"You're a good talker at any rate, just as Oreb was. Did he teach you? That's what I heard long ago about you night choughs, that when one of you learns a new word he teaches the rest."

"Man come."

"Toward us?" He sought to peer ahead into the darkness, but might as effectively have peered into a barrel of tar. Recalling the husband's slug gun and three remaining shells, he turned to look behind him; the darkness there was equally impenetrable.

He faced about again. "Now, Oreb, I want to keep going the way I was before I turned around. Am I headed right?" He tapped the ground before him with the staff as he spoke.

"Good. Good."

"There isn't a pit at my feet, by any chance? Or a tree that I'm about to knock my head against?"

"Road go."

"And so will I." He stepped forward confidently, cutting and thrusting as he walked—and seemed to hear the staff that slashed the air tapping the roadway still. Stopping, he called, "Hello!"

A distant voice answered, "Heard me, did yer?"

"Yes. Yes, I did. I heard your stick."

The methodical tapping continued, but there was no further reply.

Under his breath he asked, "Can you see him, Oreb?"

"Bird see."

"That's the way. Keep your voice down. One man alone?"

"Big man. No men."

"Does he have a slug gun, or anything of that nature?"

"No see."

Deep and rough and somewhat nearer now, the distant voice said, "Dinna have such. Yer neither, bucky."

"You're right," he said. There was a faint, metallic rattle, and he added, "What was that?"

"Yer got gude h'ears."

"Tolerably so."

Nearer still. "How's yer een, bucky?"

"My eyes?"

Oreb muttered, "Man big. Watch out."

"Ho! Won't hurt him." The roughness of the approaching voice suggested a second night chough hopping along the road, its depth a huge bird as tall as a man.

"I heard something that sounded almost like the sling swivels of slug gun."

"Did yer, bucky?" A second rattle followed the final word.

"Yes," he said. "What is it?"

"How's yer een?"

"My vision, is that what you mean? Good enough." Recalling the spectacles he had found in his pocket, he added, "A little worse than most, perhaps, for reading."

"For readin', bucky?" The rough voice was close now. "Yer can read." A deep chuckle. "H'only ther wind's blowed yer candle h'out." *Wind* rhymed with *fiend* in the stranger's mouth.

"You're not from Viron, I take it."

"Nae from naewhere." The chuckle came again, followed by the rattle.

"I believe I recognized that sound this time—a sword blade in a brass scabbard. Am I correct?"

"Smack h'on, bucky."

Something—hard leather—touched his fingers, and he was reminded again of Xiphias's pressing the sword upon him, although the hand that gripped his arm was far larger than Xiphias's had been.

"Want ter feel a' her?"

"Yes, I do. May I draw it?" His hands had found the throat of the scabbard, a throat that was covered with leather too, like the rudimentary guard and the rest of the hilt.

"Canna see me whin, can yer, bucky?"

"No. But I'll be able to—to weigh it in my hand, without the scabbard. I needn't, if you'd prefer I wouldn't."

"Yer a h'officer, bucky?"

"A military officer, you mean? No. Nothing of the sort."

"Yer talks like such. Aye, pluck."

The blade hissed from the scabbard, heavier than the knobbed staff and nearly as long. He made a few cuts, ran his fingers gingerly over the flat, then wiped it on the sleeve of his tunic.

"Got h'it h'off a dead coof," the rough voice confided. "He dinna want h'it nae mair."

"But you do, I'm sure." He sheathed it again and held it out, touching something large and solid: leather again, soft old canvas, and cool metal that seemed to be a belt buckle nearly as high as his chin.

" 'Tis me." Taking back the sword, the stranger's outsized hands brushed his. "Want ter feel a' me clock?"

"Watch out!" Oreb fidgeted apprehensively on his shoulder.

"No," he told the stranger. "Certainly not."

"Craw, ain't h'it? Thought 'twas a man. H'on me hunkers sae yer can reach. Have yer feel, bucky." His left wrist was caught between fingers as thick and hard as the staff, and guided toward a mat of coarse hair. He was conscious of a faint reek of sour sweat.

"You have a beard," he said. "So do I." The nose was wide and prominent, the cheekbones high and gaunt, framed in shaggy hair that fell to the stranger's shoulders.

"Took me rag h'off." His hand was freed, then caught again. "Here's me e'e. Stick in yer finger."

"I'd rather not," he said; two fingers were forced into the empty socket nevertheless.

"H'other's ther same. Feel a' her?"

He was forced to. "You're blind," he said. "I—I know how banal it sounds, but I'm sorry."

"Wait till me rag's back h'on," the stranger rumbled. "Want ter feel a' yern. Got ter, an' yer ken why. Yer get a notion a' me clock?"

"Yes," he said, afraid that he would be forced to touch the stranger's face again. "I should warn you, though, that Oreb doesn't like being held. He'll probably fly if you attempt it."

Oreb contradicted him. "Touch bird!"

"Dinna think he never did, not nae live 'un."

"Touch bird!"

"*Seen* lots, 'fore me een was took. H'oreb's his name?"

"It's what I call him, at least. A friend I had long ago—the friend for whom I'm searching—had a pet night chough he called that. I'm afraid I've given this one the same name to save the trouble of thinking of a new one." He felt Oreb leave his shoulder and added, "He's going to you, I think."

"Lit h'on me whin. A fin'er, H'oreb, an' speak h'up h'if h'it pains yer."

"No hurt."

He felt a pang of jealousy that he quickly suppressed. "I've already introduced Oreb, so I ought to introduce myself as well. My name is Horn."

"Horn. An' H'oreb."

"Yes," he said, and felt Oreb return to his shoulder.

"What would yer say me h'own name might be, bucky?"

"Your name? I just met you. I have no idea."

The tapping resumed. "We might's well walk h'as talk. Never heard nae name like Horn. Nor H'oreb neither."

"It means *raven,*" he explained as he strode after the steady tapping of the stranger's sword. "It's from the Chrasmologic Writings. Caldé Silk, the friend I spoke of, was an augur."

"H'oreb. Horn. Silk. Common names, like? Maybe me h'own might be Cotton, here."

"Why no, that's a woman's name." He felt vague frustration. "Surely it would be better if we called you as your mother did."

" 'Twas Freak, mostly."

"I see—understand, I mean. No doubt you're right; it would be better if you had a new name among us."

"Aye."

"You asked whether Oreb, Horn, and Silk were common names. Oreb is very unusual—I've never known a man with that name. Silk is fairly unusual, too, although certainly not unheard-of. Horn is common enough."

"Huh!"

"Here in Viron, men are named after animals or parts of animals. Silk is a male name, just as Milk is, because Silk comes from an animal, the silkworm. Addax, Alpaca, and Antbear are all common names. Do you like any of those?"

"H'ox fer me, maybe. Might do. H'or Bull. What h'about 'em, bucky?"

He smiled. "People would think we were related, but I've no objection to that."

"Gie me some mair."

"Well, let me see. Silk had a friend named Auk. An auk is a kind of water bird, as you probably know."

"Me h'own could be H'owl, maybe. Blind h'as a h'owl by daylight, dinna they say?"

"Yes, it could, if you wish it; also there are the various kinds of owls—Hawkowl, for example. I was about to say that Auk had a friend named Gib. A gib is a tomcat, so that's a male name, too. Gib was a large and powerful man, as you are."

"Pig," the stranger rumbled.

"Good name!"

"I beg your pardon?"

"Said me name's Pig, bucky. H'oreb, he likes h'it. Dinna yer, H'oreb?"

"Like Pig!"

Pig laughed deep in his chest, clearly pleased. "Never heard a' nae blind pig, bucky?"

"I don't think so, but I suppose there must be some."

"Have ter have a new name when me een's found. H'eagle, h'it could be, h'or Hawk."

"Did you say something about finding eyes?" He was startled.

"Aye. Why Pig come, bucky, doon h'out a' ther light lands. Have een ter gie h'in this Viron, bucky? Een fer me? 'Tis ther muckle place hereabouts? Yer talk like h'it."

"Yes, Viron's the city. It owns, or at least it controls, this land, and all the farms and villages for fifty leagues and more. But as to whether there is any physician in Viron skillful enough to restore your sight, I really have no way of knowing. I doubt that there was when I was here last, but that was about twenty years ago."

Pig seemed not to have heard. "Dinna drink nae mair."

"I seldom do myself. A little wine, occasionally. But I wanted to say that this is an extraordinary coincidence. You're looking for eyes, as you put it. Because I'm looking for eyes also. For one at—"

Pig had caught his shoulder, causing Oreb to flee with a terrified squawk. "Had een, yer said." Questing thumbs found them and pressed gently. "Read, yer said."

"Yes, sometimes. Not lately."

"Gude een, yer got." Fingers and thumbs traversed his cheeks, found the corners of his mouth and the point of his chin under his beard. "Snog clock, bucky. Liked ther girls, dinna yer? When yer was younger?"

"Only one, actually."

The tapping of the leather-covered brass scabbard resumed. "Them that can winna, an' 'em that wad canna. 'Tis a hard grind fer ther h'axe, bucky."

"A hard life, you mean. Yes, it is."

"Een noo. Yer lookin' fer een, yer said."

"Eyes for a chem. I have a friend—a chem who was a co-worker when I was younger—who's gone blind."

"Like auld Pig."

"Yes, precisely, except that she's a chem. Her name is Maytera Marble, and before I left Blue I promised I would find new eyes for her if I could. She gave me one of her old ones to use as a pattern, but I no longer have it."

"Yer lost it?"

"Not exactly. I was forced to leave it behind. I remember how it looked, however, or at least I believe I do; and I'd like very much to find replacements, if I can. Maytera was my teacher when I was a child, you see. I mean—"

"No talk!"

"Dinna fash auld Pig, H'oreb. Bucky, would yer make mock a' me fer h'offerin' me fin'ers ter help yer look?"

"Certainly not."

"Dinna think h'it. Yer nae ther kind. Yer lookin' fer a mon, yer said. Silk's ther name?"

"Yes, Caldé Silk. Or Patera Silk. I intend to find him, and to bring him to Blue. That's what I swore to accomplish, and I will not break my oath."

"Ho, aye. An' Silk's cauld?"

"Dead? Then I'll find new eyes for Maytera Marble and return home, if I can."

There was a silence.

"Pig? Is that what you want me to call you?"

"Aye."

"Pig, would you mind if I walked closer to you? If—if I touched you, sometimes, as I walked?"

"Shuttin' yer h'in, h'is h'it? Touch h'all yer want."

"The darkness. This dark. Yes. Yes it is."

"Like dark!"

"I know you do, Oreb. But I don't. Not this, particularly. At home—on Blue, I mean. May I talk about the way it feels, Pig? I certainly don't mean to be offensive, but I believe it might make me feel better."

"Blue's h'outside, bucky?"

"Yes. Yes, it is. It has a—the Short Sun. A round gold sun that walks across the sky during the course of the day, and vanishes into the sea at shadelow. At shadeup it reappears in the mountains and climbs up the sky like a man climbing a hill of blue glass. But before it begins to climb, there's a silent shout—"

Pig chuckled, the good-humored rumble of men rolling empty barrels.

"It's a silly phrase, I realize; but I don't know another way to express it. It's as though the whole whorl, the whorl that we call Blue and say we own, were welcoming the Short Sun with tumultuous joy. I'm making myself ridiculous, I know."

Pig's hand, twice the size of his own, found his shoulder. "Dinna naebody but yer hear what dinna make nae noise, bucky?"

He did not answer.

"Partners?"

"Surely. Partners, if you don't object to having a fool for a partner."

"Yer misses yer Short Sun."

"I do. It would be a relief, a very great relief to me, to see a light of any kind. A lantern, say. Or a candle. But most of all, the sun. Daylight."

"Aye."

"You must feel the same way. I should have realized it sooner. And if we were to encounter someone with a lantern, I would see it and see him. Even now, even in this terrible darkness, I remain singularly blessed. I should pray, Pig, and I should have thought of that much sooner."

Far away, a wolf howled.

"Yer got 'em h'on yer whorl?" Pig inquired.

"Yes, we do. Ordinary wolves, such as you have here, and felwolves, too, which have eight legs and are much larger and more dangerous. But, Pig . . ."

"H'out wi' h'it."

"That whorl, Blue, had people living upon it long before we came—people who may still be there, some of them at least. One seldom sees them. Most of us never have, and we call them the Vanished People, or the Neighbors, and children are taught that they're wholly legendary; but I've seen them more than once, and even spoken with them. I don't believe I will again, because I've lost something—a silver ring with a white stone—that was left behind with Maytera Marble's eye."

"Huh!"

"But once when I did—when I spoke with the Neighbors—I asked what they had called the whorl we call Blue, what their name for it had been. And they said, 'Ours.' "

"No cry!"

"I'm sorry, Oreb." He tried to dry his eyes on the sleeve of his tunic, then clamped the knobbed staff beneath his arm to search himself for a handkerchief. Pig's elbow brushed his ear, and he corrected his position slightly and began to tap the roadway before him as Pig was.

"When Pig had een," Pig rumbled, "Pig dinna never have nae thin' ter look fer. Dinna tell yer sae?"

"No. Tell me now." He had recalled the bloody tatters of the handkerchief that the woman had discarded in the farmhouse kitchen, and was dabbing at his own eyes with his sleeve once more. (Remora spoke in the recesses of his mind. "No, um, place of permanence for us, eh? For we mortals, no—ah—possessions. Own it, eh? But in time, hey? Another's, and another's. Do you take my meaning, Horn? We've nothing but the gods, in the, um, make a final reckoning.")

"Muckle lasses, prog an' grog." Pig mused not far away, less visible than Remora in the dark. "Nae thin' h'else ter look fer, an' thought h'it livin'."

"No talk."

"Ho, Pig can bake h'it, H'oreb, an' yer can take h'it."

"No talk. Thing hear."

"Somethin' ter hear? What's fashin' him, bucky?"

He had already stopped to listen, his head cocked, both hands grasping the knobbed staff. No wind had blown, or so it seemed to him, since he had been returned to the Long Sun Whorl; but a wind touched both his cheeks, warm and moist and fetid. Hoping Pig could hear him, he whispered, "Something's listening to us or for us, I believe."

"Huh!"

"Where is it, Oreb?"

From his shoulder, Oreb muttered, "Bird see."

"Yes, I know you see it. But where is it?"

"Bird see," Oreb repeated. " 'Bye, Silk."

Feathers brushed the side of his head as Oreb spread his wings. Clawed feet pushed against his shoulder, those wings beat loudly, and Oreb was gone.

Pig said, "Yer corbie's right, bucky. 'Tis a godlin'. Pig winds h'it. H'in ther road h'up h'ahead, most like."

Something hard tapped his shin, and Pig's hand clasped his shoulder, feeling as big as his father's when he himself had been a small child—a sudden, poignant memory. That big hand drew him to one side. At his ear, Pig's hoarse voice muttered, " 'Ware ditch, bucky."

It was shallow and dry, although he might easily have been tripped by it if he had not been warned. A twig kissed his hand; he forced himself to close his eyes, although those eyes wanted very badly to stare out uselessly at the utter darkness that wrapped him and them. "Pig?" he breathed; then somewhat more loudly, "Pig?"

"Aye."

"What are they?"

There was no reply, only the big hand drawing him deeper among whispering leaves.

"Oreb wouldn't tell me. What is a godling?"

"Hush." Pig had halted. "Hark." The hand drew him forward again, and for an interval that seemed to him very long indeed, he heard nothing save the occasional snap of a twig. Trees or bushes surrounded them, he felt sure, and from time to time his questing staff encountered a limb or trunk, or some motion of Pig's evoked the soft speech of foliage.

A faint and liquid music succeeded it, waking his tongue and lips to thirst. He hurried forward through the blackness, drawing the towering Pig after him until gravel crunched beneath their feet and he sensed that the water he heard was before him. He knelt, and felt a gracious coolness seep through the knees of his trousers, bent and splashed his face, and tasted the water, finding it cool and sweet. He swallowed and swallowed again.

"It's good," he began. "I'd say—"

Pig's span-across hand tightened upon his arm, and he realized that Pig was drinking already, sucking and gulping the water noisily, in fact.

He drank more, then explored the stream with his fingers, trying to keep their movements gentle so as not to stir up mud. "It's not wide," he whispered. "We could step across it easily, I believe."

"Aye." There was a hint of fear in the deep, rough voice.

"But the godling—whatever that is—shouldn't be able to hear us as long as we remain here. Or so I think. The noise of the water should cover the sound of our voices."

He bent and drank again. "I pumped water for a woman who had bandaged my wrists not long ago. It was good, cold well water, I believe, and I almost asked her for a glass. But we were about to eat—

so I thought, at least—and I told myself I wasn't really so thirsty as all that. I must learn to drink when I have the opportunity."

He recalled Pig's chance remark about drinking, and added, "Drink water, I should say. I thought I had learned that on Green, where there was rarely any water that was safe to drink except for what certain leaves caught when it rained."

"Bird find," a harsher voice even than Pig's announced.

"Oreb, is that you? It must be. What have you found?"

"Find thing. Thing hear."

"Did you? Good. Where is it?"

"No show."

"I don't want you to show it to me, Oreb, and I couldn't see it if you did. I want you to tell me how to avoid it. We were going to Viron, or at least I certainly hope we were. Is this thing, this godling, standing in the road waiting for us?"

"No stand. Thing sit."

"But it's in the road? Or sitting beside it?"

"On bridge."

Pig broke in. "H'oreb, me an' Horn's partners. You an' me, H'oreb, why, we're partners ter, h'ain't we? Yer h'allow such?"

"Good man!"

"Not too loudly, please, Oreb." He drank again.

"So, H'oreb, Pig needs yer ter tell where we're h'at. Will yer? 'Tis h'another road, wi' this trickle across?"

"No road."

"A medder, H'oreb? Might find coos hereabouts, would yer say?"

"No cow."

"Huh!" Pig sounded impatient. "How can Pig get him ter tell, bucky? Yer know him."

Oreb answered for himself. "Say woods."

" 'Tis where we h'are, H'oreb? H'in a wood? Canna be."

"In woods," Oreb insisted. "Silk say."

"My name is Horn, Oreb—I've told you so. I believe he's correct, Pig. We're in a wood, perhaps on the edge of a forest." He paused to search his memory. "There was an extensive forest north of Viron when I lived there. A man named Blood had a villa in it, as did various other rich men. This may well be the same forest."

"Felt yer trees h'all 'round, bucky. Could nae touch 'em, an' such could nae touch me, h'or would nae."

"No doubt they're large trees, widely separated."

"Ho, aye." Pig's rough voice contrived to pack an immense skepticism into the two words. "Big trees hereabouts, H'oreb?"

"No big."

"Not close, they be? Ane here an' h'other h'over yon?"

"All touch."

"H'oreb can tell where they're h'at an' where they hain't. Do yer h'object ter lendin' him h'out, bucky?"

He rose. "I suggest we follow this stream instead. Streams frequently go somewhere, in my experience. Are you coming?"

"Bird come. Go Silk." Oreb settled upon his shoulder.

"Pig ter, H'oreb. We'll gae h'along wi' Horn."

He heard the big man's knees crack, and said, "Then let us go in silence, if you won't tell me about the godlings."

"Dinna hae naethin' ter tell yer, bucky. 'Struth. Pas sends such ter make folk gae ter yer h'outside places."

For some time after that they walked on without speaking. Now and then the tip of the knobbed staff splashed water; now and then the end of the leather-covered brass scabbard rapped softly against a trunk or a limb; but for the most part there was silence, save for the rasp and rattle of gravel beneath their feet and an occasional warning uttered *sotto voce* by Oreb, who at length offered, "No see."

"The godling, Oreb? Are you saying you no longer see it?"

"No see," Oreb repeated. "Thing watch. No watch."

Oreb's voice had sounded strangely hollow. The tip of the knobbed staff, exploring left and right, rapped stone. "We're in a tunnel of some sort."

"Aye, bucky." Those words reverberated slightly as well.

He stared into the darkness, half convinced he could make out a lofty semicircle of lighter black before them. "There are tunnels everywhere, do you know about them, Pig? Tunnels of unimaginable length and complexity underlying the entire Long Sun Whorl."

"Huh." Nearby in the darkness, Pig's softly re-echoing voice sounded understandably doubtful.

"I was in them long ago. One must pass through them to reach the landers, which are just below the outside surface. The first Oreb was down there as well, with Auk and Chenille."

"Bad hole!"

"Exactly. But I certainly hope you're right when you say the godling can't see us in here."

"Dinna harm folk," Pig muttered, "h'or nae h'often."

"We may be in those tunnels. If so, we're approaching a cavern such as the sleepers were in. Look up ahead. I can see something there, I swear." Without waiting for Pig, he hurried forward—then halted, stunned with wonder and terror.

To the north and south, the skylands spread in splendor far greater than he recalled. Against their magnificent display, above the bridge under which he had passed, he saw silhouetted shoulders like two hills, a smooth, domed head that might have filled the farm woman's kitchen and sundered all four walls, and bestial, pointed ears.

3

Justice and Good Order

Nat has sent troopers from Dorp, who have arrested us. Dorp it appears has a standing horde (as Soldo did) which it calls its leger. There are three legermen and the sergeant. I gave him two silver cards, and although he will not let us go, it has put us on a friendly basis. I am paying for our rooms at this inn as well, one in which the sergeant, a legerman, and I are to sleep tonight, and another in which Jahlee is supposed to sleep, with Hide and the other two legermen.

Dinner and a bath! The sergeant—his name is Azijin—has been given money with which to buy provisions; I told him he might keep it, at least for tonight. He and his men, I said, could join us at dinner. There was wine, and food that seemed very good to Hide and me.

Nat is a person of importance in Dorp, it seems. We are likely to be fined and whipped. I have tried to convey to my daughter that it might be well for her to leave us, but I am not sure she understood. If she did, she may not agree; and if she tries to escape now, she may be shot.

I will not stand idly by and see her stripped, no matter what some judge in Dorp may say.

As I was writing, she came in to ask for a larger fire. The innkeeper wanted an additional payment for the extra wood, and we began to bargain over the amount. Sergeant Azijin told him to supply it, cursing him and pushing him into the corner. Jahlee got her fire and went away satisfied. I looked in on her just now, and her appearance has improved greatly.

During our argument, the innkeeper stated that he "always" made an extra charge for extra wood. I asked him how long his inn has stood here, and he said proudly, "For six years." We are so new to this whorl that we have not worn out the clothes we brought from the other, some of us; yet we talk and act as if it has been ours from time immemorial. Once I wept when I told Pig what the Neighbors had said. He must have thought me mad, but I was only tired and weak, and oppressed by the stifling darkness. A sorrow, too, pressed upon my heart. It is still there; I feel it, and must keep busy.

Azijin lets me write like this, which is a great relief to me. I have worried that he might read it, but he cannot read. So he says, and I think he is telling the truth. He seems ashamed of it, so I assured him that it is not difficult, and offered to teach him, making large letters on the same paper I took from the bandits and use for this journal.

The wounded bandit Jahlee drained told us we might take whatever we wanted if only we would spare him, which I rashly promised to do. I can see him still: his thin mouth below its thin mustache, and his large, frightened eyes. Jahlee said she had never killed before, but I know it is a lie—she killed for me when we fought Han. We flatter ourselves with our horror of them, but are we really much better?

Rereading that above, I was aghast at my candor. What if the judge in Dorp should read it? I might destroy it (perhaps I should) but what about the other two accounts? How much labor I expended on them, dreaming that someday Nettle might peruse them, as she yet may. I must hide them.

I have done what I could, but the best solution would be to see to it that our baggage is not examined. I must question the sergeant about legal procedures, and ask his men as well—for all I know, they may have more and better information, or be more willing to part with it. Although we chatted together at dinner, I do not recall their names.

Before I sleep I ought to record the notable fact that I have bathed, for which I—and all who come near me, no doubt—am most grateful. On Lizard we washed in summer in the millpond or the sea. In winter, as I washed myself here after dinner: by heating water in a copper kettle hung over the fire and scrubbing everything with soap and a rag.

When I was a boy in Viron, we had tubs for it like washtubs, but longer. Those of the poorest class were generally of wood, those of the middle class, such as my mother and I, of iron covered with enamel. In Ermine's and the Caldé's Palace, and I suppose in the homes of the wealthy generally, they were stone, which seemed very grand. Still I have washed myself in them, and it is a finer thing to bathe in the millpond. I intend to pray for an hour or so when I lay down my quill. But if the Outsider were to grant my every wish, I would bathe always in our millpond; and whenever I wished to bathe, it would be summer.

★

★ ★

Oreb is back! Drawing the whorls between this paragraph and the last makes it look as if a week at least had passed, I know. It was only a night, but a great deal has happened. News enough for a week, to say nothing of dreams. I will do my best to take everything in order.

I had asked for more firewood, curious to see whether the innkeeper would try to collect for it after what had passed between himself and Azijin. I got it without additional payment, this room became quite warm, and when the sergeant returned I asked him to open the window. He did, and came very near to receiving a cold, tired, and very hungry night chough full in the face. It was Oreb, of course; and he had come to present me with a ring set with a peculiar black gem. I will describe it in greater detail in a moment, if I am not interrupted.

Just now I said that the sergeant was nearly hit by Oreb, who had, I believe, been pecking at the shutter for some time, although I had failed to hear him above the crackling of the fire. I must add that it was snowing hard, myriads of tiny flakes flying before a whistling west wind. "Them at sea Scylla help," said Azijin.

I got a fine fresh fish and a cup of clean water for Oreb. He ate and flew into a corner near the chimney—there is a wooden brace for it there on which he perches—and has not moved from it since. Azijin and Legerman Vlug were dumbfounded, and asked more questions about him than I was able to answer. I expected them to demand the ring; so I suggested they might hold it for me until we reached Dorp, when I would explain the circumstances under which I had received it to the judge and ask that it be returned to me. They examined it very curiously but showed no desire to keep it for me.

It is too large for my fingers, so I put it in my pocket, thinking I would look through the jewelry when I could do so at leisure, find a chain, and wear it around my neck. I was afraid I would lose it, however; it is on the thumb of my left hand as I write this, which answers well.

There is a picture cut into the black stone. I took it to the window, and although the day is far from bright I was able to see that there are lines graven on it, a picture or writing. I suppose it is a seal ring, and the thing to do is to imprint it on wax so the seal may be read.

I talked about Oreb for some time, explaining that he is a pet, that he can speak after a fashion, and that he often goes away for purposes of his own. Before I could get to bed, I had to tell them a bit about Silk and the original Oreb, saying I supposed he must be dead. "On that you must not count, mysire," Azijin told me. "A parrot older than her my great aunt had, and ninety-one she was when on the lander we went. About the old bird often my mother tells." So perhaps this Oreb is the very Oreb that Silk owned after all. It is such an interesting idea that I am glad there is no way in which it can be tested. How disappointed I would be if I found it were not true!

After that I went to bed, as did the sergeant and Vlug. I can only guess how long I slept before I was awakened by a soft hand stroking my forehead—an hour, perhaps.

It was Jahlee. "My fire's dying, Rajan, and the room's getting colder and colder. Can't I come into bed so you can warm me for a minute? I don't dare get in with Hide, he's sound asleep and would kill me when he woke, and you wouldn't want me to get into the troopers' beds would you? But I'm freezing, and I'm afraid I'll freeze to death. Please, Rajan? I'm begging for my life!"

I consented, and it was a remarkable experience even before we went to Green. I put an arm over her and held her so that she could warm her back against my belly; and it was exactly as though I embraced an actual woman, one more slender than Nettle and less voluptuous than Hyacinth, but beyond question a young and attractive woman, soft, clean, and perfumed.

I have been trying to recall what it was like to sleep with Fava, there amid the stones and snow; and I was very conscious then that she was not at all what she pretended to be, that I was in fact embracing a reptile capable of changing its shape in the same way that the little lizards I caught in the borage outside my window or the honeysuckle along our fence could change color—that my position was not much different from that of a snake-charmer sleeping in a ditch, with his serpent coiled under his tunic.

I woke and sat up, determined to dress, wake Jahlee, and tell her she had to go. As I got to my feet, yawning and blinking, the room was transformed in a way I would have said was quite impossible. The shutters became a circular opening through which showed a sky of the most ethereal blue. The knife-scarred wooden walls mended themselves and petrified to soft gray stone. Jahlee rose and wrapped herself in one of the blankets, being careful to let me see that she was beyond doubt a slim human woman with flawless white skin, a slender waist, and hemispherical pink-tipped breasts I longed to caress from the moment I glimpsed them. She embraced me and I her, while within two steps of us Azijin and Vlug slumbered on, sleeping on the same beds they use in this inn, and under the same rough blankets.

When we parted, I asked where we were.

"On Green. Can't you feel the warmth, and the dampness of the air? If I were the way I was the last time you saw me, they would feel wonderful to me. Here I am as I am." She paused to smile and let the blanket slip a trifle. "And they still feel wonderful. I exult in them!" Azijin's eyes opened. He blinked and seemed to stare about him in a dazed fashion; then he shut them again and slept once more.

I crossed the room to the window and looked out, expecting to see Green's jungles. Clouds such as I had not seen since Saba lowered us from her airship spread below me, not the black-tinged rain clouds that had oppressed us through unending months on Green, but pearlescent clouds shining in the sun, a sea greater and purer than the keels of men have ever parted, and a new whorl fairer even than Blue and more turbulent.

To drink it in, I leaned as far from the window as I could, and at last stood barefoot upon its gray stone sill, and grasping the inner edge of the opening with the fingers of one hand looked out and down, then up, and left, and right.

We were in a slender tower, standing in a niche in the face of an immense cliff of the dark red stone. Above, the red stone rose until it was lost in the glory of the sky, an infinite wall of congealed blood. To my left and right, it extended without limit, lined and eroded. Below stretched the tower, taller than the tallest I have seen on any of the three whorls, a sickening height that made me shut my eyes and step down again into the room in which Jahlee and I had awakened—but not before I had glimpsed its mighty base and the cliff below it falling away into the restless sea of cloud, sheer, black with damp, and dotted with splotches of the most brilliant green.

"I wanted to be a real woman again," Jahlee said softly, "a real woman for you and Hide, and for everyone else who wants me to be what I really am. It was why I joined you. You must have known that."

"I should have driven you away, but the bandits would have killed us both if I had."

"You foresaw that?"

I shook my head.

"Our bodies are asleep in that wretched little inn on your frozen whorl. If I were to die there . . . I've overheard you and your son talking about the other one, a woman like me he meets in dreams. He's afraid of her, but he wouldn't have to be afraid of me."

"Do you want me to kill you? I can't. My own body is sleeping, just as yours is. If I were to kill you here, you know what would happen. You saw Duko Rigoglio."

She went to the window and stood upon the sill as I had, and a wind rose that stirred her blanket and set her sorrel hair fluttering behind her. "If I could be like this forever, I would jump," she told the sky.

"Before you do, will you answer a question? You've been a good friend to my son and me, and I hesitate to put us further in debt to you; but I'm curious, and it may be important."

She stepped down and turned to face me.

"We've been to various places on Green, and to the Red Sun Whorl, to the very spot on which the Duko's house once stood."

"Yes." Her eyes were bright blue now, as though they were holes bored through her skull and I were seeing the sky behind her; for a moment I wondered whether she could control their color, and then if they had drunk so much of that sky that they had taken on its very hue.

"Most of the places to which I've gone have been places where I've already been, and the street of ruins in the city they called Nessus was certainly the street on which Rigoglio had lived. I very much doubt that either Azijin or Vlug have been to Green at all, and I have certainly never been to this strange tower in this mighty cliff. Have you?"

She nodded without speaking, and I asked her when.

"When I was very young. When I'd just learned to fly, and before I'd decided to hunt your frigid, hostile Blue."

"Before you came the first time?"

She did not answer. "I was not at all sure I could make the Crossing. We heard stories. How much strength was required, how much endurance. If you're not strong enough, not a strong enough flier, you fall back to Green a failure. If you lack endurance . . ." She shrugged. "Only your frozen corpse gets to Blue. It crosses the sky there, a little scratch of fire. No doubt you've seen them. I have."

I nodded.

"That little scratch of fire, and you're gone forever. I wanted to try just the same. We all do, even if some want it more than others and many never actually try. It's something we get from you, a need to become more and more like you, until we're as human as we can possibly be."

"We feel it too," I told her, "though not always as strongly as we should."

"So I was wondering whether I could, and whether I'd be brave enough to try. I wasn't flying all that well yet, and I knew I'd have to get a lot better to fly fast enough to leave Green. One day there was a break in the clouds. You've lived on Green, you said. You must know it happens now and then."

I nodded again.

"Burning light from the sun came streaming through, but I looked up anyway and saw this little streak of gray against the cliff, and I told myself I'd fly up to it someday to see what it was, and when I did I'd be a strong enough flier to Cross."

"You did, clearly."

"Yes. I tried to for years, and there were days when I couldn't even get up above the clouds. There are strong winds at this level, and the air is thin."

I filled my lungs with it, and said, "It certainly seems better to me than the sopping air down there."

"I suppose it would. Are you waiting for the end of my story? It's ended. The day came when I was able to fly up here. I knew by then that I had much more to learn, and that I had to be stronger before I tried Crossing. But I felt I'd come more than halfway, too, and I was right. There was a corroded metal hatch over that window then. I tore it off and let it fall. When I'd explored all the rooms on all the levels, I decided to clean this one out and make it a private place just for myself, my own room in my own tower in the sky. There were bones in here and some other things, but I threw them out that window and swept this floor with my hands. When everything was tidy, I told myself I'd come back and spend hours up here after I'd made the Return Crossing, just thinking about who I was and what I had done for my children. But I never did, till now."

"I'll try to leave you here," I promised her, "and take the troopers back with me. I don't know if it can be done, but I'll try." I shut my eyes, gathering the thoughts that had fled my mind soon after we arrived. "Whose bones were they?"

"You know. They were your friends. I doubt that you want to talk about it."

Blindly, I sat down again upon the bed that been hers and mine. I hated Green then as I have hated it so often, the whorl of teeming unclean life, of violent death and universal decay. In my heart I rejected it, I hope once and for all. "Were they the Neighbors'?" I asked. "The Vanished People's?"

Perhaps she nodded. "I think that when we'd destroyed them everywhere else, they held the tablelands against us. As places of final refuge, they must have built these towers in the cliffs, with windows like this one so that—"

She was gone.

I had recalled my body as she spoke, with all its well-remembered knobs and insufficiencies, the sagging face behind my beard and the ankle that ached in rainy weather, and ached abominably in any weather whenever I had to walk far. . . . And realized with a sort of shock that I was no longer sitting on the bed, but lying in it. I opened my eyes and saw the smoke-blackened timbers that supported the roof of the inn.

"Master Incanto? Awake you are?"

It was Azijin; I asked him who had told him to call me that.

"Your son, mysire. Where he was, and you, of Master Incanto they speak, he says. About dreams you know? That also he says, Mysire Horn."

"Much less than he believes." I sat up, very conscious that Jahlee lay beside me still sound asleep.

Vlug sat up too. "Wah! Good Mysire Pas!"

I got out of bed and went to the fire. "I know what you must be thinking, Sergeant, seeing my daughter in bed with me. I can only say that nothing of the kind took place. She became frightened, as women sometimes do at night in strange places, and sought reassurance from her father."

Azijin joined me at the fire. He sleeps naked and was naked still, hairy and muscular. "Such things I never think, mysire. But me it was that the door barred. If anyone the bar took down, I would hear, I thought."

"We tried not to wake you, Sergeant. I suggest that we try not to wake my daughter as well."

"Right, mysire. Loud I will not speak."

Vlug came over wrapped in a blanket, and Azijin told him to get something for us to sit on. There are no chairs, but he carried over the mattress from his bed. He is a tall, fresh-faced boy with unhappy hair that is neither truly red nor truly yellow but brighter than either. "Morning now it is, I think," he said. "The pig who this inn keeps we wake, Sergeant?"

"Not yet," Azijin told him. "For Mysire Horn to unriddle a dream I wish."

"I too!"

"Always in my dreams I am awake, Master Horn," Azijin began.

"Not like that it is, this dream of last night. Like real it is," he tapped the hearth before him. "Most real. Not like a dream at all it is."

"With me, the same it is!" Vlug exclaimed.

"In this dream asleep I am, in my bed lying. You and your daughter not sleeping like me are, but walking past, talking and talking while on I sleep. Wake I must, I think. What if you escape? Hard with me it will go when Judge Hamer hears! To wake I try, but I cannot. My eyes open. The room bright is, sunshine everywhere there is, and my bed on the wall like a picture hangs. There I sleep and do not fall, so all right it is. Here no one but me there is, so all right too that is. Only in a dream it is that the old magician, and the strange girl his daughter, and the boy who calls him Father I must guard. No one to escape there is."

He looked at me beseechingly. "Never before such a dream, mysire. For me this dream you will explain?"

Vlug started to speak, but Azijin silenced him.

"Boy talk," Oreb suggested from his high perch.

"I think Oreb's right," I told Azijin. "Vlug's dream may well illuminate yours—or yours illuminate his, as frequently happens. Vlug, tell us your dream before you forget it."

"This I never forget, Mysire Horn," Vlug began. "Never! When white my beard is, each smallest part I remember."

Momentarily he fell silent, his hands outspread with the palms down, and his wide eyes the color of blue china; but he was a born relater of tales, whose pauses and intonations came to him as its song does to a young thrush.

"As my sergeant says it is. I sleep, but asleep I am not. Up and down, up and down, a man and woman walk. Wise and kind he is, but stern. Unhappy, discontent she is. His counsel she wishes, and it he gives. No, no, not what he suggests she will do. Herself she will kill. Soon. Very soon."

Vlug spoke to Azijin. "Jahlee and her father perhaps it was, but why?

"Mysire, once around me I too looked. Your daughter before me stood. So beautiful!" He raised his pale eyebrows in tribute to her, when my old friend Inclito would have kissed his fingers.

"A great light behind her there was. A great wind also. A cloak she wore, very big and black. This cloak the wind blew." His hands suggested its fluttering motion. "Her hair also. So long her knees without such a wind it must reach. To lay hold of me with Scylla's hundred arms—"

Oreb squawked and fluttered, perturbed.

"At me it blows. So long really it is, mysire?"

I shook my head.

"In my dream it is." He shut his eyes, trying to recapture it. "So beautiful she is. A dream? So beautiful. Her lips, her eyes, her teeth. My spirit flamed. An angry goddess, your daughter Jahlee is, mysire, in my dream."

I asked whether he could recall how she had been dressed, other than the cloak.

"Not . . ." He glanced at Azijin. "Her gown I don't remember, mysire. No hat, or only a very small cap, it could be."

"Good girl." Oreb dropped from his perch to my shoulder.

"Really, Oreb? Usually you call her a bad thing."

"Good girl!" he insisted.

"Although you can't remember her gown, Legerman Vlug, she was in fact dressed?"

He glanced at Azijin, as before. "Oh, yes, mysire."

Azijin held up a stiff right forefinger, tapped it with his left, and said, "Young he is, mysire." I doubt that he is thirty himself.

"Silk talk," Oreb declared in a decided tone.

"I suppose he means that it is high time for me to interpret your dreams, and no doubt it is. A little additional thought might further the interpretation, however, and so might bacon and coffee. What do you say we rouse my son and your other troopers, and find out what this inn can offer in the way of breakfast? Jahlee has been tired and ill—no doubt you've noticed it. With your leave, I'll throw a few more sticks on the fire before we go, and give her a couple of extra blankets. If she wakes up before breakfast is ready, she can join us. If she doesn't, sleep may help her."

We got dressed and collected Hide and his guards, whom Azijin abused roundly for having allowed Jahlee to leave their room unnoticed, and went downstairs. Everything was dark and silent, but we opened the shutters—finding that it had snowed heavily during the night—and lit every candle in the place from the smoldering remains of the parlor fire. Azijin took it upon himself to wake up the innkeeper and his wife, but returned rubbing his knuckles and looking disgusted. "Sick they are, this they say. So it may be, I think. Our breakfast Vlug will prepare. If their food he wastes, on their own heads they brought it. You can cook, Vlug?"

Vlug swore that he could not.

"Then you I teach. A legerman must cook, and shoot too. Zwaar, Leeuw, to the horses you must see. Well do it! When we have eaten, I will inspect."

Hide said, "I'll take care of ours, Father. My father's a fine cook, Sergeant. I'm sure he'll help you in the kitchen, if you ask him."

I did, of course, warming a pastry of nuts and apples, approving the cheese (these people seem to relish cheese with every meal) and contriving hearth cakes while the sausages and a ground pork and cornmeal mixture were frying.

"Not good food it is," Azijin declared when everything was ready. "For good a kitchen like my mother's we need, and my mother to cook. But worse than this in an inn I have eaten. What is it in these little cakes for us you make, mysire?"

"Honey and poppyseed." I offered a scrap of the pork and cornmeal mixture to Oreb to see whether he would like it.

"Soda, too. Salt, and three kinds of flour. Those I saw you mix. If another I eat, dreams more mad than I have already will it give?"

"Not mad mine was," Vlug insisted. "The finest of my life it was, and more real than this." He speared another sausage; he had been in charge of them and seemed proud of them.

"In a bed on the wall to sleep, and the bedroom has no roof to see!" Azijin shook his head and forked more pickled cabbage onto his plate.

Hide's lips shaped the word *where?*

"You have asked me to explain your dreams," I began, after sampling the pork and cornmeal mixture for myself. "It would be easy for me to contrive some story for you, as I originally planned to do. It would also be dishonest, as I decided while we were coming downstairs. I am not speaking under duress. You have asked me to help you understand what has happened to you. I have said I will, and am therefore bound to do it faithfully. Are you aware that the spirit leaves the body at death?"

Two nodded. Leeuw said, "With gods to talk."

"Perhaps. In some cases, at least. I must now ask you to accept—to ask you, Sergeant Azijin, and you, Legerman Vlug, particularly—to accept the fact that it can, and does, leave it at other times as well."

I waited for their protests, but none came.

"Let me illustrate my point. A man has a house where he lives for some years with his wife. They are very happy, this man and his wife. They love each other, and whatever else may go amiss, they have each other. Then the man's wife dies, and he leaves the house in which he has had so much happiness. It has become abhorrent to him. Unless the Outsider, the God of gods, restores her to life, he has no wish to see that house ever again. Am I making myself clear?"

Vlug said, "So I think," and Azijin, "To me not."

"I am speaking of the spirit departing the body at death. The body is the house I mentioned, and life was the wife who made it a place of warmth and comfort."

Azijin nodded. "Ah."

"Perhaps her husband goes to the gods, as Legerman Leeuw suggested, perhaps only out into darkness. For the moment, it doesn't matter. My point is that he leaves the home she made for him, never to return."

"Bird go," Oreb declared. He had been hopping around the table, cadging bits of food. "Go Silk."

I told him, "If you mean you wish to die when I do, Oreb, I sincerely hope you don't. In Gaon they tell of dying men who kill some favorite animal, usually a horse or a dog, so it will accompany them in death; and under the Long Sun their rulers went so far as to have their favorite wives burned alive on their funeral pyres. When I die, I sincerely hope no friend or relative of mine will succumb to any such cruel foolishness."

Zwaar, who had been silent until then, said, "When the spirit goes a man dies, I think."

I shook my head. "He dies because you shot him through the heart. Or because he suffered some disease or was kicked by a horse, as a wise friend once suggested to me. But you bring up an important point—that the spirit is not life, nor is life the spirit. And another, that the two together are one. A husband is not his wife, no more than a wife is her husband; but the two in combination are one. What I was going to say was that though the man in my little story left his house once and for all when his wife died, he had left it many times previously. He had gone out to weed their garden, perhaps, or gone to the market to buy shoes. In those cases he left it to return."

Hide said helpfully, "The spirit can leave the same way, can't it, Father?"

"Exactly. We have all had daydreams. We imagine we're sailing the new boat we're in fact building, for example, or riding a prancing horse we don't actually possess. Most of the dreams we have at night are of the same kind, and 'dreams' is the right name for them. There are others, however. Dreams—we call them that, at least—which are in fact memories returned to the sleeping body by the spirit, which left it for a while and went elsewhere."

Azijin was grinning, although he looked a bit uncomfortable; Vlug, Leeuw, and Zwaar heard me with wide eyes and open mouths.

"That is what befell you and Private Vlug," I told Azijin. "Your spirits departed while you slept, and went to sleep in another place. There Vlug's spirit—"

I rose. "Excuse me for a moment. I took off Oreb's ring while I was cooking and laid it on a shelf in the kitchen."

Before they could protest, I hurried out. The ring was where I had left it earlier when I decided I might require some such excuse. I put it on and went through the kitchen and into the private quarters of the innkeeper and his wife, finding him just struggling into his trousers.

"I heard you were ill," I said, "and thought it might be wise for someone to look in on you. If you and your wife would like a bite to eat, I would be happy to prepare something."

"So weak we are, mysire." He sat down upon the conjugal bed. "Thank you. Thank you. Anything."

I explained matters to Azijin and his troopers, and Hide and I looked after the innkeeper and his wife. As I feared, both have been bitten by Jahlee. They should recover, provided she does not return for a few days. She is still asleep at present, although it is well past noon. "Girl sleep," reports Oreb, who just flew up to our room to look; he and I are agreed that it is best to leave it so. I have arranged the blankets so that her face is scarcely visible, and of course the shutters are closed. Azijin and Vlug promise not to disturb her.

Azijin has decided not to travel today. "The cause of justice and good order," he says, "we serve as well in comfort here as by in this snow dying and the horses crippling." I second him in that with all my heart.

The ring will no longer fit my thumb, which seems very odd. I have been wearing it on the third finger.

4

He Is Silk

He felt Pig's hand close on his shoulder. "Hooses, bucky. Trust ter Pig. Hooses h'all 'round."

At that moment, he was too tired to wonder how Pig knew. "Then let's stop here and ask, if they'll talk to us."

"Pockets runnin' h'over wi' cards, bucky?"

"No," he said. "Not running over."

"Nor me. Nor H'oreb, Pig wagers. Got a card, do yer, H'oreb? Yer do nae!"

"Poor bird."

"Yet good people can be moved by charity, sometimes, and all we want is a place to rest and a little information."

"H'all yer want." The *tap-tap-tap* of Pig's sheathed sword was moving away, as was Pig's towering bulk, visible in the light of the glowing skylands. "H'oreb's hungry though. H'ain't yer, H'oreb? A bite a' een, noo. Dinna say yer never h'ate nae een, H'oreb. Pig knows yer breed."

Oreb fluttered to Pig's shoulder. "Fish heads?"

"Aye! Comin', bucky?" Pig's leather-covered scabbard rapped wood.

Silence followed, save for the tapping of his own staff and the shuffle of his feet. "Yes," he said. "I had misjudged your position a bit. How did you know there were houses here? I couldn't see them myself until you told me they were present."

"Feel 'em." The scabbard rapped the door again. "Feel 'em h'on me clock."

It seemed impossible that they had reached the outskirts of Viron already. "Are there many?"

"Both sides a' ther road. 'Tis h'all Pig can tell yer."

"It's remarkable just the same."

"Blind, aye. H'oreb can tell yer more. How many, H'oreb? Let's hear yer count 'em."

"Many house." Oreb's bill rattled.

"There yer have h'it." The leather-covered scabbard pounded the door. " 'Tis listenin' does h'it, bucky. Most dinna. Take 'em h'inside. Think they hears us knockin' sae polite? If Pig was ter kick ther door h'in, they'd have ter listen, wouldn't they? They would." A explosive thump was presumably Pig's boot striking the door.

"Don't! Please don't. We can go on to the next house."

"Aye." Another violent kick, so loud that it seemed it must surely attract the attention of the godling at the bridge, a full league off.

From inside a voice called, "Go away!"

"Soon h'as she's stove h'in," Pig rumbled. "Gae smash h'in ther next. Winna take ter lang." To prove his point, he followed the words with another tremendous kick.

A woman's frightened voice sounded from inside the house.

"What's she sayin'? Yer make h'it h'out, bucky?"

"No." The end of his staff had found one of Pig's massive boots. Raising his voice slightly, he said, "Open the door, please. I swear we won't harm you."

Golden light appeared at a crack, followed by the scrape and thump of a heavy bar lifted from its fittings and set aside.

"Ah," Pig said, "maire like, 'tis."

The door opened a thumb's width, then swung back as Pig dropped to one knee and threw his shoulder against it. The woman inside screamed.

"Please, there's nothing to be afraid of. If you'd opened when we knocked, all this fuss would have been prevented."

"Who are you, sir?" The voice that had ordered them to go away was tremulous now.

He stepped inside and laid his hand on the householder's arm, calming him as if he were a dog or a horse. "My friend is blind. You're not afraid of a blind man, are you? And certainly you shouldn't be afraid of me. We haven't come to rob you. Put away that knife, please. Someone might be hurt."

The householder stepped back, evoking a terrified squeal from his wife. He held a candle in one hand and a butcher knife of substantial proportions in the other, and seemed inclined to surrender neither one.

"That's much better. May the Outsider, Pas, and every other god bless this house." Smiling, their visitor traced the sign of addition before turning back to Pig and wincing at his first real sight of that exceedingly large face, all dirty rag, straggling hair, and curling black beard. Pig was preparing to enter the house on his knees, ducking under the lintel and working his shoulders through the doorway.

"We're looking for eyes." It seemed a happy inspiration under the circumstances. "Eyes for my friend here. Do you know of a physician capable of replacing a blind man's eyes?"

"In the city," the householder managed. "In Viron, it might be done."

It was progress of a sort. "Good. What is his name?"

"I don't know, but—but . . ."

"But they might have someone?"

The householder nodded eagerly.

"I see—though my unfortunate friend does not. We must go to the city in that case."

The householder nodded again, more eagerly than ever.

"We shall. But we must rest first." He tried to recall when he had last slept, and failed. "We must find a place to sleep, and beg food—"

Oreb lit on his shoulder. "Fish heads?"

"Something for my bird, at least, and something—I'm afraid it will have to be quite a lot—for my friend Pig. We're sorry to have frightened you; but we could hear you inside, and when you wouldn't come to the door it made Pig angry."

The householder muttered something unintelligible.

"Thank you. Thank you very much. We really do appreciate it."

Loudly enough to be overheard, the householder's wife whispered, ". . . doesn't look like an augur."

"I am not. I'm a layman, just as your husband is, and have a wife of my own at home. Does it bother you that I blessed you? A layman may bless, I assure you; so may a laywoman."

"I'm Hound," the householder said. "My wife's Tansy." He tried to give his butcher knife to her, and when she would not take it, tossed it onto a chair and offered his hand.

"My own name is Horn." They shook hands, and Pig extended his, the size of a grocer's scoop. "Sorry ter a' scared yer."

"And my bird is—"

"Oreb!"

Tansy smiled, and her smile lit her small, pale face. "I'll get you some soup."

"You can sleep here," Hound told them. "In the house here, or . . . Would you like to eat out back? It's going to be a little cramped in here. There's a big tree in back, and there's a table there, and benches."

There were. Pig sat on the ground, and the other two on the benches Hound had mentioned. "We've beer." Hound sounded apologetic. "No wine, I'm sorry to say."

"How's yer water?"

"Oh, we've a good well. Would you prefer water?"

"Aye. Thank yer."

Hound, who had just sat down, rose with alacrity. "Horn, what about you? Beer?"

"Water, please. You might bring some sort of small container that Oreb could drink from, too, if it isn't too much trouble."

Tansy arrived with bulging pockets and a steaming tureen. "I try to keep fire in the stove, you know, so I don't have to lay a new one for every meal. I'll bet your wife does the same thing."

He nodded. "You'd win that bet."

"So when we have soup, why not keep it there so it stays warm? That way I can have some hot quickly. It—it really isn't any particular kind of soup, I suppose. Just what Hound and I eat ourselves. There's beans in it, and potatoes, and carrots for flavor."

"Guid ter smell h'all ther same. Ham, ter. Pig winds h'it."

The tureen received a place of honor in the center of the table next to Hound's candle. Four large bowls clattered down, followed by rattling spoons. "I'll get some bread. What's her name, Horn?"

He looked up, surprised.

"Your wife's?"

"Oh. Nettle. Her name is Nettle. I don't suppose you knew her as a child? Years ago in the city?"

"No. It's not a common name. I don't think I've ever known a Nettle." Tansy backed away, paused for a hurried conversation with her husband at the well, and retreated to her kitchen.

"She'll bring cups or something," Hound explained, setting his water bucket on the table beside the soup tureen, "and beer for me. I hope you don't mind."

"Not at all." He paused, trying to collect his thoughts. "May I—might we, I ought to say—begin by telling each other who we are? I realize it's not the conventional way to start a conversation; but you see, I need information badly and hope that when the three of you know why I need it as badly as I do, you'll be more inclined to give it to me."

Tansy set a bread board, a big loaf of dark bread, and the butcher knife on the table, and handed pannikins around. "I can tell you who Hound and I are, and I will too, unless he wants to. Shall I?"

"Go ahead," Hound said.

Pig found his pannikin and pushed it across the table. "Better h'if yer fill h'it fer me."

"You know our names," Tansy began. "You wanted to know if I knew your wife in the city when I was a little girl, and I didn't. I grew up right here in Endroad. So did Hound. We did live in the city up until about five years ago, though. There wasn't any work out here then."

Hound said, "There isn't any now, or very little."

"So we went to the city and worked there till my father passed away, and then my mother wrote and said we could have the shop." Tansy began ladling out soup.

"Mother lives next door," Hound explained, "that's why it bothered Tansy so much when you said you'd kick in her door too."

"So that's what we do now. Hound goes into the city, mostly, and tries to find things people want that we can buy at a good price, and he's very good at it. Mother and I stay in the store, mostly, and sell the things. We have hammers and nails, we sell a lot of those. And tacks and screws, and then general tinware, and crockery."

Hound added, "We have drills, planes, and saws, all of which my wife forgot to mention. I did cabinet work before we got the shop. We own our little house. Mother owns her house and the shop. We give her so much each week from what the shop takes in, and she helps Tansy there sometimes. So that's who we are, Horn, unless you want to hear about brothers and sisters."

He shook his head. "Thank you. By rights, we strangers should have gone first. It was gracious of you to give the example yourselves." He returned the pannikin, which he had filled with well water. "Here you are, Pig. It's good water, I'm sure. When we met, you told me you were journeying west, I believe."

"Aye."

He ladled water into his own, then held the ladle so that Oreb could drink from it. "Are you willing to tell us anything more? If you aren't, that should be sufficient, surely."

"Ho, aye. Dinna like ter snivel's h'all. What yer want ter know?"

Tansy ventured, "What happened to you? How . . . ?"

Pig laughed, a deep booming. "How come yer nae sae big h'as me? Freak's what Ma said."

"How you . . ." Tansy's voice fell away. "We—we'd like to have a child, and I worry, you know, that something might be wrong with it. Not . . . Not that it would grow up big and strong. I'd like that."

Hound said, "Without offense. Could you see, when you were a boy?"

"Ho, aye. Was a trooper's h'all. Got caught, an' they dinna like me. Seen a dagger comin' h'at me een, an' 'twas ther last. Took me 'round h'after, h'only Pig canna see 'em nae mair. Heard 'em, though. Threw things h'at me, ter. 'Twas h'in ther light lands, ther mountings. Doon here's flatlands." Pig spooned up more soup and swallowed noisily. "Yer nae eatin' naethin', bucky. What's wrong wi' yer?"

"I—" He picked up his spoon. "Because you would have heard me, I suppose, if I had been—though I try to make as little noise as I can, eating soup. You came here seeking new eyes, Pig?"

"Aye. Yer knows a' ther wee folk, bucky?"

"Children, you mean? Or us? We must seem very small indeed to you."

"Smaller'n yer. Hereabout folk don't know such, but h'in ther light lands 'tis different. They comes, an' they goes." Pig held out his hand, scarcely higher than the table. "Little bits a' men, an' morts small ter them h'even. 'Fore me een's took, they dinna hardly never come. Not many's never seed such h'up close, like. H'after, they come 'round lots, knowin' 'twas safe wi' me, lang h'as they stayed h'out a' me reach."

Pig paused, his big fingers groping his beard. "They'd nae been afore, maybe. Canna say. Ane name a' Flannan come particular h'often. Still nae eatin' yer soup, bucky?"

"I suppose I'm not especially hungry—" he began.

"Bird eat!"

"Besides, I was listening to you with rapt attention." He dipped up soup, and sipped. "This was in the mountains, in the light lands, as you call them?"

"Ho, aye. Na braithrean was takin' care a' me, after 'em what had me give me h'up. Settin' h'all ter meself h'in ther sun. Settin' h'on a stone, knew 'twas h'in the sun by the warm a' h'it h'on me clock, an' here's Flannan. H'in ther west, he says, they gie new een. Gae ter t'other h'end a' ther sun. 'Tis Mainframe says h'it, Flannan says. What fashes yer, bucky?"

He had dropped his spoon into his bowl, and Tansy asked, "Yes, what is it?"

"I understand! I—what a fool! You talked about little people, Pig, and I ought to have understood you at once. They fly, don't they?"

"Do they fly, bucky? They do."

"We call them Fliers here," he said, "and I used to know one. The mountains you mentioned, are those the Mountains That Look at Mountains?"

"Aye, bucky, but 'tis lang h'on ther tongue sae Pig says mountings, mostly."

He spoke to Tansy and Hound. "The Mountains That Look at Mountains surround Mainframe at the East Pole. I went there once. We flew over them."

Wide-eyed, Tansy asked, "Can you fly, too? Like a Flier?"

"No. I was a—a passenger, I suppose I should say, on the airship of the Rani of Trivigaunte. Auk and Chenille and Nettle and me. And Maytera, too, and Patera Remora. A lot of people. We went to Mainframe and spoke with the dead. I know how that sounds, how incredible. You need not believe me, and I won't blame you in the least if you don't."

"Bird go!" Oreb declared.

"Will you, good bird?" He fished a slice of celery from his soup and offered it.

"This is . . ." Tansy pushed a lock of her long hair from her eyes. "You really are extraordinary people, Horn. Both of you are."

"Everyone is an extraordinary person," he told her solemnly. "I haven't profited from life as I should. I haven't learned very much at all. But I have learned that, a fact I know beyond all doubt and question. That's something, surely."

He turned back to Pig. "But you don't want to hear about me, and I certainly don't want to hear about myself. My mind keeps talking to me about myself all the time, and to confess the truth, I'm heartily sick of it. This Flier, Flannan—he said that they could give you new eyes at the West Pole? And that Mainframe had told him it was possible?"

"Did he say sae? He did. Soon h'as he's h'off himself, 'tis ther road fer Pig. 'Tis a lang 'un, though."

Hound asked, "To the West Pole? I've never heard of anyone traveling anything like that far. Have you, Horn?"

"No. It's hundreds of leagues, I'm sure. If memory serves, Sciathan—that was the Flier I knew—said once that it would take months for a mounted party to reach the East Pole, and I believe we're considerably nearer the East Pole than the West. It might easily take Pig years to walk to the West Pole. Or so I would imagine."

" 'Tis been a year fer me h'already, bucky." Pig inclined toward him, his great, homely face, banded with its soiled rag and lit from below by the flickering candle, desperate and resolute. "H'only ter me, h'if een can be put back there, een can be put back somewhere h'else, like h'as nae. Sae why nae h'ask h'along yer way?"

"Why not indeed?"

"Gae ter t'other h'end, though, h'if there's nae help fer h'it. Yer need nae come wi' me, h'if yer finds yer h'own short a' there."

The man Pig called *bucky* smiled, sipped his water, and smiled again. "Which brings us to me, I'm afraid. Shall I recount my tale?"

Pig grunted, and Hound and Tansy nodded, while Oreb bobbed his approval. "Silk talk!"

"My name is Horn, as you know. I was born in the city; I lived there until the age of fifteen, when a group of us boarded the lander that carried us to Blue, where we founded the town we call New

Viron. My wife, Nettle, and I settled outside the town, on Lizard Island. We manufacture paper there and sell it—or we did." He took another sip of water. "It's so hot here. I had forgotten."

Hound said, "Lately. Hot summers and short winters."

"Yes, I remember now. Mainframe is losing control of the sun, and Pas is trying to drive all of you out."

Tansy nodded. "That's what the augurs say."

"Gae h'on, bucky."

"As you wish. New Viron has grown—I won't call it a city, yet that would be only a slight exaggeration. Others have come, of course, and some have joined us, coming to live in New Viron or working land in its territory, or fishing or lumbering. Some have been from Viron itself, some from Limna and the other villages, no doubt including this one, and some from foreign cities. When a group from a foreign city lands, they are not permitted to establish a town of their own where they landed, for reasons that should be apparent. They must either join us in New Viron or leave our territory. Most choose to unite themselves to us."

Hound said, "I understand."

"Some are forced to stay and labor for us, I'm sorry to say, and are bought and sold like cattle; in any case, they too swell our population. There has been natural increase as well, as one would expect. Nettle and I have three sons, and ours is not considered a large family. Families with eight or ten children are by no means uncommon."

"Yer lookin' fer a mon a' ther name a' Silk, bucky."

"Yes, I am, and that's the most urgent point I require information on. He may be called Caldé Silk or Patera Silk. Can any of you tell me where to find him?"

Hound and Tansy shook their heads.

"Things are not as we'd like in New Viron, you see. The rich struggle with one another, each gathering such followers as he can and hoping to rule in a year or two. Stronger than any of them is the mob, those among us who acknowledge no rule but their own, and desire neither justice nor peace."

Hound said, "That sounds like Viron itself. Are you sure you're not talking about that?"

"No. I have not set foot in Viron in twenty years, and I am very sorry indeed to hear that things are in such a state. Since neither you nor your wife can tell me where I might find Patera Silk, I take it he no longer leads your government."

Tansy said, "That was years and years ago."

"I see." He paused, stirred his soup, and fished out a morsel of cabbage for Oreb. "We hoped that he could help us—and that he would. It's why I came."

Hound asked, "From Blue?"

"Indirectly, yes. I knew Caldé Silk well in the old days."

Tansy pulled a wad of colored cloth from one of the pockets of her apron. "Napkins! I brought napkins, and forgot to give them to you."

He accepted one and wiped his eyes. "I'm sorry. It's a childish weakness, one I very much regret. I happened to think again about leaving, and the last time I saw Silk. It was snowing. One of those short winters we spoke of, and I only saw half of it. Half or less. Silk walked away into the snow, and we went down into the tunnels, Nettle and I. I was very excited, and felt that we were doing something terribly brave, and that we were doing what Silk wanted, too.

"I'm sure we were, still. I know we were. And we were going to go to a wonderful new whorl; we did that, but when I think back to the days when I lived with my mother and father, and my sisters and brothers, and all of us knew Patera Silk, I call them the good old days. That seems so sad now. How very young we were!"

"Poor Silk!"

"Not really, Oreb." He smiled through his tears. "I've had a good life, one that's not over yet. I've loved a wonderful woman and a very beautiful woman, and I have been loved. Not many men can say that."

"H'on wi' yer story, bucky."

"Very well. Nettle and I built a house on Lizard, well away from the stealing and the shootings. We were poor, if you like, yet we were happy though there were times when there wasn't enough to eat." Reminded of the necessity of eating, he spooned up soup and tasted it. "This is really excellent. I'm hungry, no doubt, and that always helps. But excellent by any measure."

Tansy made him a little seated bow, her long black hair gleaming in the candlelight.

"We lived there quite contentedly, and brought up our sons. One day five of the leading citizens called on us. They talked about conditions in town, and crop failures—the corn crop, particularly, because it had failed disastrously that year. To tell you the truth, I couldn't imagine what they were getting at. Neither could Nettle, I'm sure. They had never shown any regard for our opinions in the past; and if they wanted our advice, I at least had little to give. There was Marrow, who has been one of our leading men from the beginning, and His Cognizance Patera Remora, and three more. I could name and describe the others, but it would mean nothing to you.

"They had been given a way to return someone to this Long Sun Whorl, or thought they had. Our own lander would have made that possible and even easy, of course, if only it had not been looted of nearly everything that permitted it to fly the moment it put down; but it had been, and was beyond repair. Silk had been our leader until we went into the tunnels. I ought to have said that."

"Good Silk!"

He nodded, his face serious. "He was. He was the greatest man I've known, and the best. It is said that not many great men are good men; but Silk was, and had a way of making even bad people like and trust him that I've never seen in any other man."

After giving her husband a timid glance, Tansy ventured, "I wish we'd known him."

"I wish you had too. I knew him, as I said, and it was one of the principal matters of my life. Nettle and I even wrote a book about him." He sipped more soup. "When we left, he was caldé of Viron. Can you tell me what happened?"

"Not in any detail," Hound said. "He was forced out of office. I wish my father were still alive to tell you about it. He knew more about it than Tansy and I do."

She said, "We were children then. It was—I don't know. Ten years ago? Or twelve? About that."

Hound nodded. "He wanted everyone to get on the landers and wanted to go himself, or he said he did. He kept telling people they ought to leave, and taking cards out of circulation. Nobody liked that. There were protests and riots, a lot of trouble. I know a lot of people wanted him arrested and tried, but I don't think it was ever really done. He was an augur, after all."

"He was married," Tansy objected. "Mother still talks about it. She doesn't like it."

Pig coughed and spat. "Nae gang ter h'eat yer soup, bucky? Pity ter waste h'it."

He pushed his bowl over. "You may have it, if you'll give Oreb a bite or two. I'm full. Have you had any bread, Pig?"

"Nae, bucky. What h'about yer?"

"I'll cut you some. It will be delicious dipped in that excellent soup, I feel sure."

"There's more in the kitchen keeping hot," Tansy put in, "and in the big bowl should be hotter than what you have. Let me warm yours up, Pig."

Hound said, "I know we haven't really answered your question, Horn, but we've told you everything we remember."

"You don't know what became of Silk after he was deposed?"

Hound shrugged. "I don't think he was killed or thrown into the pits. My father would have talked about it."

Tansy ventured, "People tell stories, you know how it is. Somebody's seen him in the market somewhere, or they're living in the city under new names, Silk and his wife. Or he goes around in disguise helping people. A lot of people think he's gone outside. He was always talking about that, they say."

Nodding to himself, he passed two thick slices of bread to Pig, who said, "Thank yer, bucky."

Hound yawned. "I've seen him. I ought to tell you that, Horn. My father thought he was wonderful, so when he came here, my father held me up so I could have a good look at him. They used to sell pictures of him, too, and for a while we had one over the fireplace. It's probably still up in the attic."

"We're keeping you and your wife from bed, I'm afraid."

Tansy smiled. "It's almost morning anyway."

Hound seconded her. "We were asleep when you knocked. When the sun goes dark, there isn't much else we can do."

"Candles are very dear," Tansy explained, "and so is oil for the lamps. We used to sell them—"

"We still sell oil, but it's pricey these days."

"It's all gone now, dear. Palm bought the last yesterday."

"I'll try to get some more when I go into the city tomorrow. I was going to scout around for candles anyway. Are you two going there?"

"H'are we? We h'are! Ter find me een. Right, bucky?"

"Yes. To find eyes for Pig, and for my friend Maytera Marble back home. I was about to tell you about her a moment ago, as it happens. She's a chem. I suppose there are still a few chems left?"

Hound nodded. "Not many."

"Her eyes have failed her, and I'd like to find new ones, if I can. I was going to say that when those five called on Nettle and me, they did so because we had known Patera Silk better than almost anyone else on Blue. The sole exception to that is Maytera Marble, who knew him better than either of us; but she's very old now, and—and in need of eyes, as I said."

Pig swallowed soup-soaked bread. "Dinna fash me, bucky."

"Thank you. Yet I know it must be painful. Have either of you any idea where I might find new eyes for a chem? Any idea at all?"

Hound shook his head.

"Oddly enough, I do. Do you know where I might find a male chem?"

"There should be some in the city. It's been years since I've seen a chem here in Endroad, male or female."

Tansy murmured, "Except for the soldiers."

"That's right." Hound snapped his fingers. "Twenty or thirty soldiers went through here about, let's see, a couple months ago. They were male chems, naturally, so I was wrong. But they didn't stay and they haven't come back."

"Where bound ter?" Pig inquired.

"I have no idea. Why are you looking for a male chem?"

Oreb had a question too, and stopped demolishing the slice of bread Pig had given him to voice it. "Iron man?"

"Yes, we want to find an iron man. Let me know if you see one, please."

Tansy asked, "But why?"

"Because chems can reproduce, just as bios such as you and your husband can. It's a point I should have raised with Maytera Marble the last time I spoke with her."

Hound said, "A male and a female chem can get together and build a child. I've heard that."

"It's not like we do," Tansy protested. "They have to make the parts and put them together, so it's not the same thing. Our child's going to grow in me. That's what we hope and pray for."

"Exactly. You and Hound can make a son or a daughter for yourselves. If I had time I'd look for a better word than *make,* but for the moment that will have to do. The point is that what you make is a child, not pieces that can be assembled to make up one. You don't make eyes, and afterward a nose, and then a heart or liver; so that even if—I hope you'll excuse this, Pig—even if there were a great surgeon sitting with us who could put new eyes into Pig's sockets in such a way that he could see again, you two couldn't make a pair of new eyes for him to use.

"Chems are made quite differently, of course. Each parent carries half the information necessary to make the parts and assemble them. Now follow me closely, please. When my friend Maytera Marble plucked out one of her eyes—both, as I say, had stopped functioning—she took it out quite easily, and she took it out as a unit. Am I making myself clear?"

Hound said, "Yes. Certainly."

"Both her eyes had gone blind; but they did not go blind at the same moment. If they had, she would have known, I feel sure, that the real trouble lay deeper and new eyes would not permit her to see again. What actually happened was that one failed first, and the other failed a short time afterward. I know that Maytera inherited certain new parts when Maytera Rose died; Maytera Rose was also a sibyl, and was the senior sibyl at our manteion at the time of her death. I do not believe, however, that either eye was among those parts. If I am correct, Maytera Marble had been using the eyes that failed her for more than three hundred years—presumably they simply wore out."

Pig put down his spoon. "Huh. Didn't try ter make herself no new ones, bucky?"

"You're ahead of me, clearly. No, I do not believe she did. If she had, she said nothing about that effort to me, and I feel sure she would have."

"She'd a' tried, h'anyhow. Yer can take such from me, an' lily, ter."

"I agree. Why didn't she at least attempt it? Surely it must have been because she didn't know how, and since new chems clearly require new eyes, they must be among the parts made by the male. If I can find a male chem, I'll try to persuade him to make eyes for her, and give them to me to take back to her."

Pig said slowly, "H'or yer could find a dead 'un, bucky, an' pluck his h'out."

"Yes, provided I can remove them without damaging them." He endeavored unsuccessfully to sit up straighter and square his shoulders. "I've no wish to end your conversation, friends, but I'm very tired indeed, and you say it will soon be shadeup. With your permission, I'd like to excuse myself."

Hound said, "Yes, certainly," and Tansy, "You can sleep in the house, if you'd rather do that. Or I can bring out some blankets for you to lie down on."

"I shall be quite comfortable wherever I lie down, you may be sure." He took three steps back from the table, sank to his knees, and stretched out on the coarse, dry grass.

Pig groped for his sword, found it, and rose. "Wi' yer, bucky. Guid night ter h'all."

"Horn," Hound asked, "would you and your friend like to go with me tomorrow?"

There was no reply.

"I'll be riding one of our donkeys, Pig, and leading the other two. You—now that I see you standing up . . ."

Pig's chuckle rumbled in his chest. "Nae donkey fer me, but thank yer kindly. Bucky can, an' he'll thank yer better'n Pig. Yer a buck an' a brathair."

Tansy touched Hound's elbow. "The shade's nearly up already, dear."

"I'll wait for them to get some rest," he told her. "We can camp, if we have to."

He turned back to Pig. "But there's something else we ought to talk about. You two haven't known each other long, have you?"

"Have we? We've nae. Met h'up h'on ther road ternight, we did. Yer need nae fash. Yer nae gang ter tittle naethin' what's news ter auld Pig."

"It's just . . ." Hound glanced helplessly at his wife. "We were—were all sitting there pretending. You and Tansy were, and I was, too. All of us except his bird."

"Good bird!" Oreb's tone declared that matter settled.

Tansy asked, "Do you really know what we know, Pig? You're not from around here."

"Aye."

"I do too. I think so. I—I know Hound better than anybody, and

I could tell from the way he opened our house to you, and the way he talked. I think I could, I mean, I did. I really do."

Hound drew a deep breath. "He kept saying and saying he was looking for Caldé Silk. But *that's* Caldé Silk right there. That's Caldé Silk himself, Pig. You never saw him, but people have told me he's living with his wife in the old manse, quite near here."

"Aye, laddie. Meant ter call h'on him, but he was nae ter home. Door h'open an' wife dead, layin' h'in a box. Felt a' her. Met h'up wi' him an' H'oreb h'after. Kenned who he was an' he dinna." Slowly and heavily Pig sank to the grass. "Lucky fer Pig, yer say. Huh. Lucky fer him? Time'll say. Pig dinna ken nae more'n H'oreb there."

He lay back, his sheathed sword clasped to his chest. "Yer best ter call him Horn when he wakes. An' rouse me, will yer?"

In a moment more he was snoring. Hound and Tansy stared at each other, but found nothing to say.

He was in a boat, and there was a monster greater and more terrible than the leatherskin below it, its face showing through the long smooth swell. He opened his old black pen case, dipped a black quill into the little ink bottle and began to write furiously, conscious of how short—how terribly short—a time was left to him.

I am just setting out for Pajarocu, he wrote, *knowing nothing of what is about to transpire there, not even knowing that my son Sinew has decided to track me down and go to Green with me, or that my grandson, Krait, the son of my daughter Jahlee, will soon join me as a son.*

The scratching of the quill slowed and died. He stared at the paper. Who was Krait? He had no daughter, no sons.

To the west, a lonely bird flew over the water, black as it crossed and recrossed the sun; he knew the bird was Oreb, and that Oreb was calling, "Silk? Silk? Silk?" as he flew. The bird was too far, its hoarse voice too faint to be heard. He thought of standing and waving, of calling Oreb to him, of lighting the lantern and running it up the mast for Oreb to see, so that the leatherskin or something else in the water would come to him, would come called by his burning prayer at sunset. He thought of looking over the side at the monstrous face beneath the water, of challenging it to emerge and destroy him if it could. He did none of these things.

The boat rocked, becoming the cradle he had made for Hoof and Hide, a cradle large enough for two, so that Nettle, sitting in the sea, could rock the two together, rocking with her left hand while the right drove the quill: *Enlightenment came to Patera Silk on the ball court; nothing could be the same after that.* The book that they had never been able to begin begun at last, the book that lay behind his effort to make paper, behind the paper-making that had succeeded where nothing else would succeed, the paper-making that had made him the envy of his brothers and the pride of his mother, the paper-making that had been the salvation of the family.

I am just setting out for Pajarocu. Who was Pajarocu and what had he done? He crossed out the words and rewrote them: *It is worthless, this old pen case. It is nothing. You might go around the market all day and never find a single spirit who would trade you a fresh egg for it. Yet it holds—*

Enough. Yes, enough. I am sick with fancies. That was it. That was good. He reached down to turn the page so that he might begin a new one, but there was no need; the one he had written remained blank.

He stood up and shouted, but he could not recall the bird's name and the bird would not come in any case, could not hear him, remained in his pen case no matter how wildly he shouted or how loudly he waved his arms. Something with tusks and shining eyes was swimming to him, swimming east, always and forever east, in a spear-straight line from Shadelow, its wake marked already by faint phosphorescence.

He shouted until Seawrack rose from the sea to comfort him, smoothing his hair with two smooth, white hands. "It's only a dream, Horn, only a dream. If you need anyone, Hound and I are right here."

He wanted her to stay, to lie in their boat with him and comfort him, but she vanished when he tried to hold her, and it was getting dark and Green rising, a baleful jade eye. There were water bottles in the racks; but the boat was gone and the salt sea with it, the sea that was a river called Gyoll in which corpses floated, savaged by big turtles with beaks like the beaks of parrots, the river that circled with whorl, the river over which the stars never set. He had come to the end of that river, and it was too late.

He sat up. The well-remembered walls of the pit encircled him, walls marked with dank crevices opening on ruinous passages half filled with earth and stones. "It's dirt up here," a voice behind him rasped. He turned and saw Spider sitting behind him on the tumbled column, Spider in conversation with small girls in starched frocks. "It's all dirt," Spider repeated, and added, "I can tell from how it's made."

He asked politely how he could find Hyacinth.

"Down there." The blond girl pointed. "She's down there like Spider and me."

The dark girl nodded. "Down there where you're going, and she can't ever come back. Take a cake for the dog."

Spider nodded, too, saying, "It's dirt down there. I can tell from how it's made." Spider took something green from his pocket and handed it over. It was one of the crawling green lights that lined the tunnels, and it began to crawl across his palm, gleaming in the hot sunshine until he closed his fingers around it. "Thank you," he said. "Thank you very much."

"Oh, you ain't thanked me yet," Spider told him. "You'll thank me when you're down there."

He knelt and wiggled through the opening and back onto his boat, where the crawling green light he had put upon the ceiling was Green rising in the east, a baleful eye. Pig was seated in the stern, his hand upon the tiller and Oreb on his shoulder. "Good Silk," said Oreb. Pig removed the dirty gray cloth that had covered his eyes; and when it was gone, he, who had supposed that he could see, could actually see.

And Pig's big, bearded face was Silk's.

"This is really very kind of you," he told Hound when he had washed and sipped the maté Tansy made for him, "but won't we be getting a late start?"

"Yes," Hound conceded, "but it doesn't matter much. Usually I start before shadeup, as Tansy will attest, I'm sure, because she always gets up too, even though I tell her not to, and makes breakfast for me."

Tansy laughed. "I go back to bed after he leaves."

"If I have good weather," Hound continued, "and drive the donkeys for all I'm worth, there's a nice old inn in the middle of the city that I stop at. It's not too terribly expensive, and I'm right there to start my buying the next day."

"I understand."

"But even if we left this instant, we couldn't possibly reach the city before shadelow. So we'll camp along the road someplace, or stay at a country inn I know about. It's not as nice as the one I usually stay at, but it will save us a few bits, and if we rough it beside the road, that will cost nothing. Either way, we'll finish the trip tomorrow, and I'll start my trading tomorrow afternoon."

Tansy asked, "Shall I cook something now for you two, or wait till Pig wakes up?"

"Wait," Hound told her. "He'll eat more than Horn and me put together."

"Then I'd like to show Horn our shop. Can I?"

Hound looked at him, shrugging. "Do you want see it? It's very ordinary, except for being so small."

Tansy said, "But it's where we work, so it's not ordinary to us. It's ours, and the others aren't."

Their shop was on the village square, a very short distance from the little house on the edge of the village in which they lived. He stayed respectfully behind them as they mounted its three steep steps and unlocked its door.

"I don't think we'll have any customers this early," Tansy told him, "but if we do, we'll sell them whatever they've come for, and then lock up again when we go. I'll open up for the day after you and Hound and Pig leave."

"You said it was small." He paused to look around at the shiny pots and pans suspended from the ceiling, the barrels of nails and the hammers and saws hung from nails in the walls. "But it's bigger than our house on Lizard, and we raised three children in that house."

"There are rooms up above, too," Tansy told him. "My father used to rent them out. We tried to, but we couldn't find anybody who wanted them."

Hound said, "There are so many empty houses these days. Anybody who wants a house can just move in."

"So we keep the extra stock up there, and there's a bed so Mother can nap when she gets too tired. We should have brought you here last night, then you could have slept in a bed."

"My father had a shop like this in the city. I shouldn't say like this, really, because his wasn't as big. He sold paper and quills and ink, and account books and so forth."

Hound's eyebrows went up. "That might not be a bad idea for us. You can't buy paper here in Endroad. I'll see what a ream goes for in the city."

Tansy said, "Nobody here will want that much."

"Of course not." Hound's voice was brisk. "One bit for two sheets of paper and one envelope. We'll have a big bottle of ink, too, and sell it by measure."

"You couldn't sell quills here," Tansy said. "Just about everybody hunts, or keeps geese and ducks."

"Or both," Hound added. "Look at this maul, Horn. I made it myself, so it cost us nothing, and we've got it priced at nine bits, which is what you'd have to pay for a maul like this in the city. The head is elm and the handle's ash. I finished them both with pumice and flax-seed oil."

"That doesn't burn well in lamps, but it's a good polish for wood," Tansy said.

He accepted the maul and carried it to a window to admire it; and she, somewhat timidly, stepped closer and pushed up the sleeves of his plain brown tunic. "What happened to your arms?"

He glanced down at their soiled bandages. "I cut myself somehow. I want to say reaching into some brambles, because they are injuries of that sort; but I don't remember exactly how it happened."

Hound said, "Some of those look pretty nasty."

"I saw them when he took the maul," Tansy said. "I'm going to take those off and put something on the cuts, Horn, and then I'll tie them up again for you. Sometimes somebody cuts himself in here, so I keep bandages and things upstairs." She hurried to the narrow stair at the back of the shop.

He told Hound, "I'm putting you to a great deal of trouble."

"We're glad to do it." Hound took the maul and restored it to its place on the wall. "I just wish we could do more for you, and that my father could be here to help. He'd like to, I know."

As Hound spoke, Oreb swooped though the open door to perch on the handle of a scythe. "Stand up. Big man."

"Pig's awake, you mean?"

Oreb's scarlet-crowed head bobbed. "Pig up."

"In that case, we ought to rejoin him as soon as possible."

"Go shop," Oreb explained. "Bird say. Say shop. Pig go."

Hound chuckled. "You know, I'm starting to understand him. Is your friend coming to meet us here, Horn?"

He nodded, hearing Tansy's small, swift feet again upon the stairs. "I only hope he can find it."

"If he could find his way to Viron from the East Pole, he can find our shop in this village."

"Roll up your sleeves," Tansy ordered; and then, "Wait, I'll do it for you. Hold out your arm. This may hurt."

"I hope so."

She glanced up at him. "You do? Why?"

"Because I feel that I've done something wrong, that I've failed a test of some sort and deserve to be punished."

He paused, recalling the kitchen and the woman who had tied the bandages Tansy was cutting away with scissors. "Did I say something last night about not remembering when I slept last? That's incorrect; I slept in a field of new wheat. I dreamed about Nettle sitting on the beach, and trying to warn her—trying to warn somebody anyway, and failing."

"Poor Silk!" Oreb flew to his shoulder.

"Yes, poor Silk indeed, with no one but a fool like me to search for him. He may or may not need help, but every god knows New Viron and I do."

"Hold still," Tansy directed. "This isn't the first time you've hurt your arm, is it? That's an ugly scar."

At the door a new voice asked, "You say you were the only 'un lookin' for Caldé Silk, stranger?"

Hound said, "Gods be, Merl. Is there something we can do for you this morning?"

"Mornin' to you 'n your wife." A spare, middle-aged man in a worn tunic of faded green stepped into the shop. "Saw your door open is all."

Tansy glanced up. "This is our friend Horn, Merl. He's cut himself, and I'm salving them for him. See how brave he is?"

"You're lookin' for Caldé Silk, you says?" Merl rubbed his stubbled jaw.

"Yes, I am. Do you know where I can find him?"

"Was in the old manse, only nobody hardly seen him there."

"Can you tell me where that is?"

Oreb fluttered dolefully. "No go."

"Well, I could right enough. Only he's not there no more. Not now, anyhow." Merl drew himself up. "You seen these men that got their heads all wrapped up, Hound? They got shawls or somethin' tied around them like a woman."

Hound shook his head. "You mean here?"

"Right here in Endroad. I'm tellin' you. You see 'em, stranger?"

"No see," Oreb declared for both.

"Unless you mean my friend Pig, who ties a cloth around his head to conceal his sightless eyes, I have not."

" 'Stead of a hat's what I mean. I figure they're fixin' to kill him. They got slug guns 'n swords, 'n these here big knives." Merl pointed to a corn knife on the wall. " 'Bout like that 'un, only nicer. They come to my place in the big dark of yesterday. Scared Spirea 'n Verbena to where they crawled right under the bed. Fact."

Hound asked, "How many were there?"

"There's three." Merl paused. "Foreign-lookin', 'n had foreign-soundin' names, too, to where I don't recollect 'em. Not from nowheres near here's what Myrtle says to me, 'n she had the right of it. I told how to get to the old manse, 'n I tells 'em try there. I don't know as how he's in there, I says, only you state your business with him, 'n maybe you'll find out somethin' you're needin' to know."

He asked, "Did they find him? Please, sir, this is extremely important to me."

As she knotted a clean bandage Tansy murmured, "I doubt that he knows."

"Never thought to see 'em again, I'll tell you. I did, though, just walkin' to town this mornin'. Met 'em where the road crosses. Couldn't of been a hour ago."

"Did they find Silk?" he repeated.

Merl shook his head. "Said not. Said there wasn't nobody home." Merl laughed. "They didn't like me much, I'll tell you. But I says well I told you everythin' I knew, so try in the city. They says yep, that's where they's bound for."

Hound said, "It's where I'm going with Horn here and another man, too. We've already tarried too long."

"I agree. I thank you—I can't possibly thank you and Tansy

enough for all your kindness—but if these foreign men really do intend harm to Silk, I must find him first; and the one thing everyone seems to agree upon is that he isn't here."

Hesitantly, Hound asked, "You'll be going your own way, you and Pig, as soon as we reach the city? To look for Caldé Silk, and for a doctor for Pig and so on?"

"Yes, I suppose so."

"Then I . . ." Hound glanced at his wife. "We'd like to give you something to remember us by, wouldn't we, Tansy?"

She looked up, and her smile rendered her small, sweet face radiant. "I was hoping to give them some food to take with them, if it's all right with you."

"Yes. Absolutely. But they'll eat it, and then it will be gone. I mean something that Horn can keep."

He said, "That certainly isn't necessary, and since I'll be traveling on foot for the most part—"

"On one of our donkeys, until we get into the city."

"I must travel light, of necessity. Really, I'd much prefer you wouldn't."

Hound ignored it. "This is what we have. What you see here. Choose anything you like."

Interested, Oreb flew up to perch on the edge of a stew pot and peck at a grater.

Hound said, "A little pan that you could cook in wouldn't weigh much, and I think you might find it comes in very handy."

Tansy added, "Or a sewing kit to mend your clothes, Horn. We have those, too, with needles and a pair of little scissors and everything, that you roll up in a cloth. You could carry it in your pocket."

He pointed. "If you're serious—and I repeat that you really needn't do this—that's what I'd like to have."

"A lantern?"

He nodded. "Last night—really it was before last night, I suppose, during what Merl called the big dark—I wanted such a lantern very badly indeed; I would have given far more than I possess for one. To get one for nothing is more than I prayed for, if you're still sure that you want to do this."

"Certainly we do. Hound can reach it down for you."

Merl whispered, "They got better 'uns in back. Those is the three-bit 'uns. Them in back's five."

"That's right," Hound said. "I'll get you one." He went to the back of the shop and returned a moment later carrying a black lantern somewhat smaller than the tin ones suspended from the ceiling. "This one's enameled, you see. It opens like this so you can light it, and once you've closed it, it will blow away before it blows out."

Merl leaned over the small black lantern, studying it as if he expected to receive it. "Thought you was out of candles."

"We are," Hound told him. "There's a candle in every lantern we sell, naturally, but we have no—"

The little shop was plunged in utter, blind darkness. "Look out," Oreb croaked warily. "Watch out."

5

Haunting Dorp

Morning. I went to bed exhausted, and feel that I am exhausted still; but I want to bring this account, which has fallen behind so badly, up to date; and I know that I can sleep no longer—unlike my unlucky daughter, who as far as I know is sleeping yet.

We stayed at the inn for three nights, idling and telling idle tales of ghosts, war, and riot, until food and fodder were running low and the snow had stopped. She was still sleeping, but Sergeant Azijin demanded we go, which we did—Hide, poor Jahlee, the sergeant and his legermen, and me. She cannot be awakened. Hide and I contrived a rough litter for her; it was carried by her mule and a pack horse, and gave endless trouble.

Each of us has been put into a private house, whose owners are responsible for us. I am in a third-floor bedroom, cold and drafty, whose door is locked outside. They tried to feed me when I came, but I wanted only to rest. Now I am up, wearing my coat and wrapped in a quilt. There is a little fireplace, but no fire. Eventually someone will bring me food, and perhaps I can get wood and a fire. I hope so.

I, who am so seldom hungry these days, find that I am hungry now. Given my choice between food and fire, I believe I might choose the food, which surprises me. Oreb has gone. I would like to have something to give him when he comes back.

I have been praying. Sometimes I feel that the Outsider is as near me as he was to Silk; it was like that when I sacrificed upon the hilltop. Today it seems that he is busy far away and does not hear a word. Perhaps he is angry at me for befriending Jahlee, as I confess I have tried to do. What do the family charged with imprisoning her think of her at this moment? How I would love to know! Without me to keep them away, they are bound to find out soon.

I hesitate to write that she is an inhuma, but look at this account! See how much of it there is! Scarcely a word does not condemn me. I will not destroy it. No, I would sooner perish. If it condemns me, it will show equally that Hide is innocent. The inhumi are evil creatures, granted. How could they be otherwise?

More prayer and furious thought. Pacing the floor, wearing my quilt like a robe. Jahlee's spirit cannot return to her, that seems certain. I should never have returned while leaving her there. I must go back and bring her home, although I cannot imagine how it is to be accomplished.

We will be tried, even if they do not learn that Jahlee is an inhuma. Tried for restraining the fat trader. Robbed by the law of all we took from the robbers and—as I hope—released. Or enslaved, as Azijin seemed to think likely.

Food at last, and good food, too, and plenty of it. It was brought up around midday, by a big, pleasant-looking woman named Aanvagen. She and her husband own this house. Bread, butter, cheese, three kinds of sausage (this last I shall not believe when I reread this), fresh onions, pickled vegetables of a dozen sorts mixed together, mustard, and coffee, with a little flask of brandy which I am to use to season it to suit my taste. A feast! One on which I feasted considerably before stopping to write it all down.

I asked Aanvagen whether she was not afraid I might overpower her and escape when she brought my food. She answered very sensibly that she knew I would not because I had too many possessions—our baggage and the bandits' loot. "Goods" was her word. I would stay and face the court, she said, hoping to come away with something.

"And will I?"

"That Scylla will decide, mysire," said Aanvagen, which I did not find comforting. I dream of her again and again.

"Since you're not afraid of me, might I have my staff? It reminds me of happier times, and I miss it."

"In my kitchen it is. At once you need it, mysire?"

"No, I don't need it at all. I simply would like to have it, and I certainly won't try to harm you with it. If you'll let me go down and get it, I'll carry it back up. I hate to put you to so much trouble, Aanvagen." I confess I was hoping to gain a bit of freedom, enough to let me visit Jahlee.

Some while afterward a little servant girl with hair as bright as a tangerine came, bringing my staff and an armload of firewood. Her name is Vadsig, and she is a girl in fact, hardly more than a child. Recalling Onorifica, I showed her the face on my staff and declared that it could talk. She laughed and challenged me to make it say something. I explained that it was angry at her for laughing, and would probably never talk to her after that. She appeared to enjoy it all—which was certainly what I wanted—laid the fire, and went off to fetch coals from one of the others, promising to return at once; but she has been waylaid by her mistress, I fear.

★

★ ★

What a dream! I want to record it before I forget it. Mora, Fava, and I were riding through a jungle on Green in an open carriage, the horses trotting purposefully ahead without a driver. I explained about Jahlee over and over, beginning each new explanation as soon as I had finished the last and interrupted at long intervals by pointless questions from one or the other. Mora wanted to know whether my room is above the kitchen, and Fava asked what color Vadsig's hair was; I remember those.

At last I asked where the carriage was taking us, and Scylla replied, cracking her arms like whips over the horses. Since the immense boles of the trees we passed and the monstrous, hairless beasts we glimpsed showed that we were on Green, I knew (as one "knows" all such senseless things in dreams) that we could never reach the sea unless I drove. In any event, I moved up to the driver's seat and took the reins; Mora sat beside me. Fearing that Fava might be angry, I looked behind us; she had become a dead doll, with Chenille's knife protruding from her ribs. The trees were gone. Dust swirled around us. I explained to Mora that I was taking us to Blue, but she had become Hyacinth.

That is all I can remember, although I feel sure there was more. All this, as I should make clear, took place after Vadsig came with the promised coals and lit my fire.

She wanted to know all about me, where I came from and where I had been, why I was under arrest and so on and so forth. I told her about Viron, how empty the city is now, and how a starless night can begin at midday and last for days, at which she became exceedingly skeptical. I told her I had sacrificed there, wearing the same torn and dirty robe I am wearing now, and took off the quilt (which I no longer required) and my coat so she could see it. She knows nothing of augury, poor child, and less of the gods. She said she would never believe in a god she could not see; I explained that she would never see the Outsider, who is the principal god here, and that even Silk had seen him only in a dream.

After that we talked about dreams, and she wanted me to tell her fortune, by which she meant that I was to practice augury as I had in Viron. One sausage remained, so I sacrificed it, the little fire in the grate our Sacred Window and our altar fire. She caught brandy blood in my empty cup and flung it into the flames, which gave us a fine flash of blue. After I had read her sausage (a wealthy marriage soon, happiness, and many children), and burned a piece of it, I gave her the rest. She is no plumper than my staff, poor child, although she insists that Aanvagen gives her enough to eat.

After she left, I prayed for a time and went to bed, and that is when I had the dream I have recounted. I cannot say what it means, and doubt that it means anything.

I have been trying to contrive some plan, but soon fall to rehashing my dream instead—planning seems so useless with our situation as it is. What can be planned when I have no freedom to carry any plan out? I might escape Aanvagen and her husband easily, and every god knows I care nothing for the loot. With considerable luck, I might steal a horse and escape from Dorp, leaving Hide to face the wrath of our captors alone, and poor Jahlee in her coma to be burned alive—neither of which I have the smallest intention of doing. They bind me far more securely than his cupidity could ever bind Nat.

At least I know what doll it was that searched for Hide.

How good it was to see Hyacinth, although it was only for a moment and only in a dream! When Nettle and I lived in the Caldé's Palace I disliked her, or thought I did. Each of us was jealous of the attention Silk gave the other, I think, which was as foolish as it was wrong. What a beautiful woman she was, good or bad. When someone is gifted, we think he should behave better than the rest of us, as Silk did. But in Silk's case, his goodness *was* his gift—a gift he had made for himself. It was the magnetism that drew others to him that caused his embryo to be put aboard a lander. That was the work of Pas's scientists, as Pig's size and strength were. (Recalling the Red Sun Whorl that it became, I cannot but wonder whether it did not sacrifice too much for us.)

His goodness he made for himself as a boy and a young man, as I wrote just a moment ago. No doubt he was prompted by his mother, but then all boys are. I was myself, but how much good did Mother's promptings do?

Oreb has returned, having found no one who might help us, and having nothing to report save cold and snow, dispirited and unwilling to converse.

★

★ ★

We progress! Vadsig brought my breakfast today, and with it news better than any fried mush. Jahlee is being held in a house diagonally across the street from ours. I hurried to my window, but it looks in the wrong direction.

"Then please, Vadsig, I beg you, let me go to a window from which I can see it. If only I can I see, for a single minute, the house in which my poor daughter is a prisoner, I'll feel a thousand times better. I swear to you I won't run away, and I'll return to this room and let you lock me in again the moment you tell me I must go back."

It took a great deal of pleading, but she agreed. Out we went, ten steps down a little hallway and into a bedroom only slightly larger and more comfortable than mine. It was Vadsig's own, as she explained with touching pride—a narrow bed, half smothered by an old quilt intended for a bigger one, a fireplace with a woodbox, and an old chest that I feel sure has more than enough room for her entire wardrobe. Together we leaned from her window so that she might point out the window of the room in which poor Jahlee lies. "A doctor for her they want if the court for him will pay," confided Vadsig.

"Poor thing," muttered Oreb, and I agree. Let us hope that it will not.

Afterward she showed me her most prized possessions—a sketch of her dead parents by a street artist, and a cracked vase given her by Aanvagen. She is sixteen, she said; but under pressure admitted she might be no more than fifteen after all. I would say fourteen.

None of which means much. The important points are that Jahlee is confined within a short walk of where I sit, that she like me is on the third floor of a private house, and that Vadsig is inclined to be friendly. She promises to find Hide for me, as well. (Perhaps I should note that the house in which Jahlee is confined has a stone first story and two upper stories of wood, a kind of construction that seems very common here, and that the street is narrow but carries a good deal of traffic, mostly wagonloads of bales, barrels, or boxes.)

I returned to this room as I had promised, heard Vadsig's key squeak in the lock and the solid thump of the bolt, and knelt to squint through the keyhole, hoping for another glimpse of the only friend I have in this brutal, busy, savage seaport. I did not get it, however; the key was still in the lock.

That gave me an idea. I slid this sheet of paper under my door and used the point of one of Oreb's quills to tickle the key into a position that allowed me to poke it out. It fell, and I retrieved this sheet with infinite care, hoping to bring the key in with it. The sheet returned indeed, but the key did not, and I swore.

"No good?" Oreb inquired.

"Exactly," I told him. "Either the key is too thick to slide under the door, or it hit the paper and bounced off."

"Bird find."

I thought that he planned to fly out my window and re-enter the house by another and was about to warn him that it might be a long while before he found another window open in this cold weather, but he disappeared into a triangular hole I had not noticed previously where the wainscoting meets the chimney near the ceiling. In five minutes or less he was back with the key in his beak. I have hidden it in my stocking.

All this has given me another idea. I am going to write a letter to which I will sign Jahlee's name, and have Oreb push it between the shutters of her window for her captors to find. It can do us no harm, and may be of benefit.

★

★ ★

Supper was late, as expected. Poor Vadsig looked everywhere for her key before confessing to Aanvagen that she had lost it; Aanvagen boxed her ears and so on, all of which was unfortunate but unavoidable; I comforted her as well as I could in Aanvagen's presence, and promised her a coral necklace when I am free.

"Sphigxday coming is, and you to the court going are," says Aanvagen, looking as somber as her fair hair and red face allow. She is a good woman at base, I believe. This is Molpsday, so I have nearly a week to wait. I must return Jahlee to Blue and consciousness before then. There can be no delay, no excuses; it must be done.

I left my room sometime after midnight, after Oreb reported that all the inhabitants were asleep. There are four: Aanvagen and Vadsig, "Cook," and "Master." After locating our baggage in a ground-floor storeroom off the kitchen and retrieving Maytera Mint's gift and some other things, I explored the rest of the house until I understood the plan of its floors thoroughly. It was dark by Blue's standards, although nothing to compare with the pitchy blackness of a darkday. Smoldering fires gave enough light to save me from tripping over furniture, Oreb advised me in hoarse whispers, and I groped my way with my staff.

When I felt I knew the house, I went outside. As expected, every door of the house in which Jahlee lies was locked. The key to my room will not open them, and I suspect they are barred at night, as the outer doors of this house are. Nothing more to report, save that I have asked Vadsig to bring me a lump of sealing wax so I can study the impression made by this ring. The stone is not actually black, I find; call it purple-gray.

Much shouting downstairs before lunch. Vadsig explained that she is not supposed to leave the house without permission, but that she had gone out to discover where Hide is being held. "Cook" caught her, and gave her a dressing down. "But finding him for you I am, Mysire Horn. In the house behind the house where your daughter is he is. Not happy there he is, these things the girl there tells. Up and down, up and down he walks. A thousand questions he asks."

"I see. I'm very sorry to hear this, Vadsig. I don't want to get you into any more trouble; but sometime when you are sent to the market do you think it might be possible for you to speak to him?"

"If it you wish, mysire, trying I am. Parel upstairs will let me go, that may be."

"Thank you, Vadsig. Thank you very, very much! I'm forever indebted to you. Vadsig, when we were in your room, you showed me the picture of your parents and your vase, things that are precious to you. Do you remember?"

She laughed and shook out her short, orange hair with a touch of the pride she showed in her bedroom. She has a good, merry laugh. "From yesterday not so quickly forgetting I am."

"I want to warn you that it's not wise to show precious things to everyone, Vadsig. You see, I'm going to give you something precious—the coral necklace I promised you; but it could get you into trouble if Aanvagen knew you had it. Do you think we could make it a little secret between the two of us? For the time being?"

"From me it she would take? This you think, mysire?"

I shrugged. "You know her much better than I do, Vadsig."

There was a lengthy pause while Vadsig reached a decision. "Not showing her, I am."

Oreb commended her. "Wise girl!"

"Stealing I am she thinking is. . . . After court you giving it are, mysire?"

"No. Right now." I got out my paper and opened the pen case. "First, though, I'm going to write something you can show other people to prove that you're not a thief."

I did, and gave it to her; but finding that she was unable to read I read it aloud for her: *Be it known that I, Horn, a traveler and a resident of New Viron, give this coral necklace, having thirty-four large beads of fine green coral flushed with rose, to my friend Vadsig, a resident of Dorp. It comes to her as a gift, freely given, and as of this day becomes her own private possession.*

I got out the necklace and put it around her neck. She took it off at once to admire it, put it back on, took it off again, put it on once more, preened exactly as if she could see her reflection, her large blue eyes flashing—and in short showed as much satisfaction as if she had been snatched from the scullery and made mistress of a city.

"If you're able to talk to my son, Vadsig, will you please tell him where I'm confined, and what my circumstances are, and that we are to go to court on Sphigxday, which he may not know? And bring back any message that he has for me?"

"Trying I am, Mysire Horn."

"Wonderful! And succeeding, too, I feel sure. I have great confidence in you, Vadsig."

"But forgetting I am." Very reluctantly, the coral necklace was removed for the last time, dropped into an apron pocket, and concealed beneath a soiled handkerchief. "Mistress a question asks. Every dream you understanding are, mysire? That to her I have told."

I tried to explain that dreams were a bottomless subject, and that no one knows everything about them; but that I had been successful at times in interpreting the principal features of certain dreams.

"Last night strange dreams she and Master having are. Them you for her will explain?"

"I'll certainly attempt it, Vadsig. I'll do what I can."

"Telling her I am."

That was two hours ago, perhaps. Thus far, Aanvagen has not come to have her dream explained; nor has Vadsig returned to report on her attempt to speak with Hide in person. Might Hide and I rescue Jahlee—provided that I can free him, or he can free himself? I suppose it is possible, but the chances of failure will be very high. I would sooner trust myself and them to the mercy of the court, I believe.

Aanvagen brought a most ample supper, accompanied by her portly husband, who was red-faced and panting after two flights of stairs. "My name—mysire . . . Beroep it is." He offered a very large and very soft hand, which I shook. "You Mysire Horn . . ." Another gasp for breath. "Mysire Rajan . . . Mysire Incanto . . . Mysire Silk—"

"Good man!" This from Oreb.

"Are. A man of many . . . Names you are." He smiled in a breathless fashion he plainly intended to be friendly.

"A man of many names, perhaps, but I'm certainly not entitled to all those. Call me Horn, please."

"You to my house I could not welcome . . . For the troopers watching were. Sorry I am." Yet another gasp. "Mysire Horn."

I assured him that it was quite all right, that I bore no animus toward him or his wife. "You have fed me very well indeed and provided me with firewood, wash water, and ample coverings for this comfortable bed. Believe me, I'm very much aware that the conditions under which most prisoners live are not one-tenth as good."

Aanvagen nudged her husband, who asked, "With gods you speak . . . Mysire Horn?"

"Sometimes. And sometimes they condescend to reply. But I ought to have invited you both to sit down. I have only my bed, but you are very welcome to sit there."

They did, and Aanvagen's husband got out a handkerchief with which he mopped his face and his bald head. "Nat. Him I know. A greedy thief he is."

Aanvagen added hastily, "To others this you do not say, Mysire Horn."

"Of course not."

"Judge Hamer Nat's cousin is."

Aanvagen's husband watched me for some reaction, but I tried to keep from showing what I felt.

"Already this knowing you are?"

"I knew that Dorp was governed by five judges, and that Nat was said to have a great deal of influence with them; but not that Nat was related to one. Am I to take that he's the judge who will try us?"

Aanvagen's husband nodded gloomily; Aanvagen herself poked a second time at his well-padded ribs. "You must about our dreams ask, Beroep."

"Mysire Horn not friendless is, first I say, woman. Poor, Judge Hamer him will make. Beaten, that also may be. But not friendless, he will be. Nat a greedy thief is. All Dorp knows."

I thanked him and his wife very sincerely, and inquired about their dreams.

"Beroep awake is, so he dreams. All through our house voices he hears."

Aanvagen's husband nodded vigorously. "Talking and tapping they are, Mysire Horn. Whisper, whisper and tap, tap."

"I see. You didn't get up to investigate?"

"Asleep I am. I cannot."

"I see. What did the voices say?"

He shrugged. "Psst, psst, psst!"

It was a passable imitation of Oreb's hoarse whisper, and I gave him a severe look to indicate that he was not to speak. He responded by saying "Good bird!" and "No, no!" quite loudly.

"You're not giving me a lot to go on," I told Aanvagen's husband. "Let me hear your wife's dream before I attempt to interpret yours."

"In my own house I am," she began eagerly, "in the big room for company. This room you see, mysire, when here you come."

"Yes. Certainly."

"With me two children sitting are. Darker than my cat one is, mysire. Beroep and I no children have. This you know?"

I admitted that Vadsig had so informed me.

"Girls in pretty dresses they are. Faces clean they have. Hair very nice, it is. A daughter you have, mysire?"

"Yes. A daughter and three sons."

Aanvagen's husband said, "A son by Strik kept is."

"Yes, my son Hide, who was traveling with me. My sons Hoof and Sinew are still free, as far as I know."

"From Dorp much traveling we are. To New Viron we go. Farther even, we sail." He waved a hand expansively. "Now travelers we arrest? Not good for traveling it is."

"I understand."

Aanvagen leaned toward me from her seat on my bed. "This these girls to me say. Bad with us it goes, for you keeping."

I made what I hoped was an encouraging noise.

"About your daughter they talk. Sick she is. Away with you her send we must. My cheeks they kiss." Aanvagen's formidable bosom rose and fell. "Mother, me they call, mysire. Bad things to me they don't want. Warned be! Warned be!"

Oreb interpreted. "Watch out!"

I asked, "Was there anything else about your dream that seemed significant to you?"

Aanvagen's mouth opened, then closed again.

"Was there any other sign associated with the gods?"

Her husband inquired, "One sign already you finding are?"

"Yes, of course. The two children. Molpe is the goddess of childhood, as you must surely know. Were there any animals, Aanvagen?"

She shook her head. "Just the children and me there were."

"Mice? Monkeys? Cattle? Songbirds?" I reminded myself so much of poor old Patera Remora then that I could not resist adding, "Vultures, eh? Hyenas—um—camels?"

Aanvagen had heard only the first. "No mice, no rats in my house there are, mysire."

"What about you?" I asked her husband. "Were there animals in your dream? Bats, for instance? Or cats?"

"No, mysire. None." He sounded very positive.

"I see. Oreb, I want you to speak freely. Do you think this a good man?"

"Good man!"

"What about Aanvagen here? Is she a good woman, too?"

"Good girl!"

"I agree. Beroep, could that have been the voice you heard? Could it have been my bird—or another, similar, bird? Think carefully before you reply."

He stared at me for a moment before patting his forehead with his handkerchief again. "Possible it is, mysire. Not so I will not say."

"That's interesting. My bird is a night chough; and the species is sacred to the god who governs the boundless abyss between the whorls, just as owls are to Tartaros. We have an indication of Molpe in your wife's dream, and an indication of the Outsider in yours." There was a knock at the door, and I called, "What is it, Vadsig?"

"Merfrow Cijfer here is. Through our kitchen she comes, in our front room she sits. With Mistress to speak she wants."

Aanvagen sought my permission with a glance, received it, and hurried out. "A moment only, mysire. Beroep."

"A good woman she is," Aanvagen's husband told me as the door closed, "but no more brain than her cat she has. Better we without her talk. To the court you have thought given? To Judge Hamer? Not friendless you are, I say."

I said that I had tried, but that I knew little of the politics of Dorp—only that I had done no wrong. "Speaking thus from ignorance, it would seem to me that my best chance is to get Nat to drop his charges. If I had the jewelry from my luggage—"

Beroep shook his head regretfully. "This I cannot do, mysire. The inventory Judge Hamer has, by me signed. Fifty cards pay, this to me he would tell."

"Most unfortunate."

Again the gloomy nod. "Why you here are, mysire. This do not you wonder? Why your jailer I am?"

I confessed that I had thought very little about it.

"You will escape, this they hope. A hundred cards paying I am. Ruined I am."

"Poor man!"

Aanvagen's husband patted the bed on which he sat. "Many blankets you have. A fire you have. Good food you get."

"So you won't be ruined. I understand. This is certainly very unfortunate. I take it that it would be useless for you to plead with Nat to drop the charges."

"Me he hates." Beroep wiped sweat-beaded face again. "Bribe him I might. I will, this I think. A greedy thief he is. Friends might help."

"Good. Who did you say is holding my son Hide?"

"Strik he is. An honest trader like me he is."

"Might he not assist you, too?"

"This I will discover, mysire. It may be."

"My son Hide is young and athletic. Headstrong, as all such young men are. He's far more likely to escape, I would say, than I am."

"No go!"

I looked up at Oreb on his perch near the chimney. "All right, I won't. Beroep, you need not worry about my escaping. That won't happen; I give you my word. I can't speak for my son, however, since I can't communicate with him. You might want to tell your friend Strik so."

"To him as you say I will speak, mysire. He may us help. It may be."

"What about the man holding Jahlee, my daughter?"

"Wijzer at sea is." Beroep pointed toward the floor. "That Cijfer, his wife is. But no money she gives unless Wijzer says."

"Do you know when he might return to Dorp?"

Aanvagen's husband shook his head, and I heard her voice from the stairs. "Beroep! A hus! A hus at our door was!"

He rolled his eyes upward. "A shadow it is, mysire. Of this assured be."

My door opened, revealing Aanvagen and a slightly slimmer, slightly younger woman with the same blue eyes, fair hair, and high complexion. "A hus at our door it is. Cijfer to our door it will not allow."

When Aanvagen's husband spoke, it was with a world of skepticism in his voice. "A hus it is?"

"Yes!" Cijfer's hands indicated a beast the size of a dray horse.

I went to the door and called for Vadsig, then turned back to Aanvagen and her husband. "Those are steep stairs. I hope you won't mind if I ask your servant to help me instead of troubling you."

He said, "You my guest are, mysire."

Vadsig's voice floated up the stairwell. *"What it is, mysire?"*

"Open the front door, please, and leave it open. Your master agrees that you are to do as I say. It's important."

There was a lengthy pause, then the sound of Vadsig's hurrying feet.

"Beroep, am I correct in thinking that if a hus—a wild hus—has come into Dorp, someone will shoot it?"

He shook his head, and both women protested, horrified.

"They won't?"

"Bad luck it is!" This from the women in chorus.

"Superstition it is," Aanvagen's husband explained, in the tone of one who tolerates the irrational beliefs of the ignorant. "If a beast into the town it comes, misfortune it brings. Back to the woodlands we must it drive. If killed it is, the misfortune in our town remains."

I had been listening for the clatter of Babbie's hoofs on Aanvagen's wooden floors, and had not heard it. I called, "Vadsig, did you open that door as I asked you?"

She replied, but I could not understand what she said. "Tell her to come up here," Aanvagen's husband advised.

As loudly as I could, I shouted, "Come here, please, Vadsig!" and fell to coughing.

Aanvagen said, "Tea with brandy in it you need, mysire. Get it you shall. See to it I will."

"Alone we should talk," her husband muttered. "That better would be. This hus in my house you wish."

I nodded. "Yes, I do."

"Not a wild hus it is. Not a shadow either it is. A tame hus? Yours, mysire?"

I nodded again.

"Like your bird it is."

Oreb bobbed agreement. "Good bird!"

"Somewhat like him at least. My hus—his name is Babbie—does not speak, of course. But he's a clean, gentle animal. We were separated, and he seems to have gone back to the woman who gave him to me. Some time ago, she learned where I was and promised to return him."

Vadsig bustled through the doorway. "Yes, Mysire Horn?"

I said, "I simply wanted to know whether you opened the front door as I asked, Vadsig."

"Oh, yes, mysire."

"You a big animal seeing are?" Aanvagen put in.

"Yes, mistress."

"What sort of animal, Vadsig?"

"Mules, mysire. Pulling carts they are."

"A hus you seeing are?" Cijfer inquired urgently.

"A hus? Oh, no, Merfrow Cijfer."

"Did you leave the door open, Vadsig, when you came up?"

"No, mysire. Cold in the street it is."

"How long did you leave it open?"

"Till you up to come telling me are, mysire."

Oreb dropped to my shoulder, giving me a quizzical look to indicate that he would go outside and look for the hus if asked. I shook my head—unobtrusively, I hope.

Aanvagen's husband asked, "No hus you seeing are, Vadsig?"

"No, Master."

He turned to Cijfer. "A hus at my door you seeing are?"

"Yes, Beroep. Never a hus so big I see. Tusks as long as my hand they are."

"This your Babbie is?" he asked me.

"Yes, I'm quite sure it is."

"Your Babbie Vadsig hurting is?"

"I certainly don't think so."

He made a gesture of dismissal. "Vadsig, to the door again go. If a hus you see, the door open leave and us you tell. If no hus you see, the door you close and your work you do."

She ducked in a sketchy curtsy and hurried away.

Cijfer offered him the letter I had penned a few hours before, her hand shaking sufficiently to rattle the paper. "Finding this in the sleeping girl's room I am, Beroep. It reading you are? Aanvagen, too?"

They bent their heads over it.

"Your daughter she is, mysire?" Her voice trembled.

I nodded.

"Sleeping all day she is. Sleeping all night she is not. Walking she is, talking is." She turned to Aanvagen, her voice trembling. "My pictures from the walls breaking!"

Downstairs, something fell with a crash. Vadsig screamed.

6

Dark Empty Rooms

"Somethin' there, bucky." Pig's hand, groping through darkness that for Pig had no shadeup, found his arm and closed around it, pointed nails digging into his flesh. "Hoose, maybe."

"Do you think they might let us sleep there? I don't see any lights."

"Was nae lights ter Hound's, neither, yer said."

A short distance ahead Hound remarked, "Oil that will burn in lamps is very dear, and candles almost impossible to find at any price." After a moment he added, "I really can't say how near the city we are, but we've come a long way. I for one am ready for a rest. What about you, Horn?"

Pig released his arm, and the tapping of Pig's scabbard indicated that Pig was moving to his right. He said, "Pig's been walking, while I've done nothing but sit upon the back of this wonderfully tolerant donkey of yours. I feel sure that Pig—and my donkey—must be far more fatigued than I am."

"Wall." Pig's voice sounded nearby. "Nae winders, nor nae doors neither." There was a pause. "Here's ther gate. Wide h'open, ter."

"No gate!" Oreb informed him.

"There's a vacant mansion back there," Hound explained. "I've passed it many times. We could camp in it, if everybody's willing. It should keep off the rain, and rain's likely after this heat. How do you feel about it, Horn? Would you be willing to stop?"

"Yes." He got out the striker Tansy had given him. "I'd like to see it, if it belonged to a man named Blood. Did it?"

"I haven't the least notion who it belonged to. All I can tell you is that nobody's lived in it for as long as I've been taking this road. It's pretty remote, and there are a lot of empty houses. Most are in better shape than this one."

"Then I want to stop, if you and Pig are willing." The striker flared.

"I wouldn't use up more of that candle than you can help."

Pig's voice came from a greater distance. "Gang h'in, bucky. Yer comin'?"

"Yes, I am." He dismounted.

The wall was ruinous; the tangled iron through which Maytera Marble had picked her way had vanished. "I fought in a battle here, Oreb," he whispered to the bird on his shoulder.

"No fight!"

"Sometimes one must. Sometimes you do yourself."

Oreb fidgeted, his bill clacking unhappily. "Bad place."

"Oh, no doubt. They were holding Silk here, and Chenille, Patera Incus, and Master Xiphias. Not so long ago, I imagined Xiphias was walking along beside me. I wish he'd come back." He led his donkey through the gate and raised his lantern, hoping for a glimpse of the villa that had been Blood's; but the feeble light of the candle scarcely revealed the distant, pale bulk of Scylla's fountain. Under his breath he added, "Or that Silk would."

"Bad place!"

Behind them, Hound chuckled. "It's haunted, naturally. All these old places are supposed to be."

"It is indeed." The man Hound addressed waved his knobbed staff before him, although the light from his lantern showed no obstruction. "There should be a dead talus right here. I wonder what has become of it."

"Well, I wonder what's become of your friend Pig. I don't see him up ahead."

"You're right. Oreb, will you look for him, please? If he's in trouble, come back and tell us at once."

"Now that's a handy pet." Hound caught up. "You've been here before?"

"Twenty years ago. I had a slug gun instead of a stick then, and a thousand friends instead of two. No doubt I should say I like this better, because no one's trying to kill me; but the truth is I don't." He pointed back to the gate with his staff. "The Guard floaters broke through there and came in with buzz guns blazing at the same time we swarmed over the wall—volunteers like me, and Guardsmen, and even Trivigaunti pterotroopers. There were taluses in here, but between the floaters and us, they never had a chance. Others did much more, I'm sure; but I got off a shot before—"

Oreb returned, dropping onto his shoulder. "Pig come."

"He's all right then?"

Oreb croaked deep in his throat, and Hound said, "I couldn't understand him that time."

"He didn't say anything, just made a noise. It means he doesn't know what to say or doesn't know how to say it. So something's the matter with Pig that Oreb can't explain, or that he doesn't know how to tell us. Is he bleeding, Oreb?"

"No hurt."

"That's good. He didn't fall, I hope?"

"No, no."

The fountain was dry, its basin filled with rotting leaves and its once-white stone dirty gray. One of Scylla's arms had been broken off.

"Do people still worship her, Hound?"

Hound hesitated. "Sometimes. I'm not religious myself, so I don't pay a lot of attention, but I don't think it's like it used to be. They offer ducks now, mostly, or that's what Tansy's mother told me once."

"What about theophanies?"

"I'm afraid I don't know that word."

"Girl come," Oreb explained.

"Does Scylla appear in your Sacred Windows?"

"Oh, that." Hound urged his donkey forward, and jerked the rope of those he led. "Not like it used to be, I suppose. She comes to the window in the Grand Manteion two or three times a year, or the augurs say she does."

"It wasn't like that at all, really. No god ever visited us in all the time that I was growing up, not until just before we left for Blue."

"I didn't know that," Hound said.

"What I wanted—"

Oreb interrupted them. "Man come. Pig man."

"Good." He raised his lantern. "Pig? Are you all right?"

"Ho, aye."

"We were worried about you." He hurried forward.

The fitful light of the swinging lantern revealed the huge Pig, his dirty black trousers and dirty gray shirt, his big sword just now exploring the wide doorway of Blood's villa as Pig prepared to step out.

"We're going to camp in there. There are fireplaces, I'm sure, or there used to be."

"Aye, bucky."

He turned back to Hound. "Do you require our help with the donkeys?"

"No," Hound called. "But you could start that fire."

"I will. There—I'm going to blow out my candle, Pig. Hound doesn't want me to waste it, and he's right. I haven't seen any firewood around here anyway, and I imagine all the furniture was stolen or burned long ago."

"Aye."

Oreb muttered, "Poor man."

"So would you guide me to the back of the house and help look for wood? The trees overhang the wall there, as I remember, and there must be fallen branches."

Pig's big hand found his arm, and although Pig did not reply, he followed Pig docilely.

"This is where they had the sheds for Blood's floaters, and where the horned cats were penned. A talus cared for them, the one Silk killed in the tunnels. I suppose the others, the ones we killed when we stormed the house, were the Ayuntamiento's. The rabbit hutches must have been back here, too, though I don't remember seeing them."

"Seein'?" Pig's hand tightened. "Did yer say seein', bucky?"

Oreb fidgeted on his master's shoulder uneasily, wings half extended. "Watch out."

"Yes, Pig, I did."

"Pals, hain't we?"

"Certainly I am your friend, Pig. I hope you're mine as well."

"Then tell me somethin', bucky. Tell me what yer see."

"Right now? Nothing at all. It's totally dark."

"Yer said yer'd blow h'out yer glim, an' yer did. Heard yer. Heard yer h'open, an' blow, an' shut h'up."

"That's right. I can light it again if you wish, and use it to look around for wood."

"Nae sunshine, bucky?"

"No. None."

The hand on his shoulder, tight already, tightened still more. "What h'about ther skylands? Onie light h'up there?"

"No—wait." He lifted his head, scanning the sky. "One little pinpoint of red. It's a city burning, I suppose, though just a spark to us. That's what someone told me they were."

"What h'about ther hoose, bucky? Did yer gae h'on h'in?"

"No, not yet. I intended to, of course."

"Then yer don't know h'if there's lights h'in h'it, do yer?" Pig's voice shook.

"I—I'm inclined to doubt it. The entrance was dark, and we—I—saw no lights in the windows. I didn't ask Hound, but if he had seen one he would have mentioned it, I'm sure."

"What h'about yer, H'oreb? Yer was h'in there wi' me."

"Bird go," Oreb confirmed cautiously.

"Yer een's guid h'in ther dark. Better'n onie man's, hain't that lily, H'oreb? Look 'round noo, will yer? A favor ter ane what's yer friend?"

"Bird look."

"Yer needn't be a-feared. What do yer see?"

"Pig, Silk."

"Aye. What 'sides a' us?"

"Big wall. Big house."

"What a' a woman, H'oreb? Do yer see onie woman h'about, watchin' an' listenin'?"

"No girl."

"Lookin' h'out ther winder, h'it might be."

"No, no. No see."

There was a grunt of effort, followed by a thump as Pig's knee came down on the hard, dry grass. "Bucky, will yer help me? Yer me friend, yer said sae. Will yer?"

"Of course, Pig." From the new angle of Pig's arm, Pig was kneeling before him. He groped for him and found the other hand, a hairy hand as large as good-sized ham, that grasped the pommel of the big sword. "I'll help you in any way I can. Surely you know that."

"Recollect how yer felt a' me face, bucky?"

"Of course."

"Wanted ter prove ter yer Pig has nae een, bucky. Got me rag h'over 'em, an' some thinks Pig's soldierin'. Wanted yer ter find h'out fer yerself."

"I understand."

"Yer didn't have nae glim then, but yer does noo. Will yer light h'it fer me, bucky? Fer ane second, like."

"Certainly. It will be a relief to me, actually. Wait a moment." He opened the lantern and got out the striker again. It flared, shooting yellow-white sparks that seemed as bright as thrown torches; the butter-yellow flame of the candle rose.

The rag was no longer across Pig's broad, bearded face. Widely spaced holes like the eyes in a skull stared at nothing.

"Can yer see 'em, bucky? See me een? Where they was?"

He made himself speak. "Yes, Pig. Yes, I can."

"Gaen, hain't they? They cut 'em oot?"

He lowered his lantern and looked away. "Yes, they are. They did."

"Gets dirty, sometimes. Cleans h'in 'em wi' a rag h'on the h'end a' me fin'er."

"Man cry," Oreb informed him, and he looked back. Rivulets of moisture coursed down either side of Pig's broad nose.

"I'll clean them for you, Pig, if that's what you wish. With a clean cloth and clean water."

"Went h'in." Pig's voice was almost inaudible. "H'in ther hoose ter find what might be found, bucky. An' seen her."

Silence. He opened the little black lantern again and blew out its candle, and could not have explained why.

"Dark h'again, bucky?" There was a hideous mirth in Pig's voice that hurt more than any tears.

"Yes, Pig," he said. "Dark again."

"Yer dinna h'ask h'about her, bucky."

"No talk," Oreb advised him.

He ignored the warning. "I didn't think it the moment for prying questions."

"Yer dinna care, bucky?"

"I care very much. But this isn't the time. Hound is unloading his donkeys, Pig, and expecting us to find firewood. Let us find firewood for him. We said we would."

Later, when all three were sitting before a small fire in the large fireplace that had graced Blood's sellaria, Hound said, "I'm going to have a look at my donkeys. I've never had one get loose on a darkday, and I prefer that it never happen." He rose. "Can I get either of you anything?"

"We've more than enough."

As Hound left, Pig whispered, "Noo, bucky? Want ter hear h'about her noo?"

He shook his head. "Wait until Hound comes back."

"Want him ter hear h'it? Thought yer dinna."

"Of course I do. He knows this area and the people in it. Have you ever been here before, Pig?"

"Has Pig? Pig has nae!"

"Well, I have; but that was years ago. I'll have forgotten a great deal, even if I don't think I have. I'll have distorted more, and even the little I remember will be largely obsolete. I wanted to get you alone so I could find out what was troubling you. Now that I have—and it troubles me, too—I'm eager to hear what Hound will say about it." He waited for Pig to speak, and when Pig did not he added, "Of course I don't imagine that Hound can tell us how a man without eyes can see; but he may be able to tell us a something about what he has seen."

"Man come," Oreb announced. "Come back."

"I take it your donkeys haven't strayed, Hound? You wouldn't have returned so quickly if that had been the case."

Hound smiled as he resumed his seat. "No. They're fine. I worry too much about them, I'm afraid, and I doubt that will be the last time I check on them tonight. It must seem silly to you."

"Your concern for the animals in your care? Certainly not. But, Hound, Pig has confided something extraordinary to me, and he'd like you to hear about it, too."

"If it's something I can help with, I'll do what I can."

"I'm sure you will. Pig went into this house alone when we first arrived. I needn't dwell upon how dark it was, or mention that Pig carried no light."

Guardedly, Hound nodded.

"I wish it were not necessary for me to mention that Pig is blind as well. He is, and though I never doubted it, he insisted I verify it. I did, and he's totally blind. If you doubt it, I do not doubt that he'll let you verify it as well."

"I'll take your word for it," Hound declared, "but I can't imagine what this is leading up to."

"Man see," Oreb explained concisely.

"Exactly. He saw a woman, here in this house. Is that correct, Pig?"

"Aye."

"Now you know all that I do, Hound. Let's go on from there.

"It was dark, Pig. Not the mere darkness of night, in which one can often discern large objects, including persons, but pitch dark. The depths of this ruined villa must have been utterly lightless. How was it you were able to see her?"

"Dinna know." Pig shook his head.

"Was she carrying a light? A candle, for example?"

"If she'd a' been," Pig said slowly, "Pig would nae been h'able ter see h'it ter tell yer." He stretched out his hands. "Fire here, hain't there? Auld Pig feels h'it, feels ther heat a' h'it. Can Pig see h'it, ter? Pig canna."

"Could you see anything other than the woman? The floor she was standing on, for example, or the wall behind her?"

"Nae, bucky. Nor canna recall such."

"It wasn't anybody you know?" Hound asked. "Tansy or—or some woman you've met in your travels?"

Pig turned his head, about ten degrees in error. "Would Pig know? Ter see?"

"I guess you wouldn't." Hound fingered his chin.

"Man talk!" Oreb urged.

"All right, I will. I warned you this place is supposed to be haunted. Or anyway I warned you, Horn. Pig had gone on ahead, I think."

"Haunted by a woman?"

"Yes. Do you want the whole story? It's the sort of thing children tell younger children, I warn you."

"I do. What about you, Pig?"

"Ho, aye."

"All right. Many years ago, a very rich man who had an ugly daughter lived here. This daughter was so ugly that no one would marry her. The rich man gave balls and parties and invited all the eligible young men in the city, but none of them would marry her. A witch came to his door all robed in black, and he fed her and gave her a card, and asked what he could do about his ugly daughter. The witch told him to lock her up where nobody except himself would ever see her. What's wrong, Horn?"

"Nothing, except that I've just realized for the thousanth time what an idiot I am. Go on with your story, please—I'd like to hear it."

"If you want me to." Hound held up the wine bottle from which he had been drinking, saw that it was still almost full, and sipped. "The witch told him to lock up his daughter where nobody could see her until everybody forgot how ugly she was. So that's what he did. He locked her in a dark, bare room and kept the shutters closed day and night so that nobody would see her and brought her food himself, and pretty soon everybody forgot about her except the augur who had christened her. I don't know what her name was, though no doubt the augur did."

"It was Mucor."

Hound stared.

"I'm sorry, I didn't mean to interrupt. Go on, I want to hear the rest."

"This augur would come to the rich man's house and ask about her. Each time the rich man would make some excuse, saying that his daughter was ill or away. Soon the augur became suspicious. He had a hatchet, and he would come at night with his hatchet and chop open the shutter and let the ugly daughter out. Then she would go from house to house asking people to take her in. No one would because she was so ugly, and so she played tricks on them, throwing their supper plates at them and making them hit themselves with their own fists, and so on.

"But a god told the augur to go away, and he did. General Mint killed the rich father, and there was nobody left to let the ugly daughter out or feed her, so she starved to death in her room. But her ghost still haunts the house, walking on top of the wall or on the roof, and sometimes she stops travelers. If she stops you and you're polite to her, she'll tell your fortune and bring good luck. But if you even hint at how ugly she is, she'll curse you and you'll die within a year."

"Tell good!" Oreb applauded with his wings.

Hound smiled. "There it is. That's all I know except that there's a family in Endroad who claim to have the hatchet, which they say the augur left behind. I've seen it and it's just an old hatchet, with no magic powers as far as I know. You look very thoughtful, Horn."

He nodded. "I am, because your story suggests that Silk has left Viron—that he's on Blue or Green, if he's still alive. Patera Silk was the augur who pried open Mucor's shutter with his hatchet, and thus beyond question the augur in the story. I'd guess that the wise witch in black robes represents someone's confused recollection of Maytera Rose; but Silk was the augur. There can be no doubt of that."

He turned to Pig. "No one—very much including me—ever asked what became of the other people who were living here, but we should have. Silk killed Blood, and Echidna killed Musk; Hyacinth became Silk's wife, and Silk cared for Mucor until she came to Blue with her grandmother. Doctor Crane—I almost forgot him, and I shouldn't—was killed in error by the Guard. I have no doubt that some others, many of Blood's bodyguards particularly, were killed in the battle that freed Silk and the other prisoners the Ayuntamiento was holding here. Still, there must have been two or three dozen cooks and maids and footmen and prostitutes."

Pig's eyeless face addressed the fire. "They tell yer how onie blind mon can see a woman, bucky?"

"No, Pig. Not really; but they tell me something equally important that I may have been in danger of forgetting—that real stories, real events, never really end. When Nettle and I wrote our few pages about Blood, we thought that Blood's story and this big house's were over and done with. Blood was dead and the house had been looted, and there was nothing left to do but write it down as we had heard it from Silk and Hyacinth and the old man who had built the kite. He had come with us to Blue, by the way, and didn't want us to use his name, although he told us a great deal about Musk and his birds. We never foresaw that Blood and his daughter and his house would live on in legend, but that is clearly what has happened."

" 'Tis a book h'or somethin' yer wrote, bucky?"

"Yes, that my wife and I wrote together. May I have some of your wine, Hound?"

"Certainly. You said you didn't want any."

"I know." He wiped the mouth of the bottle, and put it to his own.

"H'on me h'account, bucky?"

"Yes. You can't drink since you've lost your sight. That, at least, is what you've told me."

"Aye. A mon what drinks has got ter see, h'or falls."

"I understand. We were together, you and I, Pig—closer than either of us is to Hound, though he and Tansy have treated us so well. If you couldn't drink wine, I wouldn't. We're going to be separated for a while now, and to tell you the truth, I think a few swallows of Hound's good wine may be needed to keep off the ghosts. Here you are, Hound, and thank you."

Hound accepted the bottle. "Do you mean the ugly daughter?"

"Was nae h'ugly ter me," Pig said rather too loudly.

"Silk talk!"

"No, I'll be looking for Mucor—for the daughter in your story." He stood, aided by his staff. "I'm going to leave my lantern here with you. As you say, the candle is valuable and may be irreplaceable. I shouldn't need it to see her any more than Pig needed eyes. It had never occurred to me to ask how Silk saw Mucor when she wasn't physically present."

Pig rose, too. "Comin' wi' yer, bucky."

"I—this is something I would prefer to do alone."

"Be blind h'as me, bucky. H'oreb can tell yer, but better yer had somebody what's h'used ter h'it. Bucky . . ."

"Yes, Pig?"

"Bonnie she was, bucky. Beautiful ter me, ter auld Pig. Yer a smart mon, bucky."

He shook his head, although he knew that Pig could not see the gesture. "No, Pig."

"Yer h'are. Dinna stand nae higher 'n me belt, an' bony. Bonnie ter me, though. Ken why, bucky?"

"Yes, I believe so. Because you could see her, and she was the only thing you've seen in however long it's been. In years."

"Smack h'on, bucky. Yer ken her, dinna yer?"

"Yes, Pig. I—this will mean nothing to you, I realize—but I helped feed and care for her while she and I were living in the Caldé's

Palace in Viron." He turned to Hound. "Does it surprise you that I lived in the Caldé's Palace for a few days?"

Hound shook his head.

"I did, and Nettle and I came to know Mucor there, the woman you've been calling the ugly daughter. Much later, she gave me a tame hus. I'd like to show her that I'm here trying to repay her by finding eyes for her grandmother, and ask where Silk is."

Hound said, "You credit this ghost, both of you."

"Yes. Except that she isn't dead—or I don't believe she is. Certainly she did not starve to death in this house."

"H'if yer h'object ter me comin', bucky—"

"I do. I—yes, I do."

"What'll yer do h'about h'it? Think yer can gae sae hush naebody can hear yer?"

"Pig come," Oreb declared.

"Be talkin' ter her, bucky. An' me? Be standin' behind yer, lookin' h'over yer head. Yer hear, bucky? Said lookin'."

"Yes, Pig. I understand. If I agree to your coming, will you assist me? There's a climb, and it may be difficult. Will you let me stand on your shoulders?"

"Will he? He will!"

"Then come with me."

Together they went out into the blind dark. One of the donkeys brayed, happy to hear human footsteps; and both spoke to it, equally happy, perhaps, to hear another voice, even if it was no more than that of a friendly animal. When they halted and turned to face the villa again, the faint radiance of the fire, glowing weakly through the open doorway, seemed as remote as the burning city in the skylands.

"Where we gang, bucky?"

"To the room Hound mentioned." He found that he was almost whispering, and cleared his throat. "The room to which Mucor was confined by Blood. We're facing the villa now, and it should be to the right, though I can't be certain of that. Oreb, you can see the building before us, can't you?"

"See house!"

"Good. There was a conservatory at one end, a rather low addition with battlements like the rest, and large windows. Can you see that?"

"Bird find." Oreb took wing. "Come bird!"

"Ter yer right, bucky."

"I know." He had already begun to walk. "This was a soft lawn once, Pig."

"Aye."

"A soft, green lawn, before what was in effect a palace, an establishment more palatial than the Caldé's Palace in the city, or even the Prolocutor's Palace. It's hard to believe that all the changes that have taken place here have been—ultimately—for the best. Yet they have."

Pig's hand closed upon his shoulder. "Swing yer stick wider, bucky. Yer h'about ter hit ther wall."

"Thank you. I'm afraid I had practically forgotten to swing it at all."

"Aye. Yer see like yer bird, bucky?"

Hearing him, Oreb called, "Come bird!"

"No. I can see no better in this darkness than you can yourself, Pig."

"Then swing yer stick an' tap ther ground 'fore yer get a fall ter teach yer."

"I will. Have you found the conservatory yet, Oreb?"

"Bird find! Come bird!"

"He's nearer now, isn't he, Pig? Pig, can you judge whether the building on our left is as high now as it was? The original structure is three stories and an attic, as I remember."

There was a lengthy pause before Pig replied, " 'Tain't nae mair, h'or dinna seem like h'it."

"Then we're here." The tip of his staff found the wall. "I'm no acrobat, Pig, and even if I were I'd imagine I might have trouble balancing on your shoulders in the dark. Can you stoop here, near this wall, so I can get on? And remain near enough for me to prop myself on it as you stand up? You'll find me heavy, I'm afraid."

"Yer, bucky?" Pig squeezed his shoulder. "Had me fetch oot a donsy mon, ance. Cap'n Lann, 'twas." Pig squatted, bringing his voice to the level of his listener's ear. "A heavy mon they said, yer ther h'only ane ter carry him. Climb h'on, bucky."

"I'm trying."

" 'Twasn't easy ter find him, but he did nae weigh nae mair'n a pup. Me arms wanted ter tass him like a stick. Sae when h'all was safe 'twas back h'again an' here's yer horse. Had h'it behind me neck like a yowe. He was that fashed. Standin' noo, bucky. Got yer han' h'on ther wall?"

"Yes," he said, "I'm ready any time."

It was not as easy as he had hoped, but he was just able to squeeze through one of the ornamental crenels.

"Silk come!" Oreb announced proudly.

"Well . . ." He got his feet, puffing with exertion. "At least it's true Silk was up here once."

He leaned across the battlement, trying in vain to see his friend in the darkness. "Pig, do you think you might hand my staff up? I laid it by the wall, and I'll need it to feel my way along."

"Aye." A pause. "Here 'tis. Put h'out yer han'."

"No close. Come bird."

Oreb's owner felt a sudden thrill of fear. "Don't hit him with it by accident, as I did once."

"Got yer han' feelin' fer h'it, bucky?"

"Silk feel!"

"Yes. Yes, I—stop! It touched my fingers just then. There, I've got it."

"Guid. What h'about me, bucky? How's Pig ter get h'up?"

He straightened up, lifting the knobbed staff over the battlement and tapping the uneven surface on which he stood. "You're not. We have no way of doing that, and I'm not at all certain this roof would support your weight. I know Mucor, as I said; and she's been willing to do favors for me in the past. If I find her, I'll bring her to you." He weighed the morality of this statement for a moment and added, "Or send her."

Before Pig could object, he turned away. Once the questing tip of his staff found an aching void where the glass roof of the conservatory had been; after that, he stepped cautiously and stayed so near the battlement that from time to time his left leg brushed its merlons.

"Wall come," Oreb warned.

The tip of his staff discovered it. His hands, groping by instinct, found a window. He pushed aside what remained of a broken shutter. "Right here," he told Oreb. "Here it is, just as I imagined it. Is there anyone in there?"

"No man. No girl."

He put his staff through the window, turned it sidewise, and used it to pull himself up while the toes of his well-worn shoes scrabbled the wall. "This is the place, I feel sure. This was Mucor's room, the first room Silk entered when he broke into this house."

His staff discovered only the floor, and empty space. He asked, "Is there furniture in here, Oreb? A table? Anything of that kind?" Putting a hand on the wall, he took a cautious step, then another. "In Silk's day, the door was barred from outside," he told the darkness, "but it seems unlikely that's still the case." There was no reply. After half a minute more of cautious exploration he called, "Oreb? Oreb?" but no bird answered.

"Have you been bad?"

The voice seemed achingly remote. Aloud he said, "As if the speaker were in fact on Blue. As you are, I believe."

Silence and darkness, and the weight of years.

"I'd like to talk to you, Mucor. I've something to tell you and something to ask you, and a favor to ask as well. Won't you talk to me?"

The distant voice did not return. His fingers found the door and pulled it open.

"Have you been bad?"

He thought of Green and the war fought and lost there, of delectable nights with a one-armed lover whose lips had tasted of the salt-sweet sea. "Yes, I have. Many times."

As though she had always been there, Mucor stood before him. "You came looking for me." It was not a question.

"Yes, to tell you that I'm here, and that I'm looking for eyes for your grandmother. I promised her I would."

"You've been gone a long time."

He nodded humbly. "I know. I've done my best to find Silk, but I haven't found him. I'm still looking."

"You will find him." Her tone admitted of no doubt.

"I will?" His heart leaped. "That's wonderful! Are you sure, Mucor? Do you really know the future, as gods do?"

She stood silent before him, no larger than a child, her face a skull, her lank black hair falling to her waist.

"You look . . ." He groped for words. "Like—the way you did the first time I saw you."

"Yes."

"As if you have starved almost to death. I—I thought that sailors brought your food there on your island, that you and your grandmother caught fish."

"You've been gone a long time," she repeated. This time she added, "I haven't."

"I see—or at least believe I see. Certainly I see you, which reminds me of the favor I must ask in a moment; before I do, where will I find Silk?"

"In whatever place you go."

"In Viron? Thank you, I'm sure you must be correct. Will you, Mucor, as a great favor to me, go outside and talk—if only just for a moment—to my friend Pig?"

In an instant she was gone, and he was left in darkness. Retracing his steps, he found her window again and looked out. He could see nothing, only darkness beyond that of any natural night. He heard Pig's voice, and although he could not make out what Pig had said, that voice overflowed with joy. There was a hiatus, a half minute of silence. Pig's deep tones came again, trembling and so freighted with exaltation that he knew Pig was near to weeping.

Hound stroked the donkey's smooth, soft nose, saying, "There, there. Nothing to worry about." The donkey (it was Tortoise, not the one Hound rode) seemed in less than full agreement, although determined to be polite.

"If there were wolves about, I'd know it, wouldn't I?" Hound stepped back and twirled his burning stick, whose faint flame had nearly died away. It made a pretty pattern of sparks, and fanned the flame enough to show the fearful donkeys huddled together with their forelegs hobbled.

"Bird back!" Oreb settled on one of Scylla's outstretched arms. "Bird back. Silk back. Come fire."

"I'm glad to hear it," Hound said, "I've been worrying about him. He and Pig have been gone a long time." Hound went through the portico and re-entered what had been Blood's reception hall. "There you are! Is everything all right, Horn?"

"No." He turned away from the fire. "May I have some more of your wine?"

"Go right ahead. Empty the bottle. There's not much left."

"Thank you."

"You look tired." Hound sat down next to him. "Maybe it's just the firelight. I hope so. But you don't look well."

"Good Silk," Oreb muttered, perching on his shoulder.

"I—" He drank, and put down the bottle. "That doesn't matter. I owe you an apology, and offer it freely. Before I left, I drank your good wine for a bad reason, which is a species of crime. There's something sacred about wine. Have you noticed?"

Hound shrugged. "It belongs to some minor god or other. But then everything does that doesn't belong to one of the Nine."

"To Thyone's son. Isn't it odd that I should remember it? Supposedly, there is no less significant fact in religion, yet that one has stuck with me. I recalled it when Nettle and I wrote our book about Patera Silk, and I recall it now. May I have some more?"

"Certainly." Hound handed him the bottle again.

"Wine is sacred to Thelxiepeia because it intoxicates and intoxication is hers, like magic, paradoxes, illusions and other things of that sort. But wine in and of itself is sacred to Thyone's son. Thyone is a very minor goddess."

"I don't mean to change the subject," Hound said, "but do you know what has become of Pig?"

"I do and I don't."

"Poor Pig!" Oreb croaked.

Both men were silent, looking into the fire; then Hound said, "You can't tell me what happened to him?"

"Nor what happened to me, though I suppose I'll talk about it when I've ordered my thoughts a bit more."

"Wise Silk!"

He smiled. "That's the sort of the thing Hammerstone was always saying about Patera Incus. Is Incus Prolocutor now?"

Hound nodded. "I think that's the name."

"That's very well. He may be willing to help me. There's only a swallow left, wouldn't you like it? Here."

"I've had more than my share already. I've been trying to remember the bad purpose you mentioned, and I can't. Wine does that to you, makes you forget. All that I can think of is that you said it might keep away ghosts, but not the ghost of the ugly daughter. You wanted to see her."

He nodded. "That was the bad purpose—keeping off the ghosts.

We always go wrong when we use it for something other than itself, Hound. It's meant to be a beverage, a pleasant, refreshing drink, next to good cold water the best we have. When we use it for something else—to make us forget, which is what I meant when I said it might keep off the ghosts—or to warm us when we are chilled, we pervert it. Have you noticed, by the way, that it's no longer as hot as it was?"

Hound smiled. "You're right. Praise Pas!"

"No, not at all. Pas is the sun god, and it is blowing out the Long Sun that has cooled the whorl for us. I mentioned the son of Thyone. He's called that because no one knows his name—or much of anything else about him save that he's dark, and that wine is sacred to him. Am I boring you? We don't have to talk about this."

Hound raised the bottle, then lowered it again without drinking. "Not at all. What do you say we save this for Pig?"

"I doubt that he'll drink it, but it's a kind thought."

"You were saying nobody knows the wine god's name. Isn't that unusual? I thought we knew the names of all the gods, or that the augurs did even if I don't."

"It is unusual, yes—but not unique. I had an instructor once who made a joke about it. We studied the gods a good deal, and spent half a day, perhaps, on Thyone and her dark son. My instructor said that Thyone's son had drunk so much that we had forgotten his name."

Hound chuckled.

"He also said that Thyone's son was the only god whose name we don't know. It was years before I realized that he'd been wrong. We speak of the Outsider, but it's obvious that 'the Outsider' can't be his name—that it's an epithet, a nickname."

"Good god," Oreb remarked.

Hound said, "He's your favorite, isn't he? The god you love the most."

"The only god I love at all, if I've ever succeeded in loving him. In a larger sense, he's the only god worth loving. I've been outside, you see, Hound. I've been to Blue and to Green, other whorls quite different from this one."

Hound nodded.

"One goes outside full of high ideals, but one soon discovers that one has left the gods behind, even Pas. I told you how badly things were going in New Viron."

"Yes, you did."

"That's one of the chief reasons, I feel sure. So many of us were good only because we dreaded the gods. The Outsider—this is very like him, very typical of him—has shown us to ourselves. He tells us to look at ourselves and see how much real honesty there is, how much genuine kindness. You're hoping to become the father of a child."

Hound nodded. "A son, I hope. Not that we wouldn't love a daughter."

"There are children who sweep hoping to be rewarded, and there are children who sweep because the floors need sweeping and Mother's tired. And there is an abyss between them far deeper than the abyss that separates us from Blue."

"The gods keep telling us to go. That's what everybody says. I—"

"That is their function."

"I don't go to manteion myself, Horn. It seems to me that the gods ought to go with us, that they owe it to us."

"It must seem to them, I suppose, that we should take them with us gladly, that we owe them that and more."

Hound did not speak, staring into the fire.

"For three hundred years they let us live in this whorl, which they control. Their influence was malign occasionally, but benign for the most part. Scylla is a poor example, but because you know her better than the rest I'll use her anyway. She helped found Viron and graciously condescended to be its patron. She wrote our Charter, which served us so well for three centuries. Don't you think that the people who leave Viron owe it to her to take her along—if they can?"

"Why did you call her a bad example?"

"Because she's probably dead. She was Echidna's eldest child, and seems the most likely to have assisted in her father's murder. She may come back, of course, as he did. We don't call them the immortal gods for nothing."

Hound rose, broke a stick across his knee, and tossed both halves into the fire.

"You're ready to sleep, I suppose, and I'm keeping you up. I'm sorry."

"Not at all. My donkeys are afraid of something tonight, and I'm waiting for them to calm down. If I go to sleep now, they'll be all over the forest when I wake up."

"Have you any idea what may have frightened them?"

"It's wolves, usually. That's one reason I wanted to stop here. I'm sure a whole menagerie of small animals have moved in since the owners moved out, but the wolves haven't taken to denning in here yet, and I don't think they like coming inside the wall. Maybe the ghosts keep them away."

"Perhaps they do. They will keep me away after tonight, I'm sure. Is it really night, by the way? Where would the shade be if the sun were rekindled now?"

"I have no way of telling."

"Nor do I. Oreb, have you seen any wolves since we've been here?"

"No see."

"Something's frightening Hound's donkeys. Do you know what it is? Might you guess?"

"No, no."

"Then as a favor to me, would you go out and have a look around? If you see a wolf—or anything else that the donkeys might find frightening—stay well clear of it and come back and tell us."

Oreb took wing.

"You spoke of ghosts, Hound. I ought to tell you that I saw the woman who is called the ugly daughter in your story. She told me that Silk was in Viron, and that I'd find him there. Please don't ask me to exhibit her to you—"

"I wasn't about to," Hound declared emphatically.

"I cannot control her movements—her appearances and disappearances—though I confess there have been times when I very much wished I could. She's not a bad person, but I find her a frightening one, and I've never been more afraid of her than I was tonight, not even when I sat with her in the hut she and poor Maytera Marble built of driftwood. She was really present on that occasion, really there just as you and I are here. This time she was not, and I spoke with a sort of memory she has of herself."

Hound broke another stick. "You said she isn't a real ghost. That she isn't really dead as far as you know."

"I suppose I did."

"But Scylla is. Are you saying that if Scylla were to appear in the Sacred Window of the little manteion where Tansy and I were married she would be a ghost, the ghost of a goddess? People used to talk about Great Pas's ghost when I was a sprat, and some of them still swear by it."

"I think it likely, but I can't say with any certainty. I know less about the gods than you may be inclined to believe, and in all humility I don't think anyone knows a great deal. We suppose that they are like us, and we read our own passions and failings into them—which was the point of my instructor's joke, of course. If we find our neighbor irritating, we're confident that the gods are irritated by him to an equal degree, and so on. I've even heard people say that a certain god was sleeping and required a sacrifice to wake him up."

Hound started to speak, stopped, and at last blurted, "Horn, do you think it's possible your friend Pig's gone to sleep in another room?"

"It's possible, I suppose, though I doubt very much that it's actually occurred. If it has, it's probably the best thing we could hope for. I pray that it has."

"You're worried about him, too."

"Yes, I am. You're not sleeping now because you're worried about your donkeys. I'm not sleeping because I'm concerned for Pig—and for myself and my errand, to acknowledge the truth."

"This woman who's not a ghost, couldn't she have harmed him? You say she's not a ghost. All right, I accept that. She sounds a lot like a goddess to me, Horn, and a goddess . . . You're shaking your head."

He sat up straighter and turned away from the fire to face Hound. "She isn't. May I tell you what she is? You may know some or all of it already, in which case I apologize."

Hound said, "I wish you would. And I wish you'd sent Oreb for Pig, instead of worrying about wolves. You don't agree."

"No, I don't. It might conceivably have helped. I don't know; but my best guess was and is that it would have been very dangerous for Oreb—far more so than scouting for wolves, which are unlikely to pose a threat to a bird. He would have been in a confined space with a very large man who has a sword, acute hearing, and an amazing ability to locate even silent objects by sound. If Pig had been enraged by the intrusion, which I judge by no means unlikely, Oreb might have been killed."

"You're saying Pig needs privacy right now."

"I am."

Hound sat down again, crossing plump legs. "Because of something the ghost said to him?"

"Possibly. I don't know."

"Tell me about her."

"As you wish. You mentioned that the gods have been telling everyone to leave. The devices used to cross the abyss to Blue or Green are called landers. Are you familiar with them?"

"I've heard of them," Hound said. "I've never seen one."

"Are you aware that they were provisioned by Pas before the *Whorl* set out from the Short Sun Whorl? And that most of them have been looted?"

"All of them is what everybody says."

"I won't argue the point. There were human embryos among their supplies, ancient embryos preserved by cold far beyond that of the coldest winter nights. Sometimes the looters simply left those embryos. Sometimes they wantonly destroyed them, and sometimes they took and sold them, packing them in ice in an attempt to preserve them until they could be implanted."

"You said human embryos, Horn. I've heard of it being done with animals."

"Yes." His face was solemn in the flickering firelight, his blue eyes lost beneath their graying brows. "There were human embryos as well. There were also seeds, kept frozen like the embryos, so that they would sprout even after hundreds of years; but it is with the human embryos that you and I have to do, because Mucor was such an embryo. So was Patera Silk."

"Caldé Silk? You can't be serious!"

He shook his head. "I set out to explain Mucor, but there would be no Mucor—or so I believe—without Patera Silk. Nor would either of them exist without Pas, who was called Typhon on the Short Sun Whorl."

Hound said, "I've heard that the gods have different names in different places, sometimes."

"That seems to have been the case with Pas, Echidna, and the rest. They had other names on the Short Sun Whorl, and those persons—Typhon, his family, and his friends—continued to exist there after they had entered the *Whorl*."

"Go on, please."

"If you wish. I should say that I heard that Pas had been called Typhon from a man named Auk, someone I knew long ago, who said he had been told by Scylla. He was a bad man, a bully and a thug, yet he was deeply religious in his way—I very much doubt that he would have made such a thing up. It was not his sort of lie, if you know what I mean.

"When Pas—let us call him Pas, since we're accustomed to that name—decided to send mortals to the whorls beyond the Short Sun Whorl, he used no less than three separate means. Some he sent as sleepers, unconscious in tubes of thin glass until they were awakened by the breaking of the glass. Some—your ancestors, Hound, and mine—he simply set down here inside the *Whorl.* And some he sent as frozen embryos, the products of carefully controlled matings in his workshops."

"Why so many ways?" Hound asked.

"I can only guess, and you could guess every bit as well. Do so now."

Hound looked thoughtful. "Well, he wanted us to colonize the new whorls, didn't he? So he put people in here to do it."

"Waking or sleeping?"

"Both, I guess. He must have been afraid we'd fight in here, and kill everyone off. Or get some disease that would wipe us out. No, that can't be right, because then there would have been no one to wake up the sleepers."

"Mainframe could have done that, I believe."

"I've never met a sleeper, Horn. I've never even seen one. I take it that you have. Are they very different from us?"

"In appearance? No, not at all. They were made to forget certain things and given falsified memories in their place, but one only occasionally catches a hint of it."

"You're saying that everybody could have been asleep? All of us? No houses and no people, just trees and animals?"

"No, I'm saying Pas must have considered that and rejected it as unworkable, or at least undesirable."

Hound nodded. "He'd have had nobody to worship him."

"That's true, though I'm not sure it was a consideration. If it didn't seem so impious, I'd say now that the Chapter and the manteions seem almost to have been a joke, that Pas made himself our chief god largely because it amused him. Do you know the story about the farmer who complained all his life about getting too much rain or too little, about the soil and the winds and so on? It's no more impious than my instructor's joke about Thyone's son; and like that one, it has wisdom."

Hound shook his head.

"The farmer died and went to Mainframe, and was soon called to the magnificent chamber in which Pas holds court. Pas said to him, 'I understand you feel that I botched certain aspects of the job when I built the *Whorl*'; and the farmer admitted it was so, saying, 'Well, sir, pretty often I thought I could have made it better.' To which Pas replied, 'Yes, that's what I wanted you to do.' "

"That hits very close to home." Hound smiled.

"It does. It also explains many things, once you understand that Pas himself was brought into being by the Outsider. Pas wished to mold and guide us; and for him to do it, we had to be awake. As our chief god, he was ideally situated, though the false memories given the sleepers may have been intended to serve the same purpose. Like the farmer we complain of storms, but Pas must have foreseen that there would be storms—and things far worse—on the new whorls. How could we cope with them if we never saw snow, or a wind storm?"

"I still don't understand about the embryos. You said that you . . . that Caldé Silk was one of the people grown from them, and this Mucor was, too."

"To colonize the new whorls—speaking of storms and such, there's a wind rising outside. Have you noticed?"

"I've been listening to it. I won't bring my donkeys in unless there's an actual storm. They can't graze in here."

"To colonize Blue and Green, Pas had to make certain that some human beings reached them alive. He pretty well assured that by dividing us into the two groups—ourselves, and the sleepers. If the sleep process, whatever it was, couldn't keep them alive for three hundred years, we would supply colonists. If we were wiped out by some disease as you suggested, the sleepers could be roused by Mainframe, or by the chems that Pas put in this whorl as well.

"But though our surviving until we reached Blue and Green was necessary, it was not sufficient. We had to survive on those whorls afterward. Blue is a hospitable one; we are our own worst enemies there. Green is much harsher. It's where the inhumi breed, and there are diseases and dangerous animals. Pas felt we ordinary people might not be able to deal with those, so he took steps to see that we'd have some extraordinary ones as well, people like Mucor, who can send out her spirit without dying; and people like Silk, who was the sort of leader we weave legends about but seldom get—or deserve, I might add."

Hound stared at the fire before he spoke. "You said most of those embryos had been stolen or destroyed."

"I'm afraid so."

"Does that mean we'll fail?"

"Perhaps. On Green at least."

"I'd like to go. Am I crazy? I've never felt this way way before."

"The crossing is very dangerous—I don't deny that. But you and Tansy might make a better life for yourselves and your children on Blue than you will ever have here, and you would be doing the will of Pas."

"Not Blue," Hound said. "I want to go to Green. I want to go where I'm needed, Horn."

Before he replied, he stretched out on the floor, his hands behind his head. "You're a brave man."

"I'm not! I know I'm not. But—but . . ."

"You are."

"But I'm steady, and I've got a good head on my shoulders, and I don't drink or get so angry I ruin everything. I'm no troublemaker. I can work with my hands, and I drive a hard bargain. They could use me. I know they could!"

"I'm sure you're right."

"I'm going to have think about it. I'm going to have to think for a long time, probably until after the baby's born."

Silence descended on the ruined villa, a silence broken only by the moaning of the wind outside, the crackling of the fire, and the soft breathing of the man stretched on the floor.

When some time had passed, Hound rose, took a burning stick from the fire, and went outside again. When he returned, he got a blanket and spread it over the man on the floor, who opened his eyes and murmured, "Thank you."

"You're awake," Hound said.

"I fear I am."

"You said some things tonight that sounded pretty, I don't know, not religious. You admitted it yourself."

"The joke about the dead farmer."

"Yes, and other things too. I've got a question, Horn. It's going to sound bad, or anyhow I'm afraid it will. And it may be pretty silly."

"You're afraid I may not take you seriously."

Hound sat down. "I guess so."

"If you ask it seriously, I'll answer seriously, or try to. What is it?"

"You said that there are two gods we don't know. I mean, we know that there are gods like that, but we don't know their names. You said too that the Outsider had made Pas?"

"Yes. Both gods and Men—the human race—were created by the Outsider. It's explicitly stated in the Chrasmologic Writings, and I'm confident that it's true."

"The other nameless god, is that Thyone's son? Does anybody know who his father was?"

"Pas, supposedly. It's said that Thyone is one of his inferior concubines, less favored than Kypris."

"Then what I was going to ask about is pretty silly. I was going to ask if it isn't possible they're really the same."

The man lying on the floor said nothing.

"Since we don't know the names. That the Outsider is Thyone's son, the wine god, too."

"That isn't silly at all; it's extremely perceptive. You've amazed me twice within a few minutes. Yes, it's possible and it may well be true. I don't know."

"But if the Outsider made Pas, and Pas is the wine god's father . . . ?"

"Have you ever seen Thyone, Hound? In a Sacred Window or anyplace else?"

Hound shook his head.

"Neither have I. What about Pas? I have not."

"No."

"Then what do either of us know about the parentage of the wine god, and what such parentage may entail? What limitations the Outsider may be subject to or free from? I told you about Auk—how he was told by Scylla that Pas's name had been Typhon on the Short Sun Whorl."

Hound nodded.

"Scylla was in possession of a woman named Chenille when that conversation took place; Chenille told my wife a good deal about it not long afterward. Do you think that because Scylla was possessing Chenille she was absent from Mainframe? Or that Scylla can't have been in another woman—or a man, for that matter—at the same time?"

"I guess she could have if she wanted to."

"Certainly she could." The man who had been lying on the floor sat up. "I was going to tell you what happened to me, and to Pig, after I left you. Then I decided that it might better be left unsaid—that I'd let Pig tell both of us, if he would, and let it pass in silence if he wouldn't. Now I've changed my mind again. You need to hear this. You and your wife welcomed us, and I would be neglecting a duty if I withheld it."

"Does this have something to do with the gods?" Hound asked.

"I think it may. We went outside, as you know, and I spoke with Mucor, and asked her to talk to Pig when I was finished."

Hounded nodded.

"After that, I couldn't decide whether to come back here or visit the room that had been Hyacinth's."

"Silk's wife's?"

"Yes. She had lived in this house for a time. She was a very beautiful woman, the most beautiful I'd ever seen. I've seen one other since who might rival her, despite being maimed."

"Go on, Horn."

"Recalling her, and how beautiful I'd thought her then, I felt a sort of itch to stand in the suite she'd occupied, and touch the walls. She'd split her stone windowsill with an azoth. I wanted to feel that windowsill, if it was still there, and stand for a time at the very window Silk had jumped from. I told myself over and over how foolish it was, and that I should return here. Have I told you Oreb had left?"

Hound shook his head.

"He had. Mucor frightens him, as I should have remembered. It was utterly dark, of course, and I had to feel my way with my stick. It must have taken me five minutes to cross Mucor's room and find the door. I decided I'd try to return here to you, and if I blundered on a set of rooms that fit Silk's description of Hyacinth's, so much the better."

"That sounds sensible."

"Thank you. It may have been sensible, but it did me little good. Soon after I had left Mucor's room, I was completely lost, and bitterly regretted having left my lantern behind with you. I stumbled around helplessly for a long while. I was looking for stairs and tried to stay out of the rooms—after I had explored a few—because I felt certain one would enter the staircases from a corridor."

"I understand."

"I blundered into a suite just the same, and for a minute or two I didn't know I had done it. When I realized what must have happened, I found a door and went through, thinking I'd be in the corridor again; but it was another room, bigger than the first and, as well as I could judge, almost triangular. I don't know whether the geometers have a name for that shape, a wide triangle with two corners cut off. I felt certain then—absolutely certain, Hound—that I was standing in what had been Hyacinth's dressing chamber. I had never been there before in my life, though I was in this house long ago as I told you; but I have thought of it a thousand times, and I knew with absolute certainty that I was standing there. You're free to doubt me if you wish—I don't blame you."

"Go on," Hound said again. "What did you do?"

"Well, I thought that since I was there I might as well find the bedroom, which is where the window Silk had jumped through had been, and touch that windowsill and stand at the window and so on. I was tapping around with my stick, looking for the door, when I heard the sound of a tremendous blow, a blow and the sound of wood splintering. I can't begin to convey to you how frightening I found that, alone in the dark."

Hound raised his eyebrows. "Do you know, I think I may have heard it too. There was a loud bang way off in the house someplace, a long time before you came back. I thought Pig might have fallen down."

"Perhaps that was what it was, though I doubt it. My guess—and it is merely a guess, nothing more—is that Pig struck a wall, either with the sword that he uses in this darkness as I use my stick, or with his fist."

"That he struck the wall?"

"Yes. I doubt that there's furniture left in this house, or that there has been for many years. Blood would have had fine furniture, from what I've heard of him, and I feel sure it must have been carted away long ago. We pile up treasures, Hound, and believe in our folly that we are piling them up for ourselves, when in fact we are accumulating them for those who will come after us. May I confide something personal and rather disreputable concerning my own family?"

"Absolutely, if you want to."

"My oldest son was often difficult. He felt he was far wiser than Nettle and I—that we should do as he said, and be grateful that he condescended to rule and advise us."

Hound smiled. "I gave my own father some headaches, too."

"Once when he was angry at Nettle, he punched a cabinet I made so violently that he broke the door, as well as hurting his hand pretty badly. Have I clarified the sound you heard?"

Hound scratched his head. "What made Pig so angry?"

"The tapping of my stick, I assume."

"He was in Caldé Silk's wife's bedroom?"

"And thought that he was about to be interrupted. It's all guesswork; but yes, I believe that's what must have happened."

"I understand now why you didn't want to send Oreb to look in on him." Hound scraped together the twigs and bark that were all that remained of their firewood and added them to the fire. "What I don't understand is what Pig was doing there."

"In an empty room in this dark, empty house? It seems to me that there's very little he could have been doing, other than what I planned to do myself—listen to the silence, touch the walls and the windowsill, and try to guess where the bed and the rest of Hyacinth's furnishings had been."

"I thought Pig hadn't ever been in this part of the whorl before. He said so, I think. So did you, Horn."

"I probably did." He stood, dusting his knees and the seat of his trousers. "We need more wood. With your permission, I'm going to try to find some."

Hound said, "You don't want to talk about this any more."

"You can put it like that if you choose to. I've nothing sensible left to say about it, and I don't like sounding foolish, though I often do. Would you like examples of my foolishness?"

Hound reached for his lantern. "Yes, I would."

"It wasn't Pig I heard, but someone else. That suite wasn't Hyacinth's but someone else's. Pig's connection wasn't with her, but with someone who had occupied her suite before she did."

"Do you believe any of that?"

"Not a word of it. When—if—Pig returns, I may ask, very diplomatically, what Mucor said to him, and why he went to the suite that Hyacinth once occupied. I may—but I may not. I advise you not to question him at all, though I can't forbid it. Are you coming with me to look for wood?"

"Yes." Hound had opened his lantern and was kneeling by the fire to light its candle. "I'll take this, too. If we go outside the wall we ought to be able to find any amount of dead wood, blown out of the trees by that wind."

It was blowing hard when they left the flickering firelight and the smell of woodsmoke, and stepped through the opening that had been Blood's door, a gale with a hint of autumn in it that swung Hound's lantern like a feather on a string.

Hound went at once to his huddled donkeys. "I'm going to bring them inside. It'll pour in a minute or two."

His companion was about to tell him to go ahead, and to remark that the coming storm was probably what the donkeys had been afraid of earlier, when Oreb swooped to a hard landing upon his shoulder, croaking, "Man come! Big man!"

"Pig? Where is he?"

"Big big! Watch out!"

"Believe me, I'll be as careful as possible. Where is he?"

"No, no!" Oreb fluttered to keep his balance in the wind.

"You don't have to come with me, but where did you see him?"

"In back. Bird show." Oreb darted forward, flapping hard into the wind's eye, no higher than his owner's knees. The faint light of the lantern faded and was gone as Hound led his donkeys into the ruined villa.

"Come bird!" Oreb called through the darkness.

"Yes! I am!"

"Good Silk!" The hoarse croak was almost lost in the roaring of the wind. *"Watch out!"*

His probing staff found nothing until a huge hand closed around him, its grip enveloping him from shoulder to waist.

"Would you have light?" The godling's voice mingled with distant thunder; it was as if the coming storm had spoken.

The man the godling had addressed gasped.

"I will burn this house for you, holy one, if you wish."

He found it impossible to think, almost impossible to speak. "If you tighten your grip, I'll be killed."

"I will not tighten my grip. Will you sit upon my palm, holy one? You must not fall."

"Yes," he said. "I—yes."

Something pressed his feet; his knees, which he could not have kept straight, bent. The hand that had grasped him relaxed, sliding upward and away. He groped the hard, uneven surface on which he had been seated, discovering that it fell away half a cubit to his left and right, found the great fingers (each as wide as his head) curled behind him. "Oreb?"

It had emerged as a whisper; he had intended a shout. He filled his lungs and tried again. *"Oreb!"*

"Bird here." *Here* was clearly a considerable distance.

"Oreb, come to me, please."

He was conscious of the wind, cool and violent, threatening with gusts to blow him from his precarious seat.

"Hurt bird?"

"No!" He cleared his throat. "You know I won't hurt you."

"Big man. Hurt bird?"

The deep voice rumbled out of the darkness again. "If you fall . . ." Lightning gleamed on the horizon. For a fraction of a second it revealed a face as large as Echidna's had been in the Sacred Window so long ago: tiny eyes, nostrils like the lairs of two beasts, and a cavernous mouth. "I cannot catch you."

"Please." He gasped for breath, fighting the feeling that the wind blew every word to nothing. "You said I could have light. If I wanted it. I have a lantern. May I light it?"

"As you say, holy one." It was a hoarse whisper, like a distant avalanche.

He had shoved his own lantern into a pocket when he had seen Hound lighting his; now he fumbled with it and with the striker, nearly dropping both.

"It is very small, holy one." There was a faint note of amusement in the terrifying rumble this time.

"That's all right," he said, with a growing sense of relief. "So am I." White sparks cascaded onto the trembling wick. It was as if there were shooting stars in his hands, like the stars at the bottom of the grave to which Silk and Hyacinth had driven Orpine's body in a dream he recalled with uncanny clarity.

Here we dig holes in the ground for our dead, he thought, to bring them nearer the Outsider; and on Blue we do the same because we did it here, though it takes them away from him.

The yellow flame of the candle rose; he shut his lantern, mesmerized by the end of the godling's thumb, the smoothly rounded face of a faceless man wearing a peaked hat that was in fact a claw.

"You see me." The gigantic speaker sounded faintly pleased.

"Yes. You could see me before."

Slowly the great face descended. Slowly it rose, as a large boat might have in a long swell.

"Like Oreb. Oreb can see even when it seems to me that there's no light at all."

There was no reply, and he wondered whether the godling had heard him. "Oreb's eyes are larger than mine," he continued gamely, "though Oreb is so much smaller. Your eyes seem very small to me, but that's only because they are small in proportion to your face. Each must be the size of Oreb's head."

Rain fell like a lash.

"You speak too fast, holy one," the godling rumbled.

And it must seem to you that we move very fast as well, he reflected. That we dart about like squirrels or rabbits.

"Are you in danger, holy one? I will protect you."

"No." He held up the light, his sodden tunic clinging to his arm. This was better—far better—than the sewer on Green.

"Are you in need, holy one? I will supply you."

"That is good of you." He struggled to make himself heard.

"Bird here!" Oreb landed heavily on his head, and every limb jerked with terror. "Wet wet!" A fine spray of water joined the rain as Oreb shook himself and fluttered his wings.

"Getting in under the fingers, aren't you?"

"Good bird! Good Silk!"

Suddenly contrite, he spoke slowly to the godling. "You've made a shelter for me, and even let Oreb share it. Am I—are we keeping you out in this?"

Again the rumble seemed slightly amused, although he could not be sure he was not imagining it. "I do not suffer, holy one." There was pause in which the huge face, lit faintly from below, regarded him. "Are you in need?"

"No." It was still difficult for him to speak.

"The rest are to stay," the godling rumbled. Its breath, hot, moist, and fetid, pierced the wind; and lightning flashed as it spoke, starkly revealing colorless skin splashed with inky shadows. "Enough have gone. Tell the rest to stay. That is what I have come to tell you. Silk says it."

7

Drinking Companions

We have made the experiment, and the experiment has failed. That is the truth, so that is how I must look at it. All my planning—I shall be honest: all my scheming—has gone for nothing. I must devise a new approach.

When I was in Blanko, Fava and I found that when my mind was joined with hers we, and anyone else who was in our company, could travel in spirit. We went to Green; and later Jahlee, the Duko, Hide, and I, with some others, went to the great city of the Red Sun Whorl. We were able to, I believe, because the Duko had been there previously. Let me think.

I am going to write down everything—even the smallest details. Perhaps something will suggest itself, either when I am writing or when I read this over tomorrow.

I persuaded Beroep to take me across the street to Cijfer's. It was a serious violation of the law, he said; he and Aanvagen might lose their boats and even their house if the law found out. We waited until long after shadelow, when the street was almost empty. I was muffled in a thick twill boat cloak with a hood. It is dark gray, and reminds me of Olivine's giving me my augur's robe; what a strange whorl it is, in which we become someone else by putting on new clothes! The prisoner Horn disappeared as soon as Beroep draped him in this exceedingly voluminous cloak, replaced by the nameless captain of a nameless boat. In all the time I sailed with Babbie and Seawrack, I had no such cloak. Now I have no boat, but am equipped for one. No doubt it will soon appear.

In the same way, rubies and red and purple silk made me Rajan of Gaon. We are but the paper; our clothes are the ink.

Across the street we went, with Oreb flying well in advance so that his company would not betray my identity, and to make certain Cijfer would put out the lamps and open her door the moment we arrived.

She had and did. We hurried inside. "My servants away I have sent, Mysire Horn. This you say, and this I have done."

"Come bird!" Oreb was fluttering up the stairwell already. We ran after him—or at any rate Cijfer and I ran, and Beroep labored behind us, puffing and groaning. Up a flight—then another—and into the locked and bolted little bedroom whose window I had studied with Vadsig, and which has been constantly in my thoughts. It seemed as dark, almost, as Blood's villa; I nearly stumbled over the chair to which Cijfer directed me.

"A candle now you wish, Mysire Horn? The shutters closed are. No one can see."

It occurred to me that no one could see me well enough to recognize me even if they had been open, and I recalled Silk's saying that Mucor thought her spirit could not leave her room unless the window was open. I resolved to open the shutters of Jahlee's room, and did afterward, although nothing came of it.

Beroep arrived at the same time Cijfer brought the candle. He would have bent over Jahlee if I had permitted it. I ordered him away with a gesture that I hope brooked no argument, and he dropped gasping into the chair. It was only then, after Beroep had sat down, that I understood how it was that Cijfer served as Jahlee's jailer for so long without realizing that she was an inhuma: the sheet had been drawn up nearly to the top of her wig. "Good thing?" Oreb inquired when I lifted it.

I replaced the sheet, telling him to be quiet. "You've covered her face," I remarked to Cijfer. "May I ask why?"

"So silent she is, mysire. So cold. Like dead your poor daughter is. Seeing her so I do not like."

"Not dead," Beroep gasped, "she is?"

"No. She's in a coma—from which I intend to rouse her." I felt confident of my ability to do it, and made the declaration as certain as I could. What if Jahlee, who was been buried alive in Gaon, were buried alive a second time here in Dorp? Who would rescue her then?

"My house the ghosts will leave, mysire, if up she wakes?"

I told Cijfer I was sure of it, and ordered them out; she left obediently and he reluctantly. And what more is there to tell?

Nothing, really.

I sat with her all night, thinking of Green—its ruined city, its swamps and jungles, the rice fields of the villagers, the abandoned tower in the cliff, and the derelict lander in which I died rose before my mind not once or twice but twenty or thirty times; and as far as I am capable of it, I explored their every corner, leaf, and crevice. Two floors below me, where Beroep was talking to Cijfer and drinking the white brandy they relish here, plates fell from a shelf and Cijfer shrieked in dismay. That was a little after midnight, and was far more activity than I myself saw. I opened the shutters and closed them after half an hour during which the room became unbearably cold. I moved the candle from place to place. I poked the fire and fed it fresh wood. I pulled down the sheet and kissed Jahlee's cheek, and took her hand (very clearly the hand of an inhuma) from under the bedclothes and clasped it between my own. It was as cold as ice—no dead woman's could have been colder. In time I warmed it, but Jahlee never stirred.

I prayed again and again, imploring the help of the Outsider and every other god, told my beads, and recalled ten thousand things, from my mother's kindnesses when I was a boy to the way Pig looked and spoke when he rejoined Hound and me at the fire in Blood's villa. I listened to Oreb, and talked to him—mostly to caution him to say nothing about what we were doing. And at last, when I could no longer bear his chatter, I opened the shutters again and sent him out to look for Babbie, something I very much regret now, because he has not returned.

Dawn came and with it Beroep, rather drunk, to tell me that he could risk my absence from his house no longer. So here I sit, having accomplished nothing. But what more could I have done? I wish now that I had thought to cut my arm and smeared Jahlee's lips.

★

★ ★

Here is news, perhaps even good news. I hope so. There was an awful brawl downstairs this morning. I listened at my keyhole and soon identified Cook's voice; it was not difficult to guess who she was bawling at, so I pounded on my door and shouted for Vadsig. She was breathless when she arrived and every bit as red of face as Aanvagen, with a livid bruise on her cheek. "I only require that you talk to me awhile," I told her, "and give Cook's temper time to cool. I felt sure you'd appreciate being rescued from that situation, whatever it was."

"Going out I am, mysire. Asking her I am not." This was said in the tone of one who defies the armed might of cities. "Saying all morning she is. Lying, she is. No more than one hour it is, mysire. Less!"

"I believe you."

"Paying me she is not, mysire. A servant like me she is!"

"No doubt she became accustomed to bullying you when you were younger, Vadsig. She must learn from your speech and your deportment that you are growing up."

She nodded vigorously. "All her life a servant she is. So with me it will not be. This she sees. Our own house we will have. Children I will have, and servants like her to wait on us, it may be."

"Aim high, Vadsig. There is nothing to be gained by not doing so."

"Thank you, mysire. Very kind you are." Smoothing her apron, she turned to go. "Your son well is, mysire. Happy he is not, but well he is and love to you by me he sends."

She had gone out and turned the key before my mouth closed. Hide? And Vadsig? What a wonderful whorl we live in!

I have been walking up and down this little room, three steps and turn, worrying about Oreb. If you ever read this, dear Nettle, you will say that I ought to have been worrying about our son; but what is there to worry about? He and Vadsig will or will not marry. I cannot decide that for them, and neither could you; they must decide it for themselves. If they do not, each will regret it sometimes, and nothing you and I could say or do can change that. If they do, each will regret *that* sometimes, too; and we cannot change that either. So what is there to think about? I wish them both well. So would you, I believe, if you were here with me.

As for Oreb, I am concerned about him but what can I do? When we reached this whorl, he left me for nearly a year. At, this moment he has been gone less than a day. I have prayed that he is safe, and that is all I can do. I hope the Outsider, whose sacrifice Silk once intended Oreb to be, smiles on him.

The reason for my failure with poor Jahlee last night is obvious, surely. Her spirit is absent. I had supposed that it might be hovering about her body, and that I might somehow assist it to re-enter. It is not there, and in all probability is still on Green. I returned from Green, leaving her there and supposing that she could return as I did whenever she chose. Either she has not chosen to return, or she is unable to do so. If it is the first, well and good. I have no claim on her; she may remain as she is if she chooses.

But if she is unable to return (and I confess I believe that most likely) I must bring her back; and I cannot go without the company of another such as Jahlee is and my poor friend Fava was.

Available to me in this house are Vadsig, Aanvagen, Beroep, and perhaps Cijfer. I have tried to persuade myself that one of them might do. I cannot. Vadsig is lean enough, but the idea of an inhuma living by choice as Vadsig does—sleeping in a garret, sweeping and mopping floors, and washing dishes—is perfectly ridiculous. She has worked here, she says, for two years. She would have been detected a hundred times over. If somehow she had not been, she would have been detected at once by Oreb, who has seen her many times.

Beroep and Aanvagen can be dismissed at once; both are far too portly. As for Cijfer, I do not believe it. Oreb saw her and said nothing. She would not have covered Jahlee's face, or fetched a bio to help her. All four can be dismissed.

Leaving no one. What am I to do?

Sleep.

No dreams. Not of Fava and Mora, nor of anyone else; but I ought to have known better—Mora herself must be awake.

Dusk outside my window. Another short winter day has ended. Soon the house will be asleep, and I will go out and search the streets for someone like Fava and Jahlee who may (*may,* I say) be willing to go to Green with me and bring my poor daughter home. What else can I do? I give thanks to the Outsider, particularly, that Beroep failed to notice I was keeping his gray boat cloak.

★

★ ★

So much has happened that I despair of recording all of it. I required Beroep's cloak—I was right about that—but not to search the streets of Dorp for a helpful inhumu. I had no more than written *cloak* and put away my pen case and my dwindling supply of paper than I heard the rattle of sling swivels and the clatter of boots on the stair. In came two men with slug guns, and off to Judge Hamer we went—not to a courtroom, but to his house, where he held court in his sellaria.

"No formal session it is, Mysire Horn." He is fat and red of face, and seemed to me to be forcing his voice deeper than nature intended. "A preliminary hearing it is. This is capital cases we do."

I protested that I had killed no one.

"Nat you made your prisoner. Him you restrained, mysire. By our law a capital offense it is." He smiled, cocked his head, and pointed his forefinger down at his neck.

"Is Nat a particularly privileged individual here in Dorp, Judge Hamer?"

He looked severe. "Mysire Rechtor to me you must say, mysire, each time you speak."

"Excuse it, please, Mysire Rechtor. I am a stranger, and ignorant of your usages. Is Nat a privileged citizen, Mysire Rechtor? Or does this law you describe apply to everyone?"

"The protection of all it is, mysire."

"What about strangers such as my daughter, my son, and myself, Mysire Rechtor? Are we protected, too? Or does your law protect only your own citizens?"

"All it protects. This I say, mysire, and this so is."

"Then I protest on behalf of my daughter, Mysire Rechtor. She is being held by your order, and she had nothing to with restraining Nat—whom we soon released, by the way."

"By the law held she is, mysire. The law, the law cannot break." He addressed the troopers. "Mysire Horn's daughter, Meren Jahlee. Why not to my court fetching her you are?"

One came to attention and saluted. "Sleeping she is, Mysire Rechtor."

"Her you wake."

There was a whispered consultation; I took advantage of the time it gave me to look around. The five with slug guns I took to be leg-ermen, although their uniforms were sketchy at best. Except for them, and Judge Hamer, there was no one in the sellaria save Beroep, Aanvagen, and me.

The sellaria itself spoke of wealth and luxury, although no wealthy man in the Viron I knew as a boy would have been impressed by it. Its floors of waxed wood was smooth, and the rough wool carpet before the judge's desk not quite contemptible. Somber pictures hung on the crudely paneled walls; heavy chairs and glass-fronted cabinets containing rusted knives and swords, and split and polished stones, completed the furnishings.

"Mysire Horn!" Hamer rapped his desk with a walking stick. "About your daughter presently we see. Likewise Mysire Hide, who stands accused with you."

"Unjustly. He is my son and merely did what I told him."

"This he and you later must say. How you plead I must know, and not how Mysire Hide will, or this Meren Jahlee whose sleep brave men dare not disturb. Our laws you do not know, mysire?"

I shook my head.

"By speaking you must answer."

"No, Mysire Rechtor. I do not."

"Such criminals as you, Mysire Horn, three choices have. Innocent you may plead. If this you say, your innocence by your own speech and your witnesses you must to me prove."

"I would be free to speak then, Mysire Rechtor?"

"This I have said, mysire. If guilty you plead, almost the same it is. By your speech and witnesses for a light sentence you argue."

"I believe I understand, Mysire Rechtor."

"Not pleading also you may choose. If so you choose, a friend for you I shall appoint. Then your guilt we must show, and he our witnesses may question. For children and those who cannot speak this is done."

"You said that you would have to prove my guilt, Mysire Rechtor. I thought you were to be my judge."

"Your judge I am. If guilty you are, show it so I must. How pleading you are?"

I looked to Beroep for a hint, but he would not meet my eye. I said, "I won't plead until my trial, Mysire Rechtor."

"Now plead you must, so we for your trial can prepare."

I shook my head again.

"To me aloud you must speak!"

I was badly frightened, but I thought of Silk in the inn in Limna, and how he had longed for a public trial, though he had known that at the conclusion of any such trial he would be convicted and sentenced to die. Gathering what courage I have, I said, "You are my prosecutor, mysire. Take me before a just judge, and I will speak to him."

"Your judge I am!" He pounded the table with his stick.

"You claim the right to prosecute me in accordance with your laws, the laws of Dorp, about which I know nothing. I claim the right to defend myself by the only law I know, the law of reason. Reason demands an impartial judge, and that I be given the advice of someone who knows your law." I wanted to swallow and tried to, as I recall vividly. "Someone friendly to my cause."

Silence descended on the sellaria, save for the shuffling of the legermen's boots.

"Is that all you have to say, Mysire Horn?"

I nodded my head.

"To me aloud speak!"

I shook it and waited for the blow from behind I expected.

"Mysire Beroep!"

He stepped forward and said, "Yes, Mysire Rechtor," with a slight tremor.

"In your house Mysire Horn is staying how many days?"

There was a pause, and I saw Beroep's fingers twitch as he endeavored to count on them without making it obvious that he was doing so. I said, "For eight days, Judge Hamer."

"Me, Mysire Rechtor calling you are."

"No, Hamer."

"Him you silence," Hamer told one of the legermen, who positioned himself behind me with his hand over my mouth.

Beroep said, "Six days, Mysire Rechtor."

"Not eight it is?"

Beroep cleared his throat. "Only six counting I am, Mysire Rechtor."

There was an interruption as Hide was hustled in, followed by Vadsig and a middle-aged couple.

"This Mysire Hide it is?" Judge Hamer asked.

I jerked the legerman's hand down and said as loudly as I could, *"No!"*

"What this is you saying are, mysire?"

The legerman had his hand over my mouth and an arm around my neck; I could not speak.

"Mysire," Hamer pointed to Hide, "your name we must have."

"My name is Hoof," Hide told him.

"To me Mysire Rechtor you say, mysire. Again you answer."

"Yes, Mysire Rechtor."

Hamer's eyes rolled upward; I felt sure that like me, he was silently imploring the mercy of the immortal gods. "To this court your name you must give. It what is?"

The middle-aged man said, "Hide it is, Mysire Rechtor. In my house quartered he is. If removing—"

Hamer cut him off. "Him asking I am, mysire!"

Hide said, "My name is Hoof."

"Hide not it is?"

I saw Hide's eyes steal toward me, although I doubt that Judge Hamer did. "No," Hide said.

The woman interrupted, saying rather shrilly, "Hide always we calling him are, Mysire Rechtor."

Her husband snapped, "Silent you be, Versregal!"

"To your house confined he is, Mysire Strik?"

Hide said, "I am, but my brother isn't."

"Mysire Hide your brother is?"

Hide nodded, and one of the troopers stepped up behind him and cuffed the side of his head.

"To Judge Hamer loudly you must speak," Strik explained in a whisper.

Vadsig stepped forward, eyes blazing. "Not knowing he is! No crime he does! Why him you abuse? What justice this is?" And much more of the same—too much for me to record here even if I recalled it. When Hamer found out she was only a servant in Aanvagen's house, he had her gagged and tied to a chair.

"Mysire Hide. This Mysire Horn's son you are?"

"My name isn't Hide," Hide explained. "My name's Hoof. Hide's my brother. We're twins, and we changed places. We used to do it all the time when we were smaller to fool our father. He couldn't tell us apart."

"Mysire—"

"Hoof. We look exactly alike."

Aanvagen put in, "Mysire Horn three sons and a daughter having is."

Hamer silenced her with a glance.

Hide said, "I'd heard my brother was in trouble here, so I came to see if I couldn't help him, and we changed placed. He's on his way back home by now, I guess."

Hamer told the trooper to release me, and asked whether Hide was my son. I said he was.

"Three having you are, mysire? Saying this the woman is."

I nodded, and was knocked to my knees.

"Three sons you are having?"

I must have nodded again. (At another time I will write about Green.) When I regained consciousness, I was lying on the floor beside Hamer's desk, and he was questioning Azijin. "With Mysire Horn talking while snowbound you are. Of twin sons he spoke?"

Azijin stood at attention. "Yes, Mysire Rechtor."

"More than a yes from you I ask."

Azijin gulped; the sound was soft, but the sellaria was so still, and I lay so near him, that I was able to hear it. "Of his family to me speaking often he is, Mysire Rechtor. Of his sons who twins are, of his wife and older son, of his daughter, who asleep fell and could not we wake—"

"Not permitting it he is?"

Another gulp. "No, Mysire Rechtor. Permitting he is, but not waking she is."

Hamer grunted. "Of twins he speaks? Sons that twins are?"

"Yes, Mysire Rechtor."

I suppose he must have beckoned to Hide, because Hide came forward.

"This son with him then is, Sergeant?"

"Yes, Mysire Rechtor."

"Not the other it is?" (I held my breath and shut my eyes.)

"The other, Mysire Rechtor . . ."

"The other it is?" I did not have to see Hamer to know that his face was crimson with rage. "This you saying are?"

"No, Mysire Rechtor."

"This son it is?"

"Yes, Mysire Rechtor."

Hide burst out, "Who is this, and why's he lying about me?"

There was a lengthy silence. At last Hamer said smoothly, "Mysire Strik, charged with the prisoner Hide you were."

"Here he is!" Strik protested. "Before you he stands, Mysire Rechtor."

"No, mysire. Escaped he has. His brother his place has taken while you slept."

"But—but—"

"To me plain this is. Mysire, your name Hoof it is?"

Hide nodded. "Yes, Mysire Rechtor."

"Mysire Hide your brother is?"

"Yes, Mysire Rechtor."

"When your father Mysire Nat confined, you in your own town were?"

Hide coughed nervously. "Can I say something, Mysire Rechtor? It's about something that's been bothering me a long time."

"Speak. Of you what I ask it is."

"That man there isn't really my father at all. He says he is, and he must've talked to my real father a lot, because he knows a lot about me and my brothers and our whole family. But that's not him."

"Not your father he is? Lying he is?"

"I don't know if he's lying, Mysire Rechtor. Sometimes it's like he believes it himself."

Judge Hamer rapped his desk. "Nearly finished we are. Sergeant, Mysire Hide who with you in the inn was, this man his father calling he was?"

"Yes, Mysire Rechtor!"

"Good." Judge Hamer sighed with relief; I heard his walking stick rattle as he laid it down. "Good! From Mysire Nat a disposition I have. By Mysire Horn and Mysire Hide he was bound and beaten. Mysire Horn we have."

Hide started to protest, but fell silent.

"You may not me interrupt, mysire! Mysire Horn your father he is?"

"That's his name, Mysire Rechtor, but—"

"Then this man another Mysire Horn to me he is, because Horn himself he calls. This Mysire Horn we have. Mysire Hide we do not have. Meren Jahlee not I have seen, but little guilt she has, and ill she lies." This was said portentously, and there was a slight stir of anticipation.

"For this preliminary hearing I will decide. In the matter of Meren Jahlee, no reason to charge I find. Dismissed though absent she is."

Although she spoke softly, Vadsig surprised me enough to make me open my eyes by saying, "Thanks, Mysire Rechtor. We really appreciate it." At an angry gesture from Azijin, a legerman hurried to replace her gag, which lay in her lap.

"In the matter of Mysire Hide, escape his guilt confirms. With unlawful restraint he charged is. Not here he is to plead, so for him not pleading down I set. This the law requires. With his escape Mysire Strik I charge."

I was watching Strik through narrowed lids, and he looked stricken. Hide asked, "What about me, Mysire Rechtor?"

"With you my court no business has, Mysire Hoof. Free to go you are."

"Thank you," Vadsig said again. Azijin went over to fasten her gag himself, but Judge Hamer told him to free her instead.

Strik was trying to say something, but was silenced. "Your preliminary hearing not this is, mysire. A date for that I will set. Notified you shall be." Hamer cleared his throat. "Mysire Beroep."

Hesitantly, poor Beroep stepped forward.

"Mysire Horn you for us have kept. Mysire Strik also you must keep."

Aanvagen answered for him. "That we will do, Mysire Rechtor. Safe with us he will be."

"In the matter of Mysire Horn, for himself he cannot plead, for him also not pleading down I set." Just then Cijfer burst in to announce that Jahlee had escaped. But I must go.

★

★ ★

I have been out raising money. It was not easy, as the loot we took was mostly jewelry; but after searching and pounding on doors I was able to trace one jeweler to his home, wake him, and persuade him to buy six pieces. I stopped at a dram shop when I left him, a very foolish thing to do when I was carrying so much money; but I told myself (correctly, as it turned out) that I would be able to sit down with a glass before me and rest for an hour or so before I had to find my way back to Aanvagen's, and I might hear something of value. It was a clean, decent place, and had very few customers so late at night.

Sit down, Patera.

Auk sat across from me, more dour and more threatening than I ever imagined him when we wrote about his meeting with Silk. I blinked and he was gone, but he soon returned. Eventually I called the owner of the shop over, saying quite truthfully that my head ached, that I was very tired and much in need of company, and that I would be happy to stand him a glass of his own brandy if only he would tell me the gossip of the town.

"A foreigner you are?" He bent over my table, a bald and beefy man of more than forty.

"A foreigner much in need of companionship, mysire," I said.

"A girl you want?"

I shook my head. "Just someone real to talk to. Are you about to close?"

"No, mysire. At shadeup we close, but soon my son comes so sleep I get."

"Most people here don't say shadeup anymore," I told him, "or shadelow, either."

"For this my son at me laughs, mysire." He sat on Auk's stool, to my great relief. "The old place I do not forget. Back I cannot go, but remember I do. Old as me you are, mysire. Why come you did?"

For a moment I could not decide whether to tell him that I was told to (as I was by Silk) or that I was made to (as I was by Hari Mau and his friends); in the end I decided to change the subject and said, "For the same reasons as many others, I suppose. Would you like that drink? If you'll get it I'll pay for it, as I said."

"No, mysire. In my house sometimes, but here never I drink. For my trade ruin it is. From where to our Dorp do you come?"

"New Viron."

"A long voyage it is, but last night another from New Viron to my tavern comes. For you it is he searches?"

"I doubt it. What was his name?"

The shopkeeper scratched his bald head. "This forgotten I have, mysire. What yours is? Him I tell if again he comes."

I smiled and told him, "Horn it is, mysire. To him this you say. Mysire Horn for your company asks. Your townsman he is. With Beroep he is to be found. Help you he will."

The shopkeeper laughed. "Better talking you are, mysire."

"But not perfectly? How would you say it?"

" 'For' not you say."

As I sipped from my chipped glass, I struggled to recall just what I had said. "Mysire Horn your company asks?"

"Yes, mysire. That the right way it is. Also must you say, with Beroep to be found he is."

"I see, and I appreciate your instruction. I'll wait a bit before I try again."

"A good man where we are Beroep is." The shopkeeper winked and pretended to drink, then turned gloomy. "Soon ruined he is. Destroyed he is. His boats they want, mysire."

A younger man joined us. "Strik already ruined is."

The shopkeeper introduced him. "My son, mysire. Wapen he is."

Wapen said, "Strik tried will be. Everything they take."

"For what tried?"

Wapen shrugged. "If not wanted it is, too heavy it is."

His father told me, "They us destroy, mysire. One man and another."

"My father's tavern soon they take." The younger man was not tall, but he looked tough; and as he leaned toward me I saw a scar that must have been made by a knife or a broken bottle across one pitted cheek.

"Soon, not now, it is," the shopkeeper said.

"Better the tavern we sell and a boat buy. Back not coming, we are."

I said, "Better destroying those who would destroy you, you are."

The shopkeeper looked around fearfully, but his son spat on the floor, saying, "What more to us they will do?"

Soon after that the shopkeeper left for home, and Wapen excused himself to wait on another patron.

"They're y'are."

I looked around at the swaying woman behind me and said, "Chenille?"

"Tha' lady on Green? No, 's me." Jahlee dropped onto Auk's stool and leaned across the table her chin on her hands. "Guesh my faish's not sho good, huh?"

"Don't smile," I told her.

"I won'. I'sh jush show *hungry*. I foun' thish woman in a alley."

"Not so loud, please."

"I drank 'n drank, 'n I fell down 'n I knew I better shtop."

"Did you kill her, Jahlee?"

"Don' thin' sho. She'sh big woman." She paused, her eyes unfocused and her nose softening and seeming to sink into her face. "Never wash sho drunk. D'you like it, Rashan?"

I shook my head, wondering how long it would be before she was sober again. It could be a matter of minutes, I decided; it was also possible that what we were interpreting as drunkenness was permanent brain damage.

"I'sh jus' *sho* hungry," she repeated.

"A part of the blood you drink becomes your own blood. Surely you must know that."

"Washn't thinkin', Rashan. It'sh jush like th' cow." She waited, expecting (as I saw) to be scolded. "Sho then I shed go back to tha' big housh, only I'sh locked up there."

I nodded.

"An' I can' find it but I shaw you."

"Basically you're right," I told her. "We must get you out of sight, and it would probably be unwise to return to Cijfer's."

"My hair'sh crooked?" Her hands went up to it.

"No. But I wouldn't touch it if I were you." Seeing a face I recognized, I called, "Hoof, come over and sit with us."

He came to the table and offered me his hand. "I'm afraid I don't remember you, sir. Are you from New Viron?"

I was worried about Oreb and my trial and a dozen other things;

but I could not help laughing, just as I was to laugh a few minutes later when Hide came in with his bruised face and swollen eye, still angry and eager to fight. "Yes, I am," I told Hoof. "I'm your father, and this is your sister, Jahlee."

8

SAD EXPERIENCE TEACHES ME

"Horn!" As he stumbled, dripping, into the cavernous room that had been Blood's reception hall, Hound goggled.

"Bucky?" Pig's blind face looked not quite at him. "That yer, bucky?" Donkeys more than half asleep raised their heads and turned long ears to hear the moist scuffle of his shoes on the scarred and stained parquet floor.

"Yes, it's me." He sat down between Pig and Hound, wiping water from his hair and eyes. "Tired and exceedingly wet."

"Bird too!"

"Yes. Dry your feathers. But not on my shoulder, please. It can scarcely support its own weight."

"A godling had you. . . ." Hound sounded as if he did not believe it himself. "I told Pig."

"Did you? And what did Pig say?"

"Prayed fer yer, bucky."

He glanced at Pig, then laid a shivering hand on one of Pig's enormous knees. "You're wet, too."

"Aye, bucky. Been rainin' h'out there? H'it has!"

He turned to study Hound. "So are you."

Hound did not reply.

"It's raining outside, Pig, exactly as you said. But not in here. There's a tile roof, and tile lasts if it isn't broken."

"H'in through ther winders, bucky."

"Bird too," Oreb remarked.

His owner stroked him. "Do you mean that you fly into the house through its broken windows as the rain does, Oreb? Or that you are as wet as Hound and Pig?"

"Bird wet!" Oreb spread his wings, warming them at the dying fire.

"Indeed you are, and for very the same reason—that is to say, because you were out there with me."

"I wasn't." Hound spoke to the fire. "I've got to tell you that, and there it is. I heard the godling when it spoke to you, and I hid in here, in one of the little rooms off this one, until Pig came."

"I don't blame you."

"I tried to get him to hide too, but he wouldn't. He went out into the rain to help you."

"Good man!" Oreb exclaimed.

"Then you went out to bring him back?"

Hound nodded, still looking at the fire.

"Hung h'on me h'arm," Pig explained.

"I made him listen. And you and the godling were talking, were conversing, really, like a man and his servant. We—I couldn't make out what you were saying. Could you, Pig?"

"Nae ter speak a'."

"We could only catch a word here and there, but we knew from your voices that it wasn't going to hurt you. So Pig put away his sword again and came back here."

"Good Silk!"

"He most certainly is, Oreb, which is why we must find him. But you and Hound and Pig are good, too, each in your own way—friends far better than I deserve. You came to me while I sat in the godling's hand, and that took a great deal of courage. Hound's hiding in here was merely good sense, since he couldn't have achieved anything if he had tried to save me from what was actually a nonexistent threat. When there was a life to be saved, he acted as courageously as any man could.

"As for Pig, what he was ready to do leaves me speechless. I've sat cross-legged in the palm of that godling's hand, Pig, and the mere notion of attacking it in any way, of firing on it with a slug gun from a window of this house, for example, much less rushing at it with a sword . . ." He shook his head.

Pig chuckled. "Candy fer me, bucky. Could nae see h'it."

"But you saw Mucor? I mean the second time, when I sent her out to you?"

"Ho, aye." Pig's tone was no longer bantering.

Hound said, "Without offense, Horn. I hesitate to ask, but . . . I was terrified. I admit it."

"So was I," he said.

"I still am." Hound looked him in the face for the first time. "I'd like to know what the two of you were talking about. It wasn't . . . It isn't going to kill us or anything?"

He shook his head. "It's trying to help us, actually."

"Auld Pig'd like ter hear ter, bucky."

"I'll be happy to tell you, and in fact it's my duty to; but there are other questions. Perhaps Hound has asked them already. If so, I didn't get to hear your answers."

Hound said, "I haven't."

"Then I will. Can you tell us what Mucor said to you, Pig? It may be important."

There was a silence so long that Oreb croaked, "Pig talk!"

"Nae easy ter get h'it right," Pig muttered apologetically. "H'asked h'about me een. Knew I would, dinna yer?"

"Yes, I assumed so."

"Said she dinna know. A wee chat then, an' she said ter stay wi' yer, an' I might get 'em. Sae when Hound said h'it had yer, 'twas hoot sword, an' h'at 'em."

"I understand—or at least I understand more than I did. Did she tell you why she thought you might regain your sight in my company?"

"Did she, bucky? She did nae."

"After I left Mucor's room, Pig, I wanted to go into the suite that Silk's wife Hyacinth once occupied. It took me some while to find it, and when I did you were already there. You were angry, I believe, because I threatened to intrude."

"Aye, bucky."

For a moment or two he stared at the broad, fleshy face, made pitiable by the damp gray rag across its eyes. "May I ask what you were doing there, Pig?"

"A place ter think's h'all."

"You didn't know that the room you chose to think in had been Hyacinth's bedroom?"

"Did he? He dinna."

"You were outdoors, standing on the lawn, when you spoke with Mucor."

"Aye."

"It wasn't raining then—it can't have been, because it hadn't begun to rain yet when Hound and I went out to look for firewood sometime later. Why did you go back into the house, Pig? Was it to get out of the wind?"

"Why, bucky? Why nae? Dinna think h'about h'it."

"Did you come back here where Hound was waiting for us?"

Hound touched his knee and mouthed the word *no.*

"Dinna think sae," Pig murmured. "Crawlt h'in a winder."

"And went up to the second floor, which is where Hyacinth's suite was, to think?"

"Aye, bucky."

He felt his face and found that it had been dried by the fire, then ran his hand through his untidy hair, which was damp still. "You're fencing with me, Pig."

"H'is he?" It was not followed by the expected "he h'is nae!"

"Yes, he is. You are, and I'm too tired to fence. I've never taken fencing lessons, Pig, but Silk did and I got to know his fencing teacher, an old man named Xiphias. It seemed a glamorous business then, fencing."

"Did h'it noo?"

"Yes. Yes, it did." He recalled the ruined sword-stick, leaning forgotten in a corner of the Caldé's Palace. He (or had it been Silk?) had drawn its hidden blade to feel the place where Blood's azoth had notched it. He recalled the moment, and with it the texture of a bamboo practice sword and the swift pattering steps when there was no time to boast, time only for the mock-deadly business of winning or losing, thrust and parry, advance and retreat. "Later," he said, "when I was building my mill, I wondered why anyone bothered. Other than by arrangement, the occasions when two combatants with swords fight it out must be very rare. On Green—have I told you I went to Green, Pig?"

"Aye."

He lay down, hands behind his head. "I got a sword there; and after I had used it to clear a sewer clogged with corpses, I used it to kill red leapers and animals of that kind. There's an art to that, if you will allow—but it isn't fencing."

Pig's deep, rough voice seemed to come from very far away. "Want ter tell yer, bucky. Truly do."

"You've sworn not to?"

"Dinna know meself. Somethin' h'inside, ca'in' me. Kept goin' an' goin', till h'it felt hamy. Believe h'in ghaists?"

Hound said, "No."

"Yes. Certainly."

"Ane h'in there, bucky. Felt a' her."

A half-strangled sob elicited, "Poor Pig," from Oreb.

"Winded perfume. Kissed me, ter. Believe h'it?"

"Yes. She kissed a great many men in there, Pig."

"If yer'd come h'in . . ." The long, brass-tipped scabbard stirred, scraping the hearthstone.

There was a long silence, broken by Hound. "You said you'd tell us what the godling told you."

"So I did. It's bad news for you, I'm afraid; and bad news for me as well. I should tell you first, however, that I haven't the least intention of doing what I was instructed to do."

"You're going to disobey it?"

"I am indeed. What right has it to expect obedience from me?" Again he felt the pelting rain, the freezing wind that had driven it like sleet, and the faint warmth of the huge hand. He opened his eyes. "It is not a rhetorical question, Hound. Pig, I ask it of you, too. What gives that godling—or any other—a moral right to our obedience? You've been here for the past twenty years, as I have not. Answer me if you can."

"They speak for the gods." Hound sounded more diffident than ever.

"They say they do, perhaps; but the one who spoke to me didn't even bother to say it. I might add that augurs often make the same assertion, on dubious grounds."

"Holdin' yer, wasn't h'it, bucky? Could a' killed yer."

"That's correct. I was seated on the palm of its hand, and if I had jumped, I might've been badly hurt."

"Be dead, bucky."

"I doubt it. The distance from his palm to the ground must have been two or three times my height—approximately the fall Silk suffered when he drove through Hyacinth's window. Do you know about that, either of you?"

Hound said, "No."

"I won't bore you with the details, but Silk jumped out of her window and landed on flagstones, breaking his ankle. If I'd jumped from the godling's hand, I would've landed on wet ground. That might have been almost as bad—I doubt very much, however, that it could have been worse."

"S'pose h'it'd shut h'its han' h'on yer?"

Oreb squawked in dismay.

"I would've been crushed, no doubt. Still, I doubt that it could have. They move slowly. Even in the short time I talked with it, I couldn't help noticing that. Each of its fingers must weigh as much as you do. If that's correct, closing its hand entails moving the weight of four very large men."

"Bucky . . ."

He chuckled. "Oreb told me a big man was behind the house. I thought he meant you, and Hound and I had been worried about you, so I went with him. Afterward—while I was sitting in the hand—I was inclined to be angry with him for saying *big man* instead of *godling*, *giant*, or something of that kind that would've told me what I was to encounter. Then I realized that to him we're as gigantic as a godling is to us—that Oreb sees little difference between a large man like you and a larger one like the godling because there really isn't much, from his standpoint. What could a godling do to him that you couldn't?"

"Would nae hurt yer, H'oreb," Pig rumbled.

"No. But neither would the godling. You and Hound thought I was very brave for talking to it as I did—"

"I still think it," Hound announced.

"But Oreb's being just as brave every time he perches on my wrist and talks with me. A wild bird wouldn't do that, and I can't blame it in the least. . . ." The birds suggested trees, immense trees like mountains and graceful fern-foliaged trees that swayed in every breeze and burned like incense; the trees, islands and continents, and smiling lakes, deep blue seas, and storm-tossed oceans.

"What yer thinkin' h'about, bucky?"

"The three whorls. Two large and low, by which I mean near the Short Sun. This one near the stars. I don't know whether Green's bigger than Blue, or Blue's bigger than Green; but both are much bigger than this whorl we're in, the Long Sun Whorl. When we came to Blue, we scarcely noticed that. I didn't notice it at all, in fact, and doubt that many of us did. Both this whorl and that one were very large places to us, and that was all that mattered; yet I would guess that Blue is ten or twenty times larger—that there's more difference in size between Blue and this whorl than between the godling and ourselves. In this whorl, Pas took care to separate us with rivers and mountain ranges. On Blue there isn't much need for that. Distance itself makes us keep our distance." He closed his eyes again, seeing league upon league of open water, and feeling the gentle rocking of his sloop.

"Horn? You said you had bad news for us. What is it?"

"Not for Pig—at least, I don't believe so. For you and me, Hound. You wanted to take your family to Green after your child was born. So it sounded. Have you changed your mind?"

"No. I—no."

"Then it's bad news, as I said. For me, too, because I must find Silk and take him home with me, and that means we must find a lander in working order and places on it. The godling told me it has been decided—I don't know by whom—that enough people have left the *Whorl* now, and everyone who's still on board is to remain aboard."

Oreb whistled sharply.

"It came as a shock to me, as you may imagine, and I'm by no means certain it conforms to the will of Pas. When Patera Silk and the sleeper he had awakened went down to the surface of the whorl where the landers are, he saw the inscription Pas had caused to be cut into the steps. It read, 'He who descends serves Pas best.' My understanding has always been that everyone—the entire population of the whorl—is to leave it."

"Nae mair, bucky?"

"Correct. At least, according to the godling. Everyone in the *Whorl* is to remain. They hope to repair it." Closing his eyes again, he added softly, "That was what Echidna and Hierax wanted. It would seem they have won after all, although the godling claimed to be speaking for Patera Silk."

"Don't you think that it might be the divine Silk issuing these orders, Horn?"

He sat up a second time, eyes wide. "What did you say?"

"The minor god that augurs call Silent Silk? Or Silver Silk?" Hound cleared his throat. "I don't know much about your religious beliefs, Pig. . . ."

"Nae me," Pig told him. " 'Fraid ter get me wind h'up? H'all pals. Right, H'oreb?"

"Good Silk!"

Hound said, "He really is," then added hastily, "not that they all aren't. There are no bad gods. I know that."

"You're telling me that there's a god called Silk?"

"Why, yes." Hound drew his jacket more tightly about him, and edged a finger's breadth nearer the dying fire. "I thought you must know about him. You're looking for Caldé Silk, and I suppose Caldé Silk must have been named for him, since it's a name people can use, too. Men, I mean, or boys. It's sort of a stretch, not like Hound or Horn or Pig. But Wool's a common name." Hound fell silent, clearly afraid he was offending one or both his companions.

"Good name! Good Silk!"

"Be quiet, Oreb. Hound, I'd like to know a great deal more about this god named Silk. I haven't been here, remember."

"I shouldn't have brought him up." Hound was clearly sorry he had.

"Like ter know ter," Pig rumbled. "Yer said h'it h'ought ter be Silk's tellin'? Why sae?"

"Well, because the godling spoke to Horn, that's all, and Horn's looking for Caldé Silk and . . . and it seems like there's some connection, doesn't it? Because the names are the same."

He asked, "Why do the augurs call him Silent Silk and Silver Silk, Hound? Do you know?"

"I think so. But there's a disagreement about him. I should tell you that in case you talk to other people about him. Did I call him a minor god?"

"Yes, you did."

Oreb snapped his bill in protest.

"Well, some people don't agree with that. They say he's not a minor god at all, that he's an aspect of Pas. I don't understand aspects."

Pig stirred impatiently. "S'pose he was ter gae 'round callin' himself somethin', sae folk wadna know."

Hound nodded. "I see."

"I don't like to disagree, Pig," he said, "and hesitate to in a matter of no importance. But what you're describing is a mere lie, not an aspect. The gods are known by foreign names in many foreign cities, Hound. Are you aware of it?"

"I haven't traveled, I mean like you have, or Pig. But I've heard something about it."

"It is so. Those, too, are their names; and they have as much right to them as we have to ours. There is also the matter of personality, both the kinds of persons we are at base and the way we seem to others. You have your personality; you are always Hound, whether you are kind or cruel, whether you act well or badly. Pig is always Pig, Oreb—"

"Good bird!"

"Is always Oreb, a good bird just as he says; and I'm always myself. But the immortal gods, whose powers are so much greater than ours, can incorporate many different personalities, and do. This not some special insight of mine, by the way. Merely what I was taught in the schola."

"I see," Hound said again. "You're going to say that when a god uses a new name and a new personality, that's an aspect. Isn't that right, Horn?"

He nodded. "And a new appearance. The god is still Pas, Molpe, or whoever; but this is a view of Pas or Molpe that we haven't been privileged to see before—a new aspect of Pas or Molpe. Now, why has the god called Silk been awarded the epithet Silent?"

"Because he told the Prolocutor that he looked out of the Sacred Windows without showing himself there, like Tartaros. But Tartaros generally turns them black and speaks. Silk said he didn't speak or make the window change at all, pretty often. He just looked on."

"Thank you." He yawned and stretched. "Thank you very much, Hound. Believe me, I appreciate your information more than I can say. Is everyone ready to sleep? I confess I am—more than ready."

"No sleep. Night good!"

"It may or may not be night, Oreb. We have no way of knowing, and certainly no one should feel compelled to sleep who doesn't want to."

Hound said hastily, "You don't have to lie on the bare floor, Horn. I've got a blanket you can lie on. Folded in threes, it'll be a lot more comfortable."

"Thank you," he said. "That's very kind of you; but what we really need is firewood, I'm afraid. It's certainly getting cooler. I'll go outside and look for some, if both of you will promise to remain in here."

Pig prepared to rise. "Be ter wet ter burn, bucky."

"He's right," Hound told him. "You could catch pneumonia if you went out there again, and it would be for nothing."

"Dry, we need, bucky." Laboriously, Pig stood up. "Here's ther lad ter fetch h'it, ter. Dinna yer gae wi'."

"Pig—"

The long sword was only half drawn from its brass-tipped scabbard, but the swift hiss of the steel was like the hiss of a coiler big enough to crush and devour five men at once. Oreb squawked with dismay.

"I wasn't going to try to stop you, Pig—nor was I going to insist on going with you."

"Guid h'on yer, bucky." Pig grinned as the sword shot back into its scabbard. "Get yer rest while auld Pig tears h'up boards ter warm yer."

They sat in silence, watching Pig's broad back vanish into the surrounding gloom; then Hound said, "I'll get that blanket," and proceeded to do so.

"That is your bedding, Hound, and I decline to deprive you of it. I slept in a field night before last."

"I've got another one for myself." Hound smiled. "You ought to know me better than that by now. You'd give another man your only blanket and think nothing of it, I know. But I wouldn't. Neither would Pig."

"Good Pig?" Oreb was puzzled.

"Yes, Oreb. Pig is a good man—an extraordinarily good man, I'm sure. One who might give someone else his only blanket, unless I miss my guess."

Hound looked up from the pack from which he was extracting a second blanket. "Well, most men wouldn't."

"Of course not. That's why I said that Pig, who might, was an extraordinarily good man—among other reasons. It wasn't a tactful thing to say, I suppose, particularly while I was preparing to lie down on a blanket you loaned me; but it wasn't intended as criticism of you—far from it. May I say something personal, Hound? Without giving offense?"

Refolding his blanket, Hound nodded. "I wish you would."

"Very well. If you'd had only one blanket, you might have discovered something extraordinary about yourself. It would've surprised you, I believe; but it wouldn't have surprised me."

Hound did not reply until he had arranged his own blanket before the fire. "You said something personal to me, Horn, and it was very flattering. Can I say something like that to you? You won't think it's flattering, or I don't think you will. I'd rather that you didn't get too angry."

"Watch out!" Oreb exclaimed.

Oreb's master reached out to stroke him, smoothing the glossy black feathers with gentle fingers. "Which of us are you warning, Oreb?"

"You, I'm sure. He thinks I'm going to involve you in some sort of—of plot against Pig. I'm not."

"Good."

"I simply wanted to say that I like you. I like you a lot. So does Tansy. Pig . . ."

"Yes?"

"Never mind." Hound lay down upon his side, looking at the fire. "I talk too much. It isn't my only fault, but it's the worst one and the hardest to stop. Good night, Horn."

"Please. What you were going to say may be very important. I mean that. You asked my permission to say it, and received it. I want to hear it. I ask it as a favor."

"You said you were going to tell us what the godling told you to do, but you never did. Just that you weren't going to do it. What about that?"

"Did I? It wasn't intentional. If I tell you now, will you tell me what it was you were going to say about Pig? I'm perfectly sincere about its importance to me."

"All right. What was it the godling wanted you to do?"

"Go all over the city announcing that no one else is to leave—that they are to rebuild the tunnels beneath it, and to repair the remaining landers, if they can."

"But not use them?"

"Correct."

Hound waited for him to say more; but he did not, and at length Hound asked, "Did the godling tell you why?"

"In order that the *Whorl* can be re-launched. I confess I don't understand how such a thing is possible, but then I don't understand how it was launched originally either."

There was a second lengthy silence, which lasted until Hound ventured, "It's the will of the gods, I suppose."

"Perhaps it is. The godling didn't say so, but it may be—it's quite probable."

Oreb croaked; it was difficult to tell whether it was a croak of sympathy or a croak of skepticism.

"Aren't you going to do it, Horn? That's what you said."

"I know." Stretched on his back upon the borrowed blanket, he fingered his beard. "I said it because it's true. I'm not. I won't repeat what I said before, except to add that size and strength confer no moral authority. A strong man—Pig, for instance—may compel us to obey him; but we're entitled to resist if we can."

"No fight!" Oreb advised.

"Tell it to the strong man. You're a wise bird and a good talker, but you're talking to the wrong person."

"But the gods . . ." Hound's voice faded away.

"The gods possess moral authority, granted. Great Pas, particularly, possesses it; and in fact the rest have it only because he accords it to them. If a god were to—but *if* is a children's word. No god has spoken to me. What were you about to say about Pig?"

"Horn . . ."

He could not see Hound's face from where he lay, or much of anything other than Blood's domed and painted ceiling, writhing figures less than half illuminated by the flickering firelight; but Hound sounded alarmed.

"Horn, you ought to at least consider obeying, even so. I mean, a godling . . . They don't talk to us much, but most people accept that they're relaying the gods' orders whenever they do. Everybody I know does. Didn't you promise?"

"Good Silk!" Oreb announced loyally.

"No, I didn't. The godling issued its orders and I asked some questions and nodded. That's as far as it went."

"But your nodding implied—"

"That I had heard its answers and understood them. That's all. My task is to find Silk—the godling said he was here— and take him to New Viron. I want to get home to Seawrack and the two sons who remain to us, Hound. I think I've been away for about a year. How would you feel if you'd been separated from Tansy for a year?"

"Is your wife's name Seawrack? I thought you called her something else."

"Did I say Seawrack? I'm sorry. My wife's name is Nettle. We're getting off the point, however. The point is that I gave my solemn word. To keep my oath, I've risked everything—and lost. Are you looking at my face, Hound? I feel your eyes."

"Yes."

"This is not my face. I've had little chance to study my reflection, but I don't need to—my fingers tell me so. Nor are these my fingers. I am neither so tall nor so slender. I have lost myself, you see, in service to my town. I won't turn aside after all I've been through. No, not if all the gods in Mainframe were to command it.

"Now, what were you about to say about Pig?"

"You lost your yourself?"

"I'm not prepared to discuss it. First, because you would credit nothing I said; and second, because we have a bargain. I've carried out my part. I've told you what the godling wanted me to do. Furthermore, I've explained why I won't do it. What were you on the point of saying about Pig?"

"This isn't it, but he's been gone an awfully long time."

"I know. I don't know whether he'll return to us tonight, and he may not return at all. Fulfill your part of our bargain."

"I will, but first let me say that some of it isn't true, all right? I'll tell you what I was going to say, but I've had time to think about it, so afterward I'm going to take some of it back." Hound paused.

"This is what I was going to say. I was going to say that you and I get along fine. Hound and Horn, right? It's the name of an inn up in the mountains. But I was going to say I don't like Pig. That's the part I want to take back. I was going to say that I didn't like Pig, and I thought he was dangerous—"

"Good Pig!"

"And I was going to give you the name of the inn I'm going to put up at. It's Ermine's, and I was going to say that after we say good-bye and go our separate ways you could come there and stay with me, as long as you didn't bring Pig."

"That was generous of you. I certainly appreciate it." Still regarding the ceiling, the speaker smiled.

"Like I said, that about not liking Pig isn't really true. I'm afraid of him. He's huge and very strong, and I think his blindness makes him savage. It might make *me* savage too, being blind." Hound giggled nervously. "So I can't blame Pig for it. Just the same, he scares me. I'm still young and Tansy may be carrying our first child, and I don't want to get killed."

"Nor do we older people, I assure you. You say you don't dislike Pig. Do you like him?"

"I—" Hound hesitated. "Yes. Yes, I do. I'm still afraid of him, but I like him a lot."

"So do I. Thank you very much, Hound. For your offer of a place to sleep—I appreciate it, and may take you up on it—but most of all for confiding in me."

Hound swallowed. "You can bring Pig, if you want to."

"I thank you again, this time on his behalf. You are extremely generous."

"You said what I almost said might be important. It wasn't, and I realize it. But that's what it was. That's everything I was about to say."

"You're mistaken. It was fully as important as I thought it might be. Will you do me one more favor, Hound? You've done so many already that I hate to ask it, but I will. I do."

"Yes, absolutely. What is it?"

"Go to sleep."

"I was thinking . . . Pig's not coming back. I think we both know that. So I was thinking maybe I ought to go and see if I couldn't do what he said he was going to, find some old furniture to burn or tear off a couple of boards somewhere."

"Feed fire," Oreb elucidated.

"No. Go to sleep, please."

"It's getting colder."

"We must bear it. Please go to sleep."

Lying on his back with his hands behind his head, he talked to himself, telling himself how the Outsider had touched Patera Silk on the ball court between one moment and the next, and how he himself had played on, all unconscious of the momentous thing that had occurred, conscious only of the game, conscious that the ball had been snatched away as he was about to shoot, conscious that Patera Silk was a much better player than he would ever be, conscious of the sun-bright sky through which a flier floated, a black cross against the sun, a sign of addition that signed that something had been added to a whorl that would never be quite the same again, that the gods' god who had been outside for so long had come in, a whispering breeze stronger than Pas's howling, whirling storm.

Conscious too that he himself was a painted wooden figure in a blue coat moved by strings, a blue-coated figure atop a music box, whose blue coat was a coat of paint, unconscious of all that passed when the box was silent, when the clever, shiny spring inside no longer uncoiled to move him and his partner through the mad gyrations prescribed for the tune played by the steel comb that sang to itself of a virgin braiding her hair by candlelight, a virgin glimpsed by a vagrant stealing his supper from her father's garden, apples more precious because he had glimpsed her then, seated on her bed in her chemise, and she was the most beautiful woman in the whorl, was Kypris and Hyacinth because she had yet to learn how beautiful she was and the power of her smile.

Trampin' outwards from the city,
No more lookin' than was she,
'Twas there I spied a garden pretty
A fountain and an apple tree.
These fair young girls live to deceive you,
Sad experience teaches me.

Dark hair braided like a crown, and a smile that tore the heart. The mandola had not been played particularly well, and the sweet, soft voice of had been of limited range. And yet—and yet . . .

Stretched and felt before I dared to,
Shinnied easy up the tree,
Saw her sitting by the window.
Busy as a honeybee.
These fair young girls live to deceive you,
Sad experience teaches me.

"No sing," muttered Oreb, no singer himself. "No cry."

I'm old now, and soon must leave you,
But fairer maid I ne'er did see.
Curse me not that I bereave you,
I cannot stay, no more would she.
These fair young girls live to deceive you,
Sad experiences teaches me.

"Poor Silk!"

He sat up, then rose quietly and tossed the smoldering stubs of burned sticks into the fire. From the sound of his breathing, Hound was not yet asleep. He lay down again.

"Patera? Patera, are you awake?" He is Horn calling beneath Silk's bedroom window.

He is Silk replying from the window. "Yes, but Patera Pike's still asleep, I believe. Keep your voice down."

". . . dying, Mother says. She sent me to get you."

He knelt in prayer beside the bedside while Silk swung his beads in the sign of addition, knelt beside the praying boy while bringing the Peace of Pas to the gray-faced old woman in the bed. "I convey to you, my daughter, the forgiveness of the gods. Recall now the words of Pas, who said, 'Do my will, live in peace, multiply, and do not disturb my seal. Thus you shall escape my wrath. Go willingly—' "

Go willingly—

Go willingly . . .

The dying woman's head rolls upon her pillow. "Nettle? Where's Nettle? Nettle?"

She rises and takes the dying woman's hand. "I'm here. I'm right here, Grandma."

"I loved you, Nettle."

"I know, Grandma. I love you, too."

He watched them through two pairs of eyes.

"I want you to know, Nettle, that you've been loved. I want you to remember it. Someone loved you once. Someone may love you again, Nettle."

It echoed and re-echoed: *someone may love you, Nettle.*

He blinked and woke, not certain that he was not still dreaming. And at last sat up, shivering.

Their fire was nearly out. Hound had rolled himself in his blanket and was breathing deeply and heavily. Oreb was nowhere to be seen. Blood had said, "Did you walk out here, Patera? My floater'll take you back. If you tell about our little agreement . . ."

Arm in arm they had staggered and stumbled through this very room, he eager—no, Patera Silk eager to keep Blood beside him so that Blood would not take note of Hyacinth's azoth tucked into the back of his waistband and covered by his tunic, Musk escorting them to a floater driven by Willet, a Trivigaunti spy.

From up there (he could barely see the place) he had looked down into this room, where middle-aged men in evening clothes had stood drinking and talking while blood from the gash the white-headed one had made in his arm dripped unseen onto the carpeting.

Had stood with his back against a white statue of Thyone. He strained to see it in the darkness, and had made it out at last and started toward it when it moved.

Leaning over the balustrade, Thyone became Mucor, then faded like mist. Nodding to himself, he took out the lantern Hound had given him and lit its candle with a stick from the fire.

He heard Pig's muttered exclamation as he turned in to the suite that had been Hyacinth's and called softly, "Silk? Silk? Where are you, Silk?," reminding himself forcibly of Oreb.

"Lookin' ter get killed?" There was no friendship in Pig's voice.

"Silk, I know you're in him, and I must talk with you."

The long blade slithered from the brass-tipped scabbard. Looking through the doorway into the bedroom, he saw Pig's blind and terrible face, and the sword blade tasting the air like the steel tongue of a great iron snake.

"I have a light. I know you can't see it, but I do. Without it—"

Pig was coming toward him, guided by his voice and groping for him with that terrible blade.

"I wouldn't have had the courage. If you kill me, my ghost will remain here with Hyacinth's. Have you thought of that?"

Pig hesitated.

"Whenever you come looking for her, you'll find me, too."

"Bucky . . ."

"I like you, Pig, but I don't want to talk to you at the moment. I came here at the risk of my life to speak with your rider. Talk to me, Patera, or kill me here and now. I have no weapon, and those are the only choices open to you."

"Then I'll talk with you," Pig said, and sheathed his sword. "You knew because I couldn't help coming here, didn't you? You say you have a lantern?"

"Yes." He felt that a weight had been lifted from his shoulders. "No, and yes. That's what I ought to say. If it had only been that Pig wanted very much to be alone in this room, I don't believe I'd have guessed. I would have thought of Silk the god, of Silver Silk as the augurs call you, with Kypris and dismissed the thought. You're not with her now, I realize. As long as Pig is blind, you can't go back to her."

"Correct. Though I would try to have his sight restored in any case, just as you yourself are making a praiseworthy effort to restore Maytera's."

"You even sound like yourself, Patera." He held up his lantern, letting its glow fill the whole sad, empty room. "It's uncanny, hearing your voice from Pig's lips and larynx. The voice is surely much more a function of the spirit than I ever realized. Chenille must have sounded very different indeed when she was possessed by Kypris."

"She did. You said it wasn't merely my coming here, Horn. What was it?"

He sighed. "I wish I'd known when Nettle and I wrote our book. I would have emphasized the changes in voice more. If I didn't have a light, I'd be ready to swear Patera Silk was standing before me in person."

"Standing before you and quizzing you, Horn. How did you know? I won't make you reply, though I probably could. I'll be grateful for an answer, just the same."

"I wish I had a good one. Last night I dreamed that Pig took off his bandage; and when he did, his face was yours. So I must have sensed something. We call him Pig, and talk about him as if that were really his name; but it's just a name of the Vironese type that he chose for himself yesterday."

"I remember."

"You would of course. Tonight Hound said our names were linked—Hound and Horn, like a hunting inn. That started me thinking about Pig's name, because I feel closer to Pig than to Hound, though Hound has been so kind to us, and I recalled the old saying, that you can't make a silk purse out of a sow's ear. A silk purse generally means a purse made of silk, but it could also be purse to contain Silk."

Pig chuckled.

"Pig, or you in Pig, might have thought it amusing to give the proverb the lie—so it seemed to me. Then too, men rarely like the men they fear; but Hound likes Pig and fears him, too. You were the only man I'd known who had that kind of unconscious charm; but Pig has it. And, as you say, Pig had sought out this room, which used to be Hyacinth's, and was enraged at the prospect of being disturbed here."

"It was Pig who was angry," Pig said.

"I know. In one sense you're Silk—but ultimately you're really Pig, exactly as you appear to be. A Pig to whom certain new instructions have been given."

"What's that yer said, bucky?"

"I said that I had no wish to disturb your privacy, that I was extremely grateful to you for permitting me to spend even a few minutes in this room, and that I will return to Hound now and leave you to your thoughts."

"Never had none, bucky." Pig chuckled again. "Gae wi' yer, h'if yer dinna h'object ter me company."

"I'd be delighted to have it, and perhaps we can find some firewood. Do you think that might be possible?" He gasped.

"What yer catch yer breath like that fer, bucky?"

"This room has several windows. No doubt you discovered them for yourself."

"Did he? He did. Seadh."

"Well, the clouds parted just then—just as I finished speaking—and I saw a flash of skylight. It means that the sun is burning again. When we leave, it will be by daylight. I—I realize it makes no difference to you, Pig, but it will make an enormous difference to Hound and me, and even to the donkeys, I imagine."

"Huh! Want h'it ter make a difference ter me, bucky. Gang ter help me find een, hain't yer?"

He said, "I will do everything in my power, Pig. You have my solemn promise."

The doorway was much too small for them to leave arm in arm, though both would have liked to. As it was he hung back, letting Pig kneel to crawl through before him. For an instant then it almost seemed to him that the bare floor and mildewing walls had been swept aside and he saw again the luxury and splendor that had been: the rich, figured carpet, the pictured women of pink and gold, and the huge bed of scented wood with its black and crimson sheets. Wine and chocolate perfumed the air, and glowing lights clearer than the one he held swarmed over the ceiling, their refulgence held in check by the discretion of the murmuring couple in the bed.

Then Pig's boots were through the doorway, leaving behind them only silence, ruin, and himself. Sighing, he too went out, pursued by the mockery of Hyacinth's soundless laughter.

9

Before My Trial

It would be impossible for me to write down everything that has occurred since I last wrote. When I was back on the *Whorl,* and Silk spoke to me through my friend Pig, I was eager to hear all that had befallen him since we had gone to Mainframe. He never complied, although I was permitted a few glimpses; and now I understand why he did not. There are things that would be so long in the telling that the *Whorl* might go before any account was well begun. This is like that, but I will do what I can.

Before I start, I should say that we are very comfortably situated now in the house that was Judge Hamer's. At present it belongs to me, having been given to me by the town. Before we leave I hope to sell it; Nettle and I will need money, Hide and Vadsig want to build a house as well as a boat, and it is likely Hoof will marry before long. I have noticed that when one twin does something the other is not far behind.

Speaking of Vadsig, I should say that before my trial I questioned her at length, having observed at the hearing that she was possessed. I supposed—hoped, I should say—that Jahlee was her possessor. In that I was disappointed.

"Who are you? I know you're not really Vadsig. If you want to make us think you are, you must learn to talk as she does."

She gave me the defiant glance I had seen earlier when she had described her quarrel with "Cook." "We came to help. You should thank us."

"I certainly need help. Thank you very much."

"That's better." She smiled.

"You speak of yourselves as *we*. How many of you are there?"

She giggled. "What does it matter?"

Hide said, "So I can tell when you're all gone. I want Vadsig back."

"She's still here." Her voice changed tone. "We'll have to go soon. Onorifica will come in and wake me up." A return to the previous tone. (I will not continue to mark these changes; they were too frequent.) "That's the good thing about this. I can eat."

To entertain them I said, "You're not Mucor in that case. I thought you might be; but Mucor would be alone, I believe."

Vadsig giggled again.

Hide said, "We don't think it's funny, do we Father? Who's Onorifica? Was that the girl who thought you could make your stick talk?"

"He can!" More giggling from Vadsig.

"She was a servant at General Inclito's," I told Hide, "so Vadsig's possessors are Inclito's daughter Mora—you remember her, I'm sure—and her friend Fava."

"You said Fava was dead. You said we sat on her grave that one time, and—"

Vadsig interrupted. "Well, I like that!"

I told her, "I hope you'll remember, Fava, that without me your body would have gone unburied, and would, I believe, have been devoured by wild animals that very night. I buried you alone, digging stony ground in the bitter cold. Would you have done as much for me?"

Vadsig was silent.

Hide said, "I still don't understand about Fava. Isn't she really dead?"

"Death isn't a hard and fast line like the edge of a table. It is a process, and it can be a long time before the dead person is entirely gone—indeed, it may not end in total dissolution at all. Fava and Mora were close, so it's not surprising that Fava figures in Mora's dreams. The surprising thing is that both figure in yours."

He gawked, and I laid a hand upon his shoulder. "The three whorls are stranger places than you can imagine, my son. As you mature you will come upon less and less of that strangeness if you stay close to home, honor no god much, and busy yourself with prosaic affairs. Then you can scoff at such things."

Vadsig said, "Cruel to him you are, mysire."

"No, Vadsig. I'm causing him pain. Only children believe that there is no difference between cruelty and education."

Hide asked, "Are they gone now?" and she giggled.

"No, my son, they are not. Vadsig loves you so much that when she sensed that what I'd said had left you confused and unhappy she broke through to protest. Suppose you were on a mare, and the mare heard her foal cry out. You might be able to get her back under control, but you'd have to do it. For a moment you would have lost control, as Mora and Fava did then."

"I want them gone, Father!" Hide's fists clenched.

I said, "I would ask who it is you think that you're about to strike, but it would be useless, I'm sure. You may strike me, if you like, but I'll restrain you—if I can—should you attempt to strike Vadsig. It will not drive out her possessors, and she's done nothing to deserve it."

"I won't hit you."

"Thank you. As for making Mora and Fava leave, I suppose we might be able to if we tried, but there's little point in trying. They'll go when Onorifica wakes Mora for breakfast, as Mora told us. Meanwhile we must confer with them, and with Vadsig as well.

"Will you please let Vadsig speak? It is late already, we have a lot to talk over, and if Fava wants to eat and Vadsig allows it, I'll have to arrange for food—"

"Fish heads?"

I looked up in surprise, and found Oreb in his accustomed place on the chimney corner.

"Bird back!"

Vadsig said, "Speaking to you I am, mysire. What wanting you are?"

"First, your consent to the possession, Vadsig. Is it all right for Mora and Fava to remain with you till sunrise? It will help you and Hide in the long run, I'm sure."

She did not reply.

"Bird find." Oreb announced. "Find hus."

"That's right, I sent you after Babbie. Thank you. I haven't time to ask where he is, but I will later. Meanwhile, please don't forget."

"Hus good!"

"If helps it does, all right it is. Friends we are."

"Fine. Thank you, Vadsig. You're not only helping Hide and yourself, you're helping me, too. Now I must ask one more thing of you. Fava—I believe it's Fava—would like you to eat. I may be mistaken, but I think she'll make you eat voraciously. Is that all right? Have you objection to a big meal?"

"No, mysire."

"You'll have to talk more than that, I'm afraid. I can't be certain after hearing only two words."

"Sorry I am, mysire. Stupid I feel."

Hide said, "That was her. They couldn't fool me."

"Speaking I am, kandij. Late it is and hungry we are. If eating too much I am, stop me you can. But I won't make her hurt herself or drink blood like I used to, Incanto. I won't let Fava make her sick."

"Good. Thank you, all three. I'm hungry myself—"

Oreb croaked, "Bird eat?" from the chimney corner.

"Yes, Oreb. Certainly."

I turned back to Vadsig, wondering whose facial expression I was studying. "No doubt Hide's hungry too, and we might as well eat while we talk. Hide, would you go down and arrange for food with Aanvagen, if she hasn't gone to bed?"

"Right away, Father." Hide blew Vadsig a kiss.

"What do you want to talk about, Incanto?"

"Overthrowing the judges who rule Dorp."

Oreb whistled sharply.

"It seems to be the only course open to me. Nat is well connected and vindictive, and if I'm tried I'll certainly be found guilty and punished severely. I may be executed, and I'll certainly be flogged. Hide, Jahlee, and I will be deprived of our property. When they discover much of it missing—I've taken it out and sold it—Beroep and Aanvagen will be ruined, as Strik has been."

"A good man he is, mysire," Vadsig assured me. "This Master often says. This Parel also says. A hard trader Strik is, but as he says his goods are. Do you think we can really do it, Incanto? We overthrew the Duko, and I like to think Eco and I had something to do with that, but we had the Horde of Blanko, and they had a lot more to do with it than we did."

I told them, "Let me say first that if we succeed we should be able to restore Captain Strik's property. He helped me when I was just setting out, and I certainly intend to try; in fact I'll try to restore all the property that's been unjustly confiscated. The judges have been using their positions to enrich themselves; we will deprive them of both riches and position—if we can.

"Second, these judges recall the Ayuntamiento, the council we overthrew in Viron. By 'we' I mean not only Maytera Mint and Patera Silk, and Seawrack and I, but several hundred others who formed the nucleus of our rebellion. There were five councilors, too—Lemur, Loris, Potto, Galago, and Tarsier—and they controlled the Army and the Guard, immense advantages that the judges here lack. The Horde of Dorp is largely made up of reservists."

Vadsig looked doubtful. "These names not knowing, I am, mysire. This knowing I am. Legermen there are, and slug guns they have."

"We have weapons, too, Vadsig. The difficulty is to find men and women who'll use them with determined courage."

"She'll fight if she's fighting for Hide and a house of her own, Incanto. Mora and I will too, but then it won't be so dangerous for us."

"Boy come!" Oreb announced; and in a few seconds we heard Hide's feet on the stairs.

"The lady here . . . Aanvagen? Is that her name?"

We nodded.

"She and her husband and that fellow Strik have gone to Strik's to get some things so he can make himself comfortable, but I told the cook what we wanted, and she said she'd do it if I'd carry it up. She'll yell when it's ready."

"Down to help her I will go," Vadsig offered.

I shook my head. "We have a great deal to discuss. I mentioned the rebellion in Viron, in which I took part; I was one of General Mint's runners, was shot in the chest, and so on and so forth—none of which I need go into. The point is that it succeeded, though it faced opposition far more serious than the rebellion we will foment here in Dorp. It was sparked by a theophany, Echidna's appearing in the Sacred Window of my manteion. I doubt that any of you have seen a Sacred Widow."

Hide and Vadsig shook their heads. Oreb piped tentatively, "Bird see?"

"That's right, you were with me in the Grand Manteion, so you did indeed. You'll have to excuse me though, Oreb, while I explain to the young people."

Vadsig said, "I've heard about them." (It was probably Mora who spoke.) "Can you climb through them, like a real window?" That was certainly Fava.

"An interesting point. In a sense, the gods can. They can leave the Sacred Window in the form of unnoticed flashes of light to possess us, very much as you and Mora are possessing Vadsig. You don't do it like that, do you?"

"I don't know, Incanto. I don't think so. Into me they have walked, mysire, as one into this house might walk. Me they did not ask, but friends become we have."

"What I was going to say is that to anyone who hadn't been brought up to reverence the gods—and even in Viron many people had not—a god in a Sacred Window was nothing more than a large picture that spoke. Even so, that single theophany set off a rebellion that many had longed for but no one had prepared for. I believe something of the same sort might have the same effect here, with a little preparation."

Hide asked, "Do you, Father? Are you sure?" The simple words fail to convey his expression and voice; it was one of the few times I have felt absolutely certain that he loves me.

"No," I told him, "but I'm going to bet my life on it. I have no choice."

All of this took place before Hide went to Strik's house in hope of reclaiming his old bed and was beaten by Strik and his wife, and before Hoof joined us and Jahlee rejoined us in the dram shop. Now I would like to pray for a few minutes, and after that I must get to court. This High Judge business is becoming very reminiscent of Gaon, save that I have no wives here and want none.

★

★ ★

Rereading, I see that I promised to describe my search for Jahlee. This would be a good time to do it; but first I should say that I was puzzled for some time after I arrived. I could not imagine how I had gotten to Green from Judge Hamer's sellaria when trips of the kind had previously required the presence of an inhuma. My initial feeling was that what I had experienced was impossible, and thus that I was not really on Green at all but was experiencing a dream or hallucination. This lasted for what seemed an hour or two, although it cannot really have been long.

Subsequently, I realized that there were at least three explanations. The first and certainly the most attractive is that Fava was possessing Vadsig. The difficulty is that the "Fava" possessing Vadsig may be nothing more than Mora's dream of Fava; if that is so, the web of difficulties becomes worse than ever.

The second (which I am loath to adopt though I think it the most plausible of the three) is that an inhumu was present but unknown to me. I write "an inhumu," despite the fact that my previous partners in bilocation have been female; it is possible that a male might serve as well. If this explanation is the true one, it would be interesting—and useful, perhaps—to know who it was. Hide, Vadsig, Aanvagen, Beroep, and Azijin can be dismissed; I have been too close to all of them far too often to be thus deceived. In my judgment Cijfer can be dismissed as well. That leaves Judge Hamer himself (surely the most interesting possibility), various troopers, and others, any of whom could be an inhuma or an inhumu.

The third is that I was assisted by the Neighbors, from whom the inhumi must originally have gained this power. I have been seeing and speaking to them, although this is not the proper time to write about it. It seems possible that Seawrack's ring not only identifies me as a friend, but actually attracts them—although we are all attracted to friends, with a ring or without one. (I may be making too much of this.)

Whether or not the ring has such a power, the Neighbors may have found me before they made themselves known to me, which was not until after Hide and I questioned Vadsig—indeed, after Hoof and I met Wapen in the dram shop. They were willing to help us, and indeed their testimony was of great value to us during my trial, as I shall describe in a moment or two.

I am loath to mention it, but there remains a fourth—

Oreb has returned. I heard him tapping at the window just now. In he flew and gave me his usual jaunty greeting, although he was cold and hungry. Blackbirds fatten best in cold weather, according to the saying, but it doesn't seem to apply to Oreb; in any event, I doubt that he is strong enough to get much food from a frozen corpse.

I had sent him with a message for Nettle, something I ought to have done long before. She must be worried about Hoof and Hide, as well as me, and very worried indeed about Sinew. In a small hand, on half a sheet of this paper, I explained that he is living happily on Green where we have two grandsons, and is caldé of a thriving village. I also assured her that the twins are safe with me, and told her that we have an adopted daughter and that Krait, whom I also adopted, is dead. (This last was unwise perhaps; besides, if Jahlee was Krait's mother, he was properly a grandson—but one may adopt a grandson, surely.)

I see I have confused the rings. The one I am wearing is not the one Seawrack gave me, although it resembles it closely. This is Oreb's ring. It seems the stone changes color when it is worn; it was originally much darker, surely. I should go back and line out my mistake, I suppose, but I hate lining things out—it gives the page such an ugly appearance. Besides, to line out is to accept responsibility for the correctness of all that is let stand. To correct that or any other error would be to invite you to ask me (when you read this, as I hope you soon will) why I failed to correct some other. And I cannot correct all or even most of them without tearing the whole account to shreds and starting again. My new account, moreover, would be bound to be worse than this, since I could not prevent myself from attributing to myself knowledge and opinions I did not have at the time the events I recorded occurred. No, there really are such things as honest mistakes; this account is full of them, and I intend to leave it that way.

★

★ ★

Having been clubbed during a session of Judge Hamer's court, I found myself again in the abandoned tower in the cliff face in which I had left Jahlee. I was overjoyed at first, thinking it would be easy to find her and return her to her sleeping body.

I searched the tower, discovering many strange devices and a locked door that appeared to lead into the cliff itself, no doubt opening upon some cleft in the rock. Jahlee was nowhere to be found, however, and at last I was forced to admit that during the time she had been alone she had left the tower, abandoning hope of rescue and flying out the circular port—I described it a good deal earlier—and down to the fog-shrouded swamps in which she was born.

I have been talking with Oreb, who has recovered himself somewhat after his exhausting trip. (Yesterday he seemed very tired and weak, and tucked his head under his wing as soon as he had been fed.) I questioned him closely about my letter.

"Bird take."

"I'm well aware that you took it, Oreb. But did you take it to Nettle? Did you deliver it as I asked?"

"Yes, yes! Take girl. Girl cry."

"I see." I rose and paced the room for some while, pausing at one window or another—there are seven in all—to peer between the leading and the bull's-eye at the center of each diamond-shaped pane of bluish glass. This house is admirably situated atop a small hill and commands a fine view of Dorp; but I could not have told you what I had seen five seconds after I saw it. If the Sun Street Quarter as it was before the fire had been re-created there, I doubt that I would have noticed.

Oreb was hopping back and forth, snapping his bill and whistling softly in the way that betokens nervousness; and at last I turned back to him. "What did she tell you to tell me, Oreb? There must have been something."

"No tell."

"Nothing? Surely she said something—she must have. Are you saying she sent you back without even a word?"

"No tell," he insisted.

"This is Nettle we're talking about? The woman in the log house at the southern end of Lizard? Near the tail?"

"Yes, yes." He bobbed affirmation. I described her, and he repeated, "Yes, yes."

"Was it day or night when you found her, Oreb? Do you remember?"

"Sun shine."

"Day then. What was she doing? I mean, before you gave her my letter."

"Look sea."

" 'Look see'? At what was she looking?"

"Look wet. Big wet. Look sea."

"Ah, I see—I mean I understand. Was she looking out the window, or was she standing on the beach?" Foolish as it may seem, these details were important to me. I wanted very much to picture her as she had been when Oreb arrived.

"No stand. Girl sit."

"She was sitting on the beach? Is that what you're saying? On the shingle?" When we were much younger, we used to spread a blanket there and sit on it to look at the stars; but we had not done that for a long time.

"Chair sit!" He was growing impatient.

"So she'd carried a chair out of the house, and was sitting in it and staring out to sea. I suppose it's natural enough—both Sinew and I left by boat. Naturally she would expect us to return the same way. Was anyone with her, Oreb?"

"No, no."

"She was alone? There was nobody with her?"

He picked up my word, as he often does. "Nobody."

"I don't suppose you landed on her shoulder, so how did you deliver it? Did you talk to her first—tell her who you were, and who I am?"

Oreb looked thoughtful, cocking his head to one side and then to the other, bright black eyes half closed.

"It's not important, I suppose. Do you recall what she said to you?"

"Bird drop!"

"You flew over her and dropped my letter? Not into the sea, I hope."

"Yes, yes! No wet."

"In any event, she got my letter and read it. She must have, because you said she cried."

"Yes, yes."

"But then, Oreb," I shook my finger at him, "she must surely have given you some reply. You didn't leave as soon as you had delivered my letter, did you? You must have been tired, and though I suppose you could have gotten a drink from the stream that turns our mill, I'd expect you to ask her for food."

"Fish heads."

"Yes, exactly like that."

"Bird say. Fish heads?"

I nodded. "She was always very generous, and she must surely have recalled the earlier Oreb, Silk's pet."

He flew to the window and tapped one of the panes, a sign that he wanted to leave. "Bye-bye!"

"If you wish it." I unfastened the latch and pushed back the casement for him. "But it's cold out, so be careful."

"Girl write. Give bird." Then he was gone.

Now I should complete my account of my search for Jahlee. When I had satisfied myself that she was no longer in the tower where I had left her, I went to the circular opening in the tower wall, telling myself that I was here only in spirit, and that spirits could not be harmed by a fall; yet I could not forget what had happened to the Duko on the Red Sun Whorl, and the mindless thing we awakened when we returned to Blue.

(Another mistake. I should have written *spiritless,* or some such. The Duko's mind remained, at least in some sense. It was the thing that hopes and dreams that had gone forever. I will not line it out, although I am tempted.)

When men and women die, their spirits may go to Mainframe—so we once believed. Perhaps the Outsider or some other god sends his servants to enlist them, as they taught in Blanko. But when a man's spirit dies, that is the death beyond death.

A dozen times I told myself to jump, that no harm could come to me, and a dozen times I held back. I have written that I was afraid because of what had befallen Duko Rigoglio; but the truth is that I was afraid first, and only later discovered the reason for my fear—or if not the true reason, a rationale to justify it. Jahlee had flown, I told myself, but I could not.

As soon as my mind had formed the words, I realized they were mistaken; here, Jahlee had not been an inhuma's imitation of a human being but an actual human being, and as such she could no more have flown than I. It was possible, of course, that she had jumped—I felt certain that her fear of heights would be much less than mine.

That recalled the white-headed one, whose clipped wings had prevented him from flying away. He had tried to fly when he and Silk had fought on Blood's roof, and had fallen to his death. Standing in the circular opening I actually pushed back my sleeve to look for the scars his beak had left on Silk's arm. Needless to say, they were not there—it was Silk, not I, who fought the white-headed one, just as it was Silk who killed Blood when Blood severed his mother's arm, no matter how vividly I imagined either scene.

Frightening as it had been to stand in the opening looking down at the jungle so far below, the climb on the cliff face was worse because it took so much longer. I had thought at first to climb out the aperture itself, but I saw at once that the gray stone wall of the tower was too smooth for me to climb down. I might have done it as a boy, or Silk, who told me once that he could climb like a monkey when he was younger—but I might have fallen to my death as well. I went down toward the base of the tower, and when I judged that I was at the bottom of the outer wall, I tried to tear aside the stones, using a long pointed tool I discovered in one of the workshops. I failed, but after some time shut my eyes and leaned against the wall, telling myself that I must somehow do this, and felt it soften behind me.

The cliff face was rough enough that it seemed possible I might descend in that way. I was making good progress—or so I thought—when I risked a look below me.

It was an extremely foolish thing to do. The rolling green plain that was in fact the tops of trees taller than the tower seemed every bit as remote as it had from the aperture in the tower wall, and the dizzying void that separated me from it was terrifying. I shut my eyes and clung desperately to the stone outcrop I held, telling myself again and again that when I opened them I must not look down.

In a minute or two I tried it, but they were drawn inexorably to that plain of green. I cannot say I froze again, because I had never moved; but motion seemed more impossible than ever.

A dot appeared there, and grew. At first I thought it smoke—that someone far below the plain of leaves had made a fire of wet wood, as we had done so often there; I watched it without seeing it, as a man about to be executed watches the firing squad but sees only the muzzles of the slug guns. Around and up they swirled, drifting (as it seemed) toward me. For a moment or two I thought vaguely that the whole wet and rotting whorl had been set ablaze and was going up in smoke. Then I realized what it was I saw, and began to climb, hoping to regain the safety of the tower.

I had not gotten far before they caught up with me. Some time ago I described the way in which the inhumi who had fought for me in the war with Han laid siege to us when Evensong and I tried to escape down the Nadi. That was bad, and was made worse by the darkness. This was much worse, and was made worse still by the clear daylight that bathed me and the thousands of inhumi. Most were mere animals, like reptilian bats with long fangs and hideous snarling faces. But there were some among them whose parents had fed on human blood, naked and starved-looking, with glittering eyes in faces like our own, trailing legs no bigger than a child's, and hands and arms flattened and broadened into wings. These spoke to me and to one another, cruel words and words of a pretended kindness that was worse than cruelty—words that will haunt my dreams for as long as death spares me. Their wings buffeted my face as I climbed, and the teeth through which they draw blood were plunged into my neck and arms, my back and legs until my hands and feet were slippery with blood, although I defended myself when I had an arm or leg free with which to do it. How long the climb lasted, I cannot say—no doubt it seemed much longer than it was, and although there were times when I was forced to hoist myself from one handhold to the next, there were others when I could scramble up steep slopes of scree, in considerable danger that the whole mass might slide, but making rapid progress just the same.

Eventually I came to realize that in my haste to escape I had missed the tower, and was no longer below it but above it. I continued to climb just the same, feeling certain that a search for the tower (I did not know whether it was to my right or left) would surely doom me. At the top of the cliff, I hoped to find some level ground where I might beat my tormentors off, recalling that although numerous, they had refrained from a direct attack on Evensong and me as long as we remained awake.

That reminded me of the azoth at last, and the azoth of the sword that I had re-created for myself on the Red Sun Whorl, the sword I had flung to the wretched omophagist in the lion pit—the sword that had melted in his hands. I shaped a needler for myself then, and when it felt solid in my grasp fired again and again at the inhumi.

The effects were extraordinary. Some tumbled out of the air and fell to their deaths. Some merely seemed frightened, conscious that they had been injured in some way, wounded but bewildered as to the nature of the wound. Some seemed wholly proof against its needles and prosecuted their attacks until I actually clubbed them with it. If these had rushed me en masse, I would have fallen and been killed, without doubt; but it was my blood they wanted, not my life, and my mangled corpse at the bottom of the cliff could have supplied very little of it. That saved me.

Here I am tempted to write that the cliff-top appeared suddenly above me, for that was how it seemed to me. The truth, of course, was considerably more prosaic—I had been inching toward it without knowing what the distance was, had climbed altogether about three times the height of the tower, and so had reached it. I do not believe I could have done it in the body that lay sprawled on the floor of Judge Hamer's sellaria. Fortunately, I did not have to; the weight I lifted—clawing, sometimes, with bleeding fingers at the red rock-face—although it felt real, was substantially less than my true weight.

To have attained the top was enough at first. I lay on my back gasping and shuddering, firing the needler at any inhumi who came too near. A woman spoke. I supposed that it was one of the inhumi who had taunted me with lies during my climb, and paid little attention. Then Jahlee was bending over me, her sorrel hair brushing my cheek and her sweet and beautiful face peering into mine. "You came back! I'd given up."

"I was imprisoned," I told her. "We were already under arrest when you left, remember?" Aware that the inhumi were no longer attacking, I sat up with her assistance.

A new voice asked, "Is this your male half, Misted One? His blood does not fill our bellies." The speaker was an inhumu, in form a dwarfish, hairless, emaciated man.

Jahlee nodded. "This is my father."

He began to speak again; but I cannot recall the words; there were only two or three at most. I shot him, my needle piercing the center of his chest, and watched him die.

"Why did you do that?" Jahlee was aghast.

"I have had a sharp reminder of what we are, and what they are."

"These . . . They worship me, Rajan. They won't use the word, but that's what it is. We . . . They bring me food I can't eat. Children, and all the while I know my body's starving up there."

I was about to ask what became of the children whose blood she was unable to drink (although I was afraid I knew) when my attention was drawn to a new figure, tall and tightly wrapped in a colorless cloak, approaching us with stiff, bird-like strides. Seeing him, I realized that what I had taken to be a large black boulder was in fact a squat domed building without windows.

Jahlee was telling me (no doubt correctly) that I should not have killed her friend. I said, "Will you forgive me? I've forgiven you a great deal, and made you my daughter though you were once my slave."

★

★ ★

It has been days since I wrote. I have been very remiss, but it has been a busy time. We are about to leave. I will pass over the Neighbor—what we said will quickly become apparent. Tomorrow we sail for home; if I wish to record my trial at all, I had better do it today.

It was held in what is called the Palace of Justice, a big, solidly constructed building with courtrooms for all five judges. I had been taken from Aanvagen's house several hours before and locked in a cell in the back of the building. Oreb visited me there, slipping between the bars on my window without difficulty, and on his second visit brought Babbie.

It was very good to see him again. "You've grown," I said. "Why, just look at you! You were no bigger than a big dog when I freed you."

Are you really my old master? (This was said with Babbie's eyes; it is the only way he has of talking, but generally works well enough.)

I put my arm through the bars, and he stood on his four hind legs, with all four forelegs braced against the wall, and snuffled my fingers. His coat—cannot call it fur—was as stiff as the bristles of a hairbrush.

Yes! Yes, you are!

"I am indeed, and very glad to see you, Babbie. I need your help badly. Will you help me? It may be dangerous."

"Bird help!"

I nodded. "You've been of great help already, and I must ask more of you. You must help Babbie find the courtroom when they take me away. It will be in this building, in front."

"Bird find!"

He did, too.

Having written about Oreb, I could not resist the impulse to open the window in the hope that he might have returned. He was not there. I thrust my head out and saw several birds, but he was not among them.

I was brought into the courtroom with manacles on my wrists, which they seemed to think would shame me. I felt no shame, but a sort of urgent joy. Either we would succeed and my troubles here would be ended (as they have been, only to be succeeded by others) or we would fail and I, at least, would be killed. Very likely my daughter and both sons would be killed as well—but then, death waits for all of us, not that I wished to see them die; it was very good indeed to find all three waiting in the courtroom with my advocate.

Now that I have mentioned him, I realize I should have written about him before beginning this description of my trial, but it is too late. His name is Vent, and he is middle-aged, bald, and paunchy. I have appointed him a judge.

He rose to greet me, and Hoof and Hide stood too. Then Hamer entered, robed in black like an augur, and we all had to stand. It was only then, I believe, that I realized how full the courtroom was, and from the noise that penetrated its massive doors that there was a crowd outside clamoring to get in as well. Certainly it was then that Cijfer caught my eye, pointing to the red-faced man with her and mouthing words I did not understand. She looked very happy and almost beside herself with excitement, so that I assumed there was good news of some kind. I smiled at her and tried to look as confident as I could while puzzling over the identity of the red-faced man, whom I felt sure I should recognize.

10

Through Quadrifons' Door

Pig stopped whistling to say, "Nae sae far noo, bucky. Lookin' forward ter h'it?"

"To revisiting the city in which I was born?" (By an effort he had avoided the word *seeing.*) "To tell the truth, I dread it. It will have changed, and not for the better I'm afraid. It can scarcely be for the better. Hound, you said that Silk is no longer caldé—"

"Good Silk!" Oreb, who had been riding atop the second pack-donkey, flew to his shoulder, a sudden blossoming of black and scarlet in the bright sunshine.

"So who is?"

"Who's caldé now?" From his seat on the lead donkey, Hound looked over his shoulder. "General Mint's husband. His name's Bison. Caldé Bison."

"That's good. I know him slightly."

"You're going to talk to him?"

Oreb muttered, "Talk Silk."

"I'm going to try." He was silent after that, his mind occupied with the empty houses they had passed, and the houses (many empty too, presumably) they were approaching. Up this road Silk had ridden with Auk, and down it he had ridden in a flyer driven by Willet; but he had not said much about it. He tried to recall whether he himself had ever traveled it, concluded he had not, and then, at the sight of a narrow old house whose pink paint had faded to near invisibility and whose shiprock was crumbling, was inundated by a rush of memories.

Nettle, and a slug gun on his shoulder, Maytera Marble and the ragged crowd of volunteers singing to keep their spirits up.

Trampin' outwards from the city,
No more lookin' than was she,
'Twas there I spied a garden pretty,
A fountain and an apple tree.
These fair young girls live to deceive you,
Sad experience teaches me.

There had been other songs, many of them, but that was the only one he could remember. Nettle would know them all.

He turned to look back at the house, but it had vanished behind trees. How long had it stood empty? Twenty years, or fifteen, or ten. Its roof had leaked with no one to repair it, letting water into cracks in the shiprock. That water had frozen in winter, splitting the walls farther each year.

"Talk talk," Oreb suggested. "Talk good."

He smiled. "If you wish. You asked whether I was happy to be returning to my native city, Pig. I said I was saddened by the thought of what must have happened to it in my absence. We just passed a house that I recalled."

"Ken ther people?"

"No. But I marched past it once, when I was a boy, and we were singing a song about a house with an apple tree in the garden. I saw that one, and it did indeed have a small garden with an apple tree. I seem to remember that there were a few apples on the upper branches, though I can't be sure. It seemed a marvelous coincidence at the time, a magical coincidence and a good omen. We were hungry for good omens just then. We weren't even amateur troopers, though we thought we were."

"Ho, aye."

"Masons and carpenters with slug guns they scarcely knew how to fire, and mortar and sawdust on their knees. I had one, and a needler, and was immensely proud of both. You were a trooper, Pig. I hope you had more training than I did."

"Nae muckle."

"No talk." Oreb had caught something in Pig's tone.

"I've been wondering—I hope you won't think I'm prying,

though perhaps I am—whether you weren't given some sort of ceremony of initiation. A sacrifice to Sphigx at some manteion to dedicate you and your comrades to the art of war."

Pig did not reply.

"In some ways you remind me of a man called Auk; and Auk was quite religious, in spite of all his violence and swagger."

"Would yer gods a' let 'em take me een, bucky? Prayed ter proper an' h'all?"

He shrugged. "I suppose they could have stepped in to prevent such cruelty, but it seems they rarely do. When was the last time you were in a manteion, Pig?"

To fill the silence that followed the question, Hound said, "Tansy and I almost never go anymore. We'll have to start if she's pregnant, otherwise there'll be all sorts of trouble about having the baby washed, won't there?"

"Gi'e somethin'. That'll fix h'it."

"I'm not a wealthy man." Hound sounded apologetic. "I wish I were."

And I wish there were a great mountain here, he thought. A great mountain along whose winding pass we had been traveling all morning, so that there could be a sudden turn around a stone outcrop. We would find ourselves looking down at Viron then, Viron spread like a carpet below us, streets running northeast and southwest, and southeast and northwest, with the broad slash of Sun Street cutting across them, east to west, right through the oldest part of the city. That part was built by Pas, like the old pink house, houses and shops built before there were people here to live in them, anyone here to buy or sell. We should have declared them sacred and kept them in repair; we found a hundred things to complain of instead, and let them go one by one, and built new ones we said were better even when they were not.

The apple tree was gone, too. Cut for firewood now that candles cost so much, now that lamp oil is hard to find. Had Pas planted it? He could not have, apple trees live no longer than a man. But now that it was gone, now that it had been cut down and sawn into one-cubit logs and burned, would anyone ever plant another?

Aloud he said, "It was the first time I ever heard that song, I believe. It was a new song to me then, and I'm sure I never supposed it would be important to me."

Hound said, "Will you be going to the Juzgado, Horn? You said you wanted to talk to the caldé."

"I know I did." A rush of new thoughts.

Hound cleared his throat. "I'm going to go to that inn I told you about. Since I'm going to get a room, I might as well eat there, and they have good food. If you and Pig would like to come, I'd be happy to treat you to a meal. Then you'd know where it was, in case you can't find another place tonight."

Having come to a decision, he shook his head. "That's very kind of you, but I know where it is. I want to go to the Sun Street Quarter first, where I used to live, not to the Juzgado. Unless Viron's changed even more than I anticipate, I'll probably have to wait most of a day before I can get in to see the caldé; and if I were to come in the afternoon, I'd probably wait the rest of the day and not get in at all. So I won't go to the Juzgado until morning. What about you, Pig?"

"Wi' yer, bucky. Yer dinna mind me h'askin' h'about een?"

"Of course not. To the Sun Street Quarter?"

"Where yer gang."

"Bird go," Oreb announced. "Go Silk."

There were more houses now, not all empty, until they lined the road. Hound pointed out those that had belonged to friends and acquaintances, recounting some anecdote or describing some eccentricity. "There's the manteion for this quarter. That's where we went when we were living here."

"Thought yer did nae," Pig protested mildly.

"Oh, sometimes. Sometimes we go now with Tansy's mother, and she'd like us to go more often, I know. But in those days, we always went when her mother and father came to visit. Her father was still alive then. I think I told you that it was when he died and left us the shop that we moved back to Endroad." He hesitated. "I suppose it's abandoned now. There can't be many people left. If it's been given up, it will be locked, I'm afraid. Would you like to look inside for a minute if it isn't?"

"Aye," Pig sounded pleased. "Can he look? He canna. Like ter see h'it, though. What h'about yer, bucky?"

"If it won't delay us."

"Oh, it's not big. Not big at all. Just the usual sort of place, I'm sure, but I thought you might be interested."

"No cut," Oreb muttered.

Pig cocked his head. "What's H'oreb h'on h'about?"

"What is he saying? He's saying, 'No cut,' something the original Oreb, Patera Silk's pet, always used to say. Possibly this is the same bird."

"No cut!" Oreb repeated more distinctly.

"Do you know why he says it?" Hound inquired.

"He knows animals are sacrificed there and is afraid he may be sacrificed as well. If we understood what more animals are trying to tell us, no doubt we'd find they say the same."

Just then a flock of crows passed overhead, wheeling and cawing; hearing them, Pig asked, "What're they sayin', bucky? Yer h'always ken what H'oreb's says, sae what h'about those?"

He looked toward the skylands, and seemed for a moment to have forgotten his companions and himself. " 'Tomorrow, tomorrow, tomorrow.' I think they mean I'll find Silk tomorrow, though I've found him already; but they may also mean you'll find new eyes tomorrow. I hope so."

Hound looked back curiously. "You've found Silk already? I'm surprised you didn't tell us."

"I found the god last night, after you had told me about him; and I should not have said even that much, Hound. Please forget I mentioned it."

Hound was silent as they passed more vacant houses. Then he said, "You can read the future in the flight of birds? I've heard of that, but I forget what it's called."

"If you want a word to impress your friends, auspicatory. If you're seeking knowledge for yourself, it is simply augury, the original form of augury, now much neglected."

"Silk know," Oreb assured them.

"He very well may," he said, "but I do not."

Soon they reached the manteion; its wide front entrance was firmly locked, but Pig's questing fingers easily pulled the hasp from the side door. "Prized h'out 'fore we come," he explained. "Screws pushed back h'in but nae wood ter hold 'em."

The interior seemed dark and cavernous after the sunshine of the street. Pig made his way to the back, the scabbard rapping pews, found the altar, and laid his sword aside to grope its edges and corners for a moment.

"No cut!" Oreb declared more adamantly than ever.

"You needn't worry," his master told him. "There's no Sacred Window here. It's what they were after, I'm afraid. Was that what you're searching for back there, Pig?"

"Aye, bucky."

Hound said, "There are several manteions that are still open. Horn could take you to one, since you're going with him. Or I will, if he's busy with other matters."

"Thank yer. Thank yer kin'ly."

"Would you like me to? We can stop someplace on our way to the inn."

Pig turned toward them, the brass tip of the leather-covered scabbard tapping the side of the altar again. "Gang ter yer Sun Street Quarter, yer said, bucky?"

"Yes. I'll stop at the manteion there, though I have no way of knowing whether it's still standing—or whether it's still open if it is. I must warn you that much of the quarter burned twenty years ago."

"Gae wi' yer," Pig decided. He was standing at the ambion, his thick black nails seeming to stab its carven sides.

"Do you want to tell me what's bothering you? You needn't, of course; I'll do whatever I can whether you confide in me or not, though I may be able to assist you more intelligently if you do."

"Wad nae swaller h'it."

"Poor Pig!" Oreb flew to his shoulder, and there was a silence in which it seemed that the ghosts of sacrifices past had returned. Almost, one could smell the incense, mingled with the odors of burning hair and cedar; almost, one could hear the augur's chant and the bleat of a lamb whose time had come.

Hound coughed. "Can't you help him, Horn?"

"You went to a manteion shortly before you lost your sight." He spoke gently, just loudly enough to be heard. "You knelt there in prayer—prayers, perhaps, of which you're now ashamed, though you shouldn't be. Your gaze was fixed upon the Sacred Window. No god came at the moment of sacrifice—or at least, no visible theophany took place, no Holy Hues, none of that. But you felt peace and a deep joy that you cannot explain. You would like to recapture those, if you could."

"Were lootin'," Pig said. "Me an' na braithrean."

"I understand."

"Yer dinna. H'ever loot yerself?"

"No, Pig."

"Been h'in a toon bein' looted?"

"No, never."

"Some goes fer ther women, some fer drink, some fer cards h'or what fetches 'em. Done ane an' t'other. Said yer ken, bucky. Ken that? H'or do yer need mair? What drunk an' what ther woman was?"

His right hand made the sign of addition in the air. "It's not necessary."

"Thank yer. Fetch noo, ther Winders do. Yer right. Auld Pig dinna know h'it then, but they do. Thinkin' a' gowd cups was h'all. Ter big fer doors, bucky. Yer seen h'it. Had ter gae h'on me knees ter get h'in ter yer house, Hound. Have ter, ter get h'in ter most. Dinna like ter, but there 'tis. Dinna fash, but see ane ter stand h'in, an' 'tis h'in every time."

"We could enlarge ours," Hound told him. "I could do the work myself."

"Good a' yer. Saunt, ain't yer, bucky?"

"No," he said gently. "No, I'm not, Pig. I've told you I'm not."

"He were, ter."

"Did you kill him, Pig?"

"Ho, aye. Stood by his Winder, he did."

Pig's drew his sword as he spoke, and Oreb squawked with fear and flew back to his master.

"Had a yeller cup ter gae me. Threw it down an' broke. 'Twas chiner."

"Poor Pig."

"Did fer him. Cut doon wi' me whin." Pig held up his long blade, which gleamed faintly in the dusty sunlight.

"And then?"

"Ain't yer goin' ter say nae thing h'about h'it, bucky? Figured yer would."

He shook his head, although Pig could not have seen the gesture. "Later, perhaps."

"Suit yerself. That's ther bad a' h'it."

"It is the good of it I wish to hear, Pig."

"None ter tell."

"After you had killed him, the Sacred Window behind him caught your attention. Am I correct?"

"Nae. Told yer h'about ther doors, reck h'it? Big h'enough ter gae h'in wi'hout kneelin'. Sae did he? He did."

"Yes."

"Wasn't nae where he lay, but on me knees just ther same. Fou' ter. Most fou'. Could nae hardly, wi'hout fallin'."

"Did you speak then, Pig? Did you pray, or try to pray?"

"Nae. Tried ter. Couldn't. Could he? He could nae! Blubbed like ter a big girl. Blubbin' noo."

"Weeping, you mean. So you are, but Hound and I are not laughing."

"Guid a' yer." Pig sighed deeply and wiped his nose on a sleeve already phenomenally dirty. " 'Tis h'all, bucky. Ther lot a' h'it."

"No, it isn't. Not quite, and it will always be unfinished—incomplete—unless you tell the rest. Unless you do it now. It cannot be postponed any longer."

"Horn . . ." Hound gripped his arm.

"I'll address your concerns in a few minutes," he said. "They can wait, believe me. Go on, Pig."

"Somethin' tetched me." Pig sounded as though he had forgotten anyone was listening. "Had me een."

"Yes. Of course."

"Touched me shoulders an' me head, like h'it were standin' behind. Looked h'around. Wasn't nae thing there."

"And then . . . ?"

"Felt h'it, bucky. What yer said. Wanted ter feel h'it h'allways, but nae felt h'it nae mair."

"And you were changed, somewhat, after that. You found yourself doing things that surprised you."

"Aye."

From his shoulder, Oreb muttered, "Good Silk."

"This has been a shriving, Pig. I didn't announce it but it has been. I'm a layman, as I said; but a layman may shrive when there is need. I'd like you to kneel now. I know you don't like to, but you shouldn't withhold from the Outsider—it was he who touched you from behind, I'm sure—the obeisance you pay so many doors. Will you kneel?"

"Think he might gi'e back me een?"

"I have no idea. Will you kneel?"

Pig did.

"Good. That was the worst hurdle, the one I feared we could not get over." A swift gesture sent Hound to the front of the manteion. "Now say what I say. *Cleanse me, friend.*"

Dutifully, Pig repeated it.

"You don't like to say *I,* do you, Pig? I mean the pronoun, not the *aye* that signifies assent. Is it a superstition?"

"Dinna sound weel h'in ther light lands," Pig muttered.

"Impolite? Then you may say, 'for the Outsider and other gods have been offended by me.' After that you must recount to me everything you have done that was seriously wrong, other than the looting and murder you have already described. Oreb, you must stay with Hound until I call you both."

At the rear of the manteion, Hound had watched the kneeling Pig (so huge that even on his knees he was nearly as tall as the erect man in the worn brown tunic) until embarrassment rendered it impossible.

"Man talk," Oreb explained, lighting on the back of the pew in front of Hound's. "Talk Silk." He whistled to emphasize the importance of that talk, and added, "Bird go. Go Hound."

Hound nodded absently. Statues of the Nine still stood in niches along the walls. Who was that with the owl, he wondered? Some were only minor gods, he felt certain. Since there were more than nine statues, they had to be. He had always dismissed the minor gods as unimportant; for the first time it occurred to him that he was unimportant as well, and the important gods like Echidna (over there, holding up a viper in each hand) might concern themselves with important men and things. "Echidna, and Molpe with the thrush. But who's that with the doves?"

"Man talk," Oreb repeated in a different context.

"To myself," Hound said. "I was trying to name these gods, that's all."

One of the murmuring voices at the front of the manteion rose to intelligibility. *"Then I bring to you, Pig, the pardon of the gods. In the name of the Outsider, you are forgiven. In the names of Great Pas and Silver Silk, you are forgiven. And in the name of all lesser gods you are forgiven, by the power entrusted to me."* A quick gesture described the sign of addition over Pig's bowed head.

Hound went to rejoin them, watching the huge Pig rise and straighten his shoulders. When Pig's blind face turned toward the noise of his shoes on the cracked stone floor, he said, "I didn't hear any of that. I think I ought to tell you so, Pig. I tried not to hear, and I didn't. I was way at the back, and you both spoke softly."

"H'all right h'if yer did," Pig said. " 'Struth, bucky?"

"Why, no." He shook his head. "Neither of you are correct. Hound, you heard a part of what Pig said about looting the town in the Mountains That Look at Mountains. You also heard me say that what Pig had told me was part of a shriving, although it had not been so announced at the time."

Hound nodded.

"You may be concerned about your duty as a citizen and a member of the Chapter. Nevertheless, you must understand where your duty lies. Whenever anyone, whether an augur, a sibyl, or a layperson, overhears part of a shriving by accident, that person is honor bound to reveal nothing that he—or she—has heard. He is not to hint at it or allude to it in any way. Am I making myself clear?"

"Yes." Hound nodded again. "You certainly are."

"Then let me say this. I've said it already to Pig, but I want to say it to you. You know, just as Pig and I do, what was said earlier; and we're none of us children. For an augur to die before his Sacred Window, and particularly for him to die by a steel blade as sacrifices die, is a great honor. It is the death every augur yearns for. I don't intend to imply that it isn't wrong to kill an augur under those circumstances; but when an augur dies in such a manner, other augurs and many pious laymen must wonder whether that death was not arranged by Hierax, as a reward."

Pig said, "Hierax is dead."

Hound stared at him.

"I see. I didn't know that, though I surmised that it might be the case. No doubt it's for the best."

"Horn?"

He nodded. "Yes. What is it?"

"Before we leave—" Hound began. "Are you worried about getting into the city late? You said you wouldn't go to the Juzgado till tomorrow."

"I would like to revisit the quarter in which I used to live this afternoon. But no, I'm not. Not unless whatever you're about to propose will take hours."

"Fifteen minutes or half an hour, I hope. While . . ."

Thick with muscle and armed with thick black nails, Pig's hand engulfed Hound's shoulder. "H'out wi' h'it, mon. H'all pals."

Hound nodded gratefully. "While I was back there in the back, I was trying to name the gods. The . . . These images." He indicated them by a gesture. "You know a lot about them. I've seen that already. Tansy saw it, too. Anyway, I couldn't, or only a few. I was hoping you'd take me around and talk a little about each of them? It would give me something to tell Tansy. And Mother. I'd like it myself, too, if it would be all right with Pig."

"Silk talk?" Oreb fixed him with a bright black eye.

"Ho, aye. Do h'it, bucky. Like ter hear yer meself."

"Very well." He glanced around at the images set into the walls. "Where do you want me to begin?"

"Well, that one." Hound pointed to the nearest. "It's Phaea, isn't it?"

"Yes, you're quite correct. Phaea's one of the Seven, Pas's fourth daughter. Now that think of it, we couldn't have begun at a more appropriate place, since we hope to find new eyes for a man called Pig, and I'm carrying seed corn to Blue. Feasting Phaea's the goddess of healing, and of foodstuffs generally. She presides over banquets and infirmaries alike. You can generally recognize her images by the boar at her side."

"Yes," Hound said eagerly. "That's how I got it."

"Then I ought to add that when the boar is absent Phaea is customarily shown holding a young pig, that when the piglet is omitted as well you may know her by her thick waist, and that she is the generous patroness of cooks and physicians. Is that sufficient?"

Hound nodded. "I couldn't get this next one at all. Who is she?"

"Let me ter feel a' her." Pig's thick fingers brushed the top and sides of the image and explored the area about its feet. "Wearin' a helmet, hain't she bucky?"

"Yes, she is. A helmet with a low crest." He bent closer examining the statue. "I was about to say that the customary lion was absent, which was why you were unable to identify her, Hound—but that isn't actually the case. She wears a medallion with a lion's head, though it is too small to be distinguished at any distance. Pig, who has been a trooper, knew her by her helmet, of course; but I believe he feared—needlessly—that I might take offense if he named her before I did. She is Sphigx, the youngest of the Nine."

Hound stepped nearer to look at the medallion. "I'm glad she's still here. A lot of her statures were smashed when we were fighting Trivigaunte."

"This may be a replacement—it looks a little newer than the others. If so, that's very likely the reason her lion was reduced to a bit of jewelry. The augur here may have hoped that vandals would take her for a minor goddess."

"Good god?" Oreb inquired.

His master shrugged. "I wouldn't say so, but she's no worse than the Seven as a whole. She's reputed to be brave, at least, and in the course of my life I've found that people who possess one virtue usually have several. One can imagine an individual who's admirably brave, yet grasping, unscrupulous, drunken, envious, cruel, lewd, violent and all the rest of that sad catalogue; but one never actually meets with such a monster—or at least, I haven't."

Pig said, "Thank yer kindly, bucky."

He was taken aback. "You can't mean that seriously. I haven't known you long, but no one who's been in your company for an hour could suppose you were a mass of vices. You're generous, kind, and good-natured, Pig; and I could easily rattle off a dozen more virtues—patience and tenacity, for example."

"Guid a' yer."

Hound cleared his throat and seemed almost to choke. "I want to say that Horn speaks for me, too. I couldn't have said it as well as he did, but I feel the same way." There was an embarrassed silence.

"Shall we go on to the next? I'm anxious to get to it, I admit."

"The woman holding the snakes? I wanted to ask something else about Sphigx, but I've forgotten what it was."

"She's actually a rather interesting figure. When I was a boy, I considered her the least attractive of the Nine, and there's some truth in that; but she's by no means the least complex. One can think of her as the mirror image of her sister Phaea. If that is the case, then Phaea is Sphigx's mirror image as well, which makes her the goddess of peace. The title suits her even though she doesn't get it, at least in Viron."

Pig touched Sphigx's image again, finding the medallion. "They fight, bucky? Sounds like they h'ought ter."

"No." Leaning on his staff, he studied the image. "Despite the swords she holds, Sphigx is not merely the goddess of war, as I should have made clear. She also governs obedience, courage, watchfulness, and hardihood—all of the virtues that a trooper must have, even cleanliness and order. I mentioned that Phaea was the physicians' goddess, the goddess of healing. I used to know a Doctor Crane from Trivigaunte—this was before they went to war with us. He was a tough, brave little man; and he would tell us in no uncertain terms how much a good diet and clean hands have to do with health and healing. We have need of both Phaea and her sister, you see. One way to put that is that they need each other."

Straightening up, he turned back to Hound, smiling. "Have you remembered what you wanted to ask?"

Hound shook his head.

"Then I have a question for you. When you said that many of Stabbing Sphigx's images had been smashed, I assumed you meant by angry Vironese who saw them as symbols of Trivigaunte. A moment ago, it occurred to me that the vandals might have been Trivigauntis themselves. Statues like this are prohibited in the City of Trivigaunte and its territories, supposedly by her order, as are pictures of her; and I suppose that a deeply religious Trivigaunti might be tempted to destroy them wherever she found them. Was that what happened?"

"Mostly in the city, I think. In the Grand Manteion."

Pig chuckled. "Both sides breakin' 'em?"

Hound nodded with a rueful smile. "I'd heard that about the Trivigauntis, I suppose because they did it there. And I hoped Horn could tell us why they wanted to. That was what I was meaning to ask, what I forgot for a minute. Can you, Horn?"

He stared off into the dimness of the shuttered manteion, where a single bar of sunlight had stabbed the dusty air.

"Silk talk!"

"Oreb means me, I'm afraid." He turned back to them. "Who am I to resist a bird's demands? They wanted to because they thought it was what their goddess wanted, of course; but you understand that, surely. The real questions are whether she did, and if so why she did." He fell silent again, his clear blue eyes lost in thought.

"If she did not, then her supposed demand is presumably a lie put forth by the Chapter of Trivigaunte—whatever it's called—or the Rani's government. If that is the case, they probably say what they do to separate their people more firmly from those of other cities. Have I mentioned that there is a Trivigaunti town south of New Viron? There is."

Hound said, "I didn't know that."

"There's been a certain degree of mixing, which some on both sides have sought to prevent—Trivigaunti women marrying Vironese, and Vironese women marrying Trivigaunti men."

"Feel sorry fer ther four," Pig said.

"So do I, in a way; yet I doubt that they're much more—or much less—discontented than other couples.

"At any rate, their custom of refusing to picture the gods clearly isolates the people of Trivigaunte. This manteion would appear blasphemous to them; more importantly, so would the home of any pious person in Viron. My friend Auk, who was what is called a common criminal though he was an uncommon man, had a picture of Scylla tacked to his wall. But I am drifting away from the subject.

"If Sphigx herself issued the prohibition, I think it most likely she acted from pride or shame. She may have felt that no representation we could make could do her justice. I have seen Kypris—"

Pig's hand closed upon his elbow, its thick, pointed nails almost painful.

"Long ago, and I would defy any artist to picture a woman equally lovely. Silk's wife, Hyacinth, was dazzlingly beautiful as a young woman—but even she was not as beautiful as that."

Pig's grip relaxed.

"Or Sphigx may be ashamed of her followers, or of accepting worship at all. None of the other gods seems to feel like that, yet it would be much to their credit if they did."

Hound stared at him. "But . . ."

"But they are the gods. Is that what you would like to say? That's true. They are our gods—here, at least—and if they demand our worship, we must give it to them or perish. Do you see that niche over there?"

"Yes," Hound said. "It's empty."

Oreb croaked harshly, and his master went to it. "There is a sense in which you're wrong. In that sense, it is the Outsider's. Pig, do you want to put your hand in it? It will do you no harm."

"Nae."

"Good. Hound, do you understand why this empty niche is the Outsider's? Why it is his now, although it may originally have been intended for one of the Nine? Possibly even for Pas?"

"Because no one knows what he looks like? I think you said something about that once."

"That's one reason, at least, though there are others. I don't mean that he is as the women of Trivigaunte believe Sphigx to be. There is no harm in our trying to make pictures of him, in showing him as a wise and noble man, for example, or as the night sky we see on Blue, a great darkness spangled with points of light. There's no harm, that is to say, unless we come to believe that he actually looks like the thing we've pictured. Then this representation is best."

Hound drew a deep breath. "But this is the way they show Sphigx!"

Later, when they had left Hound at Gold Street and were making their way to the Sun Street Quarter, Pig asked, "Nae folk h'in these hooses, bucky?"

Oreb answered for him. "No man! No girl!"

His master sighed. "After we had gone through the house in which Hound and Tansy used to live, I asked Hound when we would reach the inhabited parts of the city. I spoke softly, I suppose, and perhaps you were too preoccupied to hear us; but he said that we were already there, that the street down which we walked was one of those that had not yet been abandoned. I began counting houses then, and it seemed to me that there were five empty ones for each in which someone appeared to be living."

Pig did not reply.

"Of course someone may have been living in some of those that looked empty to me. That's entirely possible, and I hope it is true."

"Yer said ther h'empty place was ther H'outsider's."

"A cheering thought—thank you. To answer your question, a few of these houses are clearly occupied, though not many."

Pig cocked his head. "Cartwheels, bucky!"

"I can't hear them. Your ears are more acute than mine, as I have observed before. I'm glad you do, however, and I don't doubt in the least that you do. May I tell a story, Pig? You reminded me of it, and even if you have no particular pleasure in hearing it, it will give me pleasure to recount it."

"Does he mind? He does nae!"

"Thank you again. I should say at the outset that I'm not sure the manteions are the same, though I suspect they are. Hound said he couldn't recall the name of the augur who'd been in charge when he and Tansy attended sacrifice occasionally. This would have been his predecessor, I expect, if it really was the same manteion. His name was Patera Ray."

"Good man?"

"Ah, that's the point of my story, Oreb. A boy—I've forgotten his name, but it doesn't matter—and his mother were returning to the city after living for a year or so in the country. You'll recall, Pig, that Hound and Tansy moved from Endroad to the city after they were married, because there was no work for Hound in Endroad. Later, they returned.

"In much the same way, this boy and his mother had moved to the country, living in a remote farmhouse where the boy, who was still quite small, was happy in the possession of a wood and a stream too wide to jump; but lonely all the same. Now they had decided to return to the city. It was a long journey as the boy measured journeys then, though he had ridden most of the way in a sort of cart pushed by his mother that carried their belongings.

"She was very tired, and they stopped on the outskirts to spend the night with a friend before going into the city to the neat little house that another kind friend—a male friend who I suppose must have slept there from time to time, since he kept a razor there—had arranged for them to occupy some years earlier. After dinner, the poor woman went to bed and to sleep almost at once, but the boy did not."

"Good boy?"

"Not particularly, Oreb, though he thought he was, because his mother loved him. He was not old enough to understand that she would always love him, whether he behaved well or badly."

They were passing empty cellar-holes, rectangular pits edged with charred wood and filled with black water. "This quarter burned twenty years ago," he told Pig. "I'm sorry that more of it has not been rebuilt. I've been in the City of the Inhumi on Green, and it's not much more desolate than this. Here's String Street, I believe. I'm sorry to see that the fire got this far."

"Wi' yer, bucky."

"I want to finish my little tale. I'll interrupt it if I see anything worth commenting on."

He paused, collecting his thoughts. "The boy decided to take a short walk. He was hoping to find another child; but he was very conscious of the danger of becoming lost, so he walked only along the road upon which the house in which he and his mother were staying stood, reasoning that he could always retrace his steps and return to her. You will have guessed what happened already. Distracted by something or other, he became confused about the direction in which he had been walking. Thinking that he was returning to his mother and the house in which they were staying, he walked a long way until he saw an old man in black weeping upon the steps of a manteion. Until that time, the boy had been afraid to ask for help; but the old man looked so good and kind that the boy approached him and, after a minute or two of silent squirming, and taking deep breaths and letting them out, and deciding on one beginning after another and abandoning each before it was begun, he said, 'Why are you crying?'

"The old man looked up, and seeing him pointed to the carts, wagons, and litters that passed them every few seconds. 'If the wrongs I have done the gods were visible,' he said, 'there would be more than those, and four men would not be enough to weep for them all.' "

They walked on in silence after that. Occasionally they passed hovels built of salvaged timbers, so that they appeared (until they were examined closely) to have been painted black. A game among children was in progress in the next street over; the shrill cries of the participants reached them like the twittering of sparrows in a distant tree.

At last Pig asked, "That ther h'end, bucky?"

He swallowed and forced himself to speak. "It is."

"Somethin' fashin' yer?"

"Boy home?" Oreb demanded. "Find home?"

"Yes, he did." He wiped his eyes. "But he was not the same boy." Under his breath he added, "And that is not the same home."

Soft though the words had been, Pig had overheard them. "See yer house, dinna yer?"

Unable to speak, he nodded; Oreb translated: "Say yes."

"This is Silver Street. We—we were walking along Silver Street, and I didn't know it. I couldn't be sure. Pig?"

"Aye?"

"Pig, I spoke of offenses against the gods. I don't really care whether Sphigx and Scylla and the rest like what I do."

"Said yer would nae break ther statues."

"Because they didn't belong to me. And because they were—are—art, and to wantonly destroy art is always evil. But, Pig . . ." He halted.

"Auld Pig's yer pal, bucky."

"I know. That is what makes this so very hard. You were blind when you left your home in the Mountains That Look at Mountains. So you told me."

"When he left na braithrean. Aye."

"You came all this way on foot, though you are blind."

"Aye, bucky. Ho, he had some tumbles."

"Then, Pig, I am going to ask a favor, one I have no right to ask. It is something I will always reproach myself—"

"No talk!"

"For. But I'm going to ask it just the same. I brought you here. I know that. You wouldn't be in this ruined quarter if it were not for me. You might not be in Viron at all."

"H'out wi' h'it, bucky."

"I thought I was going to—to show you where I used to live. The manse, and the house where I grew up. My father's shop. Where those things once stood. I would tell you something about them, what they—those places meant to me."

He wanted to shut his eyes, but made himself watch Pig's face. "Instead, I'm asking this. Hound is getting a room in an inn, and would welcome either of us—both of us, I ought to say, together or separately. The inn is Ermine's, and it's on a hill, the Palatine, in the center of the city. Would you be willing to make your way there alone? Please?"

Pig smiled. "That h'all, bucky?"

"I'll join you there, I swear, before shadelow. But I want to—I must be alone here. I simply have to."

Pig's long arms groped for him, one big hand still grasping the sheathed sword. " 'Tis h'all right, bucky. Needed me h'on ther roads. Noo yer need me ter be gone. Dinna fash yerself. Ter much hurtin' h'in ther whorl h'already, an' sae guid-bye." Pig turned away.

"I'll rejoin you, I promise," he repeated. "Tell Hound I'm coming, please, but tell him that he is not to wait supper for me.

"Go with Pig, Oreb. Help him."

Oreb croaked unhappily, but flew.

His master stood in the street, leaning on the knobbed staff, and watched them go, unable to take a single step until they were out of sight, the big man moving so slowly while towering over the few badly dressed men and women he passed, the black bird seeming unwontedly small and vulnerable upon the big man's shoulder, its dabs of scarlet the only spots of color in the ruined landscape of blacks and grays.

Slowly, ever so slowly, the tap-tap-tapping of the brass-tipped scabbard faded. The big man stopped a passerby and spoke, too distant already to be overheard. The passerby answered, pointing up Silver Street toward the market, pointing, it seemed likely, to inform the blind man who had stopped him, possibly for the bird. Their slow progress resumed until at last they were gone, faded into the black, the gray.

He himself turned then and strode rapidly away, the bare wooden tip of his staff striking at the rutted surface of the street with every step, rapping stones and splattering mud over his shoes and the cuffs of his ragged brown trousers.

Here the children had played, taking Maytera's clotheslines for jump ropes. They had jumped to Blue some time ago, the sad, half-starved little girls with the black bangs, with the long black pigtails braided with scraps of bright yarn. To Blue, and some to Green; and those would be, largely, dead.

This fire-blackened shiprock wall, these empty, staring windows, had been the cenoby's once. While the whorl slept Maytera had knelt, not to pray but to scrub this stone step so black with ash indistinguishable from mud. Maytera Mint had dressed and undressed in there, in a darkened room behind a locked door and drawn blinds, had mended worn underclothes and covered her virginal bed with an old oilcloth tablecloth, knowing that the merest shower would lend new waters to the sagging belly of her ceiling.

That ceiling would sag no more; the leaking roof on which Maytera had climbed to watch the Trivigaunti airship was all leak now, and the broad, dark door of sturdy oak that Maytera Rose had barred each night before the last thread of sun vanished had been burned long ago—whether for firewood or in the fire that had swept the quarter when the war with Trivigaunte began scarcely mattered. Anyone might go into the cenoby now, and no one wanted to.

The stone wall that had separated the garden from the street was largely intact, though the gate and rusted padlock were gone. Inside, weeds and blackberry brambles, and—yes—a straggling grape vine climbing the blackened stump of the fig tree. Enough of their arbor remained to sit on. He sat, leaned back, and shut his eyes; and in time a youthful sibyl sat down across from him, extracted a recorder from one of the voluminous pockets of her black bombazine habit, and began to play.

Sun Street had taken him to the market, and Manteion Street to the Palatine. Here was the Caldé's Palace, its fallen wall repaired with new mortar and stones that almost matched.

"Patera . . . Patera?" The voice was soft yet thick—oddly wrong. He looked around, not so much to find the woman who spoke as to locate the augur she addressed.

"Patera . . . Patera Silk?"

He stepped back and scanned the windows. The shadow of a head and shoulders showed at one on the topmost floor. "Mucor?" He tried to keep his voice low, while making it loud enough to be heard fifty or sixty cubits overhead.

"She's not here . . . She's not here, Patera."

It's the bird, he thought. The bird makes her think I'm Silk. He realized even as he formed the thought that Oreb was gone, that he had sent Oreb away with Pig.

"Please . . ."

He had not heard the rest, yet he knew what he had been asked to do. The massive doors were locked. He banged them with the heavy brass knocker, each blow as loud as the report of a slug gun.

There was no answering sound from within the palace; and at last he turned away, tramping wearily down the balustraded steps to the street. The high window was empty now, and the thick, soft voice (female but not feminine) silent. He squinted up at the motionless sun. The shade was almost down; the market would be closing. He had told—had promised—Pig that he would rejoin him in Ermine's before evening, but Ermine's was only two or three streets away.

He had just crossed the first when fingers, thin but hard and strong, closed on his elbow. He turned to see a slight, stooped figure no larger than a child, muffled in what appeared to be sacking. "Please . . . Please, Patera. Please, won't you talk to . . . Please won't you talk to me?"

"I'm not an augur. You're thinking of somebody else."

"You've forgotten . . . You've forgotten me." The muffled sound that followed might or might not have been a sob. "Have you forgotten unhappy Olivine . . . Have you forgotten unhappy Olivine, Patera?"

There was something amiss in the angle of her head, and the high, hunched shoulders. Pity almost choked him. "No," he said, "I haven't forgotten you, Olivine." It was not a lie, he told himself fiercely; one could not forget what one had not known.

"You'll bless . . . You'll bless me?" There was joy in the voice from the sackcloth. "Sacrifice, the way you used . . . Sacrifice, the way you used to? Father's gone . . . Father's gone away. He's been gone a long, long time . . . He's been gone a long, long time, Patera." She was drawing him after her, back toward the Caldé's Palace. "There's a . . . There's a woman? In the north . . . In the north, Patera."

Someone who might help her, obviously. Someone who might be able to cure whatever disease afflicted the pathetic figure before him. "A wise woman," he hazarded.

"Oh . . . Oh, yes! Oh, I hope . . . Oh, I hope so!"

They dodged down a side street. The wall of the Caldé's Palace, elegantly varied with high narrow windows in elaborate stone frames, gave way to the almost equally imposing, windowless wall of the Caldé's Garden, a wall of heroic stones, rough and misshapen yet fitted like the pieces of a puzzle.

The diminutive, limping figure drew him on far faster than he would willingly have walked. Leprosy? It had been only a word in the Writings to him. There were running sores, or pus oozing from the skin—something disgusting. Good people in the Writings, theodidacts such as Patera Silk particularly, were exceedingly kind to those who suffered this dread disease, which he had heard was rare—had heard from an augur, probably. From someone such as Patera Remora, who had attended the schola.

Abruptly they stopped. A door of iron so low that he would

almost have to crawl through like Pig was deeply set between mammoth stones, in a dark little recess that also held an empty bottle and brown, wind-blown leaves. From some recess equally dark within her sackcloth, Olivine produced a brass key bruised with verdigris; there was a dim flash, as of polished steel. Thrust into the iron door, the key rattled and squealed. A bolt thumped solidly, and Olivine whispered, *"Quadrifons . . ."*

The iron door swung back.

Ducking through the doorway, he had to bend lower still to pass beneath the massive limbs of an ancient oak. Beyond was a bed of bright chrysanthemums, glorious in the last flickering sunshine. Somewhere a fountain played. "I didn't know there were doors like that," he said, sounding inane even to himself. "I mean doors that had to have a word, and a key as well." And then, "That is a sacred name. So sacred that it's hardly ever used. I'm surprised you know it."

She stopped and looked back him. He thought he caught the gleam of thick spectacles between the rough cloth that covered her head and the fold of rough cloth that masked her face. "It's just a . . . It's just a word. The one for the . . . The one for the door. My . . . My mother." (Something deeply pathetic had entered her voice.) "I don't remember . . . I don't remember her. She was a . . . She was a sibyl? That's what my father . . . That's what my father says. She was a . . . She was a sibyl."

"Would you like to me to tell you about Quadrifons?"

Olivine nodded, the motion almost imperceptible beneath the shadowing oak limbs and the folds of cloth. "Would you . . . Would you, Patera?"

"I'm not Patera Silk," he said. "You're wrong about that. But I'll tell you what I know, which isn't much."

His back felt as though it might break; kneeling was a great relief. "Quadrifons is the most holy of the minor gods. I mean, he's called that in the Chrasmologic Writings. If it were left to me—as plainly it is not—I'd say that the Outsider is the most holy god, and indeed that he's the only god, major or minor, who's really holy at all." He laughed, a trifle nervously. "So you see why I'm not an augur, Olivine. But the Writings say it's Quadrifons, and the Chapter says that his name is so holy that it should hardly ever be used, so it won't be profaned."

"Go . . . Go on."

"I don't know you, so I really don't know whether you would be inclined to profane the name of a god—"

She shook her head.

"But I'm inclined to doubt it. You don't strike me as a fortunate person, and it's commonly the fortunate among us who do that. On the chance that I'm wrong, however, I must tell you that we don't harm the gods when we mingle their names with our curses and obscenities. We harm ourselves. I said that I didn't regard most gods as holy, but they don't have to be for our malice and mockery to recoil upon ourselves." He looked up at her shrouded face, hoping to see he had made his point, but learned nothing. "There is much more I might say, Olivine—things I may say to you another time, when we know each other better. But you wanted to know about Quadrifons."

She nodded.

"I really know very little about him, however, and I doubt that anyone knows much more than I. Just as Pas is said to be a two-headed god—do you know about that?"

"Oh . . . Oh, yes." She sounded despondent.

"Quadrifons is a four-faced one. That is to say, he has only one head, but there is a face on every side of it, so that he looks east and west, and north and south, all at the same time. He's the god of bridges, passageways, and intersections, although he's clearly more important than those few and simple things would appear to imply. I told you he had four faces."

There was no sound but the tinkling of the fountain; then she said, "I've got a little statue with the two . . . I've got a little statue with the two heads."

"I'd like to see it. You do realize, don't you, that it's only a conventional representation? We need to picture Pas to ourselves during our private devotions sometimes, and statuettes and colored prints help us do it. I should tell you that just as Pas is depicted occasionally as a whirlwind, Quadrifons is sometimes shown as a sort of monster, combining Pas's eagle with Sphigx's lion. May I talk about Sphigx for a moment? It will seem to you that I've left the subject, but I assure you that what I want to say bears upon it."

"Go . . . Go ahead." By a sort of controlled collapse, she sat down opposite him, hugging her knees to her chest. Even through several thicknesses of sackcloth, it was apparent that she had sharp knees.

"This morning two friends and I were discussing Sphigx. She's the patroness of Trivigaunte, but she won't let the Trivigauntis make pictures or statues representing her, and we talked about that."

"Uh . . . Uh-huh."

"That's what I used to say to Patera Silk." He smiled at the memory. "He'd tell me to think of the honor of our Sun Street Palaestra, and say yes instead."

"I remember when . . . I remember when you were caldé."

"When Patera Silk was, you mean. My own name is Horn."

She nodded again.

"In that case, Caldé Bison must have let you stay on when he attained to the office. That was good of him."

"I don't think . . . I don't think he knows I'm here. Were you going to say Sphigx was like Quadrifons, keeping his name . . . Were you going to say Sphigx was like Quadrifons, keeping his name secret?"

"That's very perceptive of you. Yes, I was. You see, Olivine, there used to be a woman with a table in the market who sold images of Sphigx. They would have been quite similar to your image of Pas, I suppose."

"Mine's ivory . . . Mine's ivory, Patera."

He nodded thoughtfully. "These were wood. Or at least, they appeared to be wood. This woman was a Trivigaunti spy, and what she was doing—using the little wooden images to send information—was really very clever, because no one who knew the customs of her city would associate images of Sphigx with Trivigaunte. Later on Blue, I learned that Trivigauntis who go abroad often buy images of Sphigx, which they carry home with them and hide."

"I don't . . . I don't understand." Olivine cocked her head, and again he caught the glint of glass.

"Why they want them? Because they're not supposed to have them, I suppose. Or because they feel that they provide special access to the goddess. Quadrifons' name—with your key—gives you special access to this lovely garden." He paused, looking beyond the branches that concealed them. "I used to live in the Caldé's Palace too, Olivine. It had just been reopened, and this was weeds and a few trees; but Viron itself was thronged with people. When you and Quadrifons opened the door for me, those leaves and weeds were all that I expected to see. It never occurred to me that this garden would be tended as it was in the days of Caldé Tussah when so much of the city lies in ruins. I find it heartening."

She had risen, and he rose too. "I merely wanted to say that by prohibiting the possession of her image in Trivigaunte, Sphigx has made it highly valued there. Quadrifons may have had something of the same kind in mind when he restricted the use of his name. Or he may have hoped to link himself to the Outsider, whose true name is unknown."

They left the spreading branches and crossed a bright, soft lawn. Seeing them, a white-haired man dropped his hoe and knelt.

"He wants your blessing . . ."

There seemed to be no help for it; he sketched the sign of addition over the old man's head. "Blessed be you in the Most Sacred Name of Pas, Father of the Gods, in those of his living children, in that of the patron of doors and crossroads, and in that of the Obscure Outsider, whom we pray will bless this, our Holy City of Viron."

"Come on . . . Come on, Patera." Olivine tugged his sleeve. "We've got to get some . . . We've got to get some bread." He followed, reflecting gloomily that the old man had probably noticed how very irregular his blessing had been, although he had kept his voice low and spoken as rapidly as he could.

A door (wooden, this time, although bound with iron) opened on a scullery, the scullery on the kitchen he vaguely remembered. A cook paring carrots froze as they entered, her mouth a perfect circle of surprise. The door of a cupboard rattled and banged; then Olivine was drawing him up a dark stair, her limp more pronounced than ever. Almost running, they passed a landing.

The next had a small window; he stopped before it to gasp for breath. "This floor."

"No . . . No, Patera. I was born down there . . . I was born down there, but my room's under the roof."

"I know, my child. I saw you there."

She shifted the small loaf to her other hand, and reached out to stroke his tunic. "You're . . . You're dirty."

"I've been traveling rough, I'm afraid. Last night I slept on the floor. It was a very dirty floor, too. Besides you were sitting on the ground, remember? And I knelt on it. I don't believe I even dusted my knees when I stood up. But, Olivine, I'd like to ask a personal question. May I?" She was rubbing a double thickness of his soiled tunic between her forefinger and thumb, and he had seen clearly that they were metal.

"Wouldn't you like . . . Wouldn't you like clean clothes?"

"Very much. I'd like a bath, too; but I'm afraid both are impossible."

She glanced up, her face inscrutable behind its swaddling sackcloth. "I know a . . . I know a place."

"Where I might take a bath? That's very good of you. It's wonderful of you, in fact; but before we leave this floor, there is something I must see—a certain room into which I must go, if I possibly can. I can find it for myself, I believe, and I'll rejoin you here afterward, or anywhere you choose."

"Here . . . Here, Patera." She opened a door; and he saw a corridor lined with more. He had forgotten it or thought he had, but the pattern in its carpet was like a blow.

"Yes, there. My—Nettle and I stayed here once. It was only for a few days, though it seemed forever then." He spoke to himself more than to her, but found it impossible to stop. "It was always cold, and we took blankets from other rooms—from empty rooms, I ought to say. There was a little fireplace, and the first one to get back at night would raid the woodbox in the kitchen." He paused to look at the hand that held the bread Olivine had gotten there. "And make a fire. There was an old brass pan you filled with coals to warm the bed, and we'd strip and bathe and huddle naked under the blankets trying to keep warm."

He pushed past her, stepping into the remembered corridor and half afraid it might vanish. They had not used this stair, he decided, but another larger one nearer the front, reaching the kitchen from the ground floor. "We were wonderfully happy here, as happy as we were capable of being—which was very happy indeed in those days—and happier than we were ever to be on Blue, though we were very happy there, too, sometimes."

Olivine pointed to a door.

"No, it was down that way, I'm sure."

"Where you can . . . Where you can wash? I'll find clean . . . I'll find clean clothes."

"I can't let you steal for me, my child, if that's what you're proposing."

"From an old storeroom . . . From an old storeroom, Patera. Nobody . . . Nobody cares." She stepped back into the stairwell again, and shut the door.

Shrugging, he opened the one she had indicated. A small bedroom, smaller even than the one he had shared with Mother so long ago. The bed, a chest of drawers, and a bedside table so small that it might almost have been a toy. No washstand, which presumably meant that the door that appeared to belong to a closet led to a lavatory. The thought of a bath, even a sponge bath with cold water, was irresistible; removing his tunic with one swift gesture, he threw open the door.

11

My Trial

Now that I have leisure to write again, I am ready to throw the whole thing overboard. We put out night before last, having waited half a day for a wind, and have been coasting ever since, bedeviled by light airs. I spent yesterday—or most of it—rereading everything that I have written since I began to write back in Gaon. I have covered a lot of paper and wasted hundreds of hours, all without more than mentioning my search for Patera Silk in the *Whorl*—the central reason for my trip; and (I must face the fact) the great failure of my life.

Nor have I described my trial and the overthrow of Dorp's judges, which I promised to do again and again the last time I wrote and which I intend to do in a moment. Perhaps I shall never pen an account of my return to Old Viron, of meeting my father there, and the rest of it. Perhaps it is better so.

Hoof and Hide were afraid they would be arrested. I assured them that as long as they were circumspect they had nothing to fear. And so it proved, although Wijzer and Wapen, both local men with extensive connections among the sailors and boat owners, accomplished much more. At the end (which is to say after I had been removed from Aanvagen's in chains) Beroep and Strik joined them. They had little time in which to work, but they brought us more than a hundred fighters between them—so many that the slug guns I had bought were insufficient, and they had to buy more by ones and twos out of their own pockets. Once the rebellion was under way, we were joined by many more who had only knives and clubs; but I am proud to say that all our original men had slug guns, every one of them.

In the matter of women we followed General Mint's example and used them mostly to care for the wounded and bring ammunition to the fighters. A few fought, however, and those acquitted themselves very well. There were plans for them to supply food, but our rebellion did not last long enough to require it. These women, most of them young and poor, were organized entirely by Vadsig; all she accomplished and the shrewdness and courage with which she did it are beyond praise.

But I am getting ahead of my account. First of all, I should say that I had been hoping above all else for help from Mora and Fava. As I sat in my cell in the Palace of Justice, I managed to convince myself that everything depended on them, that if they came and were able to possess Judge Hamer, I would go free. I tried very hard not to think of my punishment if they did not come, and waited with no great hope for some sign from them. My cell was dark, cold, and indescribably filthy. I felt certain that if I knew I was to be confined for years in such a place I would take my own life, and sooner rather than later. I had left my azoth with Hide, and did not know that he had entrusted it to Vadsig, fearing he would be rearrested. If I had it, I might well have killed myself then and there—or cut my way out and fled, as is more likely.

Legermen came for me at last. I asked that my shackles be removed, pointing out that I was in poor health and had as yet been convicted of nothing. They said it was up to their lieutenant. I asked them to take me to him, and they said that was what they were doing. Their lieutenant would escort me into court in person.

He was older than I had expected, thirty perhaps. "Kenbaar I am, mysire. A friend of Sergeant Azijin you are? Well of you he speaks."

It occurred to me then that my friend Sergeant Azijin might be killed if the rebellion I had been preparing actually took place. I comforted myself with the reflection that without Mora and Fava it was far more likely that he and his comrades would kill Hoof, Hide, Vadsig, and me. And hundreds more besides.

"Without an order of Judge Hamer, nothing I can do, mysire." Lieutenant Kenbaar told me as he removed my fetters. "Chained you must be he does not say, so these off I can take. But if to run you try, shoot I must."

I suppose I must have thanked him and told him that I would not attempt to escape, although I remember only that I rubbed my wrists and felt dismayed that he would be in the courtroom with his needler. I had hoped that there would be few weapons present other than the ones we brought—provided, that is, that half or a quarter of those who had sworn to come did so, and that they were not searched.

Soon I was marched into the courtroom, unchained indeed but preceded by Lieutenant Kenbaar with a drawn sword and followed by three legermen with slug guns. They too dismayed me, as can be imagined; try to conceive of my feelings when I saw almost a hundred armed legermen—Sergeant Azijin among them—along all four walls of a courtroom vastly larger than I had imagined.

(Here let me interrupt my account to say that I had been misled by the courtrooms I had seen in our Juzgado. I should have realized that in Dorp, where judges twisted the law to suit themselves, such rooms would be of far greater importance.)

I honestly cannot say whether the room was filled already when I came—although others have told me that was the case—or the audience filed in after I had taken my seat beside Vent. When we had sat there for some time, he calmly sorting and resorting the same papers and I with my head in my hands, I asked him whether it was not possible for my daughter, at least, to sit with me.

"For that no provision there is, Mysire Horn. In the row behind family and friends sit. Then so many in court we do not have. For this trial the whole of Dorp eager is. Perhaps into this courtroom even your daughter does not get."

Jahlee touched my shoulder as he spoke. Turning in my seat, I saw Hoof and Hide, Vadsig, Aanvagen, and a dozen others whose faces seemed familiar though I could put no names to them, and felt a thrill of hope.

Hamer entered with much pomp and a bodyguard of clerks, called the court to order, and asked the prosecutor, a tall thin man I had not seen before, whether he was prepared. He stood, and declared he was.

Judge Hamer then asked Vent the same question. Vent rose. "No, Mysire Rechtor." The judge waited for him to say more, but he did not.

"Why are you not ready, Mysire Advocast Vent?" This simple

question was salted with a whorl of sarcasm. "This to the court you must explain."

"If me you intend, Mysire Rechtor, if me in my person it is you ask, prepared I am. If the defense you intend, not we are—"

About than the proceedings were thrown into confusion by the arrival of a small, very erect man with a shock of white hair and one of those round soft-looking faces that breathe the very essence of stupidity. He was dressed entirely in black, and marched down the center aisle flourishing a little staff made of the vertebrae of some animal, proclaiming in a high, thin voice, "Here I am, Mysire Rechtor. Taal is here. Do not without him begin. A crush in the corridor, Mysire Rechtor, in the street worse. Delayed I was—delayed I was!"

He wedged himself between Vent and me and shook my hand very heartily, saying in a whisper that must have been audible all over the room, "Mysire Horn. An honor it is—a pleasure it is. A prince so distinguished you are. A conqueror, but humbly the gods you serve!"

Judge Hamer hammered his tall desk. "Silence! Silence! Ready you are Mysire Advocaat Taal?"

He rose with the help of his staff and seemed to require a moment to collect his thoughts. "Ready we are, Mysire Rechtor. A motion—my motion you will entertain, Mysire Rechtor? That this be dismissed ab initio, I move."

There was a buzz of excited talk, which the judge rapidly silenced. Taal's motion was denied and the prosecution was invited to present its case. Nat and others testified; I will not burden this account with the details, beyond saying that I was appalled to see matters proceed as quickly as they did.

Vent then rose and made a brief opening speech to the judge. "Mysire Rechtor, our motion to dismiss you heard. Not frivolously it we made. Here no crime is. The law we do not deny. Contrary to the law to imprison another it is. A serious offense it is. This our client has not done. This we will prove."

Another buzz of talk, and a skeptical look from Judge Hamer.

"Neither to our law subject he is. This also we will prove."

Stunned silence.

Taal rose, and seeming to strain his high, reedy voice, said loudly, "Call Mysire Ziek!"

A legerman fetched him from an adjoining room.

"A merchant you are?"

He was, and with some prompting from Taal and Vent, he told of making up the party of merchants, of Nat's forcing his way into it, and of encountering us.

"More than you they are?" (This was Vent.)

"No, mysire."

"Overpowering you they are?"

"No, mysire."

"Many servants they have, and armed these servants are? Slug guns they have? Needlers?"

"Yes, Mysire Advocaat. No, Mysire Advocaat."

"No needlers? Us tell you must."

"Three only they are. A slug gun the young man has, mysire."

Taal raised his eyebrows, which are white too and very thick. "One slug gun, mysire? Of it terrified all of you were?"

"No, Mysire Taal."

"Not, should I hope. Nat's testimony you did not hear?"

"No, Mysire Taal. It to hear, me they would not allow."

"Proper that is. Testis oculatus unus plus valet quam auriti decem. With him servants Nat had?"

"Yes, Mysire Taal. Four."

"Weapons they had?"

"Yes, mysire."

"In this court alleged it is that Mysire Horn, old he is and unarmed he was, Mysire Nat to remain with him he forced."

By that time I had practically ceased to hear them. I was watching a picture on one side of the courtroom. It was a large painting, executed in browns and various shades of orange, of robed men seated around a table. It was suspended by a tasseled cord from an ornamental hook in the shape of a leaping collarfish, and it had begun to swing.

Wijzer came forward to speak with me. "Sent to the old whorl for Mysire Silk you were? This Hide says. A good boy he is?"

"Yes. So is Hoof."

Wijzer nodded and seated himself on the gunwale, one hand grasping a stay. He is larger than most men, solid-looking, with a big, red face. "From New Viron you are? Marrow there you know?"

It reminded me irresistibly of what I had just been writing. I said, "Yes, Mysire Advocaat."

The red face became redder still as he squinted for a moment at the sun. "Me you do not know?"

"Of course I—wait. From New Viron, you mean. What a fool I've been! You're the trader who told me about Pajarocu!"

From his perch on the stay, considerably higher than Wijzer's big, freckled hand, Oreb inquired, "Good man?" Babbie (who was asleep at my feet) raised his massive head and winked, his sign of cautious affirmation.

Wijzer looked from one to the other. "Me you remember, Mysire Horn?"

"Certainly, and I should have placed you much sooner. Marrow told me he'd found a trader who might be able to help me, and the three of us ate at Marrow's—it was a very good dinner. He has a good cook."

For a moment Wijzer studied me. "Dead Marrow is."

"I'm sorry to hear it. He didn't die by violence, I hope."

Wijzer shook his head.

"He was a middle-aged man when we came here twenty years ago. Though it is twenty-two years now, I suppose." I called to Hoof, who was in the waist talking to Hide and Vadsig, and asked how long I had been gone.

"Since summer of year before last, Father."

"Nearly two years," I told Wijzer, "though when I look at my sons it seems that it must surely be longer. They were hardly more than children when I left; now they are young men."

"Brave young men they are. Gallant young men."

I agreed.

"At Judge Kenner's, them I see. Killed both will be I think, but they run and shoot, shoot and run, and after them my sailors come. Young lions they are."

I thanked him. "You must have seen them at my trial as well. I saw you in the audience, and they were sitting almost directly behind me."

Wijzer nodded. "Them in we let. Beroep and me. His family we say, so for them everyone aside moves."

"Would you be willing to give me your impressions of my trial? You would be doing me a great favor, Captain."

"Mine, Mysire Horn?" He looked back at the steersman, then out at the choppy gray-green water. "You too saw."

"Yes, but I would like to have someone else's impressions, and you are a shrewd observer."

He laughed. "Not, my wife thinks."

"Men and women frequently differ as to what is important."

"That girl Vadsig you must ask, mysire, or your daughter." He eyed me slyly.

"Perhaps I will, but I would like your impressions. I have found it difficult to write about. The details keep getting in my way."

I smiled, and Wijzer did too.

"In the course of writing all I have—not just what you see here, but much more that is put away with the clothes I bought in Dorp—"

"New clothes you buy, mysire, but old ones you wear. On a boat wise that is."

"I've learned that I have a sort of mania for writing down conversations. If you would tell me now what you remember best about my trial, I will certainly write that, and my account of it will be so much to the good."

He nodded, his eyes again on the waves and the clouds, then shouted at the young man in the stern. "What I best remember you wish to know, Mysire Horn?"

I nodded (eagerly, I hoped). When he said nothing, I ventured, "The Red Sun Whorl is what you remember best, I imagine. The tower and the pits beneath it."

"This you call that rotting town?" Wijzer shook his head. "Not, I remember. To forget I try." He raised an imaginary bottle to his mouth and pretended to drink.

"Man talk!" Oreb insisted.

"What I remember? Those leggy fellows."

"The Vanished People? I had wondered about that. Surely many of you must have thought that they were no more than tall men in masks."

"It may be, mysire, but four arms they had."

"They were not men like us, Captain, I assure you. They were the Neighbors, whom we on this side of the sea generally call the Vanished People."

"Not that men they may be I think. This others may think, I mean. Vanished Men they were, I know. My crew," he shrugged, "me they serve. These, you serve, Mysire Horn?"

"No. They are my friends, not my employers."

"A fair wind they will give?"

"Perhaps they could—I don't know. Certainly I won't ask it. Let us sail with our own wind, Captain." Now it was I, not he, who was looking out to sea; and I could not repress the thought that Seawrack was there beneath the tossing waves.

"Big wet," Oreb pronounced. And, "Bad place!"

"It's a bad place for birds, certainly—or at least a bad place for such birds as are not sea birds; but you'll learn very quickly to patrol its beaches for dead fish."

Wijzer chuckled.

"Is that the moment in my trial you recall most clearly? When the Vanished People came into the courtroom? Tell me about it, please. What you saw and heard and felt?"

"Taal I watched. Three goldcards for him I gave. This you know?"

"Yes and no. Beroep explained that you and he, with Strik and Ziek, all contributed. Taal wanted a great deal to defend me, Beroep said, because it would cost him the judges' favor; but they—you and your friends—were afraid the rebellion would never actually take place."

Wijzer nodded. "Without the rest, not it would. Without the Vanished Men, mysire."

"Perhaps you're right."

"And him." The point of his sea boot did not quite touch Babbie's broad back. "Never so much I laughed."

I confessed that I had not thought it funny at the time, though it seemed so in retrospect.

"Laugh I did and my sides hold, but out with my needler too. Why this is do you think, Mysire Horn?" He was smiling, but his clear blue eyes were serious.

"I imagine it was because you thought one of the legermen might shoot poor Babbie for chasing Judge Hamer around the room like that—it was certainly what I thought myself."

"No, mysire." Wijzer shook his head slowly. "Your daughter it was. A pretty girl she is. Not so pretty as my Cijfer, but beautiful even. Her name I forget."

"Jahlee."

"Jahlee. Yes. Too she laughs. Never laughing like hers I hear, mysire."

Oreb exclaimed, "Bad thing!" and I told him to be quiet.

"To your sons I speak. Good boys they are. Our sister, they say. Our sister. But not my eyes they meet, when this they say. Below sleeping she is?"

"When I last saw her, yes."

"My boat this is." Wijzer thumped the deck with the heel of his boot, "If no one on my boat she harms, nothing I do."

"But if she harms someone, you will be compelled to take steps. I understand, Captain."

He turned to go.

"Will you answer one question for me? How did Taal know to call the Vanished People? I hadn't even spoken with him. If the four of you instructed him to do it, how did you know?"

"Not we did, mysire." Wijzer studied me again. "This thing I know, you think? Wrong you are. Not I know."

"Good man!" Oreb assured me.

"I didn't think you did—say rather that I hoped you did, Captain. I hoped it, because I'd like very much to know myself."

"What I think, you I tell. To you they speak?"

I nodded. "Sometimes they do."

"To you alone they speak? This they say?"

He left without waiting for an answer, and after a moment I told Babbie to go below and watch Jahlee, permitting no one to harm or even touch her, to which Oreb muttered, "Good. Good."

Babbie himself simply rose to obey, thick black claws (which seem so blunt when he puts a paw in my lap in supplication, so terrible when he slashes my foes with them) clicking along the deck very much as they used to when the two of us were the sole occupants of my little sloop and there was nothing forward and nothing behind, nothing to port and nothing to starboard but the calm blue sky and the rolling sea.

I feel like going below myself. I will not—not for a few more minutes at least—because I know that it is as cold there as it is here, and dark, with a hundred vicious drafts in place of this bracing wind. Like the *Whorl* and its brave, suffering peoples, I cling to my sun as long as I can.

It was the Neighbors who had impressed Wijzer most—Wijzer who is already trying to forget the Red Sun Whorl, and who will have succeeded in convincing himself that it was only a bad dream within a month.

How many of the bad dreams I remember were not really dreams at all? Does it make any difference? We live our lives in our thoughts, or we do not live. A man imagines his wife faithful, and is happy. What difference does it make whether she is or is not, as long as he believes it? Read carefully, my sons!

Doubtless the reality (known only to herself and the gods) is that she is faithful at times and unfaithful at others, like other women.

From this we see why the gods are needed. They see what is real—or if they do not, we imagine they do. Surely the Outsider must, if it is true that Pas and the rest worship him. How do the people with whom we walk in our dreams perceive our waking? The people who speak to us there, and to whom we speak? We die to them; do our corpses remain behind until the companions of our sleep bury them weeping?

Last night I dreamed of finding this pen case in Viron—no doubt the dream was what set me writing again today. Now in reality (as I understand it) I found it between the time I left my old manteion and the time Maytera's daughter called to me from a fifth-floor window. Was it more real when I found it than when I dreamed it? How could it be, when there was no difference between the two? Was it actually where my father's shop once stood that I found it? Or is that merely a part of the dream my waking mind has not yet rejected? It seems a little too pat to be true, yet memory assures me of it now.

How tall they were, the Neighbors! Robed in dignity!

Taal's voice was a brazen trumpet: *"Upon the Vanished People, upon those once lords of this whorl, I call. The good character of my client Mysire Horn let them defend!"* Everyone must have thought it a mere trick of rhetoric, and certainly there was no one in the courtroom more convinced of it than I. I had spoken with them and explained my predicament, and they had promised to help me if they could; but I had imagined signs and wonders of the sort I hoped for (and to some degree received) from Mora and Fava, not this uncanny spectacle of walking legends mounting the steps to the judge's right and sitting one by one in the little witness chair to deliver their solemn testimony.

"Mysire Windcloud, my life to our law I have devoted, but never one of you in court I have seen. Why have you come?"

"How could I not?"

Hamer snapped, "Questions you may not ask, mysire," which I think very brave of him.

"Why not?"

Taal explained, "Contrary to our law it is, mysire."

"Then I will ask no more until Dorp's law is altered, though Dorp will lose by it. We have come because honor compels us."

"Because accused your friend here stands?"

"Because the people of your town do."

"Who accuses us?"

Hamer rapped on his desk. "To the case before us yourself you must confine, Mysire Taal."

A large picture crashed to the floor, and about half the onlookers sprang to their feet.

Taal asked softly, "That you did, Mysire Windcloud?"

"No."

Judge Hamer leaned toward him, pointing with the mace of office. "Speak you must, mysire! It who did?"

"You." There was something in the single flat word that frightened even the judge, and which I myself found terrifying.

Taal addressed the court. "Mysire Rechtor, what we do here dangerous it is. Question Mysire Windcloud I must, but not you need. With all honor to the court, this I suggest."

I felt the building tremble as he spoke; and Hamer nodded, his face pale.

"My client, Mysire Horn. Him how long have you known?"

"Since I gave him my cup." Windcloud's face turned toward me, and though I could not see his eyes—I have never seen the eyes of any of them—I felt his glance.

"In days and years you cannot say, mysire?"

"No."

"An honest man he is?"

"Too much so."

"You he serves?"

"Yes, he does." That surprised me, I confess; I am still thinking about it.

"A traitor to our breed he is?"

"No." There was amusement in the word, I believe.

"To this case alone address myself I must, mysire. This you understand. That this whorl to us you have given, not relevant it is. About that, not I may ask. About your knowledge of men's characters I may inquire, if Mysire Rechtor permits. A man as here 'a man' we say, not you are?"

"I am not, but a man of my own race."

"Many men, however, you have known, mysire? Men such as I am and as Mysire Rechtor is?"

"Yes. I was one of those who boarded your whorl when it neared our sun. In the *Whorl,* I made the acquaintance of many of your race, and I have known others since, on both the whorls we once called ours."

"Of these, my client Mysire Horn one is?"

"Yes. We became better acquainted when he was living in my house, some distance from here. I have found him to be an honorable man, devoted to your kind."

"If to our kind devoted he is, to yours a foe he must be, mysire. That do you deny?"

"I do. You spoke of your breed. You breed your own foes, who are our foes as well, those who would destroy others for gain and rob them for power." Here Windcloud paused—I shall never forget it, and I doubt that anyone who was present will—and turned his shadowed face, very slowly, toward Hamer.

"Your guest Mysire Horn was. This you have said. Invite him you did?"

"No. Another 'man' who was living in my house brought him. He was not afraid of me, as the others were."

"This you did, though living in your house without your permission he was?"

"Soon it will be spring. The white fishcatchers will return, booming, and darkening your sky which was ours in their mating flight. Two will nest upon your chimney, though you will not invite them."

Windcloud's shadowed gaze had been upon Hamer, although he had addressed Taal; at this point he directed it to Nat. "You say he has harmed you, yet I see you whole, fat, and free, while another stands beside him with a sword."

To his everlasting credit, Nat rose and tried to withdraw his accusation; but Hamer would not permit it, asking whether the statements he had made were false and warning him that he would be prosecuted for lying under oath if he acknowledged that they were.

It was only then that I truly understood what had gone wrong in Dorp. It was not that its judges took bribes or that they used their power to enrich themselves, although they certainly did. It was that they had created a system that slowly but surely destroyed all who came in contact with it. Left to work it would destroy me, as Nat had desired; but it would destroy Nat as well, and Dorp itself.

Vadsig came to talk to me. "Here you sit, Mysire Horn, writing and writing. To us you do not speak."

"Poor man!" Oreb confirmed; and I protested that I talked to him, if only to tell him to be quiet, and that I had talked to Captain Wijzer.

"You we miss. Hide and Hoof it is. Me, also, mysire. Angry with us you are?"

"Not at all. But, Vadsig, I'd much rather have you young people desirous of my company than longing for my absence."

"Me to go you want?" She jumped up, shaking her full skirt and pretending to be deeply offended. "Tell me you must! Say back to the kitchen you go, dirty Vadsig!"

I protested that no man could possibly object to the company of such a woman as she.

She sat again. "When your town we reach, married Mysire Hide and I will be. His mother's blessing he wishes. To her a good son he is."

"I know, Vadsig, and he's a good son to me as well. I couldn't be happier for you both."

"The blessing she gives, mysire? This you think?"

"Good girl?" Oreb inquired. Knowing that he meant you, dear Nettle, I nodded.

"Not she gives, I think." Vadsig eyed me sidelong to gauge my reaction.

"You're mistaken," I said, and my thoughts were full of you.

"No cards I have, mysire."

I dropped five or six into her lap, not real cards such as we used in Viron, but the shining gold and silver imitations that we see more and more here on Blue.

She would not touch them. "To Hide already so much you give, mysire."

"But I have given nothing to you, Vadsig, and I owe you a great deal."

"Mora and Fava you owe."

"I do indeed, and I'll try to repay them if I ever get the opportunity. At this moment I have the opportunity to repay you, to a small degree; and I intend to grab it. I won't detail all you did for us—you know it best. But I know it well enough, and those cards are merely a token."

"Also your son you give?" Her upper lip trembled, its minute motion piteously revealed by the brilliant sunlight.

"Are you asking whether I'll bless your union? Of course I will. I do. I'll perform the ceremony myself if you wish it, though it would be better to have His Cognizance Patera Remora. I can assist him, if he will permit it."

"A poor wife I will make." She smoothed her gown, pressing it against her body to show that she was slender to the point of emaciation.

"Before I returned here I met a young woman named Olivine, Vadsig. If she were here with us—and in a sense she is, for I have a part of her—she would point out to you that you can give a man your love and bear children. She could do neither, and she would gladly trade every one of the centuries the gods may allow her for your next year."

Vadsig's eyes melted. "Could not you help her, mysire?"

"No. She helped me."

Oreb picked up the first word, joining it to his favorite predicate. "No cut!"

I nodded. "I tried not to harm her, Oreb. It was the best that I could manage."

"Her hair?" Vadsig plunged thin fingers into her short orange tresses. "Ugly as mine it was?"

"She had none. As for yours, it is clean and straight and strong—all admirable things."

"A bad color it is, mysire."

"A good woman's hair is never of a bad color," I told her.

We talked more, she expressing her fears of you and your rejection, and I assuring her that all were groundless, as indeed I feel certain they are. Let her fear childbirth, poor child, and murderous rape in lawless New Viron; she has more than enough to worry about without fantasies.

Then, "Sometime back like you I go, mysire?"

"Back to Viron, you mean, Vadsig?"

"To Viron, yes, mysire. Also to Grotestad. To go to the Long Sun Whorl I would like. Always of it you talk, and cook, and my old master and mistress. In Grotestad they were born, mysire, but never it I have seen."

I told her it was possible she would.

"There the Vanished People went?"

I nodded.

"To greet us it was?"

"You might put it so, though they were sensible enough to find out a good deal about us—and infect us with inhumi—"

"Bad thing!"

"Before they ventured to greet even a few of us."

"Bad it was," Vadsig agreed with Oreb.

"To leave inhumi among us?" I shook my head. "It was a small price to pay for two whorls, and it enabled the Neighbors to gauge much more accurately the differences between our race and their own."

"Because our blood they drink, mysire?"

For a moment I considered how I might explain without violating my promise. "You can't see yourself, Vadsig."

"In the mirror I see."

I shook my head. "Has anyone told you that you have wonderful eyes?"

She flushed, shrugging. "Hide it says."

"But you do not believe him, because you know he loves you. You are still very young. When you are older, perhaps you will come to understand that of all the emotions—and indifference, too, because even indifference is an emotion of a sort—only love sees the unveiled truth."

"See good!"

"Yes, love sees well, and it is well to see. No matter how wonderful your eyes are, however, Vadsig, they cannot look back upon themselves. You see yourself, when you see yourself at all, in silvered glass. I used to know a very clever person who inspected his appearance in the side of a silver teapot every morning."

She smiled, as I had hoped she would. "A spoon in his pocket he might have carried, mysire."

"He knew, of course, that his image was distorted. You compare your own to that of other women you see in reality; but if you were wiser, you might compare their reflections to yours. That is what the Neighbors did. Knowing what their own inhumi were like, they gave us ours so they might compare the two. I wish I knew what they concluded, though I know what they did."

"The whorls they gave?" She looked around her as she spoke, at the beamy brown boat in which we sat, and the broad blue sea, the blue sky dotted with clouds and white birds, and the distant shore; and I dared to hope, as I do still, that she was seeing them a little differently.

"Yes. The inhumi had effectively ruined their entire race, Vadsig. I don't mean that all of them were dead, but that the civilization they had built had failed them when the shock came. Many had left these whorls already, fleeing the inhumi but taking inhumi with them."

"Their blood to drink?" She shuddered, and there was nothing feigned about it. "Not I understand, mysire."

"I said that we could not see ourselves directly, Vadsig. We need mirrors for that. We cannot run away from ourselves, either."

I heard the clicking of Babbie's claws over the creaking of the rigging as I spoke, and looked around to see Jahlee's head emerging from the little hatch. I motioned for her to join us, and Vadsig whispered, "So beautiful she is!"

We three talked together then for an hour or more. But it will soon be too dark to write, and I smell supper. I will write about all that some other time, perhaps.

12

PALACES

"You should not come in here, Olivine!" A glance showed that the tepid water was reassuringly obscured by suds and clouded with soap.

"You don't have to duck down like that . . . You don't have to duck down like that, Patera. . . ."

He snorted. "Nor do you have to look in on me every five minutes. I'm not going to drown."

"I just wanted to tell you your new clothes are out . . . I just wanted to tell you your new clothes are out here."

The door shut softly, and he stood up. The towel, like everything else in the tiny room, was within easy reach. As he dried himself, he realized that his old clothing was gone, save for his shoes. She had taken his tunic, his trousers, his filthy stockings, and his underdrawers the first time she had opened the door, beyond a doubt; he had been too busy hiding to notice. His corn, the precious seed corn he had obtained so easily, had been in a trousers pocket; but presumably his old clothes were in the bedroom. He stepped out of the tub, took the plug from the drain, and sat on the necessary stool to dry his feet.

That done, he wrapped his loins in his towel. "Are you out there, Olivine?" He followed the words with three sharp raps on the door, but there was no reply. Cautiously, he opened it.

Clean drawers, black trousers, and a black tunic waited on the bed. Beside them lay what appeared to be an augur's black robe, neatly folded; his seed corn was on that, with a clean handkerchief, new stockings, his spectacles, two cards, and his newly found pen case, the whole surrounded by his prayer beads. His old clothes and the enameled lantern were nowhere to be seen. Sighing, he dressed.

The bedroom door opened as he was tying his shoes. "Can we go up now . . . Can we go up now, Patera?"

"You were watching me, weren't you, Olivine? You came in much too promptly."

She said nothing, shifting from one foot to the other; for the first time he realized that she herself had no shoes, only strips of the coarse cloth tied around her feet.

"Through the keyhole? That was very wrong of you."

Wordlessly, she showed him a chink in the paneling that separated the room in which they stood from the next.

"To see when I was finished? Was that it?"

"If you'd put them . . . If you'd put them on. And . . ."

"And what? I promise not to get angry with you." It was an easy promise to make when he knew that pity would overwhelm whatever anger he might feel.

"And I'd never seen a bio . . . And I'd never seen a bio man. Only . . . Only father."

"Who is not a bio. I didn't think so. You're a chem yourself, aren't you, Olivine?"

She nodded.

"Hold out your hands, please. I wish to examine them both, here at the window."

"I took our bread . . . I took our bread up? While you were . . . While you were washing?"

"And got me clean clothing. Also you disposed of my old ones, no doubt. You must have been very busy."

"You took a long . . . You took a long time."

"Perhaps I did." He glanced out, thinking to gauge the distance between the setting sun and horizon, then recalled that the Long Sun never set. How profoundly unnatural a sun that moved had seemed when they reached Blue!

"I'll wash them for . . . I'll wash them for you?"

"Thank you. Now hold out your hands as I asked. I will not ask again."

One hand was an assembly of blocks and rods, the other—apparently—living flesh. He said, "Since you spied on me while I was dressing, Olivine, it wouldn't be inappropriate for me to ask you to strip, now would it?"

She cowered.

"It would be fair, and it might even be an eminently just punishment for what you did; but I won't demand it. I only ask that you take off the cloth you've wrapped around your head and face. Do it, please. At once."

She did, and he embraced her for a time, feeling her deep sobs and stroking her smooth metal skull.

When ten minutes or more had passed, he said, "You look like your mother. Doesn't Hammerstone—doesn't your father—tell you that? Surely he must."

"Sometimes. . . ."

He sat down upon the bed. "Do you imagine that you're so ugly, Olivine? You're not ugly to me, I assure you. Your mother is an old and dear friend. No one who resembled her as much as you do could ever seem ugly to me."

"I don't move . . . I don't move right."

Reluctantly, he nodded.

"I can't do what a woman . . . I can't do what a woman does. She went . . . She went away."

"She was captured by the Trivigauntis, Olivine, just as I was myself. When she got back here she went to Blue, because it was her duty to do so—the service she owed Great Pas. Do you understand?"

Slowly the shining metal head turned from side to side.

"I've been trying to remember what you were like when we left. You were still very small, however, and I'm afraid I didn't give you as much attention as I should."

"I didn't have a name . . . I didn't have a name yet. I couldn't talk . . . I couldn't talk, Patera."

Nor could she talk well now, he reflected. Hammerstone had been forced to construct her vocal apparatus alone, clearly, and the result had left something to be desired.

"Patera . . ."

He nodded. "You want me to go upstairs with you now, and to sacrifice for you and bless you, as Silk must have."

She nodded.

"For which you have dressed me in these clothes—clothes that I really should not have consented to wear, since I'm not entitled to them—and are fidgeting as we speak." He tried to recall whether he had ever seen a chem fidget before, and decided he had not. "But, Olivine, you're not going to divert me from my purpose. I'm going to the room I mentioned earlier, and you aren't coming with me. If its door is unlocked, I intend to stay there some time. Have you a pressing engagement?"

She was silent, and he was not sure she had understood. He added, "Another place to which you must go? Something else you have to do?"

She shook her head.

"Then you can wait, and you will have to. I—I'll try not to be too long."

She did not reply.

"When I come out, I'll sacrifice for you and give you my blessing, exactly as you wish. Then I would like to tell you about the errands that have brought me here and enlist your help, if you'll provide it." Unable to endure her silent scrutiny any longer, he turned away. "I'll come up to your floor and look for you, I promise."

Night waited outside the narrow window when he rose, dusted the knees of his new black trousers, and glanced around the room for the last time. Blowing out the candle, he opened the door and stepped out into the corridor again. It seemed empty at first, but as soon as he had closed the door behind him, a bit of grayish brown darkness detached itself from the shadows of another doorway and limped toward him. "You had a long wait," he said. "I'm sorry, Olivine."

"It's all right . . . It's all right, Patera."

Her head and face were swaddled in the sackcloth again; he touched it when she was near enough to touch, stroking her head as he might have stroked the head of any other child. "Do you think yourself so hideous, Olivine? You're not."

"I can't . . . I can't, Patera. Men—"

"Male chems?"

"Want me to when they see . . . Men want me to when they see me. So I try to look like one . . . So I try to look like one of you." The last word was succeeded by a strange, high squeal; after a moment he realized she was laughing.

The fifth-floor door she opened for him was five fingers thick, old and losing its varnish flake by flake but still sturdy. As he followed her into the darkness beyond it, he reflected that the room she called hers had surely been a storeroom originally. She snapped her fingers to kindle the bleared green light on its ceiling, and he saw that it still was. Boxes and barrels stood in its corners and against its walls, and metal bars, drills and files, spools of wire, and bits of cannibalized machinery littered the floor. He said, "This is where your father finished making you."

"Where we work on . . . Where we work on me." She had taken a pale figurine, a half bottle of wine, and a clean white cloth from some crevice among the boxes; unfolding the cloth disclosed the small loaf she had taken from the kitchen. She spread the cloth on the floor and arranged the other items on it.

He said, "You'll have to tell me how Silk sacrifices these things for you. We don't have a fire."

"The wine is the blood . . . The wine is the blood, Patera. The bread is the . . . The bread is the meat."

He began to protest, but thought better of it and traced the sign of addition over them, then looked up to see that Olivine was holding a book. "Is that the Chrasmologic Writings?"

"I keep it here . . . For you."

To his own surprise, he discovered that he was smiling. "I pointed out that we have no fire, Olivine. With equal or greater relevance, I might have said that we have no Sacred Window. But we can consult gods anyway, thanks to you, and perhaps they'll be in that book for us, as they are sometimes. Afterwards, I'll talk to you a little, if I may; then I'll sacrifice as you wish. Is that all right?"

She nodded, kneeling.

The Writings were small and shabby—the sort of copy, he thought, that a student might use in the schola. He opened them at random.

" 'There, where a fountain's gurgling waters play, they rush to land, and end in feast the day: they feed; then quaff; and now (their hunger fled) sigh for their friends and mourn the dead; nor cease their tears till each in slumber shares a sweet forgetfulness of human cares. Now far the night advances her gloomy reign, and setting stars roll down the azure plain: At the voice of Pas wild whirlwinds rise, and clouds and double darkness veil the skies.' "

It was customary to observe a few seconds of silence when a passage from the Writings had been read; it seemed a blessing now, although it could hardly be called silent, so beset was it with swirling thoughts.

"What does that mean, Patera . . . ?"

"I can't possibly tell you everything it means. The meanings of every passage in the Writings are infinite." (It was a stock reply.) "As for what it means to us here tonight—well, I'll try. It begins by telling us plainly that it concerns our immediate situation. 'Where a fountain's waters play,' must refer to my bath, for which I thank you again. 'There' presumably designates this palace, since I bathed here. 'They rush to land' refers to your impatience, when you wished me to end my bath and come up here with you."

"The gods are mad at . . . The gods are mad at me?"

"At you?" He shook his head. "I doubt it very much. I would say that they are offering a gentle and somewhat humorous correction, as a parent corrects a beloved child." He paused to collect his thoughts, glancing down at the book. "Next is, 'And end in feast the day.' You want me to sacrifice this bread and wine, and the day has indeed ended, which assures us that our sacrifice is what is meant. 'Feast' is probably ironic. We have no animal to offer—no real meat. We should eat a little of the bread, of course, so that it will be a shared meal. Or at least I should. And—"

"Drink some wine . . . Drink some wine, too," she suggested. "You always do . . . You always do that."

"Silk does? I'm not Silk, as I've explained several times. My name is Patera Horn—or rather just Horn, though I feel like an augur in these clothes. Now, where were we?"

"About you drinking the wine . . . About you drinking the wine, Patera."

He was tempted to insist she call him Horn, but this was not the moment for it. He nodded instead. "You say Silk does, and that accounts for the word *quaff* in the next section, 'They feed; then quaff; and now (their hunger fled) sigh for their friends and mourn the dead.' With this it would appear that the god who speaks to us has moved from our present situation to prophesy. I will sacrifice for you, the god says, and satisfy my hunger with your bread and wine. After that, we will mourn dead friends. At present I have no idea who these friends are, but no doubt it will be made clear to us when the time comes. Have you friends who are no longer with us, Olivine?"

"I don't think . . . I don't think so."

"My adopted son, Krait, is dead. He may be meant. Or someone like my late friend Scleroderma. We'll see."

He looked at the book again. " 'Nor cease their tears till each in slumber shares a sweet forgetfulness of human cares.' We will sleep then—so it appears. I know that you chems sleep at times, Olivine. Are you going to sleep tonight?"

"If you say . . . If you say to."

"Not I, but the gods. You should at least consider it. I will sleep, surely, if I can."

"My father told me to sleep while he was . . . My father told me to sleep while he was gone."

"But you didn't?"

"Over . . . Over there." She pointed to the window. "Where I could see . . . Where I could see out?"

"I didn't know you could sleep standing up."

"If I can . . . If I can lean. But I saw . . . But I saw you."

"In the street below. You have good eyes."

"I can't shut . . . I can't shut them." There were tears in the thick voice. "The . . . The rest?"

"You're right. It's my duty to explain it, not to gossip about sleeping habits." He looked down at the Writings once more, re-read the passage and closed the book. "This is by no means easy. Presumably it reflects the gods' concern for us. 'Now far the night advances her gloomy reign, and setting stars roll down the azure plain: At the voice of Pas wild whirlwinds rise, and clouds and double darkness veil the skies.' "

"Stars . . . Stars, Patera?"

"Tiny lights in the night sky," he explained absently. "We have them on Blue. You have them here, too, in a sense; but you cannot see them because they're outside the whorl. This is a difficult passage, Olivine. Why this mention of stars, when our sacrifice is taking place in the Long Sun Whorl?"

She stared at him, and although he could not discern her expression he could feel her expectancy.

"I believe it is what is called a signature; that is, a sign by which the god who has favored us identifies himself. Most frequently, signatures take the form of an animal—a vulture for Hierax, for example, or a deer for Thelxiepeia."

"There weren't . . . There weren't any. . . ."

"No, there weren't. No animal of any sort was mentioned."

He fell silent for almost half a minute, struggling with his conscience. "In honesty I must tell you that a real augur would say this passage was inspired by Pas. We have his image, to begin with; and when a god is mentioned by name, he or she is assumed to have inspired the passage. That's not invariably correct, however, and I don't believe it is in this case. The stars, which at first seem so out of place, are outside this whorl as I told you. As objects found outside it—and only outside it—they may well be signatures of the Outsider, as I feel quite sure they were in a dream I had long ago." He waited for her to protest, but she did not.

"There were horses in my dream, and horses are said to be signatures of Scylla's; but I've never felt the dream came from her. So let us look at the stars, as my wife and I used to do so often when we were younger." He tried to smile.

" 'Setting stars roll down the azure plain.' The azure plain is the sky—the sky by day, as we see it on Blue. Notice that azure itself is a shade of blue."

Olivine nodded.

"Since the stars are setting on Blue, we are warned that the influence of the Outsider will diminish there, though Blue, also, lies outside this whorl."

"Is that . . . Is that bad?"

"For the people there it is beyond doubt, and I believe I can guess why it's happening. Last night I was told by a godling that no more colonists are to leave for Blue or Green—that enough have gone, and everyone who is still here is to remain."

"I didn't know . . . I didn't know that."

"Very few people can. I was told to proclaim it, but I have not done so. At least, not yet."

He was silent again, recalling New Viron and Pajarocu. "We have very little respect for any god on Blue, Olivine. Little piety, hence little decency. Wealth is our god—land and cards and gold. What little reverence for the gods we have is found only in the newest colonists, who bring it with them. On Blue they tend to lose it. The Outsider, who is little regarded here, is virtually forgotten there."

"Don't cry . . . Don't cry, Patera. . . ."

"I used to upbraid myself, Olivine, because I paid him no proper honor. Once a year, perhaps, I tried to make some gesture of regard. Nobody else, not even my own sons—well, never mind." He wiped his face on the wide sleeve of his robe. "Your mother still honors the gods. I must mention that."

"Do you know . . . Do you know her?"

"Yes, I do. I saw her and spoke with her before I went to Green. I've hesitated to tell you so because—because—"

Olivine reached across the cloth; small, hard fingers sheathed in something that appeared to be flesh closed on his.

"She has gone blind."

The fingers relaxed; the thin metal arm fell to her side.

"She is well otherwise, and I—I feel absolutely certain she would send her love to you, if she knew of your existence. But she is blind now, like my friend Pig. To tell you the truth, I sometimes think that Pig may have been sent to me so that I wouldn't forget your mother."

He waited for some word, some comment.

"You'll say it was the judgment of the gods, I'm sure." He cleared his throat. "The judgment of the gods, for abandoning you, as she did in obedience to the gods. But I love her and can't help pitying her. She gave me one of her eyes—a blind eye, of course. They are both blind. But she gave me one in the hope that I might find working eyes for her when I got here. I've lost it. At least, it isn't in my pocket anymore."

He ceased to speak, and the silence of the Caldé's Palace closed around them. There had been someone—a cook—in the kitchen, he told himself. There had been a gardener in the garden outside. Bison was caldé now, so he and Maytera Mint, who must have renounced her vows to become his wife, lived in this high and secretive building. Yet it seemed that no one did, that not even the shrouded figure across the cloth from him was truly alive, and that the emptiness that had grasped all Viron had its center here.

"Lost . . . Lost it?" The thick, soft voice might almost have been that of the wind in a chimney.

He told himself he had to speak, and did. "Yes, I have. It's back on Green, I suppose." He wanted to say, *"With my bones,"* but substituted, "With my ring, and other things."

The shrouded figure might not have heard.

"It wasn't any good, you understand. Not to her or to anyone else. She wanted me to have it so that I would know what one looked like."

"I'm . . . I'm lucky."

He was not certain he had heard her correctly, and said, "I beg your pardon?"

"I don't work very well . . . I don't work very well, Patera."

"We all have failings. It's far better to—to have a bad leg or something of the sort than a propensity for evil."

"But my eyes are . . . But my eyes are fine. I can . . . I can see. You said . . . You said so. That's lucky . . . That's lucky, isn't it?"

"Yes, it certainly is. But, Olivine, you've let me get away from the subject again—from the passage that the god—that the Outsider, as I believe—chose for us. There's a colon in it. Do you know what a colon is? Not a semicolon, but a full colon? Two little dots, one above the other?"

She did not answer, and he floundered forward. "A colon is a very strong divider, Olivine, and colons are rarely found in the Writings. I believe—I'm guessing, to be sure, but this is what I believe—that it's intended to separate that passage about the stars rolling down the azure sky from the next so that we will understand that they concern two whorls. Blue and this Long Sun Whorl are actually like two little dots themselves, you see, if you think of them from the Outsider's perspective. The higher dot is this whorl, which is farther from the Short Sun; and the lower dot is Blue."

He cleared his throat and searched his memory. "I've shut the book, but I believe I can still quote the passage accurately. It was, 'At the voice of Pas wild whirlwinds rise, and clouds and double darkness veil the skies.' Pas himself is a wild whirlwind. That is to say, he's shown that way in art. The oldest representations of him show a swirling storm."

"I didn't know . . . I didn't know that. Is the other one . . . Is the other one—? You don't want me to say his . . . You—"

"Is he depicted as a whirlwind too? Is that what you're asking me?"

She nodded.

"No. But it's quite an intelligent question, now that I come to think about it. Pas is shown as a man with two heads, or a wind; so it's not unreasonable to think that he, who is shown as a man with four faces, might be depicted as a wind as well. He isn't, though. When a writer hesitates to set down his name—which isn't often, since so little has been written about him—he generally draws the sign of addition, a little straight mark with another little mark across it. I suppose that the idea now is that the god blesses us, though it may originally have been a diagram. Crossroads are associated with the god, as I believe I told you."

"I . . . I see."

"There's an interesting story about another god as a wind, however, and it may have some bearing on the passage in question. A certain man was hoping to have experience of the Outsider. He prayed and prayed, and a violent storm rose. At first he thought that this storm was the god, and rejoiced and shouted praise; but the storm only became more violent. Rain beat him like hail, and hail like stones. Water poured from the rocks all around, and trees were uprooted. Lightning struck the mountain on which he stood. Soon he grew terrified, and finding a little cave he hid himself and waited for the storm to pass.

"At last it did, and after it came the sun and a faint wind, a gentle breeze. And that faint wind, that gentle breeze, was the god whom he had sought."

Olivine did not speak.

"The point of the story, you see, is that Great Pas is not the Outsider. Gods often have several names and more than one personality—I was talking about this with friends not long ago—and it appears that at some time in the past people believed that the Outsider was merely another aspect of Pas. The story I just told you was probably written to show it was not the case.

"Now back to that passage. As I said, happenings in this whorl are intended—or so I would guess. Pas will manifest himself more than once, and angrily. 'Wild whirlwinds' are to rise. Notice the plural."

"Will he hurt . . . Will he hurt us?"

"That I cannot say. We have been warned by the Outsider, however, and the Outsider is a god—indeed, he may be the best and wisest of all the gods—and thus is certainly a great deal wiser than we. If he didn't believe we needed a warning, I doubt that he would have provided it.

"Now the last, and I will be able to sacrifice this bread for you. 'Clouds and double darkness veil the skies.' In one respect that is very plain. Double darkness must surely refer to the extinguishing of the

Long Sun by night. Night is coming—" He glanced toward the window. "Is already here I ought to say. It may be several days before we see the day again."

"Maybe I'll go back to sleep when you leave . . . Maybe I'll go back to sleep when you leave, Patera."

"That might be wise." His forefinger traced circles on his right cheek. "Clouds? I can't make much of that. It may mean perfectly ordinary clouds, such as we see every day. It may also refer to the god's veiling the minds of those he intends to destroy. I cannot be sure. 'Skies' presents the greatest puzzle of them all, at least to me. There have been two skies involved in the entire passage, as we have seen—the sky of Blue, and ours in this whorl. The plural must, I would think, refer to those two. The whirlwinds, clouds, and double darkness therefore refer not merely to this whorl, the Long Sun Whorl, but to Blue as well. It is dark on Blue each night, but how it can be doubly dark there I cannot imagine. An augur might give us a more exact interpretation, of course; it's a shame that there's no real augur present."

He uncorked the wine bottle. "Don't you have a glass for this, Olivine? And a knife to cut the bread?"

"I could get them . . . I could get them, but . . ." There was reluctance in the soft, thick voice that went beyond the usual reluctance to speak at all.

"But what? Please tell me."

"Father doesn't like me taking the . . . Father doesn't like me taking the things."

"I see. And you're not sure that Caldé Bison even knows you're up here?"

She shook her head.

"Doubtless your father's right. It's better not to risk your being put out of the palace, though it would seem to me that you might make Caldé Bison or General Mint a useful servant. Your father instructed you to sleep while he was away?"

She nodded again.

"I met my own father today. It was the first time I'd seen him in many years. I don't believe I told you."

"No, Patera . . ."

He smiled and shook his head. "I was walking up Sun Street,

looking for the place where our shop used to be; and he asked whether he could help me. He had seen, I suppose, that I was trying to locate a particular spot."

The shiprock walls, washed almost clean by many rains, had been crumbling into the rectangular holes that had been their cellars; cracked shiprock steps returned to the parent sand and gravel before the empty doorways. He looked above each that he passed for the painted sign he recalled so well: SMOOTHBONE STATIONER. It had proved less durable than the soot.

"Maybe I can help you." The passerby was short and stocky; his baldness exaggerated his high forehead.

"If you knew this area before it burned."

The bald man nodded and pointed. "My place was right over there for years."

"Before the fire, there was a little shop that sold, oh, quills and paper, mostly. Ink, notebooks, and so on. Do you know where that was?"

The bald man pointed as before. "That was mine."

Together, they walked to the spot. "I've been away a long time." The words had almost stuck in his throat.

"The quarter burned," the bald man said.

"I wasn't here then."

"Neither was I, I was way up north fighting Trivigauntis. Did you ever come into my shop in the old days?"

"Yes. Yes, I did."

The bald man moved half a step to his left, seeking a better angle. "Parietal? Was that your name?"

"No." Better, surely better, not to say too much too soon. "You lived here? In the Sun Street Quarter?"

"That's right. I had a wife here and children, four boys and three girls. Our house over on Silver burned too, but they got away. Went outside to one of the round whorls."

"You had a son named Horn, didn't you?" It was harder than ever to speak.

"That's right, my oldest. You knew him?"

"Not as well as I should have."

"He was good boy, a hard worker and brave as Pas's bull." The bald man held out his hand. "If you were a friend of his back then, I'm pleased to meet you. Smoothbone's my name."

They clasped hands. "I am your son Horn, father."

Smoothbone stared and blinked. "No, you're not!"

"My appearance has changed. I know that."

Smoothbone shook his head and took a step backward.

"There was a loose floorboard, right over there. After we closed, you'd pull it up and put our cashbox under it; and put a box of ledgers on top of it."

Smoothbone's mouth had fallen open.

"You didn't want me to know about it, and you were angry when you found out I had spied on you; but you continued to put it there. I know now you did it to show you trusted me, but at the time—" Tears and embraces prevented him from saying more.

When they separated, Smoothbone said, "You're really Horn? You're my son Horn, come back?"

He nodded, and they went down the street to a tavern in a tent, where the bar consisted of a plank laid across two barrels, and there were three tables, three chairs (one broken) and an assortment of stools and kegs. "You've changed out of all reckoning," Smoothbone said.

"I know. So have you. You were a big man when we went away." Memories came flooding back. "You said I was brave, but I was afraid of you. So was Mother. We all were."

The barman asked, "Wine or beer?" and looked surprised when Smoothbone asked for wine.

"How is she, Horn?"

"Mother? She was well the last time I saw her, but that was some time ago. Oxlip's taking care of her."

"I've married again. I ought to tell you."

For a moment, there was nothing to say.

"I guess you wondered why I didn't come."

He shook his head. "We thought you'd been killed."

"Not me, Horn."

"That's good." He was sick with embarrassment.

"You did all right out there?"

"Well enough. It was difficult, but then it was difficult here too. Difficult for you, I mean; and it would have been difficult for Nettle and me, if we had stayed here. It was no worse there, just different. Our donkey died." He laughed. "I don't know why I said that, but it did. That was the bottom—the worst time we had. After that things got better, but only slowly. Years of hard work. Nothing to eat, sometimes."

Smoothbone nodded. "I know how that is."

"People say there's always fish. I mean on Lizard they say that. We live on Lizard now."

"I never heard of it. Just Blue or Green is what they say."

"It's on Blue—a little island. We have a house there, a house we built ourselves, and a paper mill." Suddenly he smiled. "You have three grandsons. No, more, but the others aren't mine. Mine are Sinew, Hoof, and Hide."

Smoothbone smiled too. "This is Nettle? Nettle's sprats?"

"That's right. We married. We'd always planned to, and old Patera Remora married us there a few days after the lander put down. Do you remember Patera Remora, Father?"

"Remora?" Smoothbone tugged an earlobe reflectively. "It was Pike. Patera Pike. Then Silk, that was caldé after."

He nodded.

"We went to sacrifice with him, I suppose it must have been three or four times."

"More than that."

"You and your mother, maybe." Smoothbone drained his glass. "More wine, son?"

"No, thank you." His glass was half full.

"I'll have another." Smoothbone signaled the barman. "You know, I ought to have written all that down. I wish I had."

"On Blue, I wrote a history of Silk. Nettle and I did, I ought to say."

"Did you now!"

"Yes, Father. Nearly a thousand pages."

"I'd like to see it. My eyes aren't what they were when I was shooting Trivigauntis, but I can still read with a lens. Were you wanting to get paper and pens at our old shop, son?"

He shook his head. "I simply wanted to see it. To stand there for a little while and remember." He paused, considering. "Now that I know just where it was, I'm going to go back there and do it. It may be the only chance I'll ever have."

"Will you now?" The barman brought the wine; Smoothbone paid as before. "If you want something, I could take you to the new place. I'll give you just about anything you want there."

"No, thank you."

"Box of pencils? Pen case, maybe, with a little paper to put in it?"

"That would be nice. You're very kind to me, Father. You were always very kind to me—I'll never be able to thank you enough for all that you did to teach me our trade—but no, I couldn't impose upon you like that."

"Sure now?"

"Yes. I don't need those things, and I wouldn't feel right if I accepted them."

"Well, if you change your mind you just let me know." Smoothbone rose. "I've got to—you know. Excuse me minute?"

"Certainly."

"Promise you won't go away? I want to ask you about my grandchildren and tell you about your brothers. Half brothers, anyway. Antler's ten and Stag's eight. You wait right there."

"I will," he said.

Afterward they had talked for over an hour; and later, when he returned to the place where their shop had stood, he found a pen case, used but still serviceable, on the steps in front of it. It was of thin metal covered with thin black leather, and very like the pen cases that had been sold in that shop twenty years before. It was like the pen cases used by students in the schola, for that matter.

"I am here before you," he told Olivine, "but I am going to offer a funeral sacrifice for myself, nevertheless—for my body on Green, which lies there unburied as far as I know. I couldn't do this in a manteion. In fact I couldn't sacrifice in a manteion at all, though I might assist an augur. There has been an exchange of parts. You, I think, will understand that better than a bio would."

She nodded, perhaps a little doubtfully.

"Very well," he said; he looked up, thinking of the Aureate Path and Mainframe at its termination, although the Long Sun was hidden behind the shade. "My body does not lie here, nor is it to be found in this whorl. We offer it to you, Quadrifons, and to the other gods of this whorl, in absentia. We offer it also to the Outsider, in whose realm it lies. Accept, all you gods, the sacrifice of this brave man. Though our hearts are torn, we—the man himself, and your devoted worshipper Olivine—consent.

"What are we to do? Already your have spoken to us of the times to come. Should you wish to speak further, whether in signs and portents, or in any other fashion, your lightest word will be treasured. Should you, however, choose otherwise—"

He raised his arms, but only silence answered him.

He let them fall. "We consent still. Speak to us, we beg, though these sacrifices."

Picking up the loaf that Olivine had filched from the kitchen in which she had been born, he raised it. "This is my body. Accept, O Obscure Outsider, its sacrifice. Accept it, Great Pas and all lesser gods."

Lowering the loaf, he broke it in two, scattering dun-colored crumbs over the white cloth, then tore away a fragment and ate it.

"This is my blood." He raised the bottle, lowered it, sipped from it, and sprinkled a few drops upon the cloth.

"Can you tell what's going to happen from that . . . Can you tell what's going to happen from that, Patera?"

"I can try." He bent over the cloth, his lips pursed.

"Will my father ever come back . . . Will my father ever come back, Patera?"

"The right side—" he tapped it, "concerns the presenter and the augur. Perhaps you were aware of that already."

Olivine nodded.

"Here are two travelers, a man and woman." He smiled as he indicated them. "Converging upon another woman, who can only be yourself. It seems likely that they represent your father and the woman he has gone to seek. Since they are shown coming from opposite directions it may be they will arrive separately. You must be prepared for that."

"I won't mind a . . . I won't mind a bit!" There was joy in her voice, and it almost seemed that there was joy in her eyes as well, although that was impossible.

"Patera, why are you looking at me like . . . Patera, why are you looking at me like that?"

"Because I heard your mother, Olivine. You don't sound like her—not usually, I mean. Just then, you did."

"I've been wanting to talk to you about . . . I've been wanting to talk to you about her." Olivine's hands were at her face; there was a momentary silence, punctuated by a sharp click. "Here . . . Here, Patera. Take it to . . . Take it to her." Her hand held an eye like the one he had left on Green, save that it was not dark; the sackcloth had fallen away from her face, so like her mother's with its empty socket.

He drew back in horror. "I cannot let you do this. You're young! I forbid it. I can't let you sacrifice yourself—"

The eye fell among the crumbs and wine stains. She sprang up, limping and lurching, and fled before he could stop her. For what seemed to him a very long time, he heard her uneven footfalls upon floors bare and carpeted and stairs of wood and marble—always farther from himself, the wine-stained cloth, and the eye she was giving to her mother.

"Thank you," he said. "Thank you very much, Hound. Good evening, Pig. I hope you found this place without too much difficulty." Seeing Oreb perched upon a bedpost in the room beyond, he added, "Man back."

"Mon come ter see yer," Pig rumbled. "Gane noo."

Hound nodded. "An augur from the Prolocutor's Palace. He left his card. Where did I put it?" Hound's belongings were scattered over an old rosewood dresser; he moved one, then another, as he searched for it.

"Fashed h'about yer, bucky, him an' me both."

"You had no need to be, though I realize I'm very late. What did this augur want with me? And come to think of it, how did he know I was here?"

"I registered you." Hound put down a striker and picked up a scrap of paper, first to look under it and then to look at the scrap itself. "I had to, it's the law. This is a copy of what I wrote. Do you want to see it?"

He had dropped into a chair. "Read it to me, please. I'm tired—much too tired to do anything except sleep."

"All right. I wrote, 'Hound of Endroad, Pig of Nabeanntan, and Horn of Blue.' "

"Is that your town, Pig? That Nabeanntan? I don't believe you've mentioned it."

"From nae toon." Pig was taking off his tunic. "Has ter have a thing ter write, they says."

"Then it seems quite innocent. No doubt Ermine's had to report it to some authority in the Civil Guard—though that must be the Caldé's Guard now—and it made its way to the Palace from there by some route or other. What did he want?"

"Ter warn yer, bucky."

"Against what?"

Loudly, Oreb croaked, "No cut!"

Momentarily, Hound abandoned his search. "That was what he said when we asked what he wanted, but I think he really wanted something else."

"What was it?"

"I don't know. I told him that he could leave a message for you with us. Or write a note and seal it, if he preferred, but he wouldn't."

"H'asked h'about yer, ter. What yer look like an' where yer been." Pig rose. "Goin' ter have a wash, bucky. Want ter gae first?"

"No, thank you. I've bathed already."

"Thought sae. Smelt yer scented soap. New kicks, ter?"

"Yes, an augur's robe, and an augur's tunic and trousers—though I'm not an augur, as I have assured you. An explanation would be complex, and I'd prefer to provide one in the morning. Hound, I'm surprised you left it to Oreb to comment on them; and unless Pig understood Oreb, I can't imagine how he knew."

"Wise man," Oreb remarked.

The wise man's smile twitched at his thick black beard and heavy mustache. " 'Twas ther moth flakes, bucky."

Hound held up a modest white calling card. "I thought it might be better to let you bring up the subject yourself, if you wanted to talk about it. But it was quite a shock to see you like that only a little while after the other one left. Here's his card, if you'd like to see it."

Patera Gulo
Coadjutor
Prolocutor's Palace

"Ken him, bucky?"

"Pig, you perpetually amaze me. How do you do it?"

"Listen's h'all. Yer took a bit a' wind."

Hound said, "I noticed it myself."

"Gasped? I suppose I did. Not because I recognized his name—though I do—but because he's coadjutor. He wanted to warn me, you said? It's a matter of some importance if His Cognizance sent his coadjutor with the warning."

"Good Silk! Fish heads?"

He shook his head. "No, no food. To tell the truth, I want nothing but rest. Rest and sleep; and if I can go to bed without a supper, you certainly can. Hound, if you'll show me where I can lie down, I'll try not to trouble you and Pig further."

Hound led him to a pallet in the next room; and when he had removed he shoes and stretched himself on it, said softly, "We fed your bird when we ate. Don't worry about him."

There was no response, and Hound, moved by the sight of that tragic face, added still more softly, "You don't have to worry about anything. Pig and I will take care of it," hoping that he spoke the truth.

"Somebody to see you, Horn." It was Mother's voice from the kitchen; but he was lost in flames and smoke, groping through the fire that had destroyed the quarter, groping backward through time to reach the two-headed man in the old wooden chair Father used at meals.

"Somebody to see you."

He woke sweating, and it was ten minutes at least before he fully accepted the fact that he was older and knew that there was no returning to the past save in dreams.

When he had placed himself in time, he sat up. Hound breathed heavily in the bed; Pig more heavily in the room beyond. The window was open; curtains fluttered in a night breeze, gentle ghosts whispering of the days of Ermine's prosperity. Oreb was silent, asleep if he were present at all; and in all likelihood winging his way over the city.

This was the moment, yet he felt a strange reluctance.

His shoes were half under the bed. He retrieved them and groped in a corner for the knobbed staff, then remembered that he had left it in the Caldé's Palace—in the lavatory in which he had bathed, or possibly in the bedroom beyond it. If Hound woke, or Pig, he might say that he was going back for it. He might make the lie true, in fact, to salve his conscience; although it seemed doubtful that anyone would come to his knock at the Caldé's door at such an hour, even more doubtful that he would be admitted to fetch his staff or anything of the kind.

Neither Hound nor Pig awoke.

The key was in the lock. He turned it as quietly as he could, slipped through the door, and relocked it from outside, dropping the key into his pocket. The years had worn threadbare gray paths down the middle of the luxurious carpets he recalled. Ermine's banisters had lost a baluster here and there.

The cavernous sellaria had been stripped of much of its furniture and most of its lights. At the desk, a lofty young man with a beard as black as Pig's own stood arguing with the clerk. The clerk wore a blue tunic with crimson embroidery that seemed chosen to hold death and the night at bay, the bearded youth a long, curved saber and a white headcloth in place of a cap; neither man so much as glanced at him.

The door to Ermine's Glasshouse was locked, but the lock was small and cheap, the door old and warped.

Where Thelx holds up a mirror.

Dampness and decay scented the air; the broad blossoms were gone, the trees dead or overgrown, the colored glass gems trodden into the mud; improbably, the pond remained—light from distant skylands flashed gold in its depths.

He knelt, and closed his eyes. "It's me, Patera. It's Horn, and I've come to get you, I want to bring you back to Blue with me. You're here—I know you're here."

There was no answering touch, no ghostly voice.

"What Nettle and I wrote about you—we didn't just make it up. You told us on the airship, remember? You said a part of you would always be here." When he opened his eyes, it seemed for a moment that he saw Silk in the water; but it was only his own reflection, a reflection so faint it vanished as he stared.

"You're here; I know you'll always be here and I can't take you away. But you could talk to me, Patera, just for a minute. You always liked me. You liked me better than almost anybody else in the whole palaestra."

Not all the blossoms were gone, it seemed; the cool night air bore a faint perfume.

"Please, Patera? Please? I want this more than I've ever wanted anything. Just for a minute—just for a minute let me see you."

"I loved only you, nobody but you. Not ever." Warm lips brushed his ear. In the pool, an older Silk knelt beside Hyacinth. Both smiled at him.

The yawning maidservant who answered the Caldé's door gawked at him and jumped in her haste to get out of his way. When he found the right room at last and the husband's knobbed staff was in his hands, he heard distant shots and opened a window.

There had been three, from a slug gun. While he listened he heard two more, and saw a mounted guardsman gallop by.

The maid had waited in the foyer to let him out, still so sleepy that she called him "Caldé" when warning him against the danger of the streets. "One shot means death," he told her, smiling. "Many simply means that someone's missing a lot." He had learned that in worse streets and in the tunnels long ago. He wished for some money to give her for admitting him and for her obvious concern for him; but he had only the two whole cards, and a card was far too much.

"Here." He pushed one into her hand, and got away before she could embarrass him with her thanks.

The street was very dark, and quiet save for five hurrying Guardsmen; Ermine's lobby quieter still, although a small table had been turned over and a vase broken. There was no clerk behind the desk now, no one in the lobby at all. The stairs seemed higher and steeper than he recalled.

As he put the key back into the lock, Pig asked sleepily, "Recollect ther craws, bucky?"

It took a moment. "Why, yes. Yes, I do, Pig."

"Still say ther same?"

13

The Yawl

A tent is not the most comfortable of accommodations in winter. I have tried a cave—and various other locations—and they are all of them better; yet we are in a tent, and it is my doing. By "we" I mean Jahlee, Oreb, and myself.

Yesterday morning we made port at New Viron, after having been detained within sight of the town by contrary winds for a full day. We were all exceedingly glad to get off the boat, as you may imagine. Even Wijzer was pleased to go ashore, or so it seemed to me.

Here I must interrupt the narrative I have not really begun to say that he offered to land us on Lizard, this despite the bad weather we were then experiencing and the poor anchorage offered by Tail Bay. I explained that although I was very eager indeed to get home again, my duty forbade it. I would have to report to the people of New Viron, whose emissary I had been, and take care of various other matters. It was a torture as bad as anything the Matachin Tower might impose to stand on deck and see, through pelting rain and driving spray, the tiny golden rectangle that was the window of our little house. You were sitting up late, Nettle, reading or writing or sewing, and wondering what had become of us. I wanted very much to see you, however briefly and at however great a distance. I was sorely tempted to send Oreb to you; but you, having ridden out that same gale at home, will understand when I say that I could not bring myself to risk his small life in such a fashion.

Another digression, but there is no help for it. I intend to send him to you as soon as he has recovered his strength; the sea was not kind to him, but he will be fit enough in a day or two, I believe. Meanwhile I hope to send you a little cheerful news by the Neighbors. It seems likely that they will be in touch with me here as they were in Dorp; if so, I will try to persuade them to carry another message.

The upshot was that we put in at New Viron. Oreb has a new phrase: "No boat!" It expresses my feelings as well as his, and better than I could myself. No more winter sailing, at any rate. The rest feel the same way, I would guess—particularly Jahlee, whose vomiting blood nearly killed her, and persuaded Wijzer's crew that she was gravely ill. (Hoof knows, I believe, although I have not told him. Hide says he has not, that he has told only Vadsig. I have not asked her; and it is at least equally likely that Hoof's suspicions were roused by something he saw or something Jahlee herself said to him.)

The inns here are dangerous, and after asking various people to recommend safe and decent ones, and being disappointed with those, we settled on the following arrangement: Hoof, Hide, and Vadsig—all that they can provide beds for—are staying with my brother Calf and his wife. Jahlee and I have bought a tent and pitched it in this sandy field belonging to the town, very near the sea. The town sent me out, and for the town I labored without payment for nearly two years; it owes me this and more, as I told the men sent to dislodge us. I hope to be summoned soon to make my report.

Gyrfalcon has declared himself caldé, and seems to be making it stick. Hoof came, and we talked about it. He is a tyrant, or at least Hoof says that Calf says he is. Many think a tyrant preferable to the anarchy that prevailed earlier. That Hoof says also, and I could have guessed it for myself. For their sake, I hope they will not learn differently in a year or two.

We have been doing what we can to make the tent snug. Hide and I ditched it and cut brush that Jahlee arranged very cleverly against the sides to break the force of the wind. I should add that the weather is not as cold as it was, and that is worth any quantity of brush. We have a little copper stove, too, which keeps us warm and serves me to cook on. All in all, we are surprisingly comfortable. As soon as I have made my report and handed over my corn, I will buy a boat and go. After our storm-tossed voyage with Wijzer, I am in no hurry.

Sunshine and a mild wind; winter is about over. So I pray. When it began, I was in Gaon fighting the Man of Han; I would never have guessed that when it ended I would be nearly home. The Outsider has been very good to me. He reads this, I believe, even as I write it. The ink is not yet dry upon my thanks.

Hoof came again. We agreed that although I must remain here for the present, there is no need for him to remain as well. He will try to arrange for a boat to take him to Lizard. I gave him money for that purpose and this record, too, as far as the bandits. Without prompting, he asked if he might read it. I said he was welcome to, but asked him not to show it to you until I have a chance to speak to you. He said he would not. I begged him to keep it safe, explaining how important it is to me. He promised to make every effort. He is a good boy—too serious, if anything. He tried to tell me something but wept too much to get it out. We embraced and parted.

He has told me a little about his adventures before he found us in Dorp. I must get him to tell me more when next I see him, and set them down, with Hide's adventures in Gaon. I must not fail to do this.

When the apprentice visited me in my cell, I talked to him about writing, and the making of books. He brought a pen, ink, and paper such as they use in the Red Sun Whorl, and wrote out a few sentences for me: "You are the only client who could leave our oubliette, but chose to stay. You must have been in many terrible places if this one does not seem terrible to you." (I believe I am quoting him correctly except for his spellings; he used those of his city, which I cannot recall with any precision and which differ in many respects from ours.)

"I have been in places that were more dangerous than this, but in none more terrible," I told him.

"You must have been in Nessus. You said you walked a long way beside Gyoll."

"On another visit, yes. This time we went directly from our own whorl to the Broken Court."

"You can do that?" His eyes were wide.

"Go straight to the Broken Court? Clearly we can. We did."

He shook his head in disbelief. He does not have what is called an attractive face; although his piercing eyes smiled once or twice, I do not believe I ever saw a smile reach his lips.

"You could write a book yourself, if you chose. Nettle and I had a great many other things to do when we were writing what people call *The Book of the Long Sun* now; but every evening when the twins were asleep, one or the other of us would work on our book, and sometimes both of us worked together."

He picked up his pen and seemed about to speak.

"It's really only a matter of deciding what you would say if you were telling a friend. You have friends, I'm sure."

He nodded. "Drotte and Roche and Eata. Drotte's a little older than I am. So is Roche. Eata's a little younger."

"But you are friends, all four of you?"

He nodded again.

"Then pretend you are talking to Drotte and Roche. You must speak your best, and not show off as you might be inclined to do if you were talking with Eata."

"I see." He remained troubled.

"Unless we were writing some part of our book about which Nettle knew much more than I, I would write first."

"Like you were talking?"

"Exactly. When she had time, Nettle would read what I had written, correct my spelling and grammar—she is better at both—and add passages of her own. Still later, I would re-write, incorporating what she had written into our text and perhaps adding a few thoughts of my own. After that, she would make a fair copy and we would consider that section done."

"Look at that!" His pen jabbed at his capital *Y*. "If Master Palaemon had written it, it would have been beautiful."

"Leave beauty to your words. If your letters can be read, for them that is beauty enough."

"You said your wife copied out everything you wrote."

"She did; but that was the least of the many things she did. At times we had to imagine actions and conversations. She is very good at that. In a hundred instances, she refreshed my memory on important points. While it's true that she writes a better hand than I, that was much less important."

"I never forget. I don't understand how anybody does."

"You're fortunate," I told him, "and will have a great advantage when you come to write a book of your own."

He shook his head. "I won't, until I have a scribe to make my writing look better."

"Will you have one?" When I looked only at his rags, I found it difficult to believe; but when I raised my eyes to his narrow, intense face I found it easy.

"When I'm a master. Master Gurloes has Master Palaemon write for him, mostly. But Master Malrubius used to make a scribe come and help him twice a week. They have to, if we tell them to. They're afraid of us."

"Understandably so." I looked around my little cell for the last time, conscious I would leave it soon and a trifle wistful already; it had been a haven of rest and prayer.

"You're not."

"Can you be sure? Perhaps I'm secretly terrified."

He shook his head with an obstinacy that recalled Sinew's. "I've seen a lot of that. You're not afraid at all."

"Because I'm not really here."

"That judge is afraid."

"He doesn't know, you see." I tried not to smile. "Or if he does by this time, he may be afraid that my daughter and I will leave him here. As we might."

"She's a witch, isn't she?"

To the best of my recollection I did not answer. "What do you say we pay a call on him? Will you show me where you've put him?"

For a moment or two he considered the matter, hand upon chin. "I shouldn't let you out. . . ."

"I wouldn't ask you to. I'll let myself out."

"If one of the journeymen saw you, it would be bad." He was still considering. "Only in that black robe he might think you were one of us, if he didn't see your face."

"It would be better if I had a hood, wouldn't it?" I made one for myself in imitation of the journeymen I had seen, and added the decorations worn by Master Gurloes, thinking my white beard and hair deserved them. "Will this pass, do you think?"

"Blacker." (He was certainly a young man of courage.) "Ours are fuligin. Like soot."

I did what I could.

"I might be able to get you a sword. Want me to try?"

I shaped a sword such as I had seen in the hands of their journeymen, with a two-handed grip and a long straight blade.

"Can I hold it for a minute? Is it real?"

"Of course you can." I gave it to him. "No, it isn't."

"It feels heavy." Holding it clearly gave him pleasure.

"It's my old friend Pig's, as well as I remember it. Could you carry it for me? I'm no longer young, I'm afraid."

"We don't do that."

We went out, I through the door and he through the doorway.

★

★ ★

To town this morning, determined to make my report, sat until midafternoon in Gyrfalcon's reception room, and returned here. Tomorrow I intend to go to Marrow's first—or at least, to the house that was his. I do not doubt that he is dead; Hoof would never lie to me about such a matter. But as I sat with little to do but think, it occurred to me that Marrow may have left a message for me. That is worth investigating, surely. It cannot be a waste of time worse than I endured today.

When the Prolocutor had me sacrifice in the Grand Manteion, I thought it no worse than a minor waste of time as well. Now I see clearly that it tipped the scales toward failure. Had I not acceded to his request, I might have found Silk, whom I heard was staying at our inn, although only when it was too late. Time wasted can never be recovered. I mean time that accomplishes nothing, and in which we have no enjoyment.

I have been playing with Oreb and scratching Babbie's ears. None of which I count as time wasted. I enjoy it, and so do they. Besides, I feel entitled to a little recreation after so much dreary sitting and staring. I find I cannot pray when others who are not praying are present.

No, I find nothing of the sort. I did not try. I will go again tomorrow, and if Gyrfalcon (who sent me out as much as Marrow and the others) keeps me cooling my heels again, I will pray. Perhaps others will join me. There's a cheering thought! I'm looking forward to trying already.

Silk prayed aboard the Ayuntamiento's boat with Doctor Crane looking on. If he could do that, I can do this.

Jahlee returned, cheerful and eager to talk. Our cool, damp, dark weather suits her. "It's much better than the snow, Rajan. Much! I have to keep moving to stay active, but I've slept so much already. I feel as if I'll never sleep again. And I'm getting hungry. It's wonderful!"

I made her promise that she would not attack children.

"Or the poor. You always say that."

"Very well. Or the poor. No one who doesn't have enough to eat. You'll agree to that, won't you?"

She smiled, briefly displaying her fangs. "I won't bite myself, if that's what you're worried about. Is it all right if I go back and bite the Man of Han?"

"He's dead, I believe."

"They'll have a new one by now. No, seriously, I want a good-looking woman, someone like me. I won't kill her either."

"Or keep going back to her."

"Not more than once. You've got my word." She rose to go, the very picture of a good-looking young woman herself in her white furs. "Do you think I'd be better as a brunette?"

"Possibly." I considered her. "No, you couldn't be better. No conceivable change would be an improvement."

"Bigger breasts?" She tossed her hips, what Vadsig calls *wiggling*. "Smaller waist? I want your honest opinion."

"Bad thing!" This from Oreb.

"My honest opinion is that you shouldn't try it. You might break in two."

She laughed. She has a very pleasant laugh, but it seemed to me then that at her laugh our tent became a trifle darker. "I want to have sex with one of you. With one of your women, and feed afterward. Won't that be fun?"

She was baiting me; I waved it aside. "Jahlee, I've been wanting to talk to you about something serious. Perhaps this is the time."

"Do you want me to go? I can't blame you." Lifting her skirt, she danced toward the door of our tent.

"No," I said. "Not at all."

"That's good, because I can't keep it up long." She raised her skirt higher to display her legs. "Pretty, aren't they?"

"Very."

"But not strong. They're as strong as I can make them, though. I need to find another animal I can ride."

"You could have ridden your white mule from Dorp. It would have taken a great deal longer, of course."

She shrugged. "I might not have gotten here at all, and if I had, it would have been—you know."

"Flying."

"Don't say it. It's not wise. Anyway, I would have lost my mule even if I didn't lose my life, and I would have been separated from you. I don't want to be separated from you."

"Any other man or—"

"I don't think so. Anyway, I'm going into town to try to buy a new mule or something, if I can get a boat to pick me up."

I wished her luck.

"Merryn had trouble with animals, too," Jahlee said as she went out.

For some minutes I have been puzzling over that name. My first thought, naturally enough, was that "Merryn" was another inhuma we had known in Gaon; but there could be little point then in saying that Merryn, too, suffered difficulties with animals, since all inhumi do.

When the torturer's apprentice and I went to Jahlee's cell, there was an unhealthy-looking young woman with her, so pale and gaunt I feared that Jahlee had been feeding until I recalled that on the Red Sun Whorl Jahlee could eat (and could not eat) as I did—that the differences between our digestive systems had been erased, so to speak, since neither of us had any.

"This is my father," Jahlee explained to her, "but I don't know who the boy is."

The young woman had smiled, and seeing that smile I resolved not to trust her. "He's my brother," she said. "We're brothers and sisters, we witches and the torturers." Her voice was shrill and unpleasant.

"I brought her," the apprentice told me. "She's a witch," he indicated Jahlee with a nod, "and I thought another one might be able to help her."

Here I want to write that the young witch smiled again; but it was the same smile, which had remained upon her face as if forgotten. "She has no powers."

"You don't know her," the apprentice said.

"I sense none in her, and she says she has none." The witch rose, moving like a woman stiff with age.

"I don't," Jahlee told the apprentice. "I am a perfectly ordinary human woman." The happiness she had in saying it warmed my heart.

"I will go now," the witch announced; he opened the door for her and went out with her, locking it behind him. Through its barred window I heard him say that he wished to show us his dog. Possibly the witch made a reply that I did not hear.

Stepping through the door Jahlee said, "I'd like to see it. I love dogs." I followed her in time to see the witch's gaping mouth and the utter blankness of her large, dark eyes.

(I must remember to ask Jahlee about the secret. I cannot reveal it to Nettle, no matter how much I want her to know and understand. Jahlee could. She seemed in a good mood, and I should have detained her.)

★

★ ★

We have a boat! The Outsider, seeing we required one, has arranged that we be given one at no expense and with very little trouble. But I am ahead of my story. This morning I located the house that had been Marrow's. It had been sold, but the new owner kindly referred me to a good woman named Capsicum who is disposing of Marrow's possessions.

"Here is his letter," she said, and showed it to me. I cannot reproduce it here, because I cannot recall the precise phrasing. Suffice it to say that he addressed her as "my darling," with other endearments, and that he asked her to distribute the gifts he listed, and authorized her to retain what remained for herself.

"We were friends for years, and after his wife died there was nobody but me. If it hadn't been for me, he would never have got to be what he did." She sighed; she has eyes the color of a blue china plate in a large, round face, and at the moment it held no more expression than the plate. "He'd still be with us." I asked her to explain, but she would not. "There's no mending it. You were a friend of his?"

"He was the chief of the committee of five who sent me for Patera Silk, and he certainly befriended me afterward."

"The one who was caldé when we left?"

"Yes, exactly."

"Did you bring him?"

I shook my head. "I tried, and failed. Please understand me—I'm not looking for a reward. I'm entitled to none. But I have the seed corn we needed and would like to turn it over to someone who will make good use of it. I had supposed that when I returned I would make my report to Marrow. Learning that he had passed away, I tried to report to Gyrfalcon. I was unable to see him, and it occurred to me that Marrow might have left instructions for me—some message."

"Do you need money? I might let you have a little." She rose with the help of a thick black stick and went to a cabinet.

"No. I've more than enough for my needs, and my family's."

I had risen because she had; she motioned for me to resume my seat. "What was your name again?"

"Horn."

"I see."

"We live on Lizard—Marrow and the others came there the first time we talked."

She said nothing. She is a large woman, quite stout, with a small mouth and a great deal of white hair.

"I should not have gone. I know that now. At the time I thought it my duty."

"What were you going to make from it?"

"Money?" I shook my head. "I didn't expect any, though I would have taken it if it had been offered, I suppose. But you're right, there was something I wanted—I wanted to see Silk again, and speak with him."

"Do you need a handkerchief?"

She produced one, small and trimmed with lace, and I was reminded poignantly of the big, masculine-looking handkerchiefs Maytera Marble used to carry in her sleeves. I shook my head again and wiped my eyes. "It's the wind, I suppose, or too much writing. I've been writing a lot, mostly by lamplight."

"That's where I write letters." She pointed to a little damask-wood desk. "See how the light from the window falls?"

I acknowledge that it seemed a good arrangement.

"Only I don't write a lot of them. You could come here and use it sometime if you wanted to."

I thanked her, and asked again whether she had found any mention of me in Marrow's papers.

"There's a lot of stuff." Her eyes were vague. "I haven't gone through everything yet. I'll look. Maybe you could come back tomorrow?"

"Yes, I'd be happy to."

"You're sure you wouldn't like something to eat?"

"No, but it's very kind of you."

"I would." She rang a bell. "If there's something for you, I'll have to make sure you're really Horn."

I nodded and assured that I understood her caution and applauded it.

"You must have been just a sprat on the lander."

I admitted it, adding that I had thought myself a man.

"Seems like a real long time ago to you. It don't to me. I must be, oh, a couple years older. I'd like to give you some money, too. But I have to know."

"I don't need it, as I told you; but as for identification, my brother Calf lives here. He'll vouch for me, I'm sure."

A slave girl entered, bowing. Capsicum told her to serve tea and to send in "the boy."

When the slave girl had gone, Capsicum unlocked her cabinet and got out two cards. "Real ones, like we used to have back home. The Chapter will give you four gold ones for each of these."

She seemed to expect me to challenge her assertion, so I said, "Patera Remora, you mean? I feel sure he won't, since they're not mine."

A boy of about ten joined us, and she introduced him as her

grandson. "You have to go to the shop of a man named Calf, Weasel. This gentleman will tell you how to get there. Ask Calf to come here, please, and identify the gentleman for me. The gentleman says Calf is his brother."

My knowledge of these streets is somewhat limited, but I directed Weasel to the best of my ability and he nodded as though he understood. "Do you have a magic bird?"

I laughed and tried to explain that I had a pet bird, not a magic one. To confess the truth, I had not the heart to tell the little fellow there were no magic birds.

"Where is it?"

"I sent him to my wife, to let her know that our son Hoof is returning to her, and that the rest of us—our son Hide and his betrothed, and our daughter and I—will return to her soon."

Capsicum smiled at the prospect of a wedding. "Marrow'd have married me after his wife died, but I wouldn't let him."

I said I was sorry to hear it.

"Get along, Weasel. You go and ask the gentleman to come like we told you to, this don't concern you. We would've fought like a old dog and a old cat, Patera. I've never been sorry I said no."

"I'm not an augur. I realized that this is an augur's robe, but I'm not."

"You've got a wife, you said."

"Yes, I do. Augurs have wives, occasionally, however."

"Patera Silk did. I heard that before we left."

The slave girl came in, staggering under the weight of a tray loaded with tea and wine, cups, saucers, and wineglasses, and enough little sandwiches and cakes to feed a palaestra. I drank tea (and to please Capsicum a glass of wine) and ate a sandwich, which was excellent.

We talked about Viron for a time. I told her about the devastation that was the Sun Street Quarter, which she had supposed would have been rebuilt long since. "I don't think I'd have come, Patera, if it hadn't been for that. I had a nice place, the whole top floor in a real nice house, and my rent paid for half a year. Only it burned, and I thought, he's going away and I've lost everything, and if I don't go with him I'll lose him too. So I went."

She toyed with the cards she had taken from her cabinet, then laid them down; clearly they recalled Viron, and the rooms there she had lost. "Why are people so mean?"

"Because they separate themselves from the Outsider." I had not thought about it in those terms before and said what I did without reflection; but as soon as I had spoken, I realized that what I had said was true.

"Who's that?" she asked.

"A god." I was suddenly afraid of saying too much, of pushing too hard or too far.

"Just a god?" She took another sandwich.

"Isn't that enough for you, Capsicum? Godhead?"

"Well, there's a lot of them, and sometimes it seems like they're as mean as we are."

"Because they, too, have separated themselves from him. Nor are there really many gods, or even two. Insofar as they're gods at all—which isn't far, in most cases—they are him."

"I don't follow that." She seemed genuinely puzzled.

"You have a walking stick. Suppose it could walk by itself, and that it chose to walk away from you."

She laughed; and I understood what had drawn Marrow to her years ago; she did not laugh for effect, as women nearly always do, but as a child or a man might.

"You see," I said, "if the Outsider were to make a walking stick, it would be such a good walking stick that it could do that." I held up the staff Cugino had cut for me. "But if it chose to walk away from him, instead of coming to him when he called to it, it would no longer be a walking stick at all, only a stick that walked. And when someone tending a fire saw it go past, he would break it and toss it onto the coals."

She studied me as she chewed her sandwich, and I added, "I myself have walked away from him any number of times; he's always come after me, and I hope he always will."

"It's only a walking stick when I walk with it." She held up her own thick black stick. "That's what you mean, isn't it?"

"Exactly."

Dusting crumbs from her hands, she picked up the cards and tossed them into my lap. "These are for you."

"I don't need them, as I told you."

"Maybe you will." Her right hand scratched her left palm, a gesture I did not (and do not) comprehend.

"Wouldn't it be better to wait until I've established that I am who I say I am?"

"Horn, the man Marrow sent to bring back Silk."

"Yes. Precisely."

She shook her head. "That's for what Marrow left. This's mine, and I want you to have it. Did he say why he wanted Silk?"

"Certainly. There was a great deal of disorder here, a great deal of lawlessness. Marrow and some others had tried to set up a government; but they could not agree on a caldé, and most felt that if they had, the townspeople would not accept him. They would accept Silk, however, and the five who met with me had agreed to accept him, too."

"We don't need one anymore." Capsicum's voice was bitter. "We've got Gyrfalcon."

"Since I failed to bring Silk, that's all to the good."

She said nothing, regarding me over the top of her glass.

"You think he killed Marrow, don't you?"

"I didn't say so, and I won't."

"But you think it." I hesitated, scrambling for words that would make my meaning tolerable, if not acceptable. "I don't know that. I returned here only a few days ago."

She nodded.

"Let us suppose, however, that I did—that I knew beyond question that Marrow, who fought beside me in the tunnels and did everything he could to assist me in the mission he gave me, had been murdered, and that the new caldé here was his murderer." I laid the cards she had given me on the tray. "Even knowing that, I would have to consider what would happen to the town if he were stripped of power and tried. It would be difficult to overturn a mountain—I believe you will agree with that. But it would be easier to overturn a mountain than to replace it."

When she did not speak, I said, "I am giving you back your cards. It wouldn't be right for me to keep them."

The boy Weasel returned and reported that Calf would not come but had given him a note. Capsicum broke the seal, unfolded the note, and read it twice. I asked whether I might read it too, since it concerned me.

She shook her head, carried the note to her cabinet, and locked it in a drawer. "It says you're who I thought you were, Horn. Only there's some personal stuff in there I wouldn't want anybody else to see unless Calf said it was all right. You've been hoping Marrow left a letter for you or something?"

"Yes. Did he?"

"No. Or anyway I haven't found it. He did leave you something, though. A boat."

My face must have shown my surprise.

"He wanted to give you something, I guess. Probably he thought a boat wouldn't be any use to me, and I'd just sell it. I would have, too, if it hadn't been on the list to keep for you. I don't know much about them."

We went to the harbor to see her, walking slowly through cold sunshine, accompanied by her grandson and another boy of the same age. *Wavelily* is the name across her stern. It reminds me painfully that "Lily" was the name of Tongue's daughter, who was murdered during my absence; I will rename the boat *Seanettle.* She is a yawl (a rig I had not sailed before) with a tall mast forward and a small one aft.

"You think you can handle her alone?" Capsicum asked. "I won't be much help."

I was surprised she wanted to sail at all, and said so.

"I've been down to look at her a couple of times." Almost defensively she added, "It's what I'm supposed to do. Marrow wanted me to look after all this."

"Of course."

She turned study the yawl, her heavy black stick thumping the warped planks of the pier. "When I was younger . . ."

I pointed to Weasel and his friend, who were already on board. "Would you like to take her out?"

She is wider in beam than my old sloop, I would say, and perhaps a trifle shorter; but she handles every bit as well and rides the waves like a duck, and that is what matters. I had Capsicum take the tiller, cautioned her against putting it over too fast, and saw to the sails with the help of the boys, setting the big gaff mainsail, the little three-cornered jigsail that was furled on the mizzen boom and is probably the only sail the mizzen has, and a jib. (There is a flying jib as well, a square sail that can be set on the topmast, and two as yet unexplored bags in the sail locker.) It was obvious she could have carried more, but on a strange boat I thought it wise to be cautious. With that sail, we churned right along; the boys were delighted, and so I believe was Capsicum.

"I swore when I came here that I would never sail again in winter if I could help it," I told her, "but I maintain that I have kept my oath. This is spring sailing, really."

She nodded, her cheeks red, her nose running, and her big, round face radiant. "There's floatflowers in this wind."

A small hand tugged at my coatsleeve. "Is he coming back?"

"Is who coming back?"

"Weasel says you told him to talk to somebody else."

"Oh. Oreb. Yes, I did. I sent him to talk to my wife." I was watching the draw of the mainsail, and not paying a great deal of attention to the small solemn face before me.

"Is he coming back?"

"I hope so. He always has, though he was gone for nearly a year once."

Capsicum patted the gunwale beside her and shooed the boys away. "You're in danger. Do you know that?"

I sat. "Not from those children. At sea, one is always in some danger; but at the moment, that's not at all severe. From Gyrfalcon, is that what you mean?"

She nodded.

"Then I know nothing of the kind. I know you thought I might be when we talked about his becoming caldé—your tone and expression made that plain. But Gyrfalcon was a member of the committee that sent me after Silk. He can hardly object to my having tried to carry out his instructions, and if he punishes me for failing . . ." I shrugged.

"You said they thought that if one of them got to be caldé the people wouldn't agree."

It was not precisely what I had said, but I nodded.

"But they'd be happy with you. I think you're right." She looked pensive.

"I said nothing of the kind. I said that it was thought they might accept Caldé Silk."

She remained silent after that, I believe until I had put the yawl about and started back to New Viron. Then she began to talk about the possibility that Gyrfalcon might be overthrown. "He'll kill you, Patera, if you give him time."

"New Viron's sickness is not Gyrfalcon," I told her. "It was a cruel and lawless place without him, and it seems to me that it's better with him, if anything. A bad horse needs a big whip, as the saying goes. We overthrew the judges of Dorp. Possibly you've heard."

She was silent. The two boys drew nearer to listen.

"It was easy—so easy that a young friend and I ordered the judge presiding over my trial to convict me, because the uprising I planned might not have taken place if he had not. He wanted to dismiss the charges against me, you see, because he was afraid. Keep your heading, please. You're letting us drift downwind."

I took the tiller myself and corrected our course.

"I got to know the people of Dorp," I told her. "They're good people—brave, hardworking, and much cleaner than we. Shrewd traders, but kind and basically honest. The judges had taken advantage of their good qualities, and so the judges had to go; if I had not removed them, the people themselves would have within a few years. Gyrfalcon isn't taking advantage of the good qualities of the people, from what I've seen. He's taking advantage of their bad ones. If they are too quarrelsome to unite against him, and so violent that they'll willingly pay his taxes to be protected from one another, they have no reason to complain."

When she still appeared unconvinced, I told her, "Dorp was like Viron—it needed a better government. New Viron needs better people."

The harbor was in sight, and I instructed Weasel and his friend in lowering the mainsail, then had them stand by its halyards. A black speck in the distance caught my eye, and I waved to it before resuming my seat on the gunwale. "In its present state," I told Capsicum firmly, "New Viron couldn't be governed by a good person—by General Mint, for example."

"Or Silk."

"Or by Silk. You're quite correct. Either would have to grow worse, or give the tiller to someone else."

★

★ ★

Oreb reached our boat (I should have mentioned this when I wrote yesterday evening) shortly after we dropped the mainsail, and was soon announcing, “Bird back!” and “Good Silk!” and pulling my hair as usual. All his nonsense.

14

Luncheon at the Caldé's Palace

"Do all of you wish to see the caldé?" Bison's clerk inquired doubtfully.

Pig said, "Aye," and rose; Hound nodded, cleared his throat, and said, "Y-yes." Oreb, who had taken a dislike to the clerk, spat, "Bad man!"

"I'll have to see about it," the clerk informed them, and disappeared for the second time behind the heavy door of carved oak.

Perhaps to conceal his nervousness, Hound said, "I suppose this has changed a lot since the last time you were here, Horn?"

He shook his head. "It seems very much the same. This is a new carpet, but it seems very like the one that was here when I carried a message to Caldé Silk. That is certainly the door I remember, and I'd guess that these chairs were here then."

The clerk returned, nodded, and motioned to him; and he told Pig, "We're to go in now. Watch out for the lintel."

"Nae muckle a wait, bucky." Pig took his arm.

"No. I would call it very gracious."

The paneled room beyond held more chairs and two desks, both littered with papers; a second door larger than the first yielded smoothly but slowly to the clerk's tug at its massive handle of molded brass. A tall, narrow window overlooking the city showed through the widening crevice; beside it the edge of a functioning glass, blank but shimmering with dove-and-silver promise. A burly, smiling man appeared to assist the clerk with the heavy door. His beard was streaked with gray, and his dark hair had receded from his temples. Seeing him, Hound swallowed audibly.

The bearded man smiled. “I’m Caldé Bison. Sorry I kept you waiting, but I had a few little arrangements to make.” He offered his hand.

Hound shook it. “These are my friends Horn and Pig, Caldé. It’s Horn who really has to see you.”

Bison nodded; his smile was guarded now.

“He’s come all the way from Blue. That’s what he says. I mean, he has I’m sure. And he’s been to Green. Pig and I . . . Well, I thought I’d better come too.”

He looked at his companions desperately; the smaller said, “I’ve been sent here by New Viron, the town our colonists have founded. I’d like to tell you about it.”

Bison shook his hand and invited them to sit down. The chairs were large and comfortable, elaborately carved, with red leather seats and tapestried backs. He edged his nearer Bison, discovering that it was so heavy he had difficulty moving it.

“I’m here as the representative of the Ayuntamiento of New Viron,” he began, “and of our town as a whole; I should explain that though it has a de facto Ayuntamiento, it has no caldé.”

“Silk talk!” Oreb proclaimed.

He smiled. “Yes, that’s what we want, but I really ought to explain the situation there to the caldé before we get to that. If I don’t make that clear, he won’t understand why we need his cooperation as badly as we do.”

“Explain away.” Bison’s eyes were guarded still.

“I’ve been gone for some time now. I must tell you that. My information may not be current; and in fact, if a lander has arrived lately from that part of Blue—”

Bison shook his head.

“Very well then. Originally we saw no need of a government of any kind. We left you and General Mint behind to fight the Trivigauntis when we went down into the tunnels. You may have regarded that as a desertion, though I hope you did not.”

Bison shrugged. “I doubt that your group included a dozen fighting men. I thought you were, well, signally courageous.”

“My father remained behind to fight. I should mention that—I must. I also ought to mention that we fought Trivigauntis ourselves down in the tunnels. You spoke of fighting men. We had fighting women down there, a lot of them. And fighting boys and even a few fighting girls. Almost everyone who could hold a slug gun fought. If they hadn't, we would never have made it to the landers."

"I can imagine."

"We were three days in the tunnels, or about that. Then three weeks on the lander, very crowded, with sleepers mixed with us. They were confused for the most part; some very badly confused indeed, nearly insane. There was almost enough water—that was an enormous blessing—but little food. I've heard since of landers on which the situation was worse, but ours was bad enough. We didn't have an easy time of it."

"Yer stuck h'it, bucky. 'Tis ther thing."

"We all stuck it, Pig." He tried to put all that he felt into his voice, and could only hope he was succeeding. "There were some leaders among us, but if the rest hadn't supported them, it wouldn't have mattered; and more than half the time the people led them. So when we reached Blue, it was natural for us to govern ourselves. If there was something to be decided we met—all or most of us—and everyone who wanted to spoke before we voted on it. There were some of us, such as Marrow, who were heard with more attention than others; and if all of them spoke on the same side, the vote was largely a formality."

Bison said, "Nevertheless, you yourselves decided it, and not your leaders."

"Exactly. That was how we divided the land, for example. We agreed upon the farmsteads, less land for those with rich soil or a spring; and when all the parcels had been staked out, we drew lots. In time, the town grew. There were many other landers from here, particularly in the first few years."

Bison nodded.

"And landers from other cities—often places we'd never heard of—came down near us, and their people joined us." (It seemed best not mention that some had been forced to, and were bought and sold like cattle.) "Then too, there had been many children on the lander. I was one myself, if you like—I was only fifteen. Many more were born in the first few years."

"Your system became unworkable."

"Yes. There were too many people, and some farms were too far away. Some people abandoned theirs and became fishermen or traders or loggers, and often they were gone and missed the Assembly. Then too, in the beginning everyone had wanted to live near town. As it became crowded, and robberies, rapes, and riots increased, many who had once spoken wisely in the Assembly no longer wanted to live in town or even near it."

"Bad hole!" Oreb explained.

"We needed a caldé, and everyone saw it. I cannot say how many wealthy and powerful men wanted the office. Eight or ten, perhaps. Possibly even more."

Bison nodded, looking from Hound to Pig. "You didn't hold an election?"

"It would've meant anarchy, a worse anarchy than we endured already—open warfare among those eight or ten factions. In the end, someone would have been caldé over . . ."

"Ruins," Bison completed the thought for him. "As I am, and as my wife was before me, and Patera Silk—if I may say it—was before her."

He shook his head. "I've seen the destruction, but I've also seen that most of Viron survived its war with Trivigaunte. I doubt that a single house in New Viron would survive the war against ourselves that threatens it."

He paused to draw breath. "I said I'd have to describe conditions in New Viron, and now I have. There is no unity and no sanity, or at least very little; but there is enough for five of our most powerful citizens to ask that you send Silk to us. The people will welcome him, and all five have sworn to support him."

Hound coughed apologetically. "He . . . From what you say. The others will still be stronger than Caldé Silk, won't they?"

"No. In the first place, they could never oppose him as a block, and each would fear the others' treachery at least as much as the caldé. In the second, thousands who are committed to no one at present would flock to him. His supporters will be united, and far more numerous than theirs."

He turned back to Bison. "That is to say, they will be if you'll let us have him. That's why I'm here. I'm hoping you'll tell me where he is, and help me persuade him to go."

"You'll want a lander, too. Or do you have one?"

Oreb added his own inquiry. "Thing fly?"

"That's right, the thing that flies between whorls. No, I haven't got one, and we'll have to have one. Surely—"

Bison raised a hand. "Surely I have a dozen I'm not using at the moment. Is that what you were going to say? Well, I don't. When Silk himself was caldé, he sent off everyone who could be persuaded to go. It used to be that when a man was convicted, he was thrown into the pits." Bison laughed. "I used to think it was going to happen to me eventually. But when Silk took over they were given their choice, the landers or execution. I can't remember any choosing execution."

"If—"

Bison's hand went up again. "Just a moment. You've asked for this, and I'm not through.

"The convicts were only a small part of what we sent. Most were manual laborers of one sort or another. Laborers and their families. Carpenters and masons, and small farmers and farm laborers. Something was said a while ago about me being caldé over ruins. That's an exaggeration, but there's truth in it, and the truth is there because Silk sent out every lander he could patch up enough to fly. Not many came back, and when they they did he filled them up and sent them off again."

Bison leaned back, red-faced and scowling, then chuckled. "Well, I've got that off my chest, and I've been wanting to for a long time."

Hound ventured, "If there's no lander, Silk and Horn can't go to Blue, can they?"

Bison consulted a slim gold watch. "If they go, they'll have to get one someplace else, that's all. I may be able to help with that. Or they can wait until I have one, though I don't know when that may be."

"You'll tell me where Silk is, and help me persuade him?"

Bison stood. "Maybe, and maybe not. I haven't decided. It's lunchtime, gentlemen, and you're invited to lunch at my palace. Will you do me the honor of dining with my wife and me? We can talk about all this some more while we eat."

Bison and Pig sat on the wide rear seat of Bison's floater, the others on jump seats facing them. "I go home for lunch just about every day," Bison told them as the floater glided forward. "Generally I tell people it's because I like my cook's food."

He paused, fingering his beard. "That's true, I do. But that's not really why I go home to eat. It's because I want to talk to my wife about whatever has come up that morning. Now I want to talk to her about this. For one thing, she knows Silk better than I do."

He said, "You must mean Maytera Mint. In a book we wrote, we—my wife Nettle and I—tried to imply that you and Maytera Mint might marry; but we couldn't be certain that such a marriage would actually take place."

"Good girl!"

Bison laughed. "Don't call her Maytera, please. She isn't a sibyl anymore and doesn't like to be reminded of it. Call her General, or just Mint. She doesn't mind either one of those."

When no one else spoke, Pig muttered, "Bonny ride, bucky. Traveled far, aye, an' h'every way but flyin'. This's best. Feel a' h'it."

"I had almost forgotten about these, but I rode in the caldé's once or twice before we left." He was looking out at the city through the transparent dome. "Willet was the driver, and he promised to teach me to drive, too. That was the day before we went up to the airship, and I've wondered sometimes whether he—well, never mind. It doesn't matter."

"Ter yer, bucky."

Bison told his own driver to go slower, then spoke to Pig, first touching his knee. "Do you know about my wife?"

"Nae had ther honor."

"Then I should tell you. She's in a wheelchair. It's not that she can't walk. She can, but it's painful. So she uses the chair, mostly. I thought you ought to know. Horn does already, I'm sure."

He turned from the contemplation of empty shops. "No, I didn't. What happened?"

"Someone tried to kill her."

Hound said, "I remember people talking about it."

"Why?"

"I don't know. He was killed himself a few seconds after he fired." Bison lifted his shoulders and let them fall. "If it weren't for your friend here, I wouldn't have mentioned it."

"Poor man," Oreb muttered. It was not clear whether he intended Bison or the assassin. "Poor girl."

Their floater, already moving slowly, slowed more, then settled to the wide, smooth paving stones before the Caldé's Palace. With the whisper of one who betrays a secret, its transparent dome vanished into its gleaming sides. The driver sprang from his seat to open one side for them; from his green uniform, he was a hoppy, a member of the Caldé's Guard.

Two more Guardsmen threw back the wide front doors of the Caldé's Palace.

Pig had taken his arm. "Braw place, bucky? Feels sae."

"Handsome? Is that what *braw* means? It is indeed, with a door you won't have to duck through. Mind the steps, though."

The questing tip of Pig's sheathed sword found the first.

"I kept you waiting outside my office," Bison explained as he went up, "because I wanted to get my wife on the glass and ask about inviting you. She doesn't always feel up to entertaining, and it seemed better to find out how she was today in private. Frankly, I was amazed. She's eager to see you."

Hound was already wide-eyed. "I just wish Tansy were here. That's my own wife. She would be so thrilled . . ."

"If you live near here—" Bison began.

"Oh, no. It's—we live in Endroad. And she'd have to dress and everything. To tell you the truth, she probably wouldn't come, because she doesn't have a dress good enough."

Bison's wife Mint was waiting for them in the big dining room in which Silk had once entertained Generalissimo Siyuf. Bison hurried over to her. "My dear, I would like to present Horn, a visitor from Blue, and his friends Hound and Pig."

"Know girl!" Oreb proclaimed.

Mint smiled at all four; and although her face was pale and drawn, her smile was bright. "Welcome. Welcome, all of you. Horn, you can't have forgotten me. You used to be my runner."

He smiled and saluted. "Of course not, General."

"It's good to see you again. No, it's better than good. Wonderful, in fact. Have we been feeding you here in Viron?"

"Bountifully."

Hound said, "We breakfasted at our inn, just down the street. There was lots of very good food, but he kept giving his to Pig."

"Bird eat!"

"And to Oreb, though Oreb didn't eat as much."

"We have plenty for him here." She gestured toward the table.

"For all of you. Sit down, please. I'm seated already, and we don't stand on ceremony here, or not till shadelow. My dear, would you push me?"

Bison did.

"There, that's better." From one end of the long table, Mint regarded the silver serving dishes with satisfaction. "I've put you all on one side because I had to. We can't pass, unless there are at least three on a side. The caldé and I have to sit at a corner when we eat in here by ourselves."

She rapped her glass three times with back of a table knife, and told the maid who appeared, "We're ready, I believe. You may—no, we're not. We ought to have an invocation. Would you do it, Horn?"

He shook his head ruefully. "You think I've become an augur. I have not. I have no right to this robe."

"Better a false augur than none. If you don't do it, I'll have to ask the caldé. He'll send to the Prolocutor's Palace, and it will be time for dinner before we have our lunch."

"I—"

"Please, Horn. For me."

He rose and made the sign of addition. "Gracious Outsider, I, who learned so many prayers at the urging of this good woman, do not know the proper one to make you on such an occasion. We offer our thanks to you—inadequate thanks, yet all we have to give—for good food and for bringing us together in hospitality and friendship."

He sat, and Bison murmured, "Phaea bless our feast."

Mint picked up a platter. "Here is squab salad, Pig. It's a specialty here, or so we like to think. May I give you some?"

"Thank yer kin'ly."

She heaped his plate. "You're the most reticent of our guests. You've hardly spoken a word since you came, so it is my duty as hostess to draw you out."

"Pig talk!"

"Thank you, Oreb. Hound, you're not eating. Give him some of that salmon and caper mixture, dear, before Honeysuckle brings in the hot meats.

"Now you must help me, Pig. I'm not very good at this, so you have to pretend that I've very cleverly made you relax and babble like a brook."

"Nae sae guid meself, mistress."

"He's a difficult case," Mint told her husband. "These overgrown boys are often like that. It's hard to get them to contribute in class, but one must persevere."

"Let me try. Pig, I know why Horn came to see me this morning. He wants Caldé Silk, and thinks I can give him to him. I take it you're a friend of his. Of Horn's, I mean."

"Aye."

"Did you come with him simply to provide moral support? Or do you have some request of your own?"

"Me een."

Bison looked back to his wife; and Hound said hurriedly, "This is my fault, Caldé. I told him I thought there might be a doctor here who could help him."

Pig coughed, a self-conscious little sound that might have proceeded from an unusually mannerly mountain. "There's nae. Yer neednae say h'it. Auld Pig knows h'it."

"Then I won't, and for all I know there may be someone here who can help you. I'll make inquiries."

"Nae. Save yer pother. Yer guid wife would nae be crouchy an' sae guid a leech yer ha'." Although Pig's shaggy head did not turn, his hand brushed Mint's arm with claw-tipped fingers nearly as thick as that arm itself. "Yer sees an' Pig walks. 'Tis ther better part. A ghaist told me ter stick wi' bucky ter get me een back. If auld Pig's ter see, yer might skelp yet."

Mint looked to the man Pig mentioned. "Is that a ghost?"

"I think it must be, though the woman—Mucor, you may remember her."

Mint nodded.

"She isn't dead, or at least I don't believe she is. But she can appear to people, rather like a ghost, and she appeared to Pig. I know it sounds mad to talk of someone's appearing to a blind man, but he could see her. Couldn't you, Pig?"

"Aye, bucky."

"He thought it wonderful, as I still do. She told him that if he remained with me he might get his sight back. Isn't that correct, Pig? That's what I understood you to say."

"Aye." Pig shifted his huge bulk in his chair. "Yer will nae leave me mair, will yer, bucky?"

"I won't, and that's a promise." He spoke to Mint. "When we

got to the city, I wanted very much to be alone awhile in the Sun Street Quarter. You'll understand that, I believe, General; or at least I hope you will."

"We—I've done the same thing."

"I asked Pig to go. He did, and it wasn't until much later that I realized how cruel it had been."

" 'Tis h'all right, bucky."

"No, it isn't, and it won't happen again. Perhaps I should say here and now, so that the caldé and General Mint can hear it, that if your vision hasn't been restored by the time Silk and I leave for Blue, you're coming with us."

Mint smiled. "That reminds me. I should tell my husband, and you, that we've been haunted again. Not just the little one this time, but by Silk as well."

He stared in consternation. "Are you saying he's dead?"

"No." Her smiled was impish. "In fact, I'm quite certain he's not, Patera."

"Good Silk!" Oreb exclaimed.

He sighed and laid down his fork. "I won't tell you again that I'm not an augur—you know it, and there's no harm in your amusing yourself. Please understand, however, that this is a serious matter to me. I must find Silk and bring him to Blue. I've pledged myself to make every effort. I've kept that pledge so far, and I intend to keep it. If I had been able to find Caldé Silk, I wouldn't be troubling you like this; but I haven't. He had a house in the country, or so I'm told—"

Hound interrupted. "A cottage. That's what they say."

"But he's not there, and no one seems to know where he's living now. Hound and Tansy didn't, and they seemed to think it unlikely that anybody in Endroad did. But the caldé does—the caldé must—"

"I don't," Bison said.

Oreb spoke for his master. "No, no!"

"Darling, you must, you simply *must,* learn to be tactful." Mint's smile was gone. "Look at him. Look at his face."

His head was in his hands. "If you—this is insane."

She nodded. "It certainly is. Let me explain. It will be insane just the same, and I can't do anything about that. But an explanation may help. You've been gone since the war?"

He nodded.

"You know Silk became caldé. Do you also know that he resigned the office in my favor?"

"He was forced out, so I was told."

She shook her head. "He may have felt he was, and even said he was. But he wasn't. A lot of people disagreed with some of his policies, particularly concerning emigration. My own husband was one of them. Eventually the disagreement grew strident, and Silk made a speech. He isn't a very good speaker, and he seldom attempts it, but that was a good one. It was so good, in fact, that it's taught in the palaestras now. He said that he had sent so many people out from Viron because he felt it was his duty to the gods, to Pas and the Outsider, particularly."

Hound, seated at Bison's end of the table, leaned toward her, cupping his ear. "Could you speak up just a little, please? I can't hear you, and I—I'd like to."

"I'll try. Silk also said that he felt it was his duty to the city, to Viron. That he had been in communication with the gods, with Pas specifically, and that the whole whorl would be scourged if enough people didn't go. There were no godlings then, or anyway nobody here had seen one."

Oreb inquired, "See ghost?"

Mint smiled and shook her head. "Then he reminded everyone that he'd promised us often that he would be caldé only as long as we wanted him. After that he asked whether the people did. He was still popular with many citizens, but a lot of his firmest supporters had boarded the landers."

Bison said, "There were cheers and boos. You'll want to know whether I cheered or booed, but I doubt that any of you will ask. I cheered. You don't have to believe me, but it's the truth."

"It is. I was with him, and I cheered too. But then, and this struck us both like a lightning bolt, he said that he bowed to the popular will. As of the moment he resigned his office—Yes, what is it, Honeysuckle?"

There was a whispered conference before Mint waved her maid away. "Pig, would you be so kind as to push my chair for me? I can move it myself when I have to, but it's a rather heavy chair. Will you help me?"

"Aye, mistress. Honored ter." Pig rose. Groping fingers thrice the size of hers found the handles of her chair and drew her slowly back from the table. "Have ter tell me which way."

"To my right a quarter turn, please."

The three remaining men watched them depart in silence; when they had vanished through a gilded arch, Hound murmured, "I wonder what she wants with him."

Bison picked up the wine bottle. "What makes you think she wants anything?"

"It's—well, obvious. Or I think it is. Maybe I wouldn't think so if I hadn't been around Horn for the past couple days. But it seems obvious after what I've heard. She could have had that girl push her, or pushed herself. Or any of us could have done it, and we can see. Pig might run her into a wall, though I hope he won't. So she wanted to speak to him alone, and jumped at the first opportunity to do it. Jumped is a bad word here, I suppose. But she did."

Bison refilled Hound's wineglass. "If a few days of Horn's company has done that, I ought to keep him around myself. What do you say, Horn? Is your pupil right?"

"I don't know. It seems plausible."

"What is she saying to him? Your best guess."

"If you're asking what she's telling him, I doubt that she's telling him anything. I would guess she's questioning him about something—something she thinks he might speak openly about when the two of them are alone—"

Hound snapped his fingers and looked pleased.

"You've guessed it? What is it? I confess I have only the foggiest ideas."

Hound's mouth opened, then shut again.

Bison said, "Tell us. I'd like to know, too."

"No. I won't. I apologize, Caldé. I'm sorry, Horn. But I like General Mint, and Pig's my friend. If they want us to know, they can tell us."

Oreb bobbed approval. "Wise man!"

Bison smiled. "Shall we try to force it out of him, Horn?"

He shook his head. "He's right, and so is Oreb. Hound, you surprise me about once a day. I believe I've said something like that to you before, and it's true. I hadn't thought through the ethical implications. General Mint is an extraordinarily good woman, and a wise one. If she believes her question—and its answer—demands privacy, she's probably correct."

Hound laid a finger to his lips.

As she came through the doorway, Mint announced, "There will be four hot meats, I'm afraid, instead of the five cook planned. But Pig has tasted the shirred oysters for me and pronounces them excellent."

"Aye. H'oreb? H'oreb h'about?"

"Bird here. No go."

"Gi'e yer ae. Yer nae had ther like."

"Good Pig!"

With her chair back at the table, Mint speared an artichoke heart with her fork. "Where was I? Oh, yes, I was trying to explain about the man who shot me."

Bison gave her a concerned look.

"Yes, I was. That's what I was circling around toward. That and the ghost. Pig wants to know about the ghost. He asked me back in the kitchen."

"See ghost?" Oreb repeated.

"I didn't, Oreb, but my cook did. Horn, I want to tell you these things particularly. You say you're looking for Silk."

"I am."

Bison said, "So is someone else. I want to tell you about that before we finish lunch, but I'll let my wife go first."

"Thank you. I don't know whether these things I'm going to tell you will help you, Horn, but they may."

He nodded. "Please go on. I'm very grateful."

"I used to be caldé. I don't know whether you remember our law here. The one concerning succession says that the caldé can designate his own successor. He can tell the people whom he wants, or leave a paper in case he dies. Caldé Silk resigned, and in the speech I've described he designated me."

He nodded again.

"The Rani's government was beside itself." Mint's smile warmed them. "Here they had been saying that Vironese women were slaves, and Viron had its first woman caldé. We thought at first that the man who shot me might have been working for the Trivigauntis. But he was Vironese, and if there was a Trivigaunti connection we couldn't trace it."

Hound asked, "Isn't it possible that he shot you just because you're a woman? There are men who feel like that, or anyway they say they do."

Bison shook his head. "Not many."

"But there are some. Isn't that right, Horn?"

"Yes, there are, I'm sure. One would be sufficient."

Mint said, "I agree, but I don't think that's what it was. Neither does my husband, though he won't say so."

"I have no opinion. We've never been able to learn enough for me to form an opinion."

"I have my own, just the same. You see, when I became caldé, the sun went out. I don't mean the moment I assumed the office. It was about a week later."

"Eight days," Bison said.

"Yes, eight days. It had been hot, terribly hot, and from what we were able to find out, even hotter in Urbs than it was here. We lost about a hundred citizens to heatstroke, mostly old people, but in Urbs it was over a thousand. We conferred with the Ayuntamiento then, Caldé Silk, my husband, and I. It wasn't a formal meeting, but it lasted for hours and we learned a great deal, as did Caldé Silk, I feel sure."

Pig swallowed. "Caldé yer call him."

"Yes, he retains the title even though he's out of office, just as I do. Just as I retain my rank of general, for that matter, though I'm not on duty or fit for it."

Honeysuckle carried in a steaming tray.

"Horn, do you remember what I told you long ago about the tunnels? How they carry warm air to the surface of the whorl and return cooler air to the interior?"

He nodded.

"Spider explained it to me while I was his prisoner. He had learned it from Councilor Potto, and Potto had learned it from Tarsier. The meeting was Silk's idea, as I should have said, and he told us about a tunnel he'd seen that was entirely blocked with water. There are others, far too many, that have collapsed and are blocked with stones and earth."

"That's why it gets too hot?" Hound asked. "Is that what you're saying?"

"Why ther wee folk douses yer glim." Pig helped himself to a handful of fragrant roast pork.

"If that means what I think, you're both right," Mint told Hound. "Heat accumulates, our summers are much too hot and our winters too mild. To keep things from getting worse, Pas blows out the sun. We didn't know that then, but the gods have told us since, and so have the godlings.

"What was I was going to say was that I made two decisions at that conference. The first was that we wouldn't let anyone else leave the whorl. And the second was that we would put crews to work clearing the tunnels under Viron, directed by Councilor Tarsier. I said I made those decisions, and I did. But we all agreed, even Silk."

"We had lost too many people already," Bison explained. "If Trivigaunte had resumed the war, we would have fallen like ripe fruit. The darkness was even worse. It had everybody terrified. Clearing the tunnels may have helped, and we got Urbs to do it too. Whether it's helped or not, at least it lets everybody feel that we're doing something."

Mint smiled again. "Trivigaunte declared a victory. It was unexpected, but very welcome. They said we had capitulated to the will of Sphigx. So we said we had, too, and it would have been difficult for them to attack us after that. Why are you shaking your head, Horn? Don't you believe me?"

"Yes." He moved a lettuce leaf on his plate so as to obscure Scylla's likeness and laid down his emblazoned silver fork. "Yes, of course. I would believe you even if you said things a thousand times more fantastic than that. I was thinking that it can't be the way things are now. People are boarding landers again to go to Blue or Green. They've got to be."

"They are," Mint said. "We—"

Bison interrupted her. "Why do you say that?"

"General Mint said the gods had told you that Pas puts out the sun, and that a godling had confirmed it. I, too, have spoken with a godling. Having newly returned to this Long Sun Whorl, I may perhaps have regarded the conversation as less extraordinary than it was."

"A huge one," Hound told them. "He sat in its hand. It bent its fingers up to keep the rain off."

"None of which matters at all. What does matter is what it said—what it told me."

"Silk talk!" Oreb suggested.

"Yes, he does. Too much at times, and doesn't eat enough. These are excellent rolls." He took another, and buttered it.

Mint asked, "Isn't your name Horn?"

He glanced at her. "Of course it is. Oh, that. Oreb calls me that, that's all. He's accustomed to calling his master Silk, it seems; and he considers me his master now. No doubt he'll return to Patera Silk when we find him. Oreb seems to be looking for him, too."

Bison said, "What did the godlings say to you? I'm waiting to hear that."

"And I'm waiting to hear where Silk is. I should offer to trade information. In fact, I do. I'll tell you, of course, whether we trade or not—as caldé you have a right to know. But will you tell me? As a reward for being open with you?"

"Yes," Mint said.

Bison sighed. "My wife has a habit of committing us to more than we can do. I don't know where Caldé Silk's living at present, although I could probably find out. My ignorance is intentional. If I explain, will that be enough?"

"I'd prefer you do more," he said.

"Then I'll try. My wife told you how she became caldé. The darkdays began shortly afterward, and the first godling came."

"I understand."

"Here's what she was leading up to. We think the man who shot her may have done it because he thought Silk would be caldé again if she died. There's a feeling—"

"It's not widespread," Mint told them, "but it's there."

"A feeling among a few people that the gods are angry at Viron because he's no longer caldé."

Pig rumbled, "Wanted ter gang, mistress said."

"He resigned his office voluntarily," Mint affirmed, "just as I told you. He didn't even ask me whether I'd accept it. That may have been wise of him, because I don't think I would have. As it was, I was fool enough to take it when he named me as his successor."

Bison told her, "You had to. They'd have rioted."

"I suppose. I can only thank the gods, as I do, that I had the good sense to resign after I was shot, and to use my wound as an excuse."

"Your wound was very severe."

"It kept me from sitting at my desk." She smiled. "I can joke about it now, you see, and say that I got terribly tired of lying on my stomach. But the shot broke my right hip, and I pray for the day when I can joke about that as well. Horn, you said people were leaving in landers again."

He nodded.

"You were right. A lot of people want Silk back. Some simply feel that Silk is the caldé the gods want. Others think Silk was right, that the gods want us to keep sending people outside. I stopped it. I ordered a complete cessation, and had my Guards seize every lander. Pas had put soldiers down there to protect them originally. Did you know that?"

"Aye," Pig said.

Hound shook his head. "Well, I didn't. Did you, Horn?"

"Yes. Silk told me about one, and later we found the bodies of others in the tunnels. They'd been painted blue, not green like ours. They had been shot with slug guns."

"As I was not. He had a needler." Mint's smile turned bitter. "He wouldn't have been able to get a slug gun that close. Where was I?"

Hound said, "About having the Caldé's Guard take charge of the landers. I've never even seen one. I suppose I'm the only one here who hasn't."

"Nae me," Pig declared, and Oreb seconded him: "No see."

"The soldiers Pas had posted there so long ago were killed by men who wanted to steal the cards they knew were in the landers. We replaced them with our own. Five soldiers to each lander. Wasn't that it, dear?"

Bison nodded.

"When I was shot, my husband wanted to punish everyone who had expressed a desire to go—"

"The ones who had demonstrated and signed petitions," Bison said. "That had started after the first darkday, and I'd gone to a lot of trouble to find out who the organizers were, and then who the rest were. The Chapter was behind a lot of it."

"Good Silk!" Oreb exclaimed. "No cut!"

He nodded. "I'm not surprised."

"Pas had spoken to the Prolocutor, supposedly," Bison told them. "The usual cant."

"At any rate," Mint said, "we decided it was best to defuse the unrest as much as we could." She glanced toward Bison for confirmation, and he nodded.

"It would have been terrible to have to arrest all those people. We would have had another revolution—"

Bison snorted.

"Oh, we would have won," she said. "I agree completely about that. But what a victory! Having killed the people we should have led, we could go around congratulating ourselves."

"You decided to allow some people to go—to do the will of Pas, if you'll allow the expression."

Bison said, "Certainly. It was just that we didn't feel that it was Pas's will to destroy Viron, and we had reached that point. Under Silk so many had left that the city was about to collapse. That was why he had to go."

"Then you can't object to my taking him to Blue—but you don't know where he—"

"Lives. Exactly. And you're not the only one looking for him, Horn. Are you aware of that?"

He shrugged. "I know some men came to Ermine's last night. That was where we stayed, and supposedly—I admit I find this hard to credit—Silk was there, too."

Bison nodded. "They beat the desk clerk. They demanded that he tell them which room Silk had, and he said quite honestly that Ermine's had no guest of that name and showed them his register. They beat him pretty badly, and roamed through the corridors until the Guard chased them out."

"Bad men?" Oreb inquired.

"You didn't arrest them?"

"We tried."

Mint said, "I haven't heard of this. What do they want with Caldé Silk?"

"To take him to Blue. So they say."

Mint pursed her lips and looked thoughtful.

Hound told Bison, "We heard the disturbance outside our room, and a shot."

"Three, 'twas." Pig's big hands were groping the snowy tablecloth for more food.

Mint nudged a platter of venison madere until it was within his reach. "You said New Viron had sent you, Horn, and that you have been gone for nearly a year. Is it possible New Viron sent them out, too? When you didn't come back?"

Slowly, he shook his head. "It's possible, but I doubt it. I think I saw one talking to the clerk at Ermine's. He wasn't dressed like one of us; and though there are some very foreign-looking people in New

Viron now, I don't believe they would have sent someone like that for Patera Silk."

Bison said, "They've got a lander. They came in one, and they've set a guard on it. If you can find Silk . . ." He glanced at Mint.

"Here Silk!" Oreb sounded annoyed.

"You may be right." Mint nodded. "That's another thing we have to talk about, the ghosts. But let's dispose of this first. May I speak without interruption for one actual minute?"

Hound said, "Please do."

"Then I'll say that it's still more possible my husband's correct. You want to take Silk to Blue, and so do these strange men. If you have Silk and they have their lander, it's possible that some accommodation—"

Bison nodded. "We could take their lander, you understand. I don't know how many men they have guarding it, but it doesn't seem likely there's more than twenty or thirty. A dozen soldiers could take it, but it would mean we'd have to let another lander full of people leave, and more than that if it came back."

"Horn's shaking his head again, darling. What's the matter, Horn? Do you think we ought to send more people to your town on Blue, even if we have to kill to do it?"

"Just the opposite. You shouldn't permit anyone to go. That was the message the godling gave me, and what I promised to tell you, hoping you'd tell me where Silk is in return."

"Pah!" Bison leaned back in his chair. "This changes everything. I have to think."

Mint said, "Good. I'll have a real chance to talk while you're doing it, and I may be able to accomplish something. Did the godling tell you why, Horn?"

He shook his head.

"They never do." There was something trumpet-like in her soft, sweet voice, a distant trumpet summoning scattered troops. "If it told you anything more, anything that we should hear or can hear, I'd like to hear it right now."

"It told me that I was to proclaim its message here in Viron, its message being that no more were to go. Pig and Hound have heard all this."

"They can stand to hear it again, I'm sure. Have you proclaimed it?"

He tugged with some irritation at his thin, pale beard. "I felt that my task was to find Silk and bring him back—to do the thing I have promised to do. I felt that the godling had no right to give me orders, no matter who or what he may represent. But I haven't found Silk—"

Mint shook her head.

"I haven't, and I'm beginning to believe that may be why—that as long as I refuse to obey, I will not."

Bison said, "There may be some truth in it."

Mint nodded. "In which case, you're nearer to finding him already. You've told us. And these friends, for that matter. Proclaiming would be too strong a word for what you've done so far, but it would seem you're moving in the right direction."

"Thank you. Thank you very, very much." There were tears in his eyes.

"You think my husband's cheated you. I could hear it in your voice a few moments ago."

"No talk!"

"Oreb's right—I shouldn't say what you're suggesting. But if you could hear it, I don't have to."

"He told you the truth. He doesn't know where Silk's living now, and neither do I. After what I've told you about the man who shot me, you should be able to understand that. Quite a few people want Silk back—"

Bison leaned forward again; one thick hand struck the table. "He made my wife caldé, and she's made me caldé. We've explained all that."

Hound nodded vigorously. "You certainly have."

"So I say to you what I've said before to any number of people. If Silk were to come to me and ask me to resign the office, designating him, I would do it that day."

Mint laid her hand, small and very white, upon Pig's. "You're Horn's friend, and you're concerned about him, I know that, and it does you credit."

"So am I," Hound said.

"I feel sure you are. Horn, you must understand that Silk has friends, too. Not only personal friends, like Pig and Hound are to you, but what might be called public friends, people who love him and supported him. They're very protective of him."

"Such ken yer maun do fer him, mistress?"

"Does that mean know? If it does, they don't. Because we wouldn't. We're friends of Silk's. But many believe we might. Or if they don't believe it, they fear it. Some of them have hidden him away, probably out in the country."

Hound said, "Well, it seems to me that if you were really his friends, he would tell you where."

Mint shook her head. "He hasn't. Because, you see, he is our friend, too. If we knew, and it were known we knew . . ."

"You might be shot again," Hound said. "I see."

"Yes, or my husband might be shot. Or we both might be poisoned, or whatever you like. Horn, have you noticed that he never said he did not know where Silk was? He said he did not know where he was living. He's been hidden away by the Prolocutor, I believe."

Bison rose. "I need to talk to him. You must excuse me, darling, gentlemen. I'll see if my glass can find him."

As Bison left, Mint said, "He wants to find out where it is for you, I suppose—"

"Good man!" Oreb announced his approval.

"I doubt that's wise," Mint continued pensively, "but I doubt even more that His Cognizance will tell him. He might offer to provide a guide, but that's not likely to do much good. May I tell you about our little ghost? That might be helpful."

With a satisfied grunt, Pig pushed his plate away. "Wish yer would."

"I will. This palace, as I'm sure you understand, was built in the days of Viron's prosperity, when it had more people and far more money. After the death of Caldé Tussah, it was shut up. Councilor Lemur, who was the real ruler of the city when I was a child and a young woman, dared neither to declare himself caldé nor to hold an election he might have lost. He contented himself with actual power, and let the trappings of power go. This palace remained vacant for about thirty years."

"Caldé Silk reopened it," Hound informed Pig.

"He did. He and my friend Marble lived here at first, with her granddaughter, a Flier whose friends had been killed by the Trivigauntis, and some others. Did you live here too, Horn? I know you were with him then. Did you go home at night?"

He shook his head. "We ate here and slept in one of the rooms upstairs."

"Of which there are a great many. The first floor is devoted to public rooms like this one. There's a ballroom, a huge sellaria, the reception room you saw, and the library. And kitchens, sculleries, pantries, and so on. My husband and I sleep in a suite on the next floor, and there are more for guests, quite a lot of them. Above them are rooms for aides, maids, attendants, ladies-in-waiting, valets, and the rest of it. Above *that* is another floor with rooms for the palace staff. They're small and I've never counted them, but there must be nearly a hundred. Our own staff isn't anywhere near that large. Neither was Caldé Silk's when he and his wife lived here."

Hound asked whether some of the rooms were haunted, and Mint favored him with a smile. "They all are, if you want to call it that. Our little ghost is most often met with in the rooms we use most, but that's probably just because there is someone to see her in those. Do you have a comment to give us, Horn?"

"Silk talk!" Oreb demanded.

"Only that you haven't talked about the topmost floor, General."

She nodded. "Because I haven't been up there. I have to be carried up and down the stairs now, so I'll probably never go. I've been told that it's a perfect warren of storerooms filled with all sorts of stuff. I haven't mentioned our cellars either, for the same reason. There are nine or ten cellars on three levels."

"Knew a hizzie 'twas frighted by a ghaist h'in a cote h'in ther lightlands," Pig rumbled.

Mint smiled again. "But that ghost was a spirit, I'm sure. Ours is material. Or at least I think she is. She walks like I do to mock me, which suggests she might be a devil. I really can't believe that, however, though some devils are material. But she takes things, and she's been known to leave footprints in dust and snow. I told you so much about this palace, because I wanted you to understand why our searches have failed thus far. Do you, Horn?"

He nodded, to which Oreb added, "Yes, yes!"

"Good. If any of you would like to tour this floor when we're through here, I'll take you around and tell you as much as I know about the rooms and furnishings."

Hound said eagerly, "I would. Very much."

"Auld Pig'll push yer, mistress. Proud ter."

"Then we shall do it, and that's a promise. Horn has seen them already, I know. Perhaps he might enjoy seeing them again."

He nodded, and for Pig's sake added, "Yes. Certainly."

"I've been calling our little ghost 'her,' and none of you have challenged it. Do you want to, Horn?"

"No." He was no longer looking at Mint's small, almost colorless face, but at the room itself, half expecting to see Olivine peeping around some corner. Mucor's death's-head stare mingled with the reflections in the glass covering a picture, but faded to nothing as he watched it.

"She wears a skirt of some rough cloth," Mint was saying, "and covers her head with a shawl or scarf. So she looks female, and we assume she is. My husband thinks she is a child from one of the houses nearby who disguises herself and slips in now and then. My own guess is that she's a beggar girl who took up residence while the palace was empty and has chosen to remain. The fact that our searches have failed to find her weighs on my husband's side, I confess. Have you theories of your own?"

No one spoke. Hound shook his head.

"Horn? You were recommended to Pig by another ghost, as we heard a few minutes ago. You must have some conjecture."

Oreb croaked, "Silk talk!" impatiently.

"I have nothing to say," he told Mint, "beyond the comment that both the theories you've outlined seem implausible to me. You challenge me, very justly, to put forward a better one; but I can't."

Mint raised her eyebrows. "You have no idea whether she's female or not?"

"Why, no. If everyone who has seen her thinks her female, I would think it highly probable she is."

Beside him Pig muttered, "Have a care, bucky."

Hound said, "If she's material, not a real ghost, you might set a trap for her. My wife and I have a little shop in Endroad, and we sell them there, traps for animals, I mean. I can give you the name of a man who'll make you a bigger one."

Mint shook her head. "That would be cruel. I would much rather have a ghost to talk about than catch a child in a trap. But I haven't told you the most interesting part so far. She was seen again yesterday."

"Fient!"

"Yes, she was, Pig. By our cook. And she had Silk's ghost with her. Horn?"

"It still sounds as though you're saying Silk is dead."

"I'm not. Our cook, you must understand, thinks our little ghost is a real ghost, the spirit of someone who left this life without attaining Mainframe. All the servants—"

Bison, returning to his chair, shook his head. "I don't believe in ghosts."

"I didn't say you did, darling, I said they do. As it happens, I believe in them myself. But not in ghosts who steal and leave footprints."

Bison said, "We don't see her for months. Then somebody hears her walking on the floor above and it starts all over again. We hear her a lot more than we see her, really."

Mint nodded. "I was about to say, Horn, that even though I believe in ghosts, I don't believe in this one. And since our limping child isn't a real ghost, I doubt that Silk was a ghost either. I think it was the living Caldé Silk our cook saw. Were you able to reach His Cognizance, darling? You were at it long enough. What did he say?"

Bison hitched his high-backed armchair nearer the table. "Don't you want to finish with the ghost first?"

"I'm nearly finished. I was going to say that Silk wasn't wearing his robe. He comes to this palace in lay clothing quite often, so that isn't surprising. A caldé, even a former one, has to be extremely careful. At any rate, he was wearing ordinary clothes, according to our cook. But they must have been very dirty. She said they looked as though he'd escaped his grave."

"Did he have . . . ?" Hound pointed to Oreb.

"No bird?"

Mint shook her head. "In a robe, with his famous pet upon his shoulder, he would have been recognized by everyone. With neither, he was still recognized by our cook, who used to be his. She must have seen him every day then, or very nearly. Wouldn't you say she sees you about that often, darling?"

Bison nodded.

"After I became caldé, he and Hyacinth were often here as our guests. Shall I bring the cook in so you can question her yourselves?"

"Nae fer me, mistress."

"What do you think, Hound? Should I bring her in?"

With more spirit than might have been expected, Hound said, "I think we should all be open and honest for a change."

Oreb flapped his applause. "Silk talk!"

"Very well," he said, "I will begin. You know, obviously, that it was I and not Caldé Silk your cook saw. It was. If you want to bring her in and have her identify me, go ahead."

Mint said, "No."

"As you wish." He was about to mention the gardener, but reflected that the old man had not betrayed him; the least he could do was to reciprocate. "You want me to tell you who your ghost is. I understand that—I'd feel the same way in your place. But she reposed her trust in me, thinking I was Patera Silk; and I intend to keep faith with her."

Bison said, "She thought you were Silk."

He nodded. "I just said so."

"So does the Prolocutor. He wants you to sacrifice in the Grand Manteion this afternoon."

"I've told you I'm not an augur."

Mint said, "You would be assisting him, I would imagine," and Bison nodded.

Pig pushed back his chair. "Best gang, bucky, an' yer weel nae. Bide, an' she'll make fast."

"But we hope he will," Bison said, "and if he will there's no reason he shouldn't remain. I ask it as a favor to me, and to my wife."

"So do I," Mint declared.

"Gang h'or bide, bucky?" Pig's big hand found his forearm.

He shrugged. "Bide. I've honored General Mint since I was a boy. I can't refuse her now."

"Good!" Bison poured himself more wine. "Your friend Hound says we ought to be more honest, so here's my contribution. I knew about this when you came to my office. That is to say, I knew that the Chapter has been looking for you and that it was because the Prolocutor had heard you were here and wanted you for manteion this afternoon. I didn't want you to do it, and so—"

Hound interrupted. "Why not?"

"Because I thought he was going to tell everybody to get on landers. We've had too much of that already. Besides, I don't have landers to give them. A couple, actually, but they're not in working order. It would cost more than the city can spare to send them off." Bison sipped his wine. "But he's not going to say that. Are you?"

"No." He sighed. "No, I'm not. I'm going to tell them what the godling told me, which is that they are to remain. That Pas—well, never mind. I'll tell them to stay, and ask their help in finding Silk."

"Silk here," Oreb declared testily.

Mint nodded. "You said our little ghost mistook you for Caldé Silk."

"Yes," he said. "She did." He recalled the gardener again and added, "It happens fairly frequently."

"I dare say. Darling, I should let you finish, but I'll do it for you. Possibly I can save you embarrassment. You were going to confess, weren't you, that you arranged this luncheon to get our guests out of the Prolocutor's reach? You were going to keep them here on one pretext or another until his sacrifice was over. Isn't that right?"

Bison grunted assent.

"Very well." Mint raised a shirred oyster halfway to her mouth, then laid her fork aside. "We've had Horn's honesty and my husband's. I don't think Oreb has to unburden his conscience. He's been entirely open from the beginning. I'll go next, and after that it will be Hound's turn, and Pig's. I intend to require it of you both, gentlemen, so be warned."

"Nae meself fashes me, mistress," Pig rumbled.

"Here then is my confession,"Mint continued. "Horn, you said our ghost mistook you for Caldé Silk, and implied that our cook did as well. You say such mistakes happen often."

"Yes."He was looking around again, not for Olivine or Mucor this time, but because he wanted to see the room itself.

(I'll never come here again, he thought. Soon we'll go to the Grand Manteion, and I'll assist. I don't know where we'll go after that, perhaps back to Ermine's or the Juzgado, but we won't come back here. I'll walk out the big door, the troopers will shut it behind me, and I'll never see this any more.)

"Were you on Blue before you came here? You were sent out from there, you said, and you talk about taking Silk there."

He shook his head. "I was on Green. I spent nearly a year there; but I came there from Blue. We've a house—you'd call it a cottage—on the south end of Lizard Island, near the Tail. A house and a mill. I used to have a boat, too, though I'm afraid that's gone forever."

"I must ask you this. It may be cruel. I think it is, but I have to. Were mistakes of this kind common when you were on Green? Did people there sometimes call you Silk, for example?"

He shook his head again. "I doubt that any of them had ever seen Silk—or knew his name, unless they had heard it from me."

"New Viron must have been settled by people from here. Its name implies that. There must be many people there who've heard of Caldé Silk, and some who saw him at one time or another. Did they mistake you for Silk, Horn? Did that ever happen?"

"No," he said. And then, when no one else spoke, added, "I know what you're going to say."

"Do you? Then why don't you say it yourself and save me the trouble."

Oreb took up the word. "Say Silk!"

He ate instead, hoping that someone else would speak.

"Pig and Hound know. Are you aware of that? They have from the beginning. I asked Pig to push my chair, and as soon as we were out of earshot I explained to him that I had taught Horn, and seen him in my classroom every day."

"No see!" Oreb commented. "No boy."

"My husband told me you were calling yourself Horn when we talked on our glasses, but he thought it was to deceive the men with you. He had fallen in with the imposition, and suggested I fall in with it, too. I did, but soon came to suspect that you believed it yourself. I asked Pig, and he confirmed it. You had never been trying to deceive him, Silk. Neither had you tried to deceive Hound. You have only been trying to deceive yourself, and now even that is at an end."

"You've never had any of the pickled pilchards," he told Pig. "Would you like a couple? I'm going to try them myself."

"Horn went." Mint's face was grim. "He carried out the Plan of Pas, as we did not. It has cost me sleepless nights, Caldé. It has cost you a great deal more, I'm afraid. Horn incurred no guilt. You would be rid of yours, if you could, just as I would prefer to be rid of mine. But you cannot rid yourself of it like this."

"Thank yer, bucky. Thank yer kin'ly."

Having added three pickled pilchards to Pig's plate, he forked two more onto his own. "I know I look like Patera Silk, but I also know who I am," he said. "No one, not even you, Maytera, can make a man who knows who he is believe that he is someone else."

15

Home

Wind in the west, but it is not much of a wind and we are on the lee side of Mucor's Rock. We could have anchored in the little bay. Perhaps we should have.

Shadow for us, while all around us the blue water dances in the last light.

We set out from New Viron at first light—Hide, Vadsig, Jahlee, and I. Hide and I would be crew enough for this yawl, and I honestly believe I could manage it alone if I had to, but Vadsig is as good as a third man (far better than some men I have seen) and even Jahlee helped. This west wind was just what we wanted for our south-southwest course; we set both jibs and spread a three-cornered main topsail between the gaff and the maintop—all this over and above the mainsail and the jigger—and fairly flew. I believe I wrote earlier that the yawl was not as fast as my old sloop. I may not have allowed sufficiently for its ability to carry sail.

Here I should say that Hide has found a bonnet for one of the jibs. He is anxious to try it; so I suppose we will on the trip home, if the weather is still good.

"Hus back!" announced Oreb. I looked around the yawl, then saw Babbie swimming from the island. He had gone ashore, and Mucor asked to keep him for a while. She is finished with him, I suppose. I wish I knew what she did.

We poled through the cleft about midafternoon, the sides scraping rock. No doubt there have been other boats in the tiny harbor since I sailed out of it in the sloop, but they left no evidence of their visits—it seemed precisely as I left it, with a few scales still on the flat stone where the fish jumped for Mucor. Hide wanted Vadsig to stay behind to watch the yawl; she wanted to go ashore, and both appealed to me.

"The women's hut is at the top," I explained to them. "I've made the climb before and have no wish to make it again. You may all go. I'll take care of the boat."

There was a flurry of expostulations.

"You're mistaken," I told them, "when you say Mucor does not know you. Believe me, she knows all of you almost as well as she knows me. You'll have to introduce yourselves to Maytera Marble, and explain who you are, but there should be no difficulty about that. Tell her I'm in the boat and eager to speak with her, and ask her come down if that is convenient."

Hide wanted to know whether to take his slug gun. I told him to take it if made him feel more secure, but that I doubted he would need it. He took it; and Vadsig had her needler in the pocket of her skirt. Babbie, who has been guarding the yawl for us while it was tied to the pier in New Viron, seemed to believe I would not allow him ashore. When I told him it was all right, that he could go with the young people if he wanted, he was overjoyed.

It was just after we left that I thought I saw her among the sunlit waves. I have said nothing to the others, and it was only for a moment. Very likely I was mistaken.

Maytera Marble came down. Oreb saw her before I did, and flew up to guide her, perching upon her shoulder and exclaiming, "Silk here!" or "In boat!" every step or two. It seemed terrible to disappoint her as I knew I must, so I postponed identifying myself as long as possible.

"Patera?" Groping, Maytera found our mooring line.

I was already poling the yawl nearer. "You don't have to climb aboard," I told her. "I'm getting off."

"You—you . . . Oh! Oh, Patera. I . . . It would be so good, so very, very good to see you, Patera."

I stepped to shore, getting only a little wet, and caught her by the shoulders. I made her look up, and turn so sunlight fell upon the thousand minute mechanisms of her face, thinking that it would be difficult to insert the new eye, readying myself and her. By that time, she must surely have guessed what I was about. "Horn? I asked Horn. Such a good boy! Did he . . . Did he tell you . . . Did Horn happen to mention, Patera, I mean it wasn't important, but . . . Oh! Oh, oh! Oh, Scylla!"

That last sticks in my mind. I remember everything vividly, and the joy in her voice most vividly of all. I won't describe the way her hands—her whole spare frame—shook, or the way she hugged me, or the dance she did there on the rocks, a dance so wild it frightened Oreb, or the way she hugged me again and even picked me up like a child when her dance was done. I would describe my own joy, if I could. I cannot.

But, *"Oh, Scylla!"*

It resonates in a way that nothing else does. It is no more vivid, yet it is colored as the other memories are not. They are wonderful and warm, and I shall treasure them always; but if ever a time comes when I must justify my existence—when I must account for the space I have occupied, the food I have eaten, and the air I have breathed—I will tell about Maytera's eye first of all. I doubt that I will have to tell anything else.

Supper cooked by Vadsig and very good indeed, considering what she has to work with. Hide is fishing and promises fresh fish for breakfast, though he has caught nothing so far.

"Going tomorrow we are, mysire?" asked Vadsig.

"Tomorrow I must talk with Maytera Marble alone," I told her. "I don't think that will be difficult, and it shouldn't take long. After that we'll leave, weather permitting."

Jahlee joined us. "You talked to her alone today. You didn't think that business about staying behind to watch the boat fooled me, did you?"

I protested that I had not been trying to fool anyone.

"You made me climb way up there, and you know my legs aren't strong."

Vadsig was surprised. "The witch to see you did not wish?"

Jahlee shook her head vehemently.

"Behind she stayed, mysire. More she cannot go, she said. All right, we said, and up the steep path we climbed. To the top we got, and there she is."

"I climbed the rocks instead of the path. I told you. It was much quicker, but much more dangerous."

Jahlee looked to me, plainly in need of rescue, and I said, "I remained behind for two reasons, neither of which had to do with fooling anyone. First, Hide was worried about the boat, and would have stayed behind himself—so I feared—if no one else would do it. I wanted him to meet Mucor face-to-face, to speak with her and to gain her friendship if he could."

Jahlee said, "She knows me already, and I know her."

"I was aware of it. Also that Hide would continue to be uneasy about the boat if you were the only one who remained behind. In addition, I wanted to speak with Maytera in private."

Vadsig said, "So her sight you might give, mysire?"

I shook my head. "I would gladly have done that before thousands. So I could tell her how I was able to do it."

"No bad!" Oreb dropped from the rigging to my shoulder to tug my hair. "Give bird!"

"Oh, I'm not so down as all that," I told him.

"Bird take! Make nest!"

"Aren't I bald enough for you already?"

"Not bald at all you are, mysire." Poor Vadsig looked as puzzled as she had made me feel; I ran my fingers through my hair (it is getting much too long) and conceded that I was not.

"You wanted to be alone with that metal woman. What do we call them?"

"Chems," I told Jahlee.

And Oreb: "Iron girl."

"With that chem, but you didn't even give her the black gown you bought her. Did you tell her where you got her eye?"

"No. Perhaps I should have told her first, and given her the gown as well; but I couldn't be sure the eye would restore her sight, and if it had not . . ." I shrugged. "Afterward she was so happy, so full of joy, and the gown would have been nothing to her." I thought of Pig, and Silk.

"So you're going to give it to her tomorrow?"

"Yes, and tell her where her eye came from. She will want to know, and has a right to know. There is not a female chem left in Viron. I asked His Cognizance, and that is what he told me. Or rather, there are none left save for the one who gave the eye. He has tried to bring her to the Prolocutor's Palace, but she will not go."

"What it is of which you speak, mysire?" Vadsig's honest blue eyes went from me to Jahlee (who looked bored), and back.

"Of chems," I told her, "and young chems a-building. There is an instinct, I think, that keeps them in one place and in hiding, until they are complete. I don't believe Olivine was aware of it; but we are generally unaware of our instincts."

Hide called Vadsig then, giving Jahlee and me a moment of privacy. I said, "When Maytera received her new eye, she said something that puzzled me, as it still does. She said, 'Oh, Scylla!' Do you know that name?"

"I don't think so."

"Because I do, you see. I even dream of her at times. It is the name of the patroness of Viron, Pas's eldest daughter. Maytera is a religious woman, and lived in Viron for centuries."

"No say," Oreb croaked; I am not sure what he meant by it.

"There really isn't any reason she shouldn't have said it, though I suspect Scylla was expunged from Mainframe some time ago. She was one of the children who rebelled against Pas."

Jahlee said, "Then it doesn't matter."

"I agree, but that's what puzzles me. It seems to me that it does, and it shouldn't. Even if Scylla hasn't ceased to exist, she certainly isn't here and has little influence. Yet it seems to me it does matter—that the word matters somehow, even if Scylla herself does not. And I don't understand why."

★

★ ★

Maytera is on board—badly frightened, but on board. She sits by the cabin and holds on with both hands, and will scarcely speak. We bios can at least deceive ourselves into thinking we might survive a fall into the sea, or even the sinking of our boats. Maytera would die, and she knows it. Hoping to distract her, I asked how she reached Mucor's Rock.

"In a little boat I made."

"It was very brave of you.

"My granddaughter sat in the back. I could see then, but she told me how to go."

"Weren't you afraid?"

She nodded.

"This can't be worse."

"It's a lot worse, Patera. I—we . . ." Our bow rose upon a wave larger than most, and she gasped.

"You don't have to worry, Maytera. You really don't. It's storms that sink boats. This is just a good, stiff wind."

It seems extraordinarily foolish to write that there was fear in her eyes, when I carried one of those eyes in my pocket for so long and the other is blind and blank; yet it was so.

"Won't you be afraid on the lander, Maytera? Travel between the whorls is very hazardous. A great many people have died."

She nodded again.

To comfort her I said, "You told us once that we shouldn't be afraid of death, because the gods were waiting to receive us."

"When you came in to teach religion you mean, Patera? Yes, I suppose I did. I'm sure I did. I always said that."

"Is it any less true now?"

"When we went out to the island . . ."

"Yes?"

"It was a long, long way out over the sea." Given something else to think about, she relaxed a trifle. "I couldn't even see it from where I sat in the boat, not at first. But we waited till the sea was very, very quiet. I forget how long it was." She paused, searching her memory for the information. "Fifteen. Fifteen days, and it was the middle of summer. Then one morning there were just tiny little hills of water."

"I understand."

"I tucked my skirt up under my belt. You know how I do."

She loosed her grip on the gunwale to finger her new gown. "It's nice to have a habit again. You had this made for me. That's what Vadsig says."

"I had to guess at the size."

"It's a little big, but I like that. If I want it tighter, I can wear something underneath it, or for winter. I won't be entitled to wear a habit anymore, but it's nice."

"It's not really a habit," I told her, "just a gown in the same style—black with the wide sleeves, and so forth."

"Yes." Her hold on the gunwale resumed.

"Would you like me to leave you alone?"

She shook her head vehemently. Oreb added, "Silk stay!" apparently fearing I had not understood her.

"It isn't bombazine anyway, Patera. Bombazine is silk and wool, sort of mixed together. This is worsted twill."

"It was the closest they had."

Her small, hard hand found mine. "Do you mind?"

In appearance, hers were the hands of an elderly woman; but I said, "Not unless you squeeze."

"When I find my husband again, I'm going to hold him just like this. And squeeze. It will be a day and a night, I think, before we ever let go. Then we'll make my daughter a real woman. A complete woman. And then we'll start another. Do you think I'll ever really get there? Will I be able to?"

"I'm certain you will."

"When I rowed out to the island, Patera . . ."

"Yes?"

"I wasn't afraid. My granddaughter told me where. I didn't know how to row, nothing at all, when we pushed the boat in. She was very patient with me."

I nodded. "She's a good woman in her way."

"That was what . . . What made it so easy for me, Patera. I kept telling myself I had to look after her, that she was just a child. . . ."

"But she wasn't. I understand."

"Poor girl," Oreb muttered. "Poor girl."

"So it really didn't matter a bit if I died, and I wasn't afraid. There's my daughter now. I have to live for her."

★

★ ★

Strange dream last night. I was back in my cell on the Red Sun Whorl. The torturers' apprentice was sitting on my bed. We talked for a time; then I got up and went to the door. Through the little barred window I could see the sea, quite smooth, and a hundred women standing upon the glassy water. All were robed in black. The boy behind me was saying, "And Abaia, and they live in the sea."

I woke, not so much frightened as confused, and went out on deck. Yesterday's wind, which had driven us so far so fast, had died away almost to nothing. The sea was exactly that which I had seen in my dream, though of course there were no women on it. Did the identical women represent Maytera's progeny, and their black robes her black gown? It seems improbable, but I can make no better guess.

Oreb talked to me for a time before I returned to my bunk. "Bird go. Go girl. Say come." With much more to the same effect. I told him to go if he wished, and off he flew.

"Where is he going, Patera?"

Maytera had spoken from the other side of the cabin. I went to her. "I thought you promised me you'd sleep."

"I promised to try."

I said nothing, and she added, "It isn't easy for us. It can take days."

"Are you still afraid?"

"Not as much. Patera?"

"Yes. What is it?"

"If I were to get to sleep, and then wake up, do you think I might be the sibyls' maid again? On Sun Street?"

I shook my head.

"I don't think so either. But I've been trying to remember the last time. The last time I slept? We don't ever wake up unless something wakes us. Did you know? And nothing did until Maytera Corn came in. Then I jumped up and fixed breakfast, but it was almost noon, and I never slept after that."

★

★ ★

Home! Home at last. Hoof wrung my hand and slapped me on the back, just as though we had never been together in Dorp. Nettle kissed Vadsig, which made my heart leap for joy, and hugged and kissed me, and that was best of all. Our little house seems just the same, and the mill is running again. Hoof has been making paper.

Oreb flew over the sea, calling, "Here Silk! Here Silk!" as though to tell his fellow birds, although they are the white seabirds of Blue, with teeth and branching feathers, four legs and four wings. And I honestly do not believe we could have been happier if Silk himself had been here.

You came out to sit with me, my darling Nettle. It has always been for you, really, that I have written this account; and so I must record that fact with all the rest, and what I remember of our conversation. The Short Sun was setting in a glory of scarlet and gold, and you brought two blankets. We spread one on the sand, though it was not really damp where I had sat down to write, and you sat beside me, and we wrapped the other around us. You asked whether I was happy now.

"Very happy," I said. "While I was away—even when I was at the West Pole with Pig—I thought that if I came home without Silk I would be wretched. How wrong I was!"

Then I thought that you would ask me about Pig, and I was prepared to tell you everything about him; but you said, "Tell me this. If Silk had returned with you, what would he do?"

I replied, "He would smile and bless us and our children, surely." I said much more of the same kind, much of it foolish. But the significant thing (or so it seems to me) was said by Oreb, who croaked, "Silk here!" and "Here Silk!" over and over again until I told him to be quiet. He was wrong, of course, though it would be far, far better if he were right. Silk is behind us, in the *Whorl*. I feel his presence just the same.

Everyone has gone to bed, including me. Everyone except Oreb, that is, and I have sent Oreb away.

I slept beside you for a few hours, and woke. Even Jahlee was asleep; she will have to hunt in a day or two, I know. I was afraid I would wake you—you, most of all. Here in the mill I will not disturb you. I have lit the old lamp, and am writing at the little table where I kept our accounts.

For an hour or so I walked alone along the beach, listening for her song.

Up there, I wrote that Silk is behind us. Well, so he is. But when I myself was in that whorl which we have put behind us, Nettle, Master Xiphias walked beside me for a time.

He is dead, of course. He went to fight the Trivigauntis, and it is likely they killed him. If they did not, the twenty-two years now past surely have; he was an elderly man when I fetched him to the Caldé's Palace for Silk and asked him about swordcraft. Yet he was there and he is here, because he is in my memory and yours. "What would Silk do?" you asked. What could he? Not merely for us (in all honesty, you and I no longer matter) but for New Viron? I told Capsicum that an evil people can never have a good government.

Silk would pray, of course.

★

★ ★

Jahlee is dead. She died in Nettle's arms.

I killed her.

Nettle came in while I was praying. I heard the rattle of the latch and the opening of the door, cut short my prayers, and rose; and it was she. We talked, at first here in the mill and afterward sitting on the beach in the Greenlight, trying to find the *Whorl* among the stars. We told each other about a great many things; at some later time I may set them down, or some of them.

You fell asleep. I laid you on the sand and went into the house for blankets, thinking that I would cover you and sit beside you until you woke. Maytera was awake, and I knelt at her side for perhaps two minutes while we spoke in whispers.

When I went outside again with the blankets, I thought you had gone. That is the simple truth. Not knowing what else to do, I walked toward the place where we had been sitting. The shadow that had covered you moved, and I saw her face.

I called your name, and you woke and screamed. The azoth was in my waistband, but I did not use it. I struck Jahlee with my fists, and when she fell I kicked her like Auk. A day may come when I can forgive myself for that.

I cannot bring myself to write the details. Everyone who had been in the cabin came pouring out, Babbie first, followed by Hide with a slug gun. There was a great confusion; and I, not knowing that Jahlee was dying, I said only that she had gone into convulsions. I carried her inside and made everyone get out.

They left—or everyone save Maytera did, and I thought she might be useful as a nurse—but you soon returned with the box of bandages and salves we keep in the mill. I had laid Jahlee on our bed; she was writhing in a way that showed very plainly that she had no bones. She had never screamed, and spoke only when you took her in your arms. Then she told you that she had intended to kill you, and that I had been right to strike her.

"He won't do it again," you promised her.

I carried the candle to her bedside. It was as though the face of a beautiful woman had been molded in wax, and the heat of the flame were softening it; but the flame was death.

"I wanted him so long . . . Did you tell her about Krait, Rajan?"

I shook my head.

You said, "He told me he'd adopted a boy shortly after he and Sinew left, but the boy was killed on Green."

"Krait was one of us."

You stared at her, and I said, "She is an inhuma."

Jahlee was struggling for breath, and after a minute or two Maytera whispered, "I don't think she'll talk any more."

You were still holding Jahlee, but you were staring at me. "You brought an inhuma here? You couldn't have!"

"I thought she would do no harm." It was hard to meet your eyes, but I met them. "Krait and I . . ." I could not explain, although

I have tried to in another book, saying in cold, black words how much we hated each other, and how much we meant to each other.

It was as if a corpse spoke from the coffin. "Krait was my son. And Sinew's. You guessed, didn't you, Rajan?"

I nodded. "You knew too much about it, my daughter. And you were too concerned to learn more."

"You think we don't care. . . ."

"About your children?" I started to deny it, then realized that I have always assumed they did not.

"You do, so we must."

There was a silence. I felt certain she would not speak again. Her face was the color of chalk beneath the tinted creams and powders and rouge.

You asked, "What did she mean?" and I answered, "To pass among us, they imitate us—even our emotions. Most of their spawn are eaten by fish while they are still very young."

"Rani?" Jahlee gasped. And again, "Rani?"

Maytera told you, "She means, you I think."

You said, "She tried to kill me. I don't want to talk to her." Yet you held her still.

Something like a smile touched Jahlee's lips. "He had so many, Rani, in Gaon. I couldn't kill them all. Lean closer."

As if compelled, you did.

"Without blood, our children have no minds."

I shouted, *"Don't!"*

"Closer, Rani. It's a great secret."

"You're betraying your own kind," I told her.

"I hate my kind. Listen, please, Rani."

"Yes," you whispered. "I hear you."

Maytera touched my hand, and I knew her gesture meant, *So do I*; but I did not send her away.

"We take their minds from your blood. Their minds are yours. Here, long ago, I drank the blood of your small son. Krait was my son, the only one who lived with the mind it took from yours."

She gasped, and when she spoke again I could scarcely hear her, although I bent as close as you did. "Without you, we are only animals. Animals that fly, and drink blood by night."

Then she died, and you, Nettle, will die too, if the inhumi learn what you have learned from her. Indeed, you may die anyway if they learn I am here; they will surely assume I have told you.

I should not have come back.

[This is the end of the record that he wrote for our mother in his own hand.]

16

Hari Mau

The Prolocutor's prothonotary entered, bowed obsequiously, and handed the Prolocutor a folded paper. When he had gone, that small and pudgy worthy said, "I *implore* your *pardon*. In *all* probability it is a *matter* of no importance *whatsoever.*"

The white-haired man he addressed smiled and nodded. "I am flattered Your Cognizance has so much confidence in me."

"Good Silk!" Oreb assured His Cognizance.

"It is not *misplaced,* I feel *certain.*" He opened the note, read it, glanced gravely at his visitor, and read it again.

"You needn't confide in me, of course. I realize—"

The Prolocutor had raised a plump hand to silence him. "It concerns *yourself.* I will not conceal *that* from you. I ask you now, *openly* and *forthrightly,* whether you repose *trust* in *my judgment* and *discretion.*"

"Much more than in my own, Your Cognizance."

"Then I *tell* you *now* that this *missive* concerns *you,* but I *dare not* let you *peruse* it. Its *substance* I shall *impart* when I deem it *appropriate*. You will *willingly* assist me?"

"Very willingly, Your Cognizance."

"Exemplary." The Prolocutor looked toward a flower-decked porcelain clock. "*Less* than an *hour* remains, and we shall *each* desire to spend *precious moments* in *private prayer.* Let *me* be *succinct.*"

"Please do, Your Cognizance."

"*First,* I shall make *you* do all the *work,* though *I myself* shall read the *victims.* Prepare yourself to *address* the *devoted supplicants* of the *immortal gods.*"

The white-haired man nodded.

"*Second,* I must *warn* you that there are in *this city* certain *strangers* who are said to *purpose* to carry you *off* to *Blue.* I sent my *coadjutor* to you last night, to *forewarn* you concerning these *outsiders.* He *miscarried,* but—why are you looking like that?"

"No cut!"

"It's nothing, Your Cognizance," the white-haired man said. "Please continue."

"I was *about* to say that our *solemn sacrifice* may afford *them* an incomparable *opportunity. You,* more than *plausibly,* are *unaccustomed* to *inserting oneself* into the *devious schemes* of the *ill intentioned.* I *invite* you to *believe* it is quite *otherwise* with *me.* If it were *my* intent to *thus abscond* with you, I should consider the above-designated *solemn sacrifice* a *golden* opportunity."

"I'll be careful, Your Cognizance."

"Do so." The Prolocutor looked dubious. "You are of an *adventurous* and *mettlesome* disposition. *Inculcate* the innocence of the *dove* and the *prudence* of the *turtle.* You may need *both.*"

"I'll strive to, Your Cognizance."

"I *hope* you *do.*" The Prolocutor glanced at his clock again. "*Lastly,* that *communication.* General *Mint* desires to speak with *you.* You need fear no *bootless* delay. She is *here* in *my* Palace."

He was taken to a small but richly appointed room on the same floor by the prothonotary; a somber-faced Mint waited by the window, small hands clutching the armrests of her chair.

He bowed, Oreb fluttering on his shoulder. "This is a great honor, General. Can I be of help to you?"

She nodded and managed to smile. "Shut the door, please. We haven't time for propriety."

He did.

"The butchers may be listening, so keep your voice low." She glanced about her. "They may even be watching, but there's not much we can do about it. Sit close beside me, so that you can hear me and I can hear you. This . . ."

He waited.

"This is something I've wanted to do for a long time. And I'm going to do it right now. My husband—well, never mind. You're not Silk. We settled that."

"I hope so," he said.

"So I want to tell you something about him. That little augur kept telling me you were going to sacrifice at three. A grand affair, he said, and he wanted me to come."

"So do I."

Her eyes widened. "Do you really? Then perhaps I will. But I must tell you first." Her voice, already low, fell until it was scarcely audible. "And give you something."

He waited.

"Echidna ordered me to command the rebellion against the Ayuntamiento, I suppose because I could ride. Anyway, I did. There was a man there who had a wonderful horse, a big white stallion, and he let me have it. I jumped onto its back. In those days I could do such things."

"I remember."

"Thank you. I'm glad of that. I jumped onto its back, and it reared. I suppose that without a saddle it hadn't been expecting to be ridden. As it reared, Silk threw me his azoth." She paused. "You may have heard. It was one of the most famous incidents of the war."

"I have," he told her. "I've even written about it."

"Good, I'd like to read it sometime. I didn't stop to ask myself where Silk had gotten such a thing. I simply used it."

She reached under the shawl on her lap. "Later I learned that his wife had given it to him. Hyacinth, I mean, that woman who became his wife not long afterward. I would like to think it may have been because of the azoth."

He nodded.

Her pinched face was paler and more serious than ever; and he sensed, belatedly, that she was in pain. "That woman made him promise to, in return for the azoth. It must have been like that. He would've kept the promise and the secret. It was how he was."

"I know."

"Do you also know that I still have it? The great, the famous weapon from the Short Sun Whorl? I do."

He watched her in silence, praying for her in his heart.

"Aren't you going to ask what good an azoth is to a crippled woman in a wheelchair? Go ahead. I'm inviting the question."

He shook his head. "Legs are for running away."

She considered, her head cocked to one side. "Sometimes. Sometimes running away is the wisest thing one can do."

"You're right, I'm sure."

"I used to run away from you. From Silk, I mean. Not because I was afraid of Silk, but because I was afraid of humiliation. That was foolish."

He nodded. "Humiliation is a gift from the Outsider, I'm quite certain."

"Really? Now you sound like Silk."

Oreb croaked, "Good Silk," and stirred upon his shoulder.

He said, "I'm flattered. If that's the sort of thing Silk says, we need him badly."

"Man come!"

"I was going to say that all humiliation comes down to exclusion. The humiliated person feels himself or herself no longer a member of the group—or at least, no longer a member in good standing. As he leaves the group, he approaches the Outsider, the god the gods have cast aside."

There was a perfunctory tap at the door, which opened at once. The prothonotary said, "You must be in the Grand Manteion in fifteen minutes."

"I'll do my best."

Mint motioned for the prothonotary to close the door, and he did. "We haven't long," she said, "or I'd ask you about that. There isn't time. You're in danger. My husband told you."

"There are strangers—His Cognizance calls them outsiders, which maybe significant—here looking for Silk. Is that what you mean?"

She nodded, and the hand that had been concealed by her shawl emerged holding an azoth with a watery, somewhat purplish stone in its hilt and a bloodstone near the guard. For a moment she seemed reluctant to surrender it.

Oreb whistled, adding, "Bad thing!"

"It's a dangerous thing, certainly. It's also a valuable thing. You could sell it for a great deal of money, General."

"I could, if it were mine to sell." She sighed. "It isn't. You would have made this much easier for me, Horn, if you had asked the question. I was going to say that though such a woman could not use an azoth, she might still have the pleasure of giving it to someone who had need of it. That pleasure is mine, and I claim it. Take it, please."

"If you no longer want it, you should return it to Silk," he told her.

"I do want it. I want it very badly, but I have no need of it and you may. As for giving it back, I've tried to. Silk accepted it once but soon returned it. Cover it with your hand."

In the sacristy of the Grand Manteion, Oreb eyed the ranked sacrificial knives. "Good Silk. No cut!"

"I won't," he said, "but you must help me by remaining here. If you fly out there, the people will see you and think I've brought you to offer you to the gods, and may very well demand I do it. Will you stay here?"

"Good bird!"

He had brushed the augur's robe Olivine had given him (half shamed by the clumsy stitches with which he had sewn his corn into its seam that morning), washed his hands, and smoothed his unruly hair. Now on impulse he shaved his beard, scraping it away with a well-tended razor inlaid with the Chapter's knife-and-chalice seal. "My father's was larger," he told Oreb, "but much plainer—an ordinary bone handle. This is ivory, unless I'm badly mistaken."

"No cut!"

"I'm trying not to. A little more lather, I believe."

He whisked the badger-hair brush against the scented soap in the Grand Manteion's porcelain mug, then applied the brush vigorously to his left cheek. "Here I confess I remind myself of Doctor Crane, shaving off his beard in our inn at Limna. He kept wanting to spare a little, and so do I. But no, it must all go, as his did. With it gone, my resemblance to Patera Silk will be much less marked, I imagine; besides, it—"

"Good Silk!"

"It may throw those outsiders—to use His Cognizance's suggestive term—off the track."

"Bad men?" Oreb flew from windowsill to washstand, from which he regarded his master through an eye like polished jet.

"I wish I knew. There are about a hundred things I wish I knew, Oreb. I'd like to know whether Pig and Hound are in the congregation, for example; and I'd like very much to know whether General Mint and Caldé Bison are, to say nothing of these outsiders. I'd like to know where Silk is, why neither Bison nor His Cognizance will take me to him when it would appear to be so much to the advantage of both to have Silk out of the city." After giving his upper lip a final touch, he rinsed the razor under the tap.

"Good Silk!"

"He is, and for Caldé Bison and His Cognizance that is just the problem. For His Cognizance, Silk is a second Prolocutor, able—even if unwilling—to countermand his direction of the Chapter. For Caldé Bison, having Silk here is still worse."

Energetically applied, the washcloth dotted his black robe with dots darker still. He examined them and decided it could not be helped, and that they would dry in soon in any event. "He has General Mint, his lady wife, who's so careful not to call herself Caldé Mint. She is a second caldé, just the same."

"Good girl!"

"Of course. That's why so many people love and trust her. But behind her is yet another caldé—Silk. I wouldn't want Bison's job on any terms, and most certainly not on the terms he has it."

An augur appeared in the doorway of the sacristy. "Ready for the procession, Patera? I'll show you where we're assembling."

By now it did not seem worthwhile to object to the honorific.

Whispers swept the throng that filled the Grand Manteion as a breeze sweeps a forest in leaf, soft as it left the narthex, gathering strength as it proceeded down the nave. He had no way of knowing (he told himself) that it was because he was walking with the Prolocutor, a step behind and a step to the right as he had been instructed to. Yet he knew it was, and was subtly, inexplicably embarrassed.

There were seats for them some distance from the Great Altar, seats sufficiently removed that they would not be troubled by the conflagration a full score of sugurs and sibyls were preparing to kindle upon it—for the Prolocutor, a magnificent ebony throne austerely chased with gold, for him a chair beside and below it scarcely less imposing and likewise ebony.

A choir of . . . He tried to count the singers. Four hundred at least. On Blue they might have founded a little town of their own, called Song or Melody. Intermarried, and produced a sweet-voiced clean-faced race that would quickly become famous.

Their music rose, fell, then rose again, at once urgent and majestic. Glancing behind him at the gray shimmer of the Sacred Window, he wondered what gods listened, if in fact any did.

One did, surely, though not from the Sacred Window. Pig was in the audience. The memory of Silk and what Silk had told him in the ruined villa that had been Blood's returned, more vivid than ever.

Sunshine caught and concentrated in a wide reflector of bright gold did its work. A thread of smoke rose from the vast, ordered pile of cedar on the altar. (Wood enough to build a nice little house for some poor family, he thought rebelliously.) The white thread thickened. As the hymn reached crescendo, a tiny tongue of flame appeared.

"Rise," the Prolocutor whispered, "and *receive* my *blessing*."

He stood up, faced the throne, and bowed his head while the soft right hand of the Prolocutor traced and retraced the sign of addition over his head and the Prolocutor's plaintive voice recited the longest blessing in the Chrasmologic Writings, with extraordinary emphasis on every second or third word.

When it was over, he strode past the altar to the ambion. There was a great deal to say, and little time in which to say it; but it would be far less difficult if he could link it in some fashion to the Writings. Breathing, "Help me, O Obscure Outsider," he opened them at random.

" 'A simple way would be to admit that myth is neither irresponsible fantasy, nor the object of weighty psychology, nor any other such thing. It is wholly other, and requires to be looked at with open eyes.' "

Sighing his thanks, he closed the magnificent gem-studded volume and laid it aside. "In a moment," he said, surveying the congregation, "we will offer our gifts to the immortal gods. We will implore them to speak to us through their Sacred Window—"

There was an audible buzz of talk. He stood silent and frowning until it ceased.

"And we shall ask them to speak through the entrails of the animals we give them as well. It is easy—far too easy—for us to forget that they have spoken to us already, long before the oldest person who hears me was born.

"What the gods are saying, I believe, is that there are various forms of knowledge, of which myth is one, and that we must not confound them. It is always a temptation to throw aside knowledge—it makes life so much easier. It may well be that the kind we are most tempted to cast away is exactly that which the gods warn us to preserve today: I mean the knowledge that a thing is itself, and not some other thing. A man says women are all alike, and a woman that men are all alike. One who fancies himself wise says that one can know only what one sees, or that no one can know anything at all, and thus saves himself much labor of thought, at the cost of being wrong."

He glanced at the altar fire, gauging how much time remained. "Let us look at the myth that Pas wants everyone to leave this whorl and go to one of the whorls outside. There can be no one among you who has not heard it in one form or another, perhaps even from the lips of Patera Silk. I would certainly imagine that it has been said, with greater or less elaboration, by augurs standing at this very ambion."

There was another buzz of talk. Fingers tapping at the sides of the sculptured wave of onyx that was the ambion of the Grand Manteion, he waited for it to subside.

"Is it a mere falsehood? No, it is a myth. Is it merely an entertaining fantasy? No, again. It is a myth. Is it an exact and accurate statement of fact, as though I should say that His Cognizance, who permits me to speak to you today in his place, is a wise and good man? No, it is a myth."

He paused to wipe his perspiring forehead. "When Patera Silk went down to the first lander in the tunnels below our city, he saw the following words on the last stair: 'He who descends serves Pas best.' Those words were graven on those stone steps at the order of Great Pas himself. Plainly then, those who have thus descended stand highest in the eyes of Pas, and I believe highest in those of his father as well. From that we easily see the origin of the myth. But you to whom

I speak, the citizens of this sacred city who do not descend, serve him also."

Flames snapped upon the altar now, the voice of the fire nearly as loud as his own. A whiff of fragrant smoke reached his nostrils.

"The Writings did not say it in the passage we read; but if we had read another—one I have read often—we would have been told that the gods require us to serve in one way at one time, and in a different way at another."

He had hoped to see General Mint's chair in one of the aisles, and had failed to find it. As he spoke, he discovered her at the end of the fourth row, having presumably been lifted into her seat by an attendant who had rolled her chair away. Bison sat beside her, watching through narrowed eyes and watched himself by Oreb, perched upon a cornice.

"So it is with us. Not long ago, it was our duty to leave, to board landers and cross the abyss to Blue or Green. Many of us did, and so pleased the gods. Now they wish those of you who have not gone to remain—to remain indefinitely, in fact, presumably for the rest of your lives."

Bison was nodding and smiling, his teeth gleaming in his black beard.

"Two nights ago, I conversed with a godling who informed me of this, and told me to tell you, as I now have. I would be neglecting my duty if I did not do so, given this opportunity. I have fulfilled it instead, and I pray the blessing of the gods, of the Outsider and Silk particularly, in the days ahead."

He had watched Pig as he spoke; but if Pig's expression had altered in the slightest, the distance between them had been too great. Now a venerable augur approached the ambion carrying a gleaming sacrificial knife upon a black velvet pillow. The heat of the altar fire was palpable.

"We are ready, Patera," the augur whispered.

"No." As his hand closed on the jeweled hilt, two more augurs led a great, gray stallion into the central aisle.

"This's what we call the sacristy? It's where we all vest, even His Cognizance, sometimes." The voice of the eager young augur who had gone to get Pig and Hound floated through the open doorway.

"His Cognizance isn't in there now, or I don't think so. But Patera Horn is."

He sighed as he dabbed at the bloodstains that spattered his robe, telling himself that it was at least an improvement on "Silk."

The brass tip of Pig's long sword tapped the stone floor and rattled against the sides of the doorway. "Man come," Oreb announced superfluously.

"Come in, Pig. Most of us have finished cleaning up. I'm almost finished myself."

Pig did, forced to duck only slightly to get through the doorway and looking pleased about it.

The eager young augur followed him. "I'm sorry, Patera, but I couldn't bring the other gentleman. He had to go. A man spoke to him, and he said he had leave."

" 'Twas candles, bucky," Pig rumbled. "Couple a' hundred fer a card, an' Hound h'off like a h'arrow."

"He did appear to me to be a merchant," the eager young augur added. "I endeavored to get his name, but he was engaged with the other gentleman and did not reply. If you're concerned I could make inquiries."

"I doubt that it matters." He dried his hands on a spotless white towel, watching the blood-tinged water in the washbowl drain away, then used the towel again to mop his sweating face. "He'll rejoin us this evening, I feel sure. Pig, would you like a chair? I'll fetch you one."

"I'll do it, Patera," the eager young augur said, and did.

"Thank yer," Pig rumbled.

"Wouldn't you like a chair too, Patera Horn?"

He shook his head, trying to indicate by his expression that the eager young augur had better go.

"This is a very, very great honor for me, Patera. Was, I mean. I, uh . . . I mean you. And His Cognizance, naturally."

"One that you have more than earned, I feel certain." He motioned toward the door.

When the eager young augur had gone, Pig said, "Win't, hain't yer, bucky? Nae wonner, h'all yer done."

"Tired? Actually, I'm not. His Cognizance had me toiling like a whole slaughterhouse and more than half sick at the thought of so many valuable animals dying. But I'm not tired now. Far from it." He got his knobbed staff from a corner and twirled it, although he knew that Pig could not see the gesture. "If it were up to me, I'd be out on the streets looking for Silk this very minute."

"Good Silk!"

"Time tint be time toom, bucky."

"Wasted time cannot be recovered? Is that what it means?"

"Stray't."

"Near enough, then. But we can't go, or at least not yet. There's a crowd waiting for us. For me. Several of these augurs told me about it, and that was when I sent that one for you and Hound. I thought that since we had to wait, we might as well wait together." He paused, smiling. "They'll forget about us in half an hour or so, I imagine. Or at least they'll think we went out some other way, and go on about their business. Were you able to follow the ceremony?"

"Ho, aye. Hound tittled ter me. Bucky . . . ?"

"Yes, Pig." He grounded his staff. "What is it?"

" 'Tis nae me fash, bucky. But yer were ter h'ask h'about yer frien' Silk, were yer nae? Yer dinna."

"No. No, you're quite right. I did not."

He carried over a second chair for himself and sat down. "I didn't ask them—ask you, I should say, you of the congregation—about Silk for one simple reason."

"Good Pig," Oreb muttered.

"You're right," Oreb's master told him. "Pig is a good man, and he knows the reason as well as I. So does Hound for that matter."

"Know h'it? He does nae."

"I believe he does. I did not ask the congregation, Pig, because I knew that everyone in it thought that I myself was Silk. As you do."

Pig did not speak. The blind face was tilted upward and to the left; as the silent seconds passed, two dots of moisture darkened the dirty gray rag that covered his empty sockets.

"They left you tears. I'm glad. But if they're for me—"

"Men come," Oreb announced distinctly.

"There's no need. I know who I am, and what I am to do."

A very tall man in an immaculate white head-cloth, dark-complexioned and strikingly handsome, strode into the sacristy, followed by similar men less richly dressed. "Patera Silk."

He shook his head.

The tall man knelt, one hand holding up the gilded scabbard of a long, sharply curved sword. "We come to proclaim you Rajan of Gaon, Patera Silk. Hail the Rajan!"

"Hail!" shouted the six with him. Their swords were out almost before the first cheer. They waved them above their heads, and one fired a needler into the ceiling. *"Rajan Silk!"* Oreb fled through an open window.

"No." He rose. "I am not Silk. I appreciate the honor you seek to do him. Believe me, I do. But you are addressing the wrong man."

"Tentie noo, bucky. Tentie be."

"I don't believe they have come to harm us, Pig. They want me to go to their town, or so I imagine."

The tall man stood, and was half a head the taller. "To judge our town, Rajan. That is why we have come."

He nodded to himself. "I thought it was something like that. You created a disturbance at Ermine's. Beat the clerk."

"Yes, Rajan." The tall man's smile was as bright as the sapphire over his forehead. "We knew you were there. Someone had seen you go in. The clerk would not tell us, so with our belts we chastised him. Our belts and the flats of our swords. A donkey beaten is well next day."

"I see." He paused. "And you would like to have Patera Silk judge you."

"You." The tall man bowed profoundly, his hands together. "You, Rajan, are he."

"My proper name is Horn. This is my friend Pig."

The tall man bowed again. "Your servant is called Hari Mau, Rajan." The others bowed too, and there was a flurry of names and shining smiles. "You must come with us," Hari Mau said, still smiling.

"I will not."

"Tentie," Pig rumbled again, and stood.

"You must. Hear me, Rajan. Echidna herself demands it."

He raised his eyebrows. "You have a Sacred Window on Blue?"

"No, Rajan. Yet we still serve the gods, and they speak to us in dreams. I swore—"

There was a murmur of objections behind him.

"We swore, we brothers, that we would not return to our homes and wives without you. We will do you no hurt." Hari Mau's smile had faded; his eyes were serious. "You will live in the palace we are building you, and judge us with justice."

He sighed. "Did you read about me in a book, Hari Mau? Before your dream?"

"Yes, Rajan. Afterward, too. Many, many others had the same dream, even the priests in the temple of the goddess."

"You cannot compel me." His right hand gripped the knobbed staff; his left touched the hilt of the azoth under his tunic.

"We do not seek to compel you, Rajan. Far better that you come willingly."

"I am going to tell you now, for the final time—"

"Good man?" Oreb spoke from the windowsill.

"That I am not the one you seek—the one whom I sought too. That I am Horn, not Silk."

"Good Silk!"

"Knowing that, do you still want me to come with you?"

Hari Mau said, "We do, Rajan," and the men around him murmured their agreement.

"You have a lander—that's what Caldé Bison told me. It's below this city now, guarded by your followers?"

"It is. As soon as you are on board, Rajan, we will fly back to Gaon."

He shook his head. "That's not what I want. I will go with you—go willingly and do as you ask—if you will fly my friend Pig—"

Pig grunted with surprise.

"To the West Pole first. Will you do that, Hari Mau?"

When the operation was over and the last bandage in place, and the tiny hands that had mimicked the surgeon's every motion had withdrawn, the white-haired man who had watched it all let himself breath again. "May I see him now?"

"You are." The surgeon pointed to the glass. "There he is." The surgeon was as tall as Hari Mau, and darker.

"I don't mean that."

The bandaged figure in the glass stirred, and the man who had spoken wondered whether he had been overheard. "I'd like to sit beside him for a minute or two, and pray at his beside. May I do that?"

"It's some distance." The surgeon spoke slowly, and his voice was rich and deep. "I'll give you directions for the tunnels, but I can't go with you. I can't take the time."

"Bird find!" Oreb declared. "Find Pig!"

"I'm going to Blue, and that's a great deal farther. I don't believe I'll ever get back."

The surgeon shook his head, his eyes on Oreb. "We'll leave this system once the *Whorl* has been repaired, but that won't be for years. A lifetime, likely as not."

"And I can't take the tunnels. My—my friends are anxious to go home. If they see me now, they'll put me on the lander and leave at once, I feel sure. Can't I travel on the surface?"

"I must myself," the surgeon said; from his tone, he had not been listening. "Your name is Horn? Is that correct?"

"Good Silk!"

"Yes," he said.

"I'll tell them to expect you, Horn. And I'll guide you, at least for the first chain or so. It's not going to be easy. I hope you understand."

He said, "I want to just the same."

"All right." The surgeon touched his belt, and a hatch at the top of the room lifted silently and almost smoothly, admitting hot wind and a pinch of wind-blown sand.

"If you could only lend me a propulsion module . . ."

The surgeon shook his head. "You have been to the East."

He nodded. "They had propulsion modules there, and they even loaned us some to use until we left."

"They need them." The surgeon kicked off, drifting upward until he caught the edge. "They require them for the fliers, so they have spares. We don't need them here, and don't have them. We've learned to do without them. Aren't you coming up?"

He did, rising too slowly because he had been afraid of rising too fast. "Silk come," Oreb announced before Oreb was snatched away by the wind.

"I don't understand all this. I don't understand how you can live like this."

"In the dark?" The surgeon caught his hand; the surgeon's own was twice as long, pink at the palm and the undersides of the fingers. "It's not usually this dark." Scarlet flashes failed to illuminate a pandemonium.

"The wind, and the sand. Is it always like this?"

"Yes," the surgeon said. "Turn on your light."

"I've been trying to." His fingers, fumbling for the tiny switch on his headband, moved it by accident; at once a glow from his forehead lit up the surgeon's dark, severe features. "I didn't realize—I should have, of course—that there would be darkdays here, too. Or that you'd have so few lights."

"We don't usually need them. These," the surgeon lit his own headband, "are medical emergency equipment."

Already his feet were above his head. He snatched at the pale blur that was the surgeon's tunic to keep himself from being blown away.

"You have your radiation monitor?"

He was about to say no when he remembered that it had been pinned over his heart. "Yes—yes, I do."

"Don't ignore it. We can fix most things here, but that one's as tough as it gets."

"Bird back!" Oreb's claws closed upon his shoulder.

"I suppose that's why you're here, so close to the—the . . ."

"Reactor. Come on." The surgeon was moving away and taking him with him.

"And the whatever you call it—the place where you operated on Pig—"

"Sick bay."

"Is farther away, where the danger isn't so great. Your reactor powers the sun? That's what we were told, though I find it almost impossible to think of anything powering the sun."

"Here, grab this outcrop." The surgeon's hands, so much longer and stronger than his own, guided his to it. "Don't let yourself think you're weightless."

He gripped the sand-smoothed rock with grim determination. "That's how it seems."

"Because of the wind." The white light of the surgeon's headband was moving away. "The wind wants to pick you up and blow you away. If you let yourself believe that you have no weight, it will do it, too."

"No fly," Oreb explained.

"The heat makes the wind?" He was frightened, so much so that his teeth chattered.

"Exactly." The surgeon seemed to be waiting for him, having

perhaps noted the chattering. "A darkday makes it worse, because there's none from the sun to counter it. Eventually it would cool off and the wind would drop, but they'll restart the sun long before that. It would take months for the reactor to cool completely."

Staring at the surgeon's light, he said fervently, "I see."

"The sand blows around. One day it will be deeper than a man can dig, and next day it's bare rock. It wears the rock away, and makes more sand, and the rock cracks in the heat."

"It seems very hot now," he ventured.

"It isn't. If the sun were on, all this would be too hot to touch, almost. Keep down, so the wind doesn't get you."

"I'll try," he promised, "but it seems very windy."

"That's because we're going uphill." The white glow of the surgeon's headlamp vanished in the middle distance, but the surgeon's voice still reached him, the only calm element in that wild night. "You've got to kick off with your legs."

"No fly!" Oreb insisted.

The surgeon's light reappeared, surprising close. "Your legs are a lot stronger than your arms."

He gasped for breath and spit out sand. "I didn't even know we were climbing."

The white light had halted. "You don't weight much, but don't let that make you think you won't get hurt if the wind slams you into some rocks. It's happened to me, and it hurt like Holy Hierax. People are killed, sometimes."

He wanted to say that he would try to be careful; but it was all he could do to struggle forward, half crawling.

"We're not supposed to fix up Cargo." They were near enough that his deep-set eyes and broad flat nose showed dimly. "But I'll make exception for you. Ask for me if you get hurt."

"You made . . ." He was panting. "An exception . . . For Pig. Thank you."

The surgeon caught his arm and helped him over the final two cubits. "I ought to tell you about that."

"Please do."

"Hold on to this and you can stand up."

Again the surgeon guided his hand to it; over the whistling wind, the snapping of his augur's robe sounded like the incessant cracking of a whip.

"Look over there. Can you see my arm?"

Oreb repeated, "See arm?"

"Yes." The pale sleeve made it easy, although there appeared to be no hand at the end of it.

"That green light. Got it?"

"I think so. Is it blinking?"

"That's where you're going. That's the sick bay. It's a league or a league and a half, something like that. Tell him I said hello."

"I certainly will."

The wind was rising again, and the surgeon had almost to shout to make himself heard. "You're still going?"

"I—yes."

"You can come back with me if you want to."

He nodded, although their faces were nearly touching. "Thank you. You're very kind."

The surgeon took his arm. "Then let's go."

Oreb added his own vote. "Go now!"

"No," he said. "You misunderstood me. I didn't mean that I was going back with you, only that you've shown extraordinary courtesy. I'll always be indebted to you."

"I thought you'd want to turn around once you'd seen it."

"No," he said.

"Just to visit a sick friend."

"It's Pig." At the moment that was all the explanation he could give.

"All right. Look behind you. See the red light?"

He nodded again. "That's where we came from."

"Right. There's a box at the base of the pylon. Open it, pull the lever, and close it again and you can go inside. Not the Remote Viewing Room, but close. Ask for me."

"Will I have to go back there to get back to our lander?" The thought to making the league-long journey twice was almost more than he could bear.

The surgeon shook his head, and it was possible to think of living again, of Pig resting in a white bed, and silence, and prayer. The surgeon said, "This is in case you turn back."

"I won't."

"You might, if you're hurt." The surgeon clasped his shoulder. "If you don't . . . Well, good-bye."

"Good-bye, and thank you again." He would have turned then and gone, but the surgeon's hand maintained its grip.

"You'll be farther from the Pole. You'll have a little more weight as you get nearer the sick bay."

"That's good to know."

"I wish I could go with you."

He felt a surge of gratitude. "So do I."

The surgeon released his shoulder. "I'll tell them to expect you, and ask them to change your dressing. There'll be sand in it."

"Thank you," he said. "Thank you again."

He had started down the slope when the surgeon's hail stopped him. "What is it?"

"You thanked me for patching up your friend Pig."

"Yes!" He had to shout to make himself heard.

"They told us to. A flier did. Wait up."

He watched the surgeon's bobbing headlamp ascend the rocky slope a good deal more quickly and skillfully than he had.

"The flier said we should. Maybe I ought to tell you about it. Mainframe's the captain. You probably know."

His instinct urged caution. "I knew it was in the east. I wasn't sure you obeyed it as well."

"We do." The surgeon drew him toward a boulder that offered shelter from the wind-driven sand. "It used to communicate with us directly. It can't anymore because the cable's been cut. So it sends fliers. Or godlings, but mostly fliers."

"No fly!" Oreb advised.

"We've found the break and we're fixing it, but it isn't as simple as hooking your optic nerve up to your friend's. There are millions and millions of fibers and every connection has to be right."

"I believe I understand."

"Still, it's got to be fixed before we leave. So do a lot of other things." The surgeon paused, clearly wrestling with whatever it was he really wanted to say.

"I'm very glad you agreed to operate on Pig, in any case."

"The thing is, we can't always be sure the flier's telling us what Mainframe said. Sometimes we think he may be adding on his own, or leaving something out. You know about the animals?"

"What animals?"

"Great Passilk is supposed to be mad at his wife and half his sprats. Frankly, I don't believe it." (Doctor Crane's chuckle seemed to echo among the rocks.) "But people say they've turned themselves into animals to get away from him."

"No cut," Oreb muttered in his master's ear.

"I heard something about that," he told the surgeon.

"So when we were told to fix up somebody, and it turned out he was called Pig, well, we had to wonder. Do you follow me?"

"Well enough to guess that you're in awe of gods you do not reverence."

"I suppose that's fair." The surgeon turned to go.

"You have been very good to us—to Pig and me. You've been a friend when we needed one in the worst way. So let me assure you that you've nothing to worry about. Pig doesn't harbor Echidna or any of Echidna's children. I won't explain how I know; but I do know. You needn't fear that I'm mistaken."

The surgeon turned back to him. "Thanks. You seem like somebody who can be trusted."

"You can trust me in this, at least."

The surgeon held out his hand. "What's your name? I know you told me, but I've forgotten it."

"Horn," he said; somewhere Doctor Crane chuckled again.

"M'to. It means a river." The surgeon cleared his throat and spat. "Those little men up on the bridge think we're pretty crude here in the black gang, and maybe we are. But we're not tricky, and we know a lot more medicine, because we get a lot more people hurt."

"I doubt that their opinion of you is nearly as low as you believe. The flier who told you about Pig—was Flannan his name?"

The surgeon shook his head. "I didn't talk to him. I don't know what his name was. I've got to get back."

They shook hands again.

When he had crawled over twenty or thirty cubits of rocky, windswept ground, he heard the surgeon's voice behind him, borne on the hot polar gale. *"Don't disregard your monitor!"*

He shouted, "I won't!" hoping to be heard.

"And don't piss into the wind!"

At his elbow Crane's ghost murmured, "Is it really worth all this to fight free of Hari Mau for an hour or two, Silk?"

17

He Took Me with Him

Pretty soon after the inhuma was buried he went back to New Viron and took me with him. "I must speak to Gyrfalcon," he told me while we went down the coast in his yawl. "To do it, I'll have to get his attention some way."

Almost as soon as I had met him in Dorp, my brother told me I would have to call him Father. I said, "I've noticed, Father, that you don't have any trouble getting noticed."

He smiled. Let me say right here where I am the only one writing that he had the best smile I ever saw. It made me like him and trust him the first time I saw him in Wapen's, and I do not believe anybody was proof against it.

"I think the Vanished People might come again to help if you asked them." I said it because I had been really interested in them in Dorp, and would have liked to see some again.

Then he explained to me about the ring he had on, saying, "This was given me by a woman I called Seawrack. You don't know her, but when you read my manuscript you will learn about her." He took it off and handed it to me. It was a plain silver ring with a white jewel. There were scratches on it that could have been writing or pictures. If it was, I could not make them out. "Look through it," he told me.

I held it up to my eye. The weather was clear and cool, the wind northeast. The waves were white-capped, I would say a little bit less than two cubits. I saw all this through the round hole, but when I had been looking awhile I noticed the limb of a tree floating upright to starboard. The leaves were still silver and green, and the limb was so big it looked like a whole tree even though I would think there must have been a trunk floating the regular way since a floating tree does not stick up like that. There was somebody sitting in one of the branches, and it was one of the Vanished People.

Father took the ring back, and the Vanished Man was gone. So was the tree he had been sitting in. Only the waves were left. I asked Father to let me look again, but he would not.

"I've shown you this so that you will know how valuable it is and not bury it with me should I die," he said. "By it, the Neighbors" (it was what he called always them) "will know that you are friendly. Do you hold any malice toward them?"

I said plainly and sincerely that I do not.

"What right have they to run around on this whorl of ours, going where they please?" he asked me.

I said, "What right do I have? If someone wants to stop me, let's see him try it." He was pleased with my answer, and said that when he died I was to have the ring. I think he was afraid Gyrfalcon would kill him, and hoped that Gyrfalcon would let us claim his body afterward.

When we got to New Viron, I expected him to call up the ghosts that helped in Dorp and hoped he would ask the Vanished People to help too. But he just walked around talking to people. His bird went with him and so did I most of the time. Babbie and Cricket watched our boat.

He used to tell stories about two men trying to cheat each other. In most of the stories they both lost, but the one who first set out to cheat his friend was the only loser sometimes. He said, "If you rob someone who would help you if you needed help you only rob yourself." He said that again and again. He said stealing only made you poorer, and asked people to tell him an old thief who was rich.

"I knew the best thief in Viron," he told them. "He gave away jewels in a way that would have surprised the Rani of Trivigaunte, but he told me once that he slept in a different place each night, and his hand was always close to his needler. He made others rich; he was as poor as a beggar himself."

He also said that our cruelty stored up pain for us. "Do you imagine you can be cruel without teaching others to be cruel to you?

You glory in your cruelty, because you believe it shows you are master of your victim. You are not even your own."

Uncle Calf's wife is making a collection of these sayings, and I have told her all I can remember. The first time I was in New Viron with him, while the inhuma was still alive, Uncle Calf would not believe they were brothers. Now he tells everyone.

I think it was on the second morning we were in New Viron that he told me he had been troubled in the night. We slept on the boat the first night. Next day Uncle Calf invited us to stay with him, like Hide and I and Vadsig did before. I slept in the room that had been ours, and he slept in the one that had been Vadsig's.

"I have had a great many strange dreams in my life, Hoof," he said, "as I imagine everyone my age has; but I have never had even one as strange as this. I woke in the middle of the night, as I often do. I got up and relieved myself, walked around the room, looked out the window at the stars, and returned to bed."

"What was your dream?" I asked him.

"I was lying in bed; and Scylla was somewhere in the dark, up near the ceiling. She spoke to me, and I sat up thinking that I was awake and would no longer hear her. I put my feet over the edge of the bed. It was very strange."

I asked who Scylla was, and he said that she was a goddess, and had been patroness of Viron back in the old whorl; when he said that, I remembered Mother talking about her. There was a big lake there and Scylla was the goddess of the lake. They had gods and goddesses for all sorts of things.

"Scylla possessed a woman I knew once," he told me. "She was willful and violent."

I said, "But the Scylla you dreamed wasn't the real goddess, was it?" and I asked him if there had ever been a real Scylla.

"Yes," he said. "Yes, that's the terrible part." Then he said something I did not understand at all: "I feel sorry for Beroep." Beroep was a man we used to know in Dorp.

For the next two or three days, he stayed up late walking the streets at night or sitting in taverns. I went with him the first night. After that I got Aunt Cowslip's son Cricket to watch our boat so Babbie could come with us. We took his bird too, and even if it could not fight it made a good lookout, warning us about people behind us or watching from shadows.

Sometimes he spoke to these people, asking questions. When he thought he had their friendship, he asked them about strangers and the sick. Sometimes we looked for the sick people afterward so he could talk to them and the people who took care of them. Once we found a man that no one was taking care of and spent half a day cleaning and feeding him, and finding somebody who would. Soon people began bringing their sick and asking Father to pray for them.

"If Scylla were here, I'd ask her to heal you," he told one woman. "Scylla is not here—though she may like to think she is—and is no longer a goddess in any case, not even in Old Viron." The woman asked him to pray to Scylla just the same, and he prayed to whatever gods might hear him.

Gyrfalcon sent men for us. They wanted me to go back to Uncle's and take Babbie and the bird, but Father would not go unless we came with him. They said they would make him.

"By shooting me? Gyrfalcon will be furious when he finds out you killed me."

Their leader said, "We'll pick you up and carry you, if we have to."

"You cannot," he told him. The leader grabbed for him, but Father knocked him down with his stick. Another man aimed his slug gun at him, but Babbie knocked him off his feet and opened his leg from his knee to his belt. A lot of people were watching by then.

Gyrfalcon had a big house south of town. He met us on the walk, and shook hands. "So," he said, "have you come to take New Viron from me?" Father smiled and said he had not, and we went into a garden behind the house and sat down at a little round table. The crocuses were up, the blue cup-o'-scents, and many other beautiful flowers that grow from bulbs; but the apple trees had not bloomed yet.

Father got the little knife out of his pen case and ripped the hem of his robe. There were grains of corn in there, black, red, and white. He gave them all to Gyrfalcon. "Cross these," he said, "but always keep the pure strains for the years to come. New Viron will never go hungry."

Gyrfalcon took them, tied them up in his handkerchief, and put it in a pocket inside his tunic. Father cried then for a long time.

Servants with chains brought us wine and food, both very good. I ate and gave some to Babbie, and drank more than I should have.

"Is this your father?" Gyrfalcon asked me, and I said it was. I felt really brave.

"I don't recognize him."

I said, "Well, I do."

"If this is your father, where is Caldé Silk?" Gyrfalcon thought he was being very smart when he asked that.

"In a book my mother and father wrote," I told him.

"You are Horn? The same Horn I spoke to a couple of years ago when we got the invitation from Pajarocu?"

"I am," Father said.

"You live on Lizard, near the tail, and make paper?"

He nodded.

"Nettle's husband?"

"Yes, and the father of Sinew, Hoof, and Hide. I am also the father of Krait and Jahlee, neither of whom you know or will ever know—both are dead. If you wish to continue to explore family connections, I am the father-in-law of a woman named Bala. She is Sinew's wife. I am the grandfather of their sons Shauk and Karn, as well."

Gyrfalcon smiled. "The founder of a family. I congratulate you."

The bird seemed to understand Father was being praised, and it called out, "Good Silk!" three or four times.

"Yes, I am." For a few seconds he sat scratching Babbie's ears. "My son Hide will come here soon with my wife and my daughter-in-law to be, Vadsig. They will be married by Patera Remora. My brother Calf and his wife are making arrangements."

"Assisted by you, financially. So I've heard."

"Correct. They know the town, as Hoof and I do not."

I spoke up then even though I should not have, saying I had been learning a good deal about it recently.

"Prowling over it at night with your . . . Father? Sitting in bottle shops. Who are you looking for?"

I said I did not know.

"Who are you looking for, Horn? As caldé of our city, I think myself entitled to ask."

"By name?" He shrugged. He had not eaten a bite till then, but he picked up a sparkle and began to peel it. "For a friend, that's all. I don't know his name. Or hers. I'll learn it when I find the person."

"You have graciously answered all my questions," Gyrfalcon said. He was making fun of Father, but you could tell he admired him too. "Will you tolerate a few more?"

"If you will tolerate one from me. Will you come—or at least consider coming—to my son's wedding? It would be a great honor for him and his wife, and for our entire family. I'm taking advantage of your hospitality, I realize."

Gyrfalcon stared, then laughed. He has a big booming laugh. "You want *me* at your son's wedding?"

"Yes," Father said, "I do. I want you there very much, if you will come. All of us will be delighted, I'm sure."

"Let me think now." Still grinning, Gyrfalcon sipped a little wine. "You promised to answer some more questions for me if I would answer that one. I suppose you meant if I would give you an answer you liked."

"Why no. Any answer. And I'm only asking you to consider it. I know how many demands there must be on your time, and in all honesty you are entitled to ask all the questions you wish."

Gyrfalcon leaned back and surveyed us, looked around at his garden, and came back to us, looking at Father and me like he never saw us before. "Do you think my wine's poisoned?"

"Certainly not. I would have warned my son not to drink it if I did. Does it bother you that I haven't drunk my own?" He drank half his glass and ate some bread.

"I poison people. That's what they say in town. You must have heard it."

"I heard something of the sort."

"Well, I don't. They can't prove I do, but I can't prove I don't."

"Naturally not."

"Do you still want me to come to your other son's wedding?"

"Of course. We will all be delighted."

"Then I'll come. Let me know when the date is set."

The bird said, "Bird tell!" and I noticed Father jumped a little. Later he explained to me about Scylla.

"I've got a few more questions for you. Here's the first one. Is Silk ever coming?"

"I have no idea. I failed to find him." For a minute I thought Father was going to cry again but he did not. "That was the principal thing I promised I would do. I realize that. I failed, and that is all I have to say. I reached Viron. I talked with its present caldé, Caldé Bison, and a number of other people—I spoke with my own father, for example. But I was unable to locate Silk, and I left. I offer no excuses."

"You don't know whether Silk's coming?"

"As I said. He may, but I very much doubt it."

I whispered, "Can't you see that if he were here Gyrfalcon would have to kill him?"

"No, I don't—because it isn't true."

Gyrfalcon told me, "You're stirring our stew with your finger, young man. Better stop before you get burned."

Father was smiling. "I've dreaded this hour. Not because of what you and the others might say to me or what New Viron might do to me, but because I knew I would have to admit that I failed, that Silk is not coming. Now I've done it and I can begin to live again."

"Good Silk," said the bird. "Good Silk!"

"Can I ask a couple more questions?"

"Before you decide on my punishment? Yes, certainly."

Gyrfalcon shook his head. "No punishment. I'm not going to give you a dressing down, either. You did your best."

"I did not," Father told him. "I did what I did. I could have remained in Viron and continued to search. I didn't."

"You said you were looking for somebody here, too, but you didn't know his name. What do you want with him?"

"I want him to go on a journey with me."

"I see." Gyrfalcon sucked his teeth at that. "Going far?"

"Yes, very far indeed," Father said.

They had put us on horses for the ride out to Gyrfalcon's house, but we had to walk back. While we walked, I asked Father if he wanted me to come when he went away. It seemed to surprise him, as if it was something he had not thought about, but I saw enough of him to know that he thought about most things way far in advance. "Would you go, if I asked you to?"

I said I would, and Hide and Vadsig could look after Mother.

"We won't be gone long," he told me. I did not understand what he meant till later. I had never gone to the Red Sun Whorl, and when Hide told me he had not made me believe it. Father could not make

Juganu believe it, either. Juganu was the inhumu we found, a little old man with a bald head. We had taken him on the boat and put out to sea.

Father said, "You have no reason to worry—far less than we. If this vessel sinks, you can fly."

"Rajan!" Juganu tried to get away, climbing the rigging like two nittimonks and flattening out his arms, but I chased him and caught him and threw him down.

"You need have no fear," Father told him, "we will be your friends if you'll let us."

"I served you faithfully." Juganu moaned. "I swear by our god."

That was the first I ever heard about the inhumi having their own god, but Father paid no attention to it. "You tried to kill me when Evensong and I left Gaon, and you will call for others to kill me here as soon as I let you go."

I said we should kill him ourselves when we were finished with him, but Father shook his head. "I killed your sister. Surely that was killing enough for one lifetime. I will not call it murder—murder is something worse—but I will not kill this man, who may be her brother for all I know. After he has helped us, we will free him."

"I served you throughout the war, Rajan." (The end of Father's staff was on his neck, and Father's foot was on his chest.) "How can I serve you now?"

"By going with us to a place where you will be as human as we are." For a minute Father thought about things. "And by coming back. You will be tempted to remain, I warn you; if you do, you will die and it will be by no act of mine."

"Where I . . . ?" The old inhumu gaped at us.

"We will sleep," Father told him, "all of us except Babbie. Hoof will rig a sea anchor for us—"

From the mizzen top, his bird cried, "I go! I come!"

"Yes," Father told it. "You will come with us, Scylla. It's for your sake we're going, after all."

After that, I furled the sails and made a sea anchor from two sweeps.

(My wife was reading over my shoulder when I wrote that last, and says that many people will not know what a sea anchor is or how to make one. The others promised to let me write this by myself, because Hide and Vadsig saw more of the man who said he was our father than I did in Dorp, and Daisy hardly saw him at all, even if she writes better. She writes better than Hide, too, even if Hide will not admit it.

(A sea anchor is the sort of anchor you use when your anchor cable will not reach bottom. A boat is meant to sail, and will sail whenever the wind blows, even under bare poles. You cannot stop it, but a good sea anchor will slow it down so much it might as well be stopped. What I did was to lash together two sweeps crosswise and tie a long line to them in the middle. The longer the line on a sea anchor, the better it holds.)

Then we went to sleep. Babbie was supposed to watch Juganu the inhumu and our boat, too, while we were gone; and Father tied a line around Juganu's neck and to his wrist. I said that if we slept and Juganu did not, he would bleed us till we were dead if we did not wake up, and the line would not help. But Father said he could not, and Juganu swore he would not.

After that we went into the cabin and Father told me to lay down and close my eyes. I did, but as soon as I heard him and Juganu lay down too, and the rattle when he put down his stick, I sat up. He was on his bunk, with Juganu on the floor beside him. I remembered the sword he called Azoth was probably under his tunic, and if Juganu got it he could kill us both. I had never seen him use it, but he had told me what it could do and so had Hide. I took it up on deck and hid it. It was not that I was afraid to go to the Red Sun Whorl, but I was very nervous about it. I cannot explain it more than that.

Babbie was on deck and looked at me with his little fierce eyes in a way that told me I was supposed to be in the cabin asleep. I have never been sure how much Babbie understands, but he understands a lot. I know he understood that, and you could ask him to bring you almost anything except food and he would go get it if he felt like it. He would even bring Father food, but he would not do that for Hide or me. Babbie has gone away, I think into the woods on the mainland, but Vadsig says Witches Rock.

This is going to be hard to explain, but I will try to do it better than Hide and the others have.

I did not feel asleep at all. (Hide says for him it was like going to sleep, but not for me.) It was more like looking through Father's ring than anything else I have done, but that was not it either. Everything began to change. Our boat was water, and Babbie was a hairy man with thick arms and real big shoulders, and glasses, and a couple of Babbie's eyes (the little ones). The bird was the bird asleep on the mizzen top with its head under its wing and another bird, a bird too fat to fly that was flying around just the same. I kept blinking and blinking, trying to blink them away; but they just got realer.

I felt like I had to hold on to something, and I tried to hold on to the sky. I have no idea why that was what I picked, except that it did not seem like it was changing, and I had tried to hold on to everything else, and everything else was changing anyhow except the sky and the water.

So I tried to hold on to the sky, the beautiful Blue sky with little dots of clouds all around and high thin wispy clouds way up behind them. Just when I thought I had it and Father could not take it away, it got darker and I thought, "Watch out, a big storm coming!" But it was not a storm, it was stars pulling the daylight in. Then the boat rolled under me a little, and I knew it was not our boat.

It had four masts, and it was higher, a lot higher, at the bow and stern than in the middle; but even the middle was about five or six cubits above the water. I had heard of boats with three masts, but I have never heard of one as big as that. It was so big it had a boat as big as ours upside-down forward of the mainmast. It steered with a wheel instead of a tiller, and the man at the wheel was staring at us like his eyes were going to roll right out of his head and yelling, "Captain!"

Father's bird landed at his feet about then, a fat bird that came up to his belt. The funny thing about Father—I know Hide said something about this but I want to say it too, like I did the changing. He looked more like our father there, not really like him, but more than on Blue. He was shorter and thicker, and his hair had some black in it. His face was more like father's, and his eyes were not sky-colored anymore.

There was a man with him I had never seen before, a man with yellow hair and a big hawk nose. His eyes were not sky-colored either. I have seen ice in the winter that was that color when the sunlight hit it, big chunks of ice floating in the sea. This man was looking at his hands, and then he bent down and felt his knees, and hit one, too, pretty hard with the side of his fist. He told Father, "I would never try this!"

Father said, "Yet this is what you are. Try to remember."

About then the captain came running up. He looked sly and he had a big curved sword hanging from the widest belt I ever saw; the blade must have been wider than my hand. He talked in a way I had trouble understanding.

Father told him, "I am sorry to commandeer your boat, but commandeer it I must." He held out his hand, and it was full of big round disks of gold with pictures on them.

The captain opened his mouth, and closed it again.

"Here," Father said, "take it. There will be as much again when we leave you—I hope to repay you in other ways as well."

I told the captain, "You better do what Father tells you."

Babbie said, "Huh! Huh! Huh!" and his eyes made the captain step back.

Father wanted to know who that was, so I said, "It's Babbie, Father."

Then he said, "I didn't intend to take him with us, but the boat will be all right, I'm sure, provided we're not too long."

The fat bird said, "Good boat!" and flew up on the railing to look down at the water. It was a big, thick railing with carving on it, and the place where we stood was ten cubits over the water. It could have been more.

Father had the captain hold out his hands, and put the gold in them, saying, "You must take us out to sea. We will leave you there—or at least, I hope we will."

The captain looked hard at the man at the wheel, but the man at the wheel was pretending he had not heard anything. When the captain saw the man did not look like he was listening, he turned around and ran down some steps into the middle of the boat, and I heard a door slam.

Father asked the fat bird, "Well, Scylla?"

There must be a word for the time when we see something we have seen before turn out to be something else, like when a stick is a snake without moving. My wife knows more words than most people. She knows more than anybody except Father. But she does not know a word for that.

When Father said, "Well, Scylla?" I saw the bird was really a girl old enough to take care of other sprats but not old enough to get married. I do not mean she looked like a girl dressed up like a bird. She looked like a girl that looked exactly like a fat bird but was really a big girl that would be a woman in another year.

"See, see!" the girl said. Then she hopped down onto the deck and spread her wings, and said, "Go sea!" After that the two started pulling apart. (This will not be the way it really was, but as close as I can come.)

The bird was in front, and it started getting smaller till it looked like it had on our boat and back on Lizard. When it got smaller you could see the girl behind it. Then she stood up, a skinny girl with an angry face and straight black hair. She said, "No here. No god. Go sea," and some other things. It scared the bird and it flew away, circling up above the boat.

"Scylla here possessed Oreb," Father told me. "It took me nearly a year to realize what had happened because she exercised no influence—or almost none—once she had brought him back. When I returned to Blue, he went away at once to search for a Window for her, or anything that might function as one. They found none, and she brought him back, earning my gratitude—though she already had it. I grew up in her Sacred City of Viron, after all."

Scylla snapped, "Gyoll? It is? Nessus? It is? Where is?"

Father nodded. "Ask the man at the wheel. He'll tell you, surely."

"Plain man!"

"Exactly," Father said, "and plain men know such things. They must."

The hawk-nosed man muttered, "I don't care where it is." Then he threw back his head and shouted, *"I want to stay!"* at the dark sky.

"You may not, Juganu," Father told him, "and in fact we're going back right now, all of us." He took my arm and Juganu's, and told Juganu to take Babbie's and me to take Scylla's. She tried to hit me and I caught her wrist. Then we fell, not up or down but to one side, faster and faster, rolling over.

I woke up on deck with Babbie licking my face. I thought at first he had hurt me because it stung, but what really happened was that I had fallen and hit it. I got in my sea anchor then and put out sail.

When Father came up out of the cabin, I said I saw now that we just fell down like that wherever we happened to be, and if he had told me he would have saved me a pretty good bruise.

"I would not," he said. "You would have disobeyed me in any case."

I had a lot of questions, and I knew he was angry, so I thought I would volunteer to cook and made a fire in the sandbox. It was too early, but he knew I did not like to cook (he had done all the cooking) and I wanted to show I would try to help without being told. While I got the fire going, I was planning what I thought we ought to have, keeping in mind what I could cook and get right and make taste good, because I knew I was not as good at it as he was. I knew what we had, and we had not done any fishing, so I decided potatoes, bacon, and onions; and when the fire was going pretty well I went below to fetch them.

Juganu was sitting on my bunk with his head in his hands. I told him to get off and stay out of my way.

He said, "Now that you know, you hate me."

I said, "I knew all along, and I don't." The first part was a lie, because I had not known he was an inhumu until we got him on the boat and Father told me. But it is what I said.

"That place . . ."

"It's where we real people come from." I thumped my chest. "I guess that's why you're one of us there, and Babbie too."

I had not thought it would bother him, but it did. He said it was what he was in his heart, that the blond man on the deck of the big boat was the real Juganu, the man he was in dreams.

I asked, "Do you really dream you're a human man like me?"

"Yes!"

"I don't believe you." I pushed him out of the way so I could open up the little cupboard where we kept most of the food. I got out potatoes, enough for father and me with some left over for Babbie, and a slab of bacon, onions, lard, and stuff.

I turned around and Juganu said, "Sometimes I do. Sometimes I really do." He followed me up on deck.

Father said I had brought too much, but I explained I had wanted to give some to Babbie and the bird, and Babbie would eat a lot. That was the first time I really thought about the bird and the girl; I was not even sure that they had come back with us. Then the bird flew down out of the rigging somewhere and perched on his shoulder. I looked around for the girl because I thought she would want to eat, too.

"We will not have to feed Scylla," he told me, "though she is surely here. Will you speak with us, Scylla?"

He had turned his head so as to look at his bird, and it said, "Bird talk?"

"Certainly, if you wish to."

"Good bird!"

"She is possessing Oreb, you see. She is in his mind—what there is of it. More accurately, there is an image of her there which she herself placed there; that image was the Scylla we saw on the Red Sun Whorl. You won't have forgotten what your mother and I told you concerning Scylla and Echidna—how they tried to destroy Great Pas, and the vengeance he took. Are you going to boil those potatoes you're peeling?"

I said I had not planned to.

"Do it. Fill a pan with seawater and bring it to a boil. Drop them in for ten minutes before you fry them. They're old—the new crop's not in yet—and that will help." In all the time I knew him, he never looked less like our real father or sounded more like him.

Juganu began to explain the same things to Father that he had to me; but Father cut him off, saying he already knew.

I said, "My sister was an inhuma, Juganu. Her name was Jahlee, and she and Father did that a lot."

He said, "She was a young woman there, you see. Quite an attractive young woman."

Then Juganu thanked Father for taking him there. "It was the high point of my life," he said. He looked just like a little old man with gray skin and no teeth; and I wondered how old he really was, because the blond man with the big hook nose had not looked as old as Father.

Father said, "You mustn't think that it will never happen again. Would you like to go back tonight?"

I used to watch Sinew play tricks on Mother, and Hide and I played some good ones too, but I had never seen anyone look that surprised. "Will you? Oh, Rajan! Rajan, I—I . . ."

Father put a hand on his shoulder. "We'll go after Hoof and I eat."

"No sea!" the bird objected.

"No, the boat will not have reached the sea yet; but it will be well for me to get a better feel for its speed. It is sailing with the current, of course, so it should make good time."

After that we were all quiet, thinking, except that he told me to use a little celery salt instead of the yellow sea-salt I brought with the pepper. "But only a little. And you should be starting your bacon, and browning the onions. Cut up the onions now. Cubes, not rings."

Then he said, "I should explain to you both why we cannot go to the sea directly, as I did to Scylla several days ago. In order to go to a place we must have with us someone who has been there, or at least been in the area. I don't know why that is so, but that is how it seems to be. I can go to Green—as I have at times—because I have been there in the flesh. I can go to the Red Sun Whorl, too, as we did a few minutes ago, because Jahlee and I went there in the company of Duko Rigoglio of Soldo. He had been a Sleeper on the *Whorl,* and so had been there in the flesh. I cannot take us to the sea there, because I have never been on it. Scylla has, to be sure; but ultimately Scylla is not among us."

His bird croaked. But it was only bird noise, not a word.

"There is another factor. When we go, we often seem to arrive in a place resembling the one we left. That was why I lured you onto this boat, Juganu. I had promised Scylla that I would take her to the sea of her native whorl if I could. Once I walked along a road that runs beside Gyoll and looked at the boats plying its water, so I hoped that if we left Blue from a boat we would arrive aboard a boat there. So it proved. That it was going downstream was sheer good fortune. Slice your potatoes. Be careful, though. They'll still be hot."

While they were frying I asked him whether we were here or there when we were there, because I had been thinking about the way he had said that the girl had not been with us, not really.

"We are in both places. The philosophers—I am none—tell us that it is impossible for a single object to be in two places at once. We are not indivisible wholes, however."

I said, "Part of us was here, and part there?"

He nodded. "And now that we've been on that boat on the river we should be able to return, though the boat itself will be in a new location. We'll test that supposition tonight."

While we were eating he explained that he had brought us back fast because he had been worried about the boat, especially because Babbie had come and would not be around to take care of things here. "That was a surprise, and a rather unpleasant one," Father told me, "though it was interesting to discover just how human Babbie is." He stopped speaking to study the western horizon.

Juganu said, "What about me?"

Father shook his head. "I knew you were human in spirit. Remember that I had an adopted daughter—one I mourn. I had an adopted son once, too." He sighed, and I saw then how hard it was for him to keep a cheerful face, as he generally did.

His bird dropped onto his shoulder. "Have bird!"

"Yes. A great blessing." He gave the bird a bit of bacon, then put his plate down in front of Babbie. He had eaten two or three mouthfuls. "I hate to disturb your meal, son, but I believe we'd better take in the jigger and reef the main."

We did, and the wind came as I was tying the last knot. I have been in worse blows, and in fact I was in a couple when we sailed with Captain Wijzer; but it would have been foolish to go back to the Red Sun Whorl until things had quieted down, three or four hours after daylight.

Down in the cabin, Father and Juganu and I took off our clothes and dried ourselves as well as we could. It felt very good to lie on my bunk then and shut my eyes, so I did not see things change the way I had before.

After a while somebody shook my shoulder. I opened them, and it was dark again.

"Get up," he said. "You don't want to sleep through this."

That was exactly what I did want, but after a minute or so it sort of soaked through to me that I was lying on wood instead of my bunk, and the boat was not rocking the way I remembered.

Some people that read this may not know about boats, so I am going to say here that they're all different. Two that are about the same size and look about the same will act about the same sometimes, but they are never exactly the same. The *Samru,* which was the big river boat we were on, was a roller, and when you were up on the high parts, it really rolled a lot, just like you had climbed up the mast of a regular boat.

Our boat was more of a rocker. Rocking is not the same as rolling. Rolling is smoother, but to me it always feels like it is just going to keep on till the boat turns over. Our boat was more of a pitcher, too, because it was only about a quarter as long.

Anyway, I sat up then but it was so dark I could not see much. I asked the man who had my shoulder who he was, and he said, "Juganu," which made me jump.

Just then there was a white light that lit up everything, and I saw Father out on the bowsprit holding it up. His bird was on his shoulder, and the girl he said was Scylla was out on the bowsprit too, farther out even than he was.

Then he shut his hand and the light was gone, and everything was as black as inside a cave. I heard the watch asking each other questions. Afterward I found out they had been sleeping on the deck, mostly. I heard boots, too, but I did not pay much attention to them.

I was trying to get forward, and afraid of bumping into a mast or something worse. I was not even sure this boat had a railing all the way around, because ours did not have any railing at all, and I was afraid of falling off. So while I was worrying about all that, I bumped somebody short and hairy and as hard as rock. I knew who that was right away, and how dangerous he was, too, so I said, "It's me, Babbie. It's Hoof," very quick.

Something happened then that surprised me as much as just about anything I saw on the Red Sun Whorl, except for the part right at the last. Because Babbie threw his arms around me and gave me a great big hug, saying "Huh! Huh! Huh!" and lifted me off my feet. Babbie's arms were shorter than mine, but thicker than my legs, and he was the strongest person I ever met.

About then the mate came up, and Babbie put me down. The mate had a lantern, and he kept holding it up in my face, and then in Babbie's and then in Juganu's. Neither of them liked it. I did not like it much myself. After a while I decided that he was looking for Father but he had probably been down in the middle of the boat when Father held up his light, so he had not seen him.

I was afraid that if I told the mate where Father was, he would make him fall off. So I said, "What's the trouble? If you need help, we'll lend a hand."

All those people were hard to understand because of the way they talked, and he was one of the hardest. He said something and I had to get him to say it over two or three times before I understood it. "Taught y'as gun." He talked like that all the time, but I am not going to write it like that, or not much.

"We're back," Juganu told him.

"Where'd y'go?" he wanted to know.

I pretended I had not understood that either and said, "You're looking for Father, aren't you? Wasn't that why you were shining your light in our faces?"

He agreed.

"Father has hired this boat. He'll want a full report. Where are we?"

"Half day from the delta. Where's he?"

"What time is it? How long till morning?"

"Not long."

By that time I had seen his face well enough to realize that he was not the man Father had given the gold to. I said "You're not the captain. Where is he?"

"Sleepin'."

"Bring him here. Father will want to see him."

The mate started to argue, and I said, "Bring him at once!"

He swung at me then. I ducked, and Babbie grabbed his arm and threw him down so fast and hard that he might as well have been a girl's doll. The lantern fell down and went out.

Father must have heard the noise, and he was there like he had flown. He opened his hand to let some light get out, and Babbie was sitting on the mate and had both his arms together in one of his hands. His hands were a lot bigger than his real ones back home, but he still had the really thick nails he walked on, and only two big fingers on each hand. Father made him get off and told the mate to sit up. He was a big, strong-looking man with one of those faces that are all cheeks and chin.

"I'm sorry you were hurt, if you were," Father told him. "Babbie can be too quick to take offense. I realize that."

Babbie was pointing to his mouth. "Huh-huh-huh." I thought he wanted Father to change him so he could talk, and I did not think Father could do that. But Father knew right away what he wanted. He gave Babbie a big curved knife with a double-edged blade, and then another one just like it, telling him he had to be careful how he used them.

The mate tried to say something, what he was going to do to Babbie someday, but Scylla told him to fetch the captain or we would make him jump overboard. Father's hand was almost closed then so she was hard to see, but she took hold of the mate like she was going to turn him around, and her hands and arms did not even come close to being as much like ours as Babbie's were. They were like snakes, with sucking mouths all along them. The mate kept backing away from her, and they got longer, till finally he ran away. Juganu said, "Blood," and it sounded like he was praying.

Father's light went out, I think because he did not want me to see Scylla.

She said, "No do? You do?" and Juganu said, "No. Never."

I was thinking that it was probably a lot easier to change your shape like she had if you were not really here. I tried to touch her, but I could not find her in the dark.

Father asked if we knew what we were doing, why we wanted to find the sea, and Juganu and I both said no.

"I'm tired," he told us. "I need to rest my back. Shall we go home? It will be safer, as I must tell you."

Juganu begged then. I will not write what he said or what happened. I could not see much of it, but I still heard it even when I looked the other way. Finally Father said all right, we would stay till daylight.

We went over to the railing and sat down. It was pretty dark, but not really completely dark. There was a red lantern at the top of one mainmast, and two hanging over the high deck aft. Those were white, but that was a good long way away at night, and that deck was higher than the one we were on, even though our deck was higher than the middle of the boat. I asked Father why we came back to this deck when we had been on the other one, but he said he did not know, he was just thankful we had ended up in the boat and not in the water.

Scylla was sitting on one side of me, which I did not like, but there was nothing I could do about it. She wanted to know when we would get to the sea, and that was when it came to me that what I smelled when I first got there was the sea, not ours but Ocean, the sea of the Red Sun Whorl. It smelled different, maybe because it was bigger or had more salt in it, or just because it was older. I got so interested in thinking about that I never heard what Father told Scylla. Probably it was that nobody could say because it depended on the wind.

His bird did not like her and would not come to me because I was next to her. I tried to find out whether it knew she was the one who had been in it, but it would only say "Bad girl!" and "No eat." It said, "No, no!" and "Good bird!" a lot too, no matter what I wanted to know.

"In the *Whorl* I was told that the inferior gods had turned themselves into animals to escape Pas," Father told me. "It embarrasses me now, but I must admit I thought it a mere legend. It was in fact a myth, that is to say a story containing an important element of truth. His Cognizance Patera Incus honored me by asking me to assist him when he sacrificed at the Grand Manteion, which of course I did. Scylla—as she has told me—seized the opportunity to possess Oreb, having overheard my conversation with His Cognizance through his glass."

I thought he meant a glass like you drink out of, but then I remembered the reading about the things you can see and talk through in my real father's book.

He told Scylla, "I still don't understand how you managed to escape Pas for so long."

She said, "Good place. No find."

She had sounded as if she was about to cry, and he said, "It's been twenty years and more. He will forgive you, surely."

"No, no. Never."

After that nobody said anything. Green came up, bigger and brighter than we ever see it on Blue. Or want to, either. The captain saw us and came running. He did not have his sword this time, but the mate was behind him and he had a long stick that smelled like smoke. From the way he held it, I knew it was some kind of weapon; and I kept my eye on it the whole time.

"Welcome," the captain said. "Welcome! We thought you deserted us."

Father explained that we had other affairs to attend to and would be leaving from time to time. The captain asked if we were hungry and invited us to join him at breakfast. Father thanked him but said we would stay where we were, and the captain and the mate went away.

"He was a long time fetching him," Juganu said, "and I wouldn't mind trying some of your human food."

I said I would have thought that just blood every time would get boring, but he said it did not, that there were hundreds of different kinds.

Father said, "Go ahead, if you wish. I'm sure he'll be happy to feed you. Just remember that if we are forced to leave without you,

you won't be able to return on your own. We'll do our best to safeguard your physical self."

Juganu trotted away, and I told Father I thought he would stay here all the time if he could.

Scylla said, "No me."

"Even if you could do that with your arms?" I asked her.

She looked so bad I was sorry I said it. The bird said, "Poor girl! Poor girl!" and I tried to touch her, to pat her back or something, but she did not feel right and I jerked my hand away.

Father said, "She is less even than we. If Oreb were to die she would not be here at all."

His bird kicked up a fuss when it heard him say that, and he had to quiet it down.

We talked awhile, and I said, "This is the Red Sun Whorl. When are we going to see the red sun?"

He pointed astern, and I stood up and looked, and then I climbed up the ratlines to see it better. The Red Sun was rising behind us, and the old falling-down city was between us and it. It was so big and so dark, like a great big coal buried in ashes. You could look right at it, and the whole city was black against it, thin towers and thicker ones, and there were some you could see through and see the little thin lines of the beams holding them up.

You could see how big that city was, and it was bigger than I had ever imagined when we first went on the boat in the river and were in the middle of it. It went on forever to the north and the south, and down the river, too, almost to where we were, walls falling down and broken towers and so many little ruined houses nobody could ever live in anymore that my brother and I could have spent our whole lives trying to count them all, and when we died we would only have just started.

But up against the Red Sun like that, you saw how little the city was, too. This is hard to explain. The city was immense. Just immense. Huge. Nobody will believe this, but if you had taken all the towns on Blue and bunched them together, and then added all the cities that Father used to talk about up in the old whorl, you could have taken all that and set it down in this city; and then if you had gone away for a year and come back, you would not have been able to find it.

There was a wall around it. Just off at the edges you could see that, way far away to the east and so far to the north and south you could not be sure you were seeing it at all; but it must have been about as tall as the tallest towers, and it was a wall. It was probably the biggest thing that people had ever made, but it was dead and rotting like the rest.

So it was all so big that when I looked at it, it was hard to breathe. But the sun kept on rising and rising, and Nessus was little. Finally I shut my eyes and would not look at it anymore. I had seen the way things really are, and I knew it. I knew that I was going to have to forget it as much as I could if I wanted to go on living. After Father left I was still curious about the Vanished People, and I asked a man I met one time about them because he seemed like somebody who might know something. He said there were things that we are not supposed to know. I think he was wrong, but right, too. I do not think that there is anything about the Vanished People that we should not know, just a whole lot that we do not. But the way things really are is something that we cannot deal with. I had to shut my eyes, and if you had been there you would have had to shut yours too.

When I looked back down at the foredeck, Father and Babbie were still there, right where I had left them, but I could not see Scylla at all. I climbed down the ratlines and there she was again, then when we went back to our boat she was gone.

We could have used her, because there was another boat, and it was full of men with slug guns. I shook out the mainsail fast and set the big jib we had not used before. Father stood up at the tiller and tried to talk to them, but they shot at him. I went and got his sword, Azoth, and gave it to him. He did not want to use it at first, but when I was shot he cut off the whole front of their boat.

"I did my best not to kill them," he told me, "but I killed two. Their bodies are back there in the water." I said it did not make any difference since the others would drown, and he said he hoped not. Later while Father was resting, Juganu flew back to get some of them. It was nearly dark then where we were.

Here I want to tell you about how Scylla went out to talk to the Great Scylla, but there are a couple other things I ought to tell about first, about the knives Father gave Babbie and what Scylla told Father at night in the dark.

So I am just going to put all that in here. Some of it he told me while we were waiting for daylight on the river boat, and some was while Juganu and Babbie were holding me down and he was straightening out my wound and bandaging it. (I was wiggling around quite a bit and he kept talking to me, I think mostly to try to keep me still.) Some was after that, too, while he was making potato soup with the fish.

To tell the truth, I am not exactly sure what he said where, so I am putting it all here.

About the knives. I wanted to know where he got them. I had been watching as good as I could in the dark and did not see him take them from anyplace. So he told me we could make things there that were not really real but were like real for as long as we wanted them. He said he had made the gold like that, but the captain probably did not know it was not there when he was not around because he had locked it in a strongbox. Naturally I wanted to know if I could do that, too; and he said I could but I would have to be careful or they would know it was a trick. I said I would be.

Scylla was Pas's daughter. Father talked like there were a lot of them, but he said she was the oldest one and the most important. She and her mother and some of Pas's other sprats had tried to kill him because they did not want people leaving the old whorl to come to Blue where they would not be the gods. So they tried to kill Pas, and for a long while they thought they had done it, and nobody would ever get to come. But Pas came back, and they had to hide.

There were two ways to hide, Father said. One was to hide in Mainframe. Scylla had talked about that, and he said she would know a lot more about all that than he did, but Mainframe was like the tunnels under the old whorl. There were branches and side tunnels and rooms and caves nobody knew about. So Scylla and the others that had tried to kill Pas hid in them, but not the way we would have. It was like I could hide my finger over here and my thumb over there. They had hidden little pieces of themselves all over, and Pas was still hunting for them and killing every little piece when he found it.

The other way was for them to hide in people. I had read about Patera Jerboa in the book, so I told him about it, and he said I was right. (This was while we were eating the soup. I remember now.) A god could hide in anybody who looked at a Sacred Window or even a glass, and once he was in there he did not have to do anything. If he just went in and kept quiet, it was just impossible for anybody to find out he was there.

But Scylla and the others found a new place. They found out that if they did it right they could go into animals. What usually happened, Father said, was that someone would bring an animal to sacrifice, for instance a goat. When they were getting ready to kill it, it would naturally be in front of the Window. Scylla or whatever god it was would get into it and break loose from whoever was holding it and run away.

"Pas soon realized what was happening," Father said, "and warned his worshippers. Thus when an animal went wild, they knew it had been possessed and hunted it down and killed it."

I said, "So it didn't work."

"Let us say it often failed. Some of the animals made good their escape, horses and birds particularly. There were other difficulties however. No doubt that was why the technique was almost never used until Scylla, Echidna, Hierax, and the rest were desperate to escape Pas. For one thing, most animals are not long-lived. You mentioned Patera Jerboa."

I nodded and said yes, I had.

"He was middle-aged when Pas possessed him, yet he yielded up his fragment of the god thirty years later. A horse may live for fifteen or twenty years, if it's well cared for; but that's extraordinary."

I said, "They can't talk either, except for Oreb."

"You are right." Father put down his soup. "But that is part of a larger and more serious problem. No horse or bull or bird has anything like the brain of a human being. If we think of the gods pouring themselves into us as wine is poured from a great cask into bottles, animals are small bottles indeed. If Scylla had possessed me instead of Oreb, the Scylla we would see on the Red Sun Whorl would still be far short of the Scylla who once existed in Mainframe. As it is, the Scylla we see is no more than a sketch of the original Scylla—of the daughter of the tyrant who assumed the name Typhon, the daughter who had pledged herself in secret to one of the sea gods of the Short Sun Whorl that would in time become our Red Sun Whorl."

I told him I had not known anything about that.

"She did," Father said. "It was a form of treason, of rebellion against her father. Abaia, Erebus, Scylla and the rest had taken possession of the waters, and were plotting to gain the land as well. According to what I was told on one occasion, they still are."

Juganu said, "Are you saying that our Scylla, the girl who comes out of Oreb, wants to ask this Red Sun goddess for help?"

"Yes. I thought you knew. She possessed Oreb, as I told you, because she knew he would soon be brought here. She felt sure—she told me this one night—that Pas would not have peopled Blue unless he had some way to go there himself to rule them. 'Lord it' was the phrase she used. She was wrong, as I could have told her. In Oreb she searched this whorl for nearly a year, finding nothing better one or two landers with their glasses half intact. They would not or could not accept her—'Upload' was the word she employed. She'd been to the Red Sun Whorl with Jahlee and me, but hadn't let us know she was present. A few nights ago she spoke to me through Oreb, and from the way he talked and what he said, I knew the speaker was not he. She revealed her presence, and implored me to take her there again."

"Did she say Pas would kill her if he could?"

Father nodded and sipped from the wine bottle; sometimes it seemed like he was just pretending to eat and drink, and this was one of them. "That is indeed what she said, but I am not certain it's true and I'm not Pas."

Juganu had been listening to us, and had even swallowed some soup. He was a little and old again, about half the size he had been. "Pas will be angry with you. Isn't he your chief god?"

Father shook his head. "The Outsider is my chief god."

I said, "The only god you trust," because I was pretty sure from things like that he had said that I knew who he really was.

"Whom I don't trust half as much as I ought to, my son."

The bird lit on Father's shoulder about then. "Bird eat?"

"Of course. You brought the fish, so you are entitled to some of the soup."

I said it had already had the head and guts.

"Yes." Father smiled and shrugged. "Oreb's diet can't have been pleasant for Scylla, though she's never complained about it. Perhaps she is accustomed to it now; and since such things taste good to him, they may taste good to her, I hope so." He held up his spoon so the bird could get some in its beak. I had finished mine, and I do not think his could have been very hot.

I asked him about Pas. "You said she said she didn't think Pas would let anybody come here unless he could come, too. She must have known him for a long time."

Father agreed she had. "For three hundred years."

"Then why wasn't she right about that?"

He shrugged. "Are you so certain she was wrong?"

"You said she and the bird couldn't find anyplace."

"Correct. Pas has not yet come, perhaps. Or perhaps he has, and Oreb simply failed to find the place that Pas found or created. You pointed out that she had long years in which to learn the nature of her father."

He grinned at me then, and I laughed too.

"Yet she believed that she and her mother—with Hierax and Molpe, though Molpe cannot have been of much help—would prove strong enough to destroy him. She was clearly wrong about that; she underestimated him, and badly."

He stopped to think and give the bird more soup. It would pick flakes of fish and cut-up potato out with its beak. "Would you like my opinion?"

I nodded, and Juganu said, "Very much, Rajan."

"Then I believe Pas knows that as the years pass we will come to realize how much we need him, and bring him. New Viron sent me for Silk. That was foolish, because no mere man could repair all the evil there. Silk did his best for Viron itself, but left it scarcely better than he found it. The same impulse will be applied to Pas in another generation, surely."

I asked if he thought a god could do it, and he said that the people themselves would have to, even if a god helped them.

We both wanted to know why Scylla wanted to talk to that other Scylla in the Red Sun Whorl, and he said, "She wants to describe her efforts in the Long Sun Whorl, and to obtain the Greater Scylla's advice. No doubt she is hoping for help as well, though she will not say so. If she were to leave Oreb and return to Mainframe—we would have to visit the Long Sun Whorl, of course—she would be destroyed. At least she believes she would be, and that's deterrent enough. If she simply remains where she is, she will perish when Oreb dies."

"No cut!" the bird said, which made me and Juganu laugh.

Father also said, "I am by no means eager to overhear their conversation, if it takes place; but I would like a word with that Greater Scylla myself."

He got his second wish, but not the first one, when we went back to the boat on the river.

We sailed through the delta. The river breaks into five big streams there, the captain told us, and so many little ones that nobody could count them. They were always changing anyway, he said, so we had to pick our way along.

Scylla went out on the bowsprit. It was long and she went almost to the end. I sat on the big carved railing and let my feet hang over. I had left my wound behind on Blue, mostly. There were no bandages anymore and I was not bleeding, but it sort of hurt and I did not feel strong. Father had said I could make things, but he had worried about me making cards or anything like that. So I did a couple little things I did not think would bother him or anybody, a nail was one, and a seashell. The way you did it was to hold your hands together and think about what you wanted, them pull them apart slowly getting whatever it was right. When I had each thing the way I wanted it, I tossed it in the water.

Then I looked around to see if anybody was watching, and I made Hide. That was a lot harder. It was nice to have him with me and be able to sit and talk to him about everything; but it was hard, too, to keep him there, and after a while I let him go. Now he says he cannot remember being there or anything we said.

What it was, was like I remembered him better than I have really remembered anything in my life. As long as I did, he was there with me. But the delta was interesting, everything very green and wrecked ships up on the islands, some mostly buried in the mud and little shacks that did not even seem to know they were just little shacks made out of driftwood where it had been palaces and forts. You saw walls leaning so far it seemed like they couldn't stand another day. And one time I got to looking at an old statue there that seemed to me like if only I could have talked to her it would have been the most wonderful thing in my life, and then I looked around to say something to my brother, and he was nearly gone. He came back fast and said, "Sorry!" Right after that I let him go.

The delta was all swampy, and the water was black. Before I guess I thought it was only black because it was night, but now the Red Sun was up and it was still black. Looking at the delta, that bright green everywhere, I got the feeling that I was looking at a body so old moss was growing on the bones and the hard dead meat of it. About then I saw there was nobody around anywhere, that the little driftwood shacks had nobody in them, and what had happened was the stone forts and palaces had lasted because they had been built the best, and the shacks because there had been people in them not so long ago and they had not had time to fall down. But they were empty now, and the houses and buildings that had been between the palaces and the little shacks had rotted away or maybe burned, and there would never be anybody there again, but people like us.

When we got out of the delta, that was the open sea that they call Ocean. It was like our sea and it was not. If you wanted to look for what was the same, there was a lot. But if you wanted to look for what was different, there was a lot too. The smell was different. The color was not the same, either, but it was hard to say just what was changed. That may have been the dark sky, mostly, and the stars. This sea knew night was coming, when everything would die. There was more foam, and I think this Red Sun Sea had more salt in it.

Out on the bowsprit, the girl started calling. She did not say a name or anything. She did not say any words. It was like people sitting on the sand clicking shells together and sometimes blowing through them. It did not sound bad, it was almost like music. Only you knew she was calling something, and when it came it was going to be bigger than anything and you were not going to like it.

That went on for a long time, so long that I got worried about us back in our boat. I think Babbie did, too, because a couple times he came up to Father and pulled on his sleeve. Babbie never could talk but you generally knew what he wanted. He had tied a piece of rope around him and put the knives Father gave him through it.

Here I want to say something else about them. This may not be the best place, but I want to make sure I say it so everybody who reads this understands and this is where I am writing. After I got shot, when Juganu and Babbie were holding me down, Babbie was trying to smile at me. He is not very good at it and does not try much. This time he did, I think because he knew how much it hurt and he wanted me to see that he was not holding me out of meanness, but he liked me and was trying to help. People hunt huses and shoot them and eat them. Sinew used to a lot, and I have done it myself. But after getting to know Babbie the way I did on the boat I could never do it again.

Anyway, his mouth was sort of open, not just the ends of the lips turned up, and looking in it I saw those knives. They were the big ripping tusks in his bottom jaw. The curve was the same and the shape was almost the same except the knives were longer. The tusks he had here were the knives in the Red Sun Whorl.

If I had been the girl, I would have given up after an hour or so. Maybe not even that long. She did not, and after a while I just wanted to get away from there. I went down in the waist, which was what you call the middle of a boat, and watched Juganu wrestle a sailor.

When I went back up on the foredeck, she was still singing. The bird was on her shoulder, and Father was out on the bowsprit too, maybe four cubits behind her. He called me over, and when I had come as far as the grating, he told me to tell the captain to strike all sail. I took Babbie with me, and the captain did it. After that we just drifted, rolling a little. We were on the open sea, out of sight of land.

People started coming up out of the water up ahead. I borrowed the second mate's telescope to look at them, and they were all women. The ones closest to us were smaller, and the ones farther away were bigger, so they all seemed like they were about the same size. Some of the farthest-back ones were as tall as Father, Juganu, and me put together. A lot had on black robes and cowls, but some were naked, especially the big ones farther back. The closest ones talked and sang, and called to us. I have never seen or even heard about anything else that was like that.

The girl kept singing to them, and they got quieter and started to come toward us. It was like they were standing on something under the water that moved. The sailors were scared, and I saw them charging the swivel gun and told Babbie not to let them use it, and went forward again. By that time they were all around our boat. Two sort of rose up and talked to the girl and Father then, their robes getting longer and longer as they came up out of the water until they would have dragged behind them clear across the deck if they had been walking on the boat. There was something under them that the women were standing on, if those women had any feet.

I went out on the grating deck again to look at the women, and one looked at me and smiled, and she had little sharp pointed teeth like tacks. Her eyes were all one color and sort of glowed or gleamed under the cowl. I went back as far as the foremast then, which is why I did not really hear anything they said or that Father and the girl said. I wanted to make myself a sword like Azoth, and I did, but it would not work for me, so I put a regular steel blade on it.

After a while the women went back into the water, and Father and the girl came to tell me to tell the captain he could sail again and we would be leaving him for good. He gave me a ruby, too, that I had seen one of the big naked women give him. He said it was real, and the captain would still have it when we had gone. I told him about the woman who had looked at me and smiled and said, "Was that Scylla?" The girl was mad about it.

After that we went home to our boat on Blue.

It was night went we got back, and I said I would take the first watch, because I knew that with all I had to think about I would not sleep for a while. I told Juganu he could have my bunk if he wanted it, but pretty soon he came up and flew away. I knew he was going to look for blood to eat, and I wondered who he would find.

Babbie was the only one on deck with me, but Babbie was asleep. So after that I just sat at the tiller the way you do with my slug gun across my lap and looked at the sea and the sky. It was calm and you could see a lot of stars. Green was up above the mainmast, and it seemed like if we put up the main top it would touch it. Our Green is not as big as theirs, but ours was plenty bright. The nicest thing was to see the reflections of all the stars dancing on the water.

I thought about a lot then. You can imagine. Most of it was things I have already written down. I thought about shooting Juganu when he came back, too; I really wanted to. But I knew the shot would wake up Father and he would know. Even if it did not, he would ask me, and I would not be able to lie to him about it very long.

Then the bird came and talked to me. That was not as nice as it sounds. For one thing, it was afraid. It would not come near enough for me to touch it. For another, I was talking to the girl too. She was not there to see, but she was there. The bird was up forward on the cabin deck, which is what we call the roof of the little cabin (it is planked and tarred like a regular deck and plenty strong enough to stand on) about halfway between me and Babbie. I could see it hopping around. I could not see the girl, but I knew she was in there. This is hard to explain.

Out on the water there were the stars and quite a bit of light from Green; for nighttime it was really pretty bright, but there was sort of a shadow between the side and the water. Green was halfway up over to starboard. So to port there was this shadow, and I felt like she was down there, watching and listening, and she could make the bird talk for her when she wanted to.

I had whistled to it, and it had whistled back. I could whistle better than it could, but it could whistle louder than I could, so for a little while we had fun like that. I would whistle "Tomcod's Boat," and the bird would whistle back the first three or four notes.

"Like bird?"

"Sure," I said. "But I'd like you better if you liked me better." I knew it would not understand, but it was somebody to talk to.

"Good bird!"

I said, "Sometimes, maybe."

That made it mad and it said, "Good bird!" and "Bad boy!"

"If you're such a good bird, what were you doing out on the bowsprit with Scylla?"

That was the first time. The bird said, "I bad?" but I knew it was not really the bird talking.

I admit I had to think about it. In the first place I did not like her. Then too, I felt like Father and Juganu and I, and even Babbie and the bird, had been real on the big river boat, but she had not been. I had not liked that. Then on our boat I felt like we were really real but she was not real at all. She could not make us see her or talk without Father's bird. Maybe none of it had to do with her being bad, but I felt like it did. So I said, "Well, you're sure not good, Scylla."

"Good girl!"

"Sure you are," I said. To tell the truth I was hoping she would leave the bird in charge and never come back.

"You good? Good Hoof? Like Silk?"

I figured there was no use fooling around with who is Silk? I knew shaggy well who Silk was. "No. He's a better man than I'll ever be."

"Your pa? Tell lie!"

"If he told them who he is, they'd want to make him caldé and Gyrfalcon would kill him."

"Good Silk!" She laughed, sort of bubbling and giggling.

"Bad Scylla," I told her. "Why don't you go fishing?"

"He kill? Kill pa."

I said, "I don't think so."

"Good girl! Not kill!"

"Oh, sure. Well, you wanted Auk to kill that old fisherman for you once. I read all about it."

"My man!"

I said, "Maybe. But you don't own me."

She laughed some more and got me real mad. I said, "Nobody ought to own other people, and if they do they shouldn't kill them unless they've done something terrible. Besides, you tried to kill your father. That's why you've got to hide. You wanted to and if you had you'd be a murderer. I think you are anyway."

The bird whistled, and I thought she had gone away. We whistled back and forth, then it said, "We slaves. Pas own."

I said, "That's the way Sinew used to talk."

"Who?" I think it had surprised her.

"Our other brother. He's older than Hide and me. Father says he's still alive on Green and has two sprats, but he used to talk like that a lot. Our real father would try to get him to help in the mill, and there would be big fights. Or he would start some kind of work and go away, so our father would have finish it, or Hide and me would."

"Like slave!" That had gotten to her. "Pas say. I do."

I said, "He was your father. He fed you and gave you a place to live, and clothes."

"I fed! Eat sheep. Eat boy."

"Like Juganu."

She let the bird talk a while after that, and I tried to get it to come to me, but it would not. "Bad boy! No, no!"

Pretty I stopped trying. I let out a reef in the mainsail, and trimmed it a little.

"Kill bird?"

I said, "You think I'd wring your bird's neck if I could catch it?"

"Yes!"

I spat.

"You would!"

I showed the bird my slug gun. "See this? If I wanted to kill you,

I could just shoot your shaggy bird and throw it over the side. It would take about ten seconds. Only I'm not going to do it. Or wring its neck, either. In the first place you stole it. It's Father's bird. Besides, just because I don't like somebody doesn't mean I want to kill them. That's what you gods used to do, from what I hear. But I'm not like you."

"No need," she said. "I die."

"Sure, when the bird does."

Juganu said, "Tomorrow. Didn't the Rajan tell you?"

I had not known he was back, but he was right at my elbow.

"We're going back tomorrow. I wanted to go back at once, but he wouldn't agree. We'll have to find the grave of Typhon's daughter Cilinia. It's in a place called the Necropolis."

I said, "What for?"

"That will be the last time. The Rajan said after that I might as well leave you, and I probably will."

I wanted to know if he knew why Father wanted to go to Cilinia's grave, and the bird said, "Why ask?"

"He made an agreement with Scylla," Juganu told me.

"What was it?"

Juganu shrugged and sat down on the gunwale. His arms had gotten short and round again, and his legs and his feet were not big and flat anymore like they are when they fly. He was just a little old man, naked, with blood on his breath; and I thought how if it had been Jahlee she would have made big tits to tease me. He said, "I thought you might know."

I said I did not.

"Would you tell me if you did?"

"Unless he said not to."

The bird laughed. I had heard it laugh before, but I did not like it.

"He made an agreement with that monster in the water," Juganu said again. "Favor for favor. He told me that much. He promised to take Scylla to the grave. That was his part of their bargain, but I don't know hers."

I was thinking about finding the grave. "It's been three hundred years. That's what they say."

Father was coming up out of the cabin, and he said, "It's been much longer than that, but I have a friend who knows the place like the back of his hand."

I am stopping here so that the others can write for a while. It has been a lot of work, a lot more than I expected. So I will let them tell about what Juganu did and all that. I will just help. I will get Daisy to go over this and fix it up, too. Or Hide and Vadsig would.

18

How He Came to Blue

"Yer come ter see auld Pig. 'Twas good a' yer, bucky." Pig's beard and shaggy hair were gone, but his head was still huge.

"No, Pig." Pig's visitor shook his own much smaller head, knowing that Pig could not see it. "I came so that you might see me."

Pig touched the bandage above his nose, the self-sterilizing pad that had replaced his gray rag. "They winna take h'it h'off, bucky. Gang ter do h'it yerself?"

He looked at the nurse in the glass, who nodded. "Yes," he said. "Yes, Pig. I am."

His fingers located the knot, and he slipped one slender blade of the surgical scissors beneath it. "Silk found scissors like this in the balneum, and later Doctor Crane used scissors of the same kind when he treated Silk. I don't know why that should touch me, but it does." Savoring the sensation, he cut.

"Bucky . . ."

"If you cannot see, you will be no worse than you were."

The nurse said, "And we'll find out why, and fix it." There was a warmth in her voice that made each word a benediction.

Pig said nothing, but his big hands were shaking.

"You haven't had much practice lately, Pig." The bandage was loose, lying limply across Pig's eyes. "That's what they told me, and I must tell you the same thing. If you can see—"

Apropos of nothing, Oreb announced, "Good Silk."

"What you see may be blurred until you re-learn how to interpret visual images."

The room had darkened as he spoke, the lights on the ceiling fading to mere specks of gold; he looked at the glass and saw the nurse manipulating a control. She nodded, and he lifted the bandage away.

"Bucky . . . ?" One of Pig's hands found his.

"Your eye is still closed, Pig."

"He kens h'it, bucky. Sae braw? He's nae!" Pig's eyelids fluttered.

"Braver than I would be."

Pig's head rolled on the pillow.

The nurse said, "It doesn't exactly go with his coloring."

Pig's right hand left the sheet in a peremptory gesture. "Wants ter see yer, ter see ther twa a' yer tergether. Dinna never want ter forget yer."

"See bird?"

"Aye." Naked now, the wide, thin-lipped mouth curved upward. "Pig sees yer, ter, H'oreb. Bucky . . . ?" Pig choked, coughed, and at last recovered.

"You have a blue eye now, Pig. Like my own."

When the nurse's glass had faded to silver-gray, Pig ventured, "Yer gang ter stay wit' me, bucky?"

He nodded, knowing Pig could see his nod and glorying in it. "Until Hari Mau finds me, and makes me go with him."

"Bird go?"

"Yes, Oreb. Certainly, if you want it. I'll be flattered."

"Pig ter, bucky?"

He was taken aback. "Would you want to?"

"Aye." Pig's voice was firm.

Slowly, he shook his head.

"Seen me h'ears."

"That has nothing to do with it. I am flattered, Pig. I'm humbled. But unless a god were to tell me otherwise, my answer must be no, for both our sakes."

"Auld Pig'd gae, bucky."

"I realize that—you would go, and endeavor to help and protect me in every way possible."

"Yer did sae fer him."

"Of course. I am your friend, as you are mine." He paused, his right forefinger tracing small circles on his cheek.

" 'Twill be a lang walk ter na braithrean wi'hout yer."

He nodded, and gloried a second time. "You'll go back to them, at the other end of the whorl?"

" 'Tis me h'only kin."

"Mercenaries. You were a mercenary trooper, Pig?"

"Ho, aye! Was he? He was! Fightin' ter make 'em gae, bucky. Paid ter. Moss-trooper, ter, an' there was nae better."

"Perhaps you'll find someone on the way, Pig. A woman who loves you. Or friends who like you as much as I do."

"Found yer h'already, bucky."

"Yes," he said sadly. "You have. And if I could take you back to New Viron with me, I would do so in an instant. The problem—one problem at least—is that I am not going there. I am going to a town very far from there, to which I promised Hari Mau I would go."

"Dimber wi' me."

"I will be a prisoner, Pig. They want me to judge their disputes, and arrange compromises for them. There are many disputes in which both sides are in the wrong, and many more in which no compromise acceptable to both parties is possible."

He sighed. "I cannot give them all that they hope for, and their disappointment is certain to turn to violence in time, unless I can escape them."

"Would yer do h'it, bucky? Gang awa'?"

Solemnly, he nodded. "I would. I will—if I can. I've promised Hari Mau that I'll go with him to his town, and that I will judge it to the best of my poor ability. But not that I'll remain there indefinitely. I will keep my promise if they'll let me. But when I've done what I can, I'm going home. I've been halfway around Blue already, and home cannot be farther than that."

"Need auld Pig then, bucky."

He sighed again. "No doubt I will, but I won't have you. In the first place, Hari Mau and his friends will learn where I am very quickly—if not today, certainly tomorrow. They'll hold me to my promise then, and insist we leave. You must have expert care for months. Your flesh may not accept your new eye. There are things that can be done should that occur, but they are difficult things and require an expert physician.

"In the second, you would be more of a prisoner than I, and in considerably greater danger, a focus for the discontents of every man I ruled against. I said that you will require months of care, because that is what your surgeon told me, and what they tell me here. If you were to come with me, I doubt that you'd live for months."

Something in Pig's face had changed. He said, "And in the third, Horn?"

"Patera!"

Oreb whistled shrilly.

"I would be a positive danger to you," Pig said. "Strength and a stout heart are hazardous qualities where they cannot prevail."

"Yes." He wiped his eyes.

Naked and subtly altered, the face was still Pig's; Silk's well-remembered voice issued from its lips. "Still, you would take me if you could."

"Yes. Yes, I would. If we reached New Viron, I would not have failed. Or even if you reached it alone."

"You do not wish to fail." Pig's big hand tightened on his.

He said, "I would give my life not to fail," and meant it.

"You already have."

"You must lie here, on this acceleration couch." Hari Mau bent over him. "You must be strapped in, as well. I apologize, though it is essential."

"I know, I've been on them before. I'm worried about Oreb."

Hari Mau's smiled widened. "There under your arm he will be safe. The lighter one is, the less strain. Oreb is very light." A wide strap snapped closed, pressing the azoth into the tense muscles under it. "For yourself you are not afraid, Rajan Silk?"

If they wished to call him that, that was what they wished to call him. Not wanting to stare, he looked from Hari Mau's bearded face to the woven matting that had replaced—what? He tried to remember the interior of the lander that had brought him from Blue to Green, but he could recall only the long rows of crude brown couches, the cramped little galley that had fed them sparsely and badly, the shooting and the shouting, the twisted steel grip of Sinew's knife protruding from the back of a man whose name was forgotten.

Hari Mau repeated, "For yourself you are not afraid?"

"Of dying?" He shook his head. "No, not of that. In a way it would be a relief, a mitigation of failure. May I confide in you?"

"Of course! I am your friend."

"What I fear is showing fear. I am afraid I'll scream when the—the push comes, and the explosion."

Hari Mau brought cotton for his ears, and he stuffed it in them gratefully. "You must put your head under your wing, Oreb, and pretend you are going to sleep. Keep out as much of the noise as you can."

"No hear?"

"Yes," he said firmly. "No hear," and watched with approval as Oreb tucked his head beneath his wing.

He had wanted a couch near the others, perhaps next to Hari Mau's, but Hari Mau had hustled him away, farther down, nearer the front of the lander, nearer the strange place to which Silk had once gone from which one could—while still in the whorl—see the stars. He was . . .

He craned his neck in a vain effort to see behind him.

Two or three rows farther down. Three rows at least, he decided, and more likely four. At least this lander was not jammed like the one in which he and Nettle had come to Blue.

Where was she now? He tried to imagine her and what she was doing, but found that he could only picture a much younger Nettle renting folding stools. I am distracted, he told himself as a slight tremor shook the lander. Under such circumstances as this, I am bound to be distracted.

Matting, woven of the split stems of some tropical plant. It would be warm in Gaon. He shivered.

Someone had ripped open the very walls to steal wire. If he and Hari Mau and all the rest were lucky, that someone would have left the insulation strewn about so it could be replaced and confined behind the matting. If they were not, it was gone and had been replaced with something else, the coarse and dirty hair of slaughtered cattle or something of the sort.

No, they did not eat their cattle in Gaon. Hari Mau had said so. Cattle were the mother goddess, were Nurturing Echidna, just like snakes. Snakes were understandable, of course. It was that way in Viron, too, to some extent. But cattle? Though cattle were associated with both Echidna and Pas, now that he thought of it. Rain from Pas, grass from Echidna; it was an old saying. Rain, the intercourse of the gods.

In Gaon, Hari Mau had said, cattle were offered to Echidna, but never eaten. The entire animal was burned on the altar. That said something about the size of altars in Gaon, and the supply of wood as well, surely.

The monitor's face appeared in a glass to his right, nearly human, though blurred about the mouth. "We'll cast off for the planet called Blue in thirty seconds. Your couch is secured."

"Yes," he said unnecessarily. "Yes, I think so." He wanted to ask whether they would get there, whether they would arrive and whether they would make a safe landing, but did not.

"If you suffer from heart disease, it would be best for you to remain in the *Whorl*," the monitor reminded him.

"I don't." There was a momentary roar, deafening even through the cotton. The lander trembled with a violence that its builders could not possibly have intended. He asked, "Is everything all right?"

"I am verifying our capabilities, Patera Silk."

It was maddening to be thus mistaken by a mere machine; what was almost worse, Oreb had taken his head from beneath his wing to listen. "Good Silk!"

"I am not Silk," he told the monitor. "You have been misinformed."

"Your name is on my passenger list, Patter Silk."

"Supplied by Hari Mau, of course." He could not keep the bitterness from his voice.

"I will first cast off from the *Whorl*," the monitor was saying. Higher up, others were saying the same thing. "When I have attained sufficient altitude, I will fire my engines. As soon as they are silent, you may move about the lander, Hari Mau. You will be unwell. Please employ the housekeeping tube to keep your area clean."

It struck him that it had been at least two minutes since the monitor had said they would leave in thirty seconds. He groped for his housekeeping tube and found that it was missing.

"It will activate upon access. You are responsible for your own area, Hari Mau."

That was because he had insisted that he was not Silk, he decided. Aloud he said, "I have no housekeeping tube, Monitor, and I will not be sick. I've traveled on landers before. I even flew here on this one. On no occasion was I sick."

"No sick," Oreb confirmed.

"I will first cast off from the *Whorl,* Potter Sulk." The blur around the monitor's mouth was spreading over its face like a cancer; the lower half of that face moved to the right, then jerked back into place. "When I have attained attitude, fire my engines. You may move about my. Plus deploy the housekeeping." The monitor's blurred gray face flickered, then vanished.

This was death, death's overture. This lander had been damaged too badly to fly. Although they had flown to the Pole in it, it could never return to Blue. It would explode when the rockets fired or crash when it tried to land, or leave them floating in the abyss to starve, visited perhaps by inhumi.

"I got there. I did it. I got back to Viron, where I could look for Silk." Suddenly aware that he was speaking out loud, he clenched his teeth.

"Good Silk!"

"Put your head under your wing, or you will be deafened. You may well be deafened anyhow."

Obediently, Oreb tucked his scarlet-capped head beneath a jet black wing.

"No, fly." It was a whisper. "Stay here."

It had been the best part of his life, the days when he had been with General Mint, with Silk in the Caldé's Palace. How few they had been! How very, very few. The hours in Silk's palace, and the hours in the boat with Seawrack. "I've been happy twice," he told the bird in a voice that he himself could scarcely hear. A shellback comb floated before his eyes. He murmured, "Most men are not happy even once," and was violently, messily ill.

Sitting in what had been the lowest part of the lander, he seemed suspended in the sky. The Short Sun blazed to his left, mercifully obscured by the darkened canopy. To his right, stars shone, and Blue lay at his feet like a lost toy. Home.

Hari Mau joined him, strapping himself into the seat. "No one should see this twice, but I cannot get enough. It is like women."

He smiled. "Yes, in a way I suppose it is."

"My friends will not look. Mota and Roti? Those fellows? They came up here for as long as it takes to eat a banana. It was enough for them. I cannot satisfy myself, ever."

Oreb had been left out of the conversation long enough. "No eat," he declared.

"No," his master told him, "you cannot eat the stars, save with your eyes. I . . ."

"What is it Rajan?" Hari Mau leaned toward him and touched his neck, as though to gauge its temperature or feel his pulse.

"I just realize that the *Whorl* is no longer my home. I grew up there, Hari Mau, and Nettle and I, in our real home on Lizard Island, used to say 'home' when we spoke of it. In those days, we never thought it would be possible to go back. Now I have, and if I had not, perhaps she would have gone instead." He was tempted to say that she might even have succeeded in finding Silk; but he knew it would make Hari Mau angry.

"It did not make you happy, Rajan?"

"It did at first, and often after that." He sighed. "Or at least I would have told you I was if you had asked me."

"But you weren't?"

"Perhaps I should say that what I had, when I realized I was not only back in the *Whorl* but near Viron—and when I re-entered the city—was not true happiness. Only the anticipation of it."

"So I feel when everything is settled back there," Hari Mau jerked a thumb over his shoulder, "and I can come up here. Here I am happy. But looking at happiness is no bad thing, Rajan."

"No," he agreed, "it isn't. Nor is it happiness we ought to seek in life. For one thing, only those who seek something else find it."

"Work or war?"

"Yes, sometimes. Peace, too, and home. I don't mean to say that wherever one lives is good. Sometimes people try all their lives to make a home, and succeed just before the end, and are happy. Some—like me—succeed much earlier, but are not happy because they don't know. When you came here, I almost said that I didn't think a man who never saw the stars could ever be truly happy."

"There is much truth."

"Then I realized that there are millions like Hound—"

"Good Hound!" Oreb explained.

"Yes, he is. He's honest and humble; and he works hard, I believe. His wife wants children, and so does he, and he will love them when they get them. But he lives in the *Whorl* and has never seen the stars. In all probability he never will, though it is he and others like him who will touch them for us all."

"I do not understand, Rajan."

"The *Whorl* will leave our Short Sun," he pointed to it, "when the repairs are completed. I'm surprised you didn't learn about it when we were at the pole. After we had finished talking about Pig, it was one of the first things they told me."

"Oh, that." Hari Mau shrugged.

"Yes, that. It may take twenty years, or fifty. Or several hundred. There's still a great deal they have to learn. But the raw materials are there, and there's an abundance of labor. They will conquer the heat, rain will fall as it never has in living memory, and Lake Limna—all the lakes—will be sweet again. Streams that have not flowed in a hundred years will run as pure and clear as on the day when Pas's finger traced their courses."

"Perhaps. But you and I will never see it, Rajan."

"No. For us a little point of light in the sky will brighten, then fade until at last it vanishes."

"You will be happy in Gaon, Rajan."

Oreb clucked unhappily.

"No doubt I will. Certainly I will try to be. What about you, Hari Mau? Will you be happy, too?"

"Delighted, Rajan. Elated." Hari Mau's tone left no room for doubt. "I will be the one who found you, who brought you to our town. You will be our foremost citizen, and I will be second only to you. We will be respected and admired, and all of us will live in peace and justice for the rest of our lives. It is not a small thing to be second in a such a town."

"No," he agreed, "it isn't. Indeed, it may well be better than being first."

Hari Mau laughed. He had a warm laugh, full of joy. "You would not talk like that, Rajan, if you could see the house we are building for you. The work had begun before we left, and it will be finished by now. We have been in Gaon only fourteen years. Perhaps I told you?" He paused, counting on his fingers. "Fifteen now. It became fifteen while we were looking for you in the foreign city."

"You mean Viron?"

"Yes. We were there only eleven days. Were we not fortunate to find you so quickly?"

The man he called Rajan looked mildly surprised. "Why no."

"But we were, Rajan. Not fortunate, to find you so quickly out of so many thousands? Echidna favored us greatly."

Oreb cocked his head. "Good luck?"

"Certainly not, Oreb—or at least it wasn't lucky as luck is usually reckoned." His master turned back to the bronzed young hero beside him. "First of all, you were not lucky because you did not find the man you were looking for. I know you think I'm Silk; many people do. Nevertheless, I'm not. I've stopped objecting where your friends may overhear me, but I know who I am."

Hari Mau started to protest, but was silenced by a gesture.

"Second, because it was carefully arranged that you should find me and take me away. I believe Caldé Bison must have had a hand in it, and quite certain His Cognizance the Prolocutor did."

"Are you sure, Rajan? If you are, Gaon owes them much."

"Gaon owes them nothing, because they were not concerned to benefit it. They wanted me out of the way, and being decent men at base were happy to accomplish their end without murder. They thought I was Silk, you see, just as you do; and as Silk I was an embarrassment, an encroachment on their authority. Caldé Bison, I would guess, sent the merchant who conveniently offered my friend Hound candles at a bargain price."

"Rajan . . . ?"

He sighed. "I sincerely hope they carried through their ruse, and Hound actually got the candles to take back to Tansy and her mother in Endroad. What is it?"

"Your temple. Trumpeters were sent through the city to announce that you would offer many beasts to the gods there. It cannot be that they were not proud of you."

"Did they? I hadn't heard about that. It was while I was talking with His Cognizance and General Mint, I suppose. In that case, Caldé Bison's involvement—"

"Bad man!"

"Is quite certain. The Chapter doesn't have trumpeters, but the Caldé's Guard does. No, he isn't, Oreb. That's what I've been telling you. A bad man would have had me killed. Councilor Potto would have been delighted to arrange it, and giggled over it afterward."

"If they wished you away, Rajan, why pay you such honors?"

"So they would not be blamed for my disappearance, to begin with." He laughed, and there was something of a gleeful child in that laughter. "We plot and plan so very hard to do the Outsider's will, Hari Mau. We think ourselves, oh, so wise! I understood at the end. Have I told you?"

"No, Rajan." Hand together, Hari Mau made him a little seated bow. "I would be pleased to learn."

"They took away Hound, you see. Or at least Bison did, and it's even possible his wife helped, though I doubt it. They left me Pig, thinking he would be easy for you to deal with. Because he was blind, he would be no protection to me."

"Nor was he, Rajan."

"I didn't want protection, I wanted Pig's sight restored, and I knew that if the Fliers said it could be done at the West Pole, it could be. Most people have never spoken to a Flier, but I knew one once. They are Crew, and know a great deal we do not." He paused, chuckling. "Patera Gulo came to Ermine's to warn me. I'm sure I haven't told you about that."

Hari Mau shook his head.

"I didn't think so. Patera Gulo was my acolyte long ago. Pardon me—I misspoke. He was Silk's acolyte. I don't know how I came to make such a mistake."

Hari Mau said, "One that I can easily forgive, Rajan."

"He was Silk's acolyte, but he's coadjutor now. I supposed in my stupidity that His Cognizance had sent him, and was quite surprised that he would use the such a high-ranking prelate for a mere errand. Normally he would have sent a page with a note, or his prothonotary.

"The truth of the matter, as I came to understand afterward, was that Gulo had come on his own. He owed his high position to his past association with Silk. When His Cognizance learned of his little visit—as he surely did very soon—he saw to it that it wasn't repeated, and claimed credit for it. He even went so far as to warn me about you and your Gaonese, as Bison did. Neither, of course, took steps to prevent your taking me. Did you have much trouble finding me in the sacristy, Hari Mau?"

"One of your priests told us where you were, and pointed it out to us when we told him we desired to speak to you. But, Rajan, you would not think they had treated you ill if you could see your house. It will be the biggest in Gaon. A house, a garden, and a fountain, all beautiful. Your wives will choose the furnishings."

"My *wives?*" He stared.

"Only four when we left, Rajan, but the most beautiful in Gaon, and we have suggested to other towns that they send their daughters. Most will. That is what Rajya Mantri thinks, and he is wise in such matters. Besides why would—"

"You must send them back!"

"No girl?" Oreb inquired sleepily.

"No. No, indeed. In the first place, Hari Mau, I have a wife already. In the second I have never even seen these women. Nor have they seen me."

"You will disgrace them, Rajan. No one wants a cast-off wife. Besides, you must have wives to cook and clean."

Sitting in the little horse-drawn tonga, he recalled that conversation. From the way the men running ahead (they were good runners here) were pointing, this was certainly it, this three-storied stucco structure with turrets and peculiarly shaped windows, behind this low plastered wall. The gray-bearded man with the big scarlet head-cloth, bowing as soon as the Rajan's eye fell upon him, was presumably Rajya Mantri.

The curtain of one of the upper windows was twitched aside just long enough to reveal two lovely, laughing faces with frightened eyes, then let fall again.

19

The Last Time

Juganu and Scylla wanted to go back to the Red Sun Whorl right away; but Father said there was no point in going from the boat and most likely we would end up back on the river boat if we did, which was not where we wanted. What we needed was a nice safe house where things would be all right the whole time we were gone. That meant we had to go back to New Viron, and what with bad wind and no wind it took three days. Juganu did not like it, but there was nothing we could do about it.

I thought we would go to Uncle Calf's, but Father decided on another place instead, in a good big house that belonged to a lady named Capsicum. Hide had met her already and she never did get over thinking I was him. But she was a nice old lady.

Father explained what we wanted, and she said she had just the place, it was a guest room that only had one window but there were two beds in it. We went in there, and it was a big window but there were bars on it. She did not call them bars and they were twisted around pretty to make a flower in the middle, but they were bars. I grabbed hold and tried to pull them out, and I could not even get them to bend a little.

She went away, and we shut the door and bolted it, and lay down on the beds, Father and me on one and Juganu on the other. After that I stared at the ceiling for a long time and nothing happened. It was about two o'clock and the sunshine in there was pretty bright. It was an interesting ceiling, because somebody had painted it like you were upside-down and looking down at a garden. There was a fountain with Green reflected in it, and those big white flowers that bloom at night, and even a bat. But after a while I got pretty tired of it.

I guess Father did too, because he said, "What are you thinking about Juganu? You're fighting me in some way."

Juganu said he was not, and they talked about that awhile. The bird started to talk, sometimes on its own and sometimes Scylla. I did not like that, and I think Father must have seen it, because he told it to be still. Then he said for Juganu to come over and lie down where I was, and for me to lie down in his bed. I did not like that either, because I was naturally worried about Father. But I did it.

Then he started talking to Juganu about the place we were trying to go to. I never heard him talk like that before, or anybody. I am going to write down all I can remember, but I do not think I can make you hear it the way I did, lying on my back looking at the bat and watching how the room got dark.

"Think of a whorl so old that even its seasons have worn out," Father said, "a whorl on which they had jungles like yours once, with wide-leafed plants and many flowers and huge trees. It is too cold for that in our time, and when the people of that whorl speak of the present they intend five hundred years.

"The sun is red. Shadeup is always cold, and it is cool even when the red sun is at its highest. You can see the stars all day long, unless they are hidden by clouds. Think of a whorl where beggars kill stray dogs for their pelts."

He talked a lot more, and then he said, "What fills your mind's eye, Juganu? Where do your thoughts fly? Be honest with me."

"I was thinking about the whorl you described," Juganu said, "about the whorl we visited, and the boat of the winged woman."

"What else?"

"That I'll be a man like you there, a better man than you, Rajan, because I'll be younger and stronger, as young and strong as your son, and I won't have to feed from him to make me strong. Do you know how we breed, Rajan? We of The People?"

"I know that your eggs must be hatched in sun-warmed water. Nothing beyond that."

The bird said, "Not man. People? Never! No *Whorl*," and I knew it was Scylla. "No there. Good! Bad things!"

Juganu sat up. "We were there! They brought us! We're everywhere!"

Father made him lie back down and told Scylla to be quiet if she wanted to do what the Great Scylla had told her to. She did not say much after that. Maybe not anything.

"How do you breed, Juganu? If it's not too personal, I would be interested to know."

"The man must build a hut for decency's sake," Juganu began in his old, cracked voice. "He selects a good place, a private place where the sun you call short kisses the water. He builds it of little green branches woven together. Weaving is difficult for us but we can do it, and if a man wishes to mate that is what he must do."

Father said, "This is on Green."

"Always on Green. Your waters aren't warm enough for us, and haven't the right life in them. There must be life of the right kind in the water, or the children will starve.

"He builds the hut and trims it with flowers, and he goes away for a day. When he returns there is no one, perhaps, and his flowers have wilted. He takes them far away and throws them into the water, and in the morning he gathers fresh ones, more than before, and trims the hut again. Once again he goes away.

"At evening he returns. The flowers he picked that morning have faded, and the leaves of the green branches from which he built his hut are flaccid and yellow. He destroys it, and carries the withered branches far away to throw in the water. Next morning he begins a new hut, higher and longer and more cunningly woven than the first. Its building requires a day. Next day he trims it with flowers both inside and out. And then he goes away."

I was about ready to go away myself by then, but Father was lying there very quietly waiting to hear more. Their bed was only about two cubits from mine, and he was lying on the side nearest me. So I could see his face pretty good just by turning my head, and he looked like he was hearing something important.

"This time a woman has come," Juganu said. "She is lying in his hut. How does he know? By a thousand signs, and none. Perhaps some small plant that he spared for the beauty of its foliage has been trodden upon. Perhaps she has taken a single blossom from his hut to wear.

"He knows. He reshapes himself then, becoming a man both young and strong. Within—"

I said, "You can't do that." It got me a look from Father.

"She has made herself such a woman as young men dream of. You have told me about your daughter Jahlee, how lovely she was. Your son has told me, too. That is how the woman looks when he sees her in the dimness of the hut he built and made beautiful for her. All these things, you understand, are their promises to each other. Their promises concerning the children they will have. You, Rajan, will understand what I mean by this. Your son will not, and should not."

Father said, "Yes, I understand. Please continue."

"In his hut they love as men and women love. There is a game they play. I think, Rajan, that you can guess what that game is."

His pet said, "Tell bird."

"He is a human man for her, and she is a human woman for him. He tells her that he came to Green on a lander, as human men do, and she tells him that she ran away from her father's house and happened upon his beautiful hut. It is not a lie."

I wanted to say that it was, but Father said, "No, it isn't. I understand. It is a drama."

"Exactly. They are the audience as well as the actors. I have been an actor, Rajan."

Father said, "I understand," again.

"This lasts all night. In the morning, when the sun's hot kisses fall on the water, they say, 'We must wash ourselves after so much love.' They swim together, and she releases her eggs and he his sperm, and it is over."

Neither of them said anything after that. The bird talked a little, but it was not Scylla and did not make sense. Finally I said, "Father wanted to know what you're thinking about that keeps us from going where we want to go, Juganu."

Father told me to be quiet, and I said, "Well, I think he ought to. You're going to take him somewhere where he can be a real man. I think he owes it to you to tell you."

"He has," Father said, and that shut me up.

I do not know how long it was before Father started talking again, but it was a long time. I guess he was thinking of what to say. When he started again his voice was so quiet I could hardly hear.

"Soon it will be evening," he said. "If we still haven't gone, we'll go up onto the roof of this house. Standing on the tiles I will point and you will peer until at last you see a certain dim red star. It's a long, long way from here. Think of it now, the sky like black velvet strewn with diamonds in the bottom of a grave, and among the diamonds a minute drop of blood.

"There is a whorl circling that star, an ancient whorl. On that whorl, Juganu, there is an old city you have seen, and through it a river. Its waters are turbid and foul, and seem scarcely to move. You know that river; you have sailed on it. There are women in that river, women who swim up from the sea. I do not speak of the feignings of the sea goddess, but of real women. Some are as tall as towers, some no larger than children. Their hair is green and streams behind them when they swim, their nipples black, and their eyes and lips and nails as red as blood.

"Steps wet and black with river water lead from the river to a street of crumbling tenements. There are women in nearly every room of those tenements, women who will sell their bodies for a round piece of stamped metal. Some are beautiful, and many are less than beautiful in ways you may find attractive."

He said more about that, but I do not remember most of it, and I am not going to write it.

Then he said, "Follow the street higher, and you meet with the iron gates of their necropolis. It is to that necropolis, that silent city of the dead, that we go; but first we must visit the lander beyond it, the ancient lander where the torturers ply their trade. The torturers are men, but there are fair women among their prisoners. They are helpless and afraid, confined to underground cells and grateful—those who have not lost their reason—to anyone who befriends them. Many were the concubines of the caldé of the city, and these are the fairest of the fair. Day after day they groom and perfume themselves for the rescuer of whom they dream, the rescuer who for most will never come. Tall and fair they think him, and a thousand times they have practiced the kisses they will give him . . . the caresses that have made him their own. . . ."

Father stopped talking, and it seemed to me that he had stopped a long time ago someplace a long way from where I was. I opened my eyes and saw daylight and stars, like there were stars painted on the ceiling instead of the white flowers, and broken stuff like glass. I sat up just as the bird flew through the break, and the first person I saw was the girl that had been inside it. Here I wish I could really say how she looked. It was not exactly happy and was not exactly angry either. She looked the way a person does when all the deciding and worrying is over, and her eyes could have burned right through you.

Father sat up then, and Juganu. Juganu looked the same as on the river boat, but Father looked the way he had in Capsicum's big house, only younger. Before he had looked a lot like our real father, and Hide says that is the way he always looked on the Red Sun Whorl. Now he did not. He looked serious, but he had two eyes again and they just shone. He got up as if he did not weigh anything, and helped me up.

The girl said, "That it?" and pointed.

Naturally I looked where she pointed. There was a little paved place down below with a post in the middle, and on the other side of it a pretty big wall that had fallen down in one place to where it was just a pile of slabs.

On the other side was a cemetery so big it seemed like the whole whorl had to be dead and buried in it. There were graves with every kind of monument, statues of men crying and women crying and I guess of the people who were dead and all sorts of things, and pillars with things on top. Between them were trees and bushes and grass, and little narrow paths that looked white. I found out later that they were made of bones. It all went on for a long way down the side of the big hill, and past it you could barely make out the buildings Father had talked about, and the river.

The girl had taken hold of his arm and was trying to pull him over to the hatch in the middle of the floor, but he would not go. She said, "We here! Why wait?"

He said, "For shadelow, of course. Do you imagine that we can simply go down there and wander about?"

He always wore that black robe that he had the corn in, but it was different, and it started changing more right then while I looked. The main thing was that it kept getting blacker and blacker. It got so black I thought it could not get any blacker, then it kept on getting blacker after that until it looked like what Azoth did when the blade came out and cut through that boat. Finally it was like it was not there at all, but like you were blind in the part of your eye that was looking at it.

There was a hood, too, with red trim on it.

Juganu went over and lifted the hatch while Father and the girl were arguing and said he was going down but if he got caught he would not tell about us. Father explained that they could not hold him anyway, and helped him make one of the black robes for himself and a big straight sword that was sharp on both sides, and told him the name of his friend and told him to send him up if he met him.

Juganu went, and for a long time nothing happened. Father talked to the girl, but I did not pay much attention. Mostly I looked at the other landers around ours, and the river and the city. I will not try to tell about it, because I could not. You could not imagine it, no matter how hard you tried. Some of the buildings were like mountains, but in it they were not huge or even big, they were just bumps. Father used to talk sometimes about the jungle where Sinew was, how dangerous it was. But that city looked worse to me, leagues and leagues and leagues of stone and brick, and millions and millions and millions of people that were worse than any animal. I would have gone home right then, if I could.

The bird came back saying, "Good place! Good hole!" I never did like it much, and I think it was afraid of me because I look like my brother but I am somebody else. Anyway, I liked it less after that, and I am not sorry that it went with him.

Then a boy came up. He was one of the apprentices. From the way Father had talked, I thought he was going to be my age, but he was younger. He was pretty big already, though. You could see he was going to be tall.

We sat on the floor then, Father, the girl, the boy, and me. The boy asked Father about his book, whether he was still writing it. Father said, "No, I've put it aside forever. If my sons or my wife wish to read what I have written, they may. But if they want it finished, they will have to finish it themselves. What about yours? The last time we spoke, you said you were going to write someday. Have you begun it?"

The boy laughed and said, no, he was going to wait until he had more time and more to put in it. Then he said something I have remembered a lot. He said, "I won't put you in it, though. No one would believe you."

It is exactly the way I feel about Father. I knew how right it was as soon as I heard it, and it is still right. The others are going to write all the other parts of this, about the wedding and all that. My part is almost over with. So I am going to try to say it, to tell you about Father the way he seemed to me right here. Even if you do not believe me, even if you think that what I say cannot have been true, you will know anyway that I thought it was. It will let you see him the way we did, a little.

Father was good.

That is the hard part to explain to everyone, and it is the thing my aunt is trying to explain, too. If you meet her and she starts telling you about him, how scary he could be, and things moving themselves and the Vanished People coming down the street and knocking on her door, that is what you have to remember if you want to understand.

If somebody frightens people, everybody thinks he has to be bad. But when you were around Father you were practically always scared to death, scared that he might really find out one day the way you were and do something about it.

I was not going to tell why I did not like his bird, but I will just to get you to understand. It was not really a nice bird at all. It was dirty, and it did not sing. It was noisy sometimes when I did not want it to be, and it would eat fish guts and rotten meat. After I got to know Father (this was in Dorp and on Wijzer's boat) I could see that the bird was exactly like me, except that it was a bird and I was a person. Father knew exactly how bad we were but he loved us just the same. Deep down, I think he loved everybody, even Jahlee and Juganu. He loved some people more than others, our mother especially. But he loved everybody, and until you meet somebody like him, you will never know how scary that was.

He was good, like I said up there. He was probably the best man alive, and I think that when somebody is really, really good, as good as he was, the rules change.

"A long time ago," he told the boy, "this girl was a sort of princess here on your whorl. Her name was Cilinia. Have you heard of her?"

The boy said he had not.

"She died here many years ago—many centuries, I believe. Now she must find her grave."

"You're ghosts." The boy looked around at us. He was not afraid, or if he was he did not show it. But he did not smile, either. He did not have a good face for smiling, anyway. "When you were here before you said you weren't."

"That was because you meant the spirits of the dead," Father explained. "My son and I are not dead, and neither is Juganu, the man who sent you to us. This girl is, however, and we must help her. Will you help us?"

He did, too. He took us to an old stone building where there were lots of coffins. They were supposed to be up on stone shelves, but most of them were not, and a lot were empty.

"Here," the girl said, and she went into the darkest corner. I did not think there was anything there, but Father was making a light with his hand, and she was right. There was a little coffin only about half the size of the others in there, pushed way over. There were spiderwebs all over it, so it was a lot easier to miss than to see.

She looked down at it awhile, and Father asked if it would be better if he put out his light. She said no, but he closed his hand until it was almost dark. Finally she said it was no good, we would have to take the lid off for her. It took a special tool, but Father made one and gave it to the boy. He said that since the boy was the only one who was really here, it at would be better if he did it.

The boy asked, "I'm just pretending you're really here?" But Father had stepped back into a corner and would not answer him. (It seemed right then like Father was not much more than a shadow and a little gleam of light, like there was a chink in the wall there that let the sunlight in.) Finally I said, "That isn't quite it either. You better take out those screws like Father told you." I am not sure the boy heard me, though.

He did it anyway. I do not think the tool Father had made felt right, because he kept stopping to look at it. He would use it awhile, maybe taking out one. Then he would stop and study it, and shut his eyes, and study it some more. So it took a while, but eventually the last one was out and he looked around for Father and asked if he should take the top off.

Father was on his knees drawing the sign of addition over and over the way he did sometimes and did not answer, but the girl said, "Yes! Oh, yes! Do it!" That was funny, because I could see the boy could hear her but could not see her.

I went over so I could look inside, and the bird sat on my shoulder. It was about the first time he was that friendly, and I was not so sure I liked it. I am still not sure.

Only it was not as easy as we thought it was going to be. The lid stuck and I had to kneel down at the other end and wrestle with it. The boy could see me then and hear me too, and I could see he felt better about that. It told me something about the way we were in the Red Sun Whorl that I had not known before. We got more real there when we did things with people who were really there. When we did not, we got less real, even to each other.

Maybe even to ourselves, but I am not sure about that.

Just the same, I think that when Father wanted to bring us back that was what he did. He thought about us, and not at all about the Red Sun Whorl, and somehow, by what he said and the way he acted, he made us think that way, too.

We got the lid off after a lot of fooling around. We thought for a while there might be some kind of secret catch, but it was just stuck. There were metal corners on the box part and on the lid, and they had rusted together. When they came loose, the girl got a lot more real and even pushed us away. Her face was just terrible. It was like the only thing in the whole whorl she wanted was inside the coffin.

Maybe it was, but she did not get it right then. There was a casket (I guess that is what you call it) inside all soldered out of sheet lead. The boy had a little knife and he cut the lead for her, along the big end and down both sides. We grabbed hold of it then and were able to peel it back.

There was not much inside, just some dirt and hair and old bones, and a little jewelry. Not much. I thought the boy would take the rings and so forth, but he did not. After I had seen the inside I looked back up at the girl to see what she thought of it, and she said, "I died young. It can't have been long after I was scanned for the *Whorl*." She was talking to Father then, not to me, and she had stopped talking like his bird.

He opened his hand all the way. It got so bright it hurt my eyes. The bird has this thin filmy sort of eyelid he uses in bright sun, and next time I looked at him he had it.

Then Father said, "I imagine so, Cilinia." From the way he said it, you knew it was the last thing he would ever say to her. I wish I knew how to do that with my voice. I have tried it, but for me it never sounds right.

Father had gotten a lot solider-looking when the light got bright. I do not know about me and the bird, I was not paying much attention to us just then, but the girl got all wispy.

After that, she went. It was like she was water in a bowl, and the dirt in the lead casket was the ground, and somebody we could not see was pouring her out. Maybe the light was.

When she was gone, Father closed his hand again. The boy wanted to know if he should put the lid back. Father said yes, and, "I can't say what may happen if you open it again. Probably nothing. Still, I advise you not to."

The boy said he would not. He screwed the lid back down, which did not take nearly as long as it had to get it off, and we shoved it back in the corner again.

When it was done, the bird said, "Bad thing. Bad girl." You could tell it was not quite sure she was gone.

I thought that was funny and said something about it to Father, and he said, "Nor am I. Back on Blue, she may possess Oreb just as she did; and in fact, I think it more likely than not, though I hope I am wrong."

After that we went back outside. It was practically night, what old people call shadelow, the time when there are shadows everyplace. There was a great big rosebush growing right by the door of the stone building with about a hundred purple roses on it. I had not noticed the smell when we came in, or anyway I do not think I did. But when we went out I noticed it a lot. The night seemed to bring it out, and it was almost like it followed us. Maybe we got it on our clothes. It was sweet but heavy, the kind of smell you like at first, but after a little while it makes you tired. Now, just about anytime I smell anything like that I think about the girl, and the dirt that was inside the lead box. She was right at the mean stage a lot of girls get in, but she would probably have gotten over it when she got older. She might have turned out to be a pretty nice person after all.

While we were walking, the boy told Father he wanted him to see his dog. He said he had wanted to show it to him the last time Father was here, but Father had not gotten to see it, so could he show him now? Father said sure.

That got me to thinking about what we were doing now instead of the girl and whether she had really gone away. I mean died, because that is what it was, I know. So I asked if we were just going back to the tower to see this dog, and I said that if that was all it was maybe it would be better for us to go home.

Father said, "We've accomplished the task we set out to do, but the most difficult part of our trip remains, my son. We must persuade—or force—Juganu to return with us."

I wanted to say, "Don't you think Juganu will want to go?" but that would have been dumb because I could see from what he had said that he did not. So I said, "You told him what would happen if he didn't."

Father did not say anything. If you asked him a question that really was a question he just about always answered some way, I think because he was so polite. But if you just said something like that to show you would like to know something, pretty often he did not say anything back. By that time I knew all about that so I did not do it very often anymore.

The boy said, "Do you want to look for your friend first, or see Triskele?"

"Both," Father told him.

After that, nobody said anything until we got to the little gate. Then the boy knocked and called out, "We are returning, Brother Porter!"

That was the torturer at the gate, a big fat man with a big sword. He stared at us through the little window, and it was the first time it soaked through to me that I should have had a black robe and a sword too, like Father had helped Juganu make.

So I made them as fast as I could while he was looking at me, and it was probably a mistake. The sword was not sharp, for one thing, and the robe was really just kind of a black sheet tied around my neck, and I still had on the tunic that Mother had made for me back home. Brother Porter opened the gate for us anyway, but he was trembling so bad that Father stayed behind to talk to him and sort of tell him it was all right.

The boy and I went on. Father made a little motion to say we ought to, and I think that was right, because the boy helped me with my robe and I found out I could make my sword sharp by pinching my fingers together and running them down the edge. I tried to make my tunic go away, too, but it would not, so the boy showed me how to pull my robe together and keep it that way, the way a real torturer would. We went back in the tower after that and down into the Juzgado part, because I had asked the boy if there were women torturers, and he said no. So I was pretty sure that was where Juganu would be. I thought maybe I could find him and get him to go back, and that would save a little time. Besides the boy said it was where his dog was.

Pretty soon we heard Juganu's voice. It was noisy down there, with somebody yelling or screaming all the time. But in a way it was quiet, too, because nobody was listening. When somebody talked the way Juganu did, just the way a person usually does so that somebody else will hear him and understand what he said, it sort of stood out. We went to the room he was in and looked through a little window pretty much like the one in the gate, and he was in there with a nice-looking woman.

She had big eyes that looked like they cried a lot, only she did not look like she was going to cry any more ever just then, if you know what I mean. She looked like life was just so wonderful there in her little room that she loved the whole whorl and nothing could ever make her unhappy again. She looked up at me when I tapped on the door with my sword, but then she looked back at Juganu like looking at anything else was just a big waste of time.

When we had gone out to the cemetery that they called the necropolis, Father and I had just walked though the wall, the bird and the girl flew over, and the boy had climbed it where it had fallen down. And I had been thinking it would probably have been better if we had come back the same way and not gotten the fat man all upset. So right then I tried to see if I could just walk through that door, too, without Father there to tell me how. I tried, and I did it. It worked fine.

There was something funny about being in there just the same. I kept thinking about what if it did not work fine when I tried to go out? What if it did not work at all? I thought about being locked in there like the woman with the big eyes, and never seeing daylight, and what did Father need me here for anyway? He could have left me on the boat with Babbie. When I told the others about that, we all laughed. But it was not funny then. It was hard to keep from turning right around and going out, one of the hardest things I have ever done.

Juganu wanted to know what I wanted, but I think he knew. I said it was time to go, and she cried and held on to him. He said, "Are you saying that we're going to leave this moment? Where's the Rajan?"

So I explained about the dog and said that we would just go down and look at it because the boy wanted us to, and Father would be along soon to see it, and then we were leaving.

He did not say anything to that for a minute. Then he said, "I have to think."

Just then I heard a new voice through the little window in the door. I turned and looked, and it was a man I had not seen before. A big, heavy man with a big heavy face had hold of the boy. He was telling him to come along, and from the way he said it, it sounded like the boy was in for a whipping. The boy said, "I will, Master. I'm sorry, Master. I meant no harm."

Then the bird came yelling, "Watch out! Watch out!" like it did sometimes. The big man stopped to look at it and said, "What's that doing in here?"

"It belongs to Master Malrubius, Master," the boy told him, and the big man he called Master hit him across the face. He did not do it like he was angry with him or anything. He did not sneer either. He just did it, the way you would swat a fly. Then Father came up behind him and put his hand on his shoulder. He turned around and saw Father, and his mouth dropped open. He did not say anything, just backed away. I think he must have run after that, but there was so much noise I could not be sure.

Juganu stayed with the woman with the big eyes, and Father and I and the bird went down to see the dog. It was dark, and there was mud your feet sank into, but a solid floor underneath. The boy said the dog had been hurt and it was better that it was there in the dark because it could rest then and get well. I was not so sure. It was pretty damp.

The dog had blankets though, old torn blankets and lots of rags, and it had tunneled into them and made a little nest for itself. That was good, because it had short hair that did not look warm. Its head was as big as a bull's without the horns, and its mouth could have held my head and bitten down on it like a cherry. I know because it opened its mouth when we came. I think it was saying it was glad to see us. The boy had bread and meat in his pocket. It did not seem like much, but he gave it to the dog and said he would come back with more. It stood up for a minute when he patted its head. It was so big through the chest that it seemed like there was something wrong with it, but I think it was just strong.

What was wrong was that its front leg was gone. The boy had bandaged it where it had been cut off, but blood had soaked through. That dog had been hurt in a lot of other places, too. The boy took the bandages off, and he and Father talked about what to do. I could see that the dog was afraid of Father and liked him at the same time. It lay down again and put its head by his feet and looked up at him and trembled a little. Father said the boy knew a lot more about treating wounds than most people did, and they talked about a woman he had known who got her arm cut off. It did not mean anything to me then.

The boy put new bandages on after that, and we went back. Juganu would not come out of the woman's room, so we went in to talk. Father told him he had to come with us or he would die. Juganu said, "I'm going to stay with Tigridia and free her."

"Free, she'll have you exorcised," Father told him. He took his arm and Juganu went for him. I think he would have choked him to death if I had not been there. He was ten times stronger than he had been when I had pulled him off the mast back on our boat. The woman got in it, and we had a real fight going until the boy ran off and got the key to her room.

Then we went back, Father and me, Juganu, and the bird. When we woke up in Capsicum's house, Juganu just fixed his face and went out. He never said a word to us. We watched to see if he really left the house, and he did. I think he was afraid we would kill him, and I would have if Father had not stopped me.

After that, Hide and Vadsig came with Mother from Lizard for the wedding, so this is everything I have got to write about, the things that I was the only one to see. I will let them and Daisy do the rest. I will criticize like they have been doing to me.

20

The Wedding

Wijzer gave the bride. Her dress was a simple one of white silk with a white lace veil, but her pearls and her beauty set the manteion buzzing. Gyrfalcon came, with an armed bodyguard of twenty men. If he had not, things would almost certainly have gone very differently, and we would not be writing this.

Nothing of that was known, of course, when Wijzer led her to the altar. What was known, and to half the town, was that a family that had never been considered prominent other than as the source of *The Book of the Long Sun* (a chronicle, generally factual, of events prior to the founding of New Viron) was now conceded to be very prominent indeed in politics and religion. Nettle, particularly, was courted by women who had previously scarcely deigned to speak to her; few, if any, dared ask whether the man assisting His Cognizance was in fact her husband.

He himself seemed happier than anyone had seen him before. At the bride's request, he read the second victim, a waterhorse. Everyone expected the usual platitudes.

Seconds built minutes, piling up like grains of sand. The whispered conversations fell away, and still he stood staring at the entrails of the snow-white victim he himself had provided.

"Mysire . . . ?" the bride whispered.

Startled, he looked up. "I'm sorry. There is a great deal here."

Another minute passed.

"His Cognizance was good enough to permit this," he said when his gaze left the carcass of the waterhorse at last. "It may have been a mistake, as such things are commonly counted."

Everyone present sensed that he was inviting them to silence him, but no one attempted to.

"I see the hand of a god in it," he told them, "and since this victim was offered to the Outsider, we can assume that it is his. That being the case, I take this opportunity to tell you that he is the god of Blue. Have you never wondered who it is? We have other gods here already. There is a Scylla greater than the one we knew, for example. You should fear and respect—but not worship—her, lest you come to ill."

One of the wedding guests called out, "Pas!"

"He is not yet here, or at least, I do not believe he is. He will come, however. You or others like you will bring him, and Silk with him—Silk, whom you sent me to bring and whom I failed to bring."

He paused, regarding those who heard him through an eye that very few could meet. "They will come. But never forget what I tell you today: you belong to Blue, and to the Outsider."

He studied the carcass. "No doubt His Cognizance has often said here that one side of the victim represents the givers and performers of the sacrifice; the other, the congregation and the community. I repeat it because I know that there are some present who have seldom honored the gods since childhood.

"The presenters of this fine white waterhorse are my son Hide and my daughter-to-be Vadsig. For them, a long marriage and a largely, though not entirely, happy one."

There were chuckles.

"They will have six children."

He hesitated, and bent lower to see more clearly. "I see a great deal of paper as well."

Scattered laughter.

"Quills and ink, and a partnership with another couple.

"The performers are His Cognizance and myself. We shall soon separate, parting in friendship and regret. One shall be highly favored by a god."

From the congregation, Gyrfalcon asked, "Which god, Patera?"

He straightened up, clearing his throat. "Where no other identification is made, it is safe to assume that the god to which a prophecy refers is the one to whom the victim is offered. The other augur—if augur is meant—also shall win the favor—"

At that instant, Oreb flew in through a window. *"Watch out! Watch out!"*

"And undertake a long journey, from which he shall not return. Death may be intended."

"Bad things!"

Raising a finger to his lips, he gave the bird a stern glance; it settled upon his shoulder, repeating, "Bad things! Things fly!"

"The god's prophecy concerned with all of us is about to be fulfilled, I believe. Certainly the entrails warn that it is very imminent. Some of you have slug guns, I see. You will need them. Others may have less obvious weapons of other kinds, as I do. You may wish to consider how best to employ them. I remind those of you who are unarmed that no man or woman of courage and resource is ever entirely helpless."

"Good Silk?" his bird croaked; and then, "Silk fight?"

He turned to the Prolocutor. "Your Cognizance, I suggest that this victim be offered to the flames entire, and that the remainder of the ceremony proceed as swiftly as possible. We haven't much time."

As has been said, Captain Wijzer led Vadsig down the aisle, he proud and tearful in crimson velvet tunic and trousers, she radiantly lovely in watered silk dripping with pearls. Her bridal bouquet was of pink-and-white seaspume; its gracious perfume soothed the very smoke of sacrifice. Aunt Oxlip's daughters Sweetbay and Madrone were her train-bearers, and Capsicum's grandson bore the ring on a black silk pillow.

Everything went normally and even magnificently, until the lovers had exchanged vows, kissed, and started back up the aisle, bathed in the fervent good wishes of their guests, among whom Hoof and I were of course numbered.

"Watch out!" Oreb croaked. And then with an urgency that few if any had heard before: *"Watch out!"* A flying shape not quite a man swooped over the pews. It struck Hide with such violence as to knock him off his feet, an apparition of fangs and terrible claws that fell in a welter of blood and slime, cut through the waist.

The blade of an azoth, a thing more terrible than any inhumi, vanished as swiftly as it had appeared, then darted forth again to spear a second inhumu at an open window.

No coherent description of that famous fight is possible. Patera Remora (this is widely known) defended himself and his altar with the knife of sacrifice, as was written two hundred years ago of another augur favored by the gods. Capsicum, it is said, stabbed Gyrfalcon in the melee; certainly she herself was shot and killed by a member of his bodyguard. Weasel, her grandson and Marrow's, is said to have killed an inhumi and an inhuma, though he was only a boy. Captain Wijzer, five inhumi, twice strangling one with each hand.

It would be possible and even easy to multiply such reports to fill a hundred pages. Because they are omitted from all the other accounts, what we must emphasize here are the indescribable noise, the welter of blood, and the wild confusion. Everyone was screaming. Everyone was fighting, even those who would have fled if they could. No count of the numbers of the inhumi was or is possible. It has been said that half the inhumi on Blue at the time took part in the attack, but the assertion rests upon their own testimony, and of what value is that?

Those skilled in war report that an attacking force will scarcely ever sustain its attack when it has lost a third of its number. The best count of the dead inhumi (that of Legume, who was charged with burning their bodies) is one hundred and ninety-eight. If it is correct, and they fought as crack troopers do, their number was about six hundred. It seems probable, however, that it was considerably larger. We would propose one thousand.

What seems certain is that without the azoth, Gyrfalcon's needler, and the slug guns of his bodyguard, the subject of this volume would have perished, and the wedding party with him.

Afterward, he visited Patera Remora, and they sat side by side talking for a time in the little garden between the manse and the manteion. "It is—ah—coming," Patera Remora told him. "In process, hey? If not in my, er, time, then in my acolyte's we will have a working Window, um, Horn."

He said, "Without Mainframe, no god can come to it, Your Cognizance."

"Better, hum? Better so. In—ah—Viron, eh? Thirty years? In, um, Old Viron, as we say now."

He smiled. "No doubt you're right, Your Cognizance."

"What all men, and most—ah—females, require is not theophany, not the divine, um, palpability. Tangibility. It is the—ha!—possibility."

"And yet Mainframe, too, will come. Not in your lifetime, I believe. In your acolyte's."

"He, um, welcome it." The Prolocutor nodded to himself, tossing back the lank gray hair that had fallen over his eyes.

His visitor gave him a piercing glance. "Not you?"

"Er, yes. To be sure."

"It would be presumptuous—very presumptuous—for me to proffer advice, Your Cognizance."

"Yet I should welcome it, er, Horn."

Oreb corrected him.

"Patera Quetzal de-emphasized the worship of Great Pas, Your Cognizance, knowing that Pas was dead. He chose—doubtless wisely—to emphasize that of Scylla instead."

Patera Remora patted his forehead with a worn and yellowed, but neatly folded, handkerchief. "I remember it well." It was the first warm day of summer.

"You, Your Cognizance, might choose to emphasize that of the Outsider, for example."

"I, um."

"He, at least—"

"Good god," Oreb remarked.

"Will not come to your Window, Your Cognizance. I believe I can assure Your Cognizance of that. Not in your time, nor in your acolyte's, nor in his."

Patera Remora nodded slowly at first, then more rapidly. "I, er, comprehend."

"Mainframe may reach Blue, Your Cognizance, before the *Whorl* puts out again; but Mainframe can never have the power here that it had there, the reins of the sun. Meanwhile it might be well for New Viron—for all of Blue—if you were to exercise your discretion."

"I, um, have. In another matter, hey? But—ah—first, Pat— Er, Horn. May I say that you are most, um, perspicacious? You are correct. I, ah, apprehend it now. I would, um . . . On my own, eh? Having been given the, er, hint? No, intimation. By you. During the—ah—the ceremony, eh? Your, um, son's nuptials. I would have, um, come wise?" He chuckled.

"I feel certain you would, Your Cognizance."

"Was it this? This the, er, topic? Upon which you, eh?"

"No, Your Cognizance." His visitor sighed. "Or at least, only partially."

"In that case, um . . . ?"

"It is wrong to take one's own life."

He waited for a reply, but none came.

"Is it also wrong to put oneself in harm's way, in the hope that one's life may be taken?"

"Poor Silk!" Oreb exclaimed, and fluttered from his shoulder to an overhanging branch.

"You, um, did. You arranged for the . . . ah? At the wedding?"

"Yes, Your Cognizance."

Remora pushed back his sweat-damp hair with bony fingers. "Not, um, sufficient. Tell me."

"Your Cognizance will recall the first inhumu, who attacked Hide. His name was Juganu, or at least that is the name by which I knew him. He was infatuated with a human woman, a murderess. He wanted to free her. She is in a prison, as I ought to have told Your Cognizance."

"You, um, opposed this? Quite right."

"I opposed it, Your Cognizance, in such a way as to stir up Juganu's ill will as much as possible." Each hand warred with the other, twisting and tearing. "I didn't—I've searched my conscience on this, Your Cognizance. I didn't imagine that Juganu would enlist hundreds of his kind for a public attack."

Remora grunted.

"I believed it most probable that Juganu would come for me alone. I would feign sleep and permit him to drink his fill, which would be much. If I lived, so be it."

Remora nodded to himself. "But if you, hum?"

"So be it. Possibly he would bring a companion. I foresaw that. Possibly he would bring two or even three; in either case I would certainly die."

"So—um—et cetera, Patera?"

"Yes, exactly, Your Cognizance. It would be what I wanted. I wanted someone else to kill me, so that I would not bear the guilt myself. You know the result of my folly—the deaths of a round dozen people and hundreds of inhumi."

"Evil, eh? Vile, um, miscreations that deserve to—ah—perish, my son."

"Yes, Your Cognizance." He straightened up and squared his shoulders. "I have been on friendly terms with three, however. No, four, because I was briefly on such terms with Juganu himself. With two inhumus, Your Cognizance, and two inhumas. I made a covenant with evil, one I bitterly regret, though those I have known have been no worse than we. I wish to be shriven of that, as well. Shall we begin?"

"No. Um, no." Remora shook his head. "First, Patera, you must tell me why you wish to—ah—ascend."

"Isn't it obvious?" His voice was angry, so much so that Oreb fled to a higher branch. "I failed! I gave my life, and still I failed."

Remora leaned back, his fingers forming a lofty steeple whose apex touched his chin. "My son, you—ah—adverted a moment ago that the, er, our attackers were no, um, not inferior to—ah—morally. I let it pass. Ignored it, hey?"

"Your Cognizance—"

A bony hand waved him to silence. "Hear me out. The—ah—implication, hum? We no better than, er, they are. It—ah—will not argue. Possibly. Possibly."

"Bad things!" Oreb declared with unshakable conviction.

"Worse things than birds," his master agreed, and added sadly, "but so are we. I thought perhaps—oh, never mind."

"Possibly," Remora repeated. "I—ah—concede that. I, er, myself—"

"I intend nothing personal, Your Cognizance, believe me."

"Um, do. Yet I myself, eh? Conscious, always conscious of many shortcomings. Now, um, Gyrfalcon, eh? A bad man? You would, um, acquiesce, my son?"

He shrugged. "Many people say he was, now that he's dead."

"Was Gyrfalcon as, er, iniquitous as an inhumu? As this, hum, Juganu you once—ah?"

"I imagine so."

"As do I. The—ah. Old Quetzal. Recollect him, Patera?"

"Of course."

"Knew, Lemur, eh? Many, um, discussions. I, er, likewise. With

Gyrfalcon. I—ah—understood him. Boasting, eh? Yes, boasting. Don't often, hey? But the truth. Talk with, er, him. Dined. Shrived him, eh? A bad man. In—ah—concordance on that point. But he—ah. Hear me here, Patera."

"Yes, Your Cognizance."

"Gyrfalcon, um, dispatched you, eh? One of, um, five of, er, us. The worst. Possibly. Possibly the worst of the, er, group. Even he would not, um? Blame someone who, er, expired. So you told me. Who—ah—died in the attempt. Do you take my meaning, Patera?" Remora shook his head violently. "Not so bad a man as that, eh? Not so bad a man as you are, Patera?"

There was silence.

"Do you still, um?"

"Want to end it?" He sighed. "Yes, I suppose I do, really. Nettle will have Hoof and Hide and Vadsig. She'll be all right."

"No die!"

Remora smiled. "Who is Nettle, Patera?"

"My wife. You know her, surely."

"An, er, dark day for me, eh? Boasted. Now I'm about to—ah—intrude. Did you, eh? And she? Husband. Lengthy absence, eh? One, um, expects the—hum—warm commerce."

"No, Your Cognizance. She didn't want to, and neither did I; but if we had, there would have been nothing wrong in that, surely."

"I, um, suspend judgment, hey? Shriving, likewise."

"You can't be so cruel, Your Cognizance."

"No? I, um, consider otherwise. You still, um? Reject the gift, hey? The gift of life, Patera. Look at me, eh? Look at me, and tell you no longer desire, er, release. Can you do it?"

His eyes were on the ground. "No, Your Cognizance. If I had brought Pig—if some way I could have . . ."

"Forbear. For children, eh? For sprats, these ifs."

There was no reply.

"The, um, ceremony. Nuptials, eh? You recall them?"

"Yes, Your Cognizance."

"Well? Ah—distinctly?"

"Very distinctly, Your Cognizance."

"I, um, homily. Curtailed, eh? Yes—ah—abbreviated while the sacred fire, eh? But the, um, reading first. You were not, er, inattentive."

"I hope not, Your Cognizance."

"I, um, advanced to the ambion, eh? Took up the Writings?"

"Yes."

"And, um, then? What next, Patera? Please elucidate."

"You found the passage in which marriage—"

"No! You—ah—erroneous. Previous to that."

"Wait a minute." His forefinger drew small circles over his right cheek. "I remember. You opened the Writings, apparently at random, read a passage, and appeared to reject it. You turned to the passage on marriage then."

"Did I, er, communicate the first passage, Patera?"

"Read it aloud, you mean? No, you read it silently, then opened the book at a different place."

"Have you—ah—formed an, er, theory to account for um?"

"Only the obvious one, Your Cognizance." As he spoke, he felt an icy tendril of dread that he could not have explained. "The initial passage was not suitable for a wedding."

A toss of Remora's head cleared his eyes of his lank hair. "It was, um, suitable, Patera. Your own word, eh? It was—ah—cogent. Very. I, um, declined, eh? Nonetheless. An error. Ah—hubris. Knew better than the gods, eh? At my, um, time of life, I should be wiser." Remora rose. "If you will, er, be unoffended by a brief absence? I shall return presently. Will you, um, enjoy the fine weather?"

"Certainly, Your Cognizance. I'll be here when you return."

"Capital. I shan't be long."

"Good Silk!" Oreb called by way of farewell.

His hands were still now as he watched Remora's retreating back. A minute passed, then two. A rockwren sang in the tree in which Oreb perched, then flew away, singing still.

"Poor Silk," Oreb remarked with simple sympathy. "Poor, poor. Poor Silk!"

He rose and began to pace the length of the little garden, left toward the docks and the sea, right toward the farms and the mountains, then left again. "I am a prisoner in a cell," he told Oreb, "and that tall man in black will return with my death warrant. I know it, and can't do a thing about it. Tell Nettle I loved her, please. Will you do that?"

"Bird tell."

"Thank you." He sat again, his head in his hands. "I loved Sinew, too. And Hoof and Hide and Krait. Jahlee and Seawrack. I should not have loved any of them—they were almost as selfish as I am, Oreb. But I did, and I asked the Greater Scylla on the Red Sun Whorl how I could find Seawrack again."

Oreb whistled sharply.

"She taught me how to communicate with her sister here. That was our bargain; but I have not used the information. I would never have used it while Nettle was alive."

"Good Silk!"

"Most of all, I loved Silk. I tried to model myself on him, and see what a mess I made of it. When at last I was given the chance to actually do something for him, I failed."

Returning with a worn volume, Remora had caught the last few words. "You did not—um—miss the mark. Ah—Horn. Yes, Horn."

"You are too kind, Your Cognizance. I did."

Resuming his seat, Remora said, "Possibly you have—um—observed that I have been calling you Patera?"

"Yes, Your Cognizance. Many people do, because of the robe, though I am aware that I am no augur. I've grown tired of objecting and generally let it pass."

"I, er, comprehend." Remora held up his book. "The Chrasmologic Writings, hey? From, um, your own Sun Street Quarter. Salvaged from the—ah—conflagration. By me, Patera. See where the cover's scorched?"

"Yes, Your Cognizance." He touched the discolored leather tentatively, as though it were a serpent. "This was Silk's? He used to read from this—from this copy—at manteion when I was a boy?"

"Um—ah—no. Not, er, exactly, Patera. Yet you are—hum—nearly correct. A—ah—near miss. To the point now, eh? Permit me."

"Of course, Your Cognizance."

From his branch, Oreb called, "Watch out!"

"It was from this that I read at the, er, nuptials. I have—ah—searched? Scrutinized it to discover the passage I rejected. Erroneously, eh. Hubris. I, um, conceived that it would be better if you did not, hum? But in error. In error. Not irretrievable, eh? I retrieve it now. Right the wrong."

The vague ache he felt in his chest at times had returned. He took as deep a breath as he could manage, recalling the swords of the torturer's tower. Men were required to lay their heads upon the block, to be lopped off by those swords; and they did it, often with great courage.

"Will you—ah—peruse it, Patera? I have, um, marked the place."

Someone else, someone very far away, said, "I cannot imagine that there is anything in the Writings that I should not read or hear read, Your Cognizance."

"It's, um, here."

The open book lay in his lap. He grasped it with both hands and raised it until his shadow no longer fell upon the print.

Though trodden beneath the shepherd's heel,
the wild hyacinth blooms on the ground.

He wept; and another distant voice, Remora's, said, "Horn did not fail us, Patera. Caldé. You see that now?"

Silk nodded.

Afterword

The three volumes of this account were written almost entirely by their protagonist, the former Rajan of Gaon, who described in considerable detail his (?) search for the fabled town of Pajarocu and tragic adventures on Green, as well as his reign in Gaon and journey to New Viron. These we have left as he composed them, save for correction of obvious errors, division into chapters, and titling those chapters and his volumes.

He left us no written record of his brief sojourns in Old Viron and the West Pole, but he spoke of them often. In this volume we have re-created them to the best of our ability, based upon those conversations. What is most certain is the point most frequently doubted by those who have read earlier drafts of the present volume: that he abandoned his search for Silk in order that his chance-met friend's vision might be restored. He agreed to accompany Hari Mau to Gaon if Hari Mau would transport Pig to the West Pole. Both men might easily have broken their promises; both men kept them. We three who knew him well (as this account shows) find it easy to believe that he acted as he did. Readers who did not must bear in mind that he could not be certain that Silk was still in the *Whorl*. It may have seemed to him that Silk had quitted Old Viron, and might well have left the *Whorl* for Blue. It should also be borne in mind that the divine Silk was possessing Pig. (Pig appears to have visited the manse in which Silk had lived with Hyacinth for this reason.) In benefiting Pig, he was also benefiting Silk.

We are indebted to His Cognizance Patera Remora for his account of their final interview. His Cognizance could not reveal the details of our protagonist's shriving; nor would we wish him to.

Following that interview, he was seen only by Daisy, who was returning to her father's boat for her sewing basket and found him provisioning the *Seanettle*, assisted by a strikingly beautiful young woman who had only one arm. Just as Hoof wrote his own accounts of certain events in which the rest of us played no part, Daisy will append hers of their meeting.

This *Book of the Short Sun* (as we have titled it) has been issued by us, two brothers and their wives, residents of Lizard Island and citizens of New Viron. We are Hoof and Daisy, Hide and Vadsig. This is the second year of Blazingstar's caldéship.

At the time, I knew Hoof (who would so quickly become my husband) only as a friend and fellow student. We lived in Lizard on Lizard, as they say. That is, in the village called Lizard on Lizard Island. My father and my brother are fishermen. My mother and I usually remained ashore, although we assisted them in cleaning and smoking their catch, and sometimes accompanied them to New Viron to sell it.

When I was younger, my mother had wanted me to learn to read, write, and cypher, things she herself could not teach me. She had become acquainted with Nettle and sent me to her to be taught with her sons. For that we paid one large or two small fish per week. This arrangement ended a year before the opening of the present narrative.

We were invited to Hide and Vadsig's wedding, as everyone on Lizard was, and sailed to New Viron to attend. Our boat required recaulking, and my father decided to put it in dry-dock there, where there were ample supplies of tar and tow. Thus we remained there several days after the other guests from Lizard had returned to their homes.

While returning to our boat for the reason mentioned above, I was very much surprised to encounter the tall, white-haired man Hoof and his brother called Father. He was carrying a sack of potatoes, and had slung two large sacks across the shoulders of a tame hus. I think one held apples and the other a ham and other smoked meats.

Having seen me a few days ago at the wedding, he recognized me and congratulated me upon having survived the attack of the inhumi. I told him quite truthfully that I would have perished had Hoof not come to my rescue, and showed him the bandage on my neck. We talked about the wedding and the battle that had followed it in a friendly fashion, and when we reached his boat, he introduced me to Seawrack, who was stowing supplies on it and who plays so large a role in the first volume of this book. Although she was strong for a woman, she had difficulty handling certain things, and I was able to help her as well as the iron-faced sibyl. Lovely though Seawrack was, with her snowy skin, blue eyes, and fair hair, there was something animal about her. It seemed clear to me that she trusted only "Father," and would have put her long knife into any other person as readily as I would gut a fish.

"We will sail tonight," he told me. "Would you be willing to make my farewells to Hoof and Hide? Nettle is making her own, and cannot be bothered with mine."

I hesitated, and he said, "I've been dreading it—in a sense, I have killed their father, though the Outsider surely knows that I never meant him the least harm. I don't want to have to face his sons, and we have a great deal to do before we go. Won't you do it for me?"

"Bird say!" his pet announced.

"I know you did," he said, "but I'd like this girl to do it, too. Will you, Daisy? Will you say good-bye for me?"

I asked where they were going, and Seawrack said, "To find Pajarocu. There will be a lander that can fly there. Or one will come, and if they will not give it to us, we will take it."

"Back to Viron," the old sibyl confided.

And he: "To the stars."

Soon after that I left them and went to my father's boat for my sewing things, thinking only about the wedding and how beautiful it had been before the inhumi attacked. And never thinking at all of these books he left behind on Lizard, which I knew nothing about then but over which I have labored for hundreds of hours now.

The faint, blinking star that old people call the *Whorl* is fainter than ever. I went outside to look at it a moment ago, and although I could make it out with the telescope, it is no longer visible to my naked eyes.

They are in it, I hope, he and his eerie young woman, Nettle, the old sibyl, and their bird, on course upon a greater sea to strange new islands. Good fishing! Good fishing! Good fishing! Good fishing! Good fishing!

★

★ ★